Doomed with a kiss . . .

"Witch," he whispered, this time the word more endearment than accusation.

Quivering with terror, Holly eased her head back around. She expected his eyes to be as dark as the rest of him, only to find herself gazing into orbs of glacial blue. It wasn't the absence of threat in those eyes that paralyzed her. It was the pained brew of dread and anticipation. With unspeakable tenderness, the knight's big hand smoothed back her hood, baring her face to the moonlight.

Holly resisted the urge to flinch. Not even when being displayed on a dais before a potential suitor had she felt so exposed.

At the sight of her face, a shudder rocked the powerful masculine frame beneath her. The unspoken confession of vulnerability robbed her of conscious will. This man wore no mask to shield her from his desire. Holly knew instinctively that in that moment, he was as defenseless as she.

He slid his fingers beneath her hair to capture her nape with gentle mastery, drawing her mouth down to his. . . .

BANTAM BOOKS BY TERESA MEDEIROS

THIEF OF HEARTS
A WHISPER OF ROSES
ONCE AN ANGEL
HEATHER AND VELVET
FAIREST OF THEM ALL

TERESA MEDEIROS

FAIREST OF THEM ALL

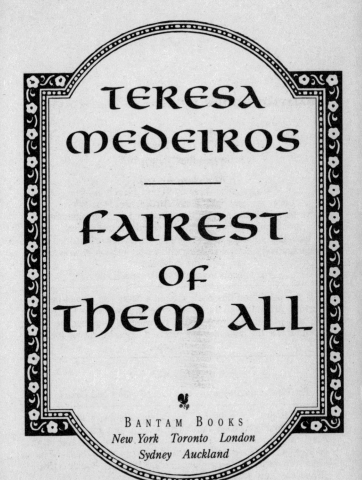

BANTAM BOOKS
New York Toronto London
Sydney Auckland

FAIREST OF THEM ALL
A Bantam Book / June 1995

ISBN 0-553-56333-5

Published simultaneously in the United States and Canada

Bantam Books are published by Bantam Books, a division of
Bantam Doubleday Dell Publishing Group, Inc. Its trademark,
consisting of the words "Bantam Books" and the portrayal of a
rooster, is Registered in U.S. Patent and Trademark Office and in
other countries. Marca Registrada. Bantam Books, 1540
Broadway, New York, New York 10036.

PRINTED IN THE UNITED STATES OF AMERICA

OPM   0 9 8 7 6 5 4 3 2 1

DEDICATION

No knight in shining armor, however valiant, can compare to a husband who does the grocery shopping while his wife is on deadline and who was always the first to say, "Let's eat out tonight, honey." You're the best, Michael, and this one's for you.

To the good Lord for turning all of my curses into blessings.

FAIREST
of
THEM ALL

PROLOGUE

WALES
518 A.D.

His body burned for her. Burned with a flame hotter
and brighter than the lust for victory that had consumed him as he faced his mortal foe on the battlefield. His hauberk was spattered with the rust of
blood, yet the satisfaction of a battle well fought, an
enemy well slain, eluded him. His loins still surged
with the same rhythmic thunder as the beast clasped
between his legs. The beast that would carry him
home to her arms.

Rhiannon.

Sinuous and sweet. Sly and tender. Mocking and irresistible.

He had found her in an ancient forest much like the one he drove his mount through now. A fey creature, darting from birch to willow, her hair glimmering in a snarl of spun gold. She had taunted him, teased him, enticed him to pursue her until he thought he would go mad for want of her. Only when he'd stumbled and fallen heavily to his knees, only when he'd buried his face in his hands in dark despair, had she come to him.

She had threaded her fingers tenderly through his hair and pressed his bearded face to her naked breasts, crooning his name, fierce and sweet. He had never dared ask her how she had known his name. Known his heart. Known his very soul. His braies had fallen away beneath the coaxing of her fingertips, and she had straddled his rigid staff, mating him with inhuman abandon until the roar of her name from his lips resounded like thunder through the forest.

Rhiannon.

He spurred the stallion onward, indifferent to its heaving flanks, the sweat lathering its neck, the gouts of steam puffing from its flared nostrils. He would drive both himself and the beast beyond endurance and let kingdoms fall for nothing more than a taste of his Rhiannon's lips.

As he topped the crest of a steep hill furred with conifers, the thatched roof of a cottage came into view. The cottage where he and his mysterious lady had frolicked naked for a fortnight like naughty children enslaved by some sensual spell, indulging every appetite, both natural and unnatural, until they lay exhausted, but never sated, in the cocoon of each other's arms.

A glimpse of gold through the cone-laden boughs whetted his eagerness. The men he commanded would have never recognized the joyous smile that split his dark visage. That smile faded as the trees parted, giving him a stark view of the clearing below.

Rhiannon standing in the embrace of another man. Rhiannon, her head thrown back, the crystalline chimes of her laughter wafting on the wind. That innocent tableau distorted itself in his mind. He saw pale, naked limbs spread upon the grass; faces contorted with unholy pleasure; Rhiannon mounting a stranger, her generous body milking the seed from a staff as swollen and bewitched by her charms as his own had been.

Without slowing, without thinking, without counting the cost of this madness to his soul, he drew his sword from its scabbard and raised it high over his head. Through the haze of blood in his eyes, he caught a glimpse of a man's shocked eyes, a swirl of gold around a woman's face bleached of both color and hope. The man sought to shove her behind him, but she resisted with inhuman strength, throwing herself in front of him, her arms outflung as if to plead for mercy.

An unearthly roar of rage and betrayal shook the clearing as he brought the sword down, plunging it through her treacherous heart, impaling both she and her lover upon its blade with a single mighty blow. Blood gushed from her snowy breast as they fell as one into the grass.

He wheeled the rearing horse around at the edge

of the clearing, an icy chill seizing his heart as he realized what he had done. Clenching his teeth against a spasm of grief, he slid off the horse and walked back to where they had fallen, each footfall a whisper of dread in the unnatural silence.

A man lay crumpled in the grass, a sword protruding from the narrow cavity of his chest. No, not a man —a boy, his whiskerless jaw still bearing a hint of baby fat, the fine gold of his hair now pale and lank around his lifeless face.

The voice came from behind him, a virulent hiss ripe with contempt. "My brother, you faithless fool. My *mortal* brother."

He spun around. Rhiannon stood a few feet away, garbed in robes of shimmering white, her breast unblemished by the kiss of death.

"Mortal?" he croaked.

"Aye, for I am faerie. And you, sir, are a murdering bastard."

A gust of warm wind whipped through the clearing.

He took a step toward her. If he could only touch her. If he could only stroke the wheaten silk of her hair, bury his lips against the satin of her throat, beg on bended knee for her forgiveness. He stretched out his hands, beseeching her silently.

"No!"

Her scream excoriated him. He fell back with a bellow of terror. The wind gathered force, whipping the writhing tendrils of her hair away to reveal a face as terrible and beautiful as God's, yet utterly without mercy.

She lifted her arms as if to bestow upon him an

unholy benediction. Her chiming voice swelled with a grim finality that mocked the paltry rage of man with the damning wrath of a woman wronged. "You sought to bind with your blade what I would give you freely. My heart. My loyalty. My love. May God curse your soul, Arthur of Gavenmore, and the souls of all your descendants. From this day forward, let love be your mortal weakness and beauty your eternal doom."

With a final surge of desperation, he lunged for her, preferring eternal damnation to the unthinkable prospect of never holding her in his arms again. Never drinking the honeyed nectar of her lips or hearing the husky velvet of her voice ripple across his skin in the darkness of night.

His grasping hands sought the softness of her flesh, but closed on naught but air. Last to fade were the mocking notes of her laughter, tinkling like invisible shards of glass in his ears.

Desolation buffeted him. He fell to his knees, this Arthur of Gavenmore who would someday rule all of Britain until a beautiful queen would prove his doom, buried his face in his hands and wept like a baby.

PART 1

Who is she that looketh forth as the morning, fair as the moon . . . ?
SONG OF SOLOMON

Rarely do great beauty and great virtue dwell together.
PETRARCH

CHAPTER 1

ENGLAND
1325

> Sweeter than the winds of heav'n is my
>   lady's breath,
> Her voice the melodious cooing of a dove.
> Her teeth are snowy steeds,
> Her lips sugared rose petals,
> That coax from my heart promises of love.

Holly smothered a yawn into her hand as the minstrel strummed his lute and drew breath for another verse. She feared she'd nod off into her wine before he

got around to praising any attributes below her neck.
Which might be just as well.

A soulful chord vibrated in the air.

> The envy of every swan is my lady's
>   graceful throat,
> Her ears the plush velvet of a rabbit's
> Her raven curls a mink's delight.
> But far more comely in my sight—

Holly cast the generous swell of her samite-clad
bosom a nervous glance, wondering desperately if
teats rhymed with *rabbit's*.

The minstrel cocked his head and sang, "are the
plump, tempting pillows of her—"

"Holly Felicia Bernadette de Chastel!"

Holly winced as the minstrel's nimble fingers tangled in the lute strings with a discordant twang. Even
from a distance, her papa's bellow rattled the ewer of
spiced wine on the wooden table. Elspeth, her nurse,
shot her a panicked look before ducking so deep into
the window embrasure that her nose nearly touched
the tapestry she was stitching.

Furious footsteps stampeded up the winding stairs
toward the solar. Holly lifted her goblet in a half-
hearted toast to the paling bard. She'd never grown
immune to her father's displeasure. She'd simply
learned to hide its effects. As he stormed in, she con-
soled herself with the knowledge that he was utterly
oblivious to the presence of the man reclining on the
high-backed bench opposite her.

Bernard de Chastel's ruddy complexion betrayed
the Saxon heritage he would have loved to deny.

Holly's trepidation grew as she recognized the seal on the wafer of wax being methodically kneaded by his beefy fist.

He waved the damning sheaf of lambskin at her. "Have you any idea what this is, girl?"

She popped a sweetmeat in her mouth and shook her head, blinking innocently. Brother Nathanael, her acerbic tutor, had taught her well. A lady should never speak with her mouth occupied by anything other than her tongue.

Flicking away the mangled seal with his thumb, her papa snapped open the letter and read, " 'It is with great regret and a laden heart that I must withdraw my suit for your daughter's hand. Although I find her charms unparalleled in my experience' "—he paused for a skeptical snort—" 'I cannot risk exposing my heir to the grave condition Lady Holly described in such vivid and disturbing detail during my last visit to Tewksbury.' " Her father glowered at her. "And just what condition might that be?"

Holly rid her mouth of the sweetmeat with an audible swallow. She briefly considered lying, but knew he'd hear of it soon enough. Brother Nathanael was also partial to lurking behind tapestries in the gleeful hope of catching her in just such a wicked fable.

"Webbed feet," she blurted out.

"Webbed feet?" he echoed, as if he couldn't possibly have heard her correctly.

She offered him a pained grin. "I told him the firstborn son of every de Chastel woman was born with webbed feet."

Elspeth gasped in horror. The minstrel frowned thoughtfully. Holly could imagine him combing his brain for words to rhyme with *duck*. Her father wadded up the missive, flushing scarlet to the roots of his graying hair.

"Now, Papa," she soothed. "You mustn't let yourself get so wrought up. You'll work yourself into an apoplexy."

When he had gathered enough composure to speak, his voice resonated with a false and dangerous calm. "A fortnight ago you informed Baron Kendall that the full moon provoked murderous madness in every other generation of de Chastel women, yet your own mother was meek as a lamb."

Holly nodded. She rather thought that one of her more imaginative ruses. Elspeth was signaling frantically toward the bench, but was too timid to interrupt her father.

"A sennight ago," he continued, his voice rising with each bitten off word, "you feigned crippling blindness and set fire to the plume in Lord Fairfax's favorite hat with a flaming pudding."

"How was I to know it was his favorite hat? He didn't trouble himself to—"

"And only yesterday," her papa's voice climbed to a roar, "you painted red spots on your face and intimated to Sir Henry that an unfortunate case of the pox contracted from the seat of a poorly scrubbed garderobe had rendered you barren!"

The swell of masculine laughter from the bench drained the color from her father's face. His complexion went bilious as a slender man garbed in black and silver arose, chuckling and wiping his eyes. "'Tis a boon to discover my rivals for Lady Holly's affections dispatched with such celerity. The explanation is simple, my lord. Your charming daughter is saving herself for me."

"Montfort," her father whispered, realizing he'd just defamed her before her most eligible suitor. "I had no idea . . ."

"Obviously. Although I must confess webbed feet might be just the thing for paddling about the moat."

Holly found Eugene de Legget, the baron of Montfort, by far the most infuriating of her suitors. His lands bordered their own and she'd done much of her growing up beneath his piercing dark eyes. He had first petitioned her papa for her hand when she was only twelve. When the earl rejected him, pleading her youth as his excuse, Montfort had sworn to someday possess her. His impassioned vow hadn't stopped him from taking a thirteen-year-old bride to his bed while he waited for Holly to reach maturity.

Possessed of a keen intelligence and a wicked wit, he parried each of her tart rejections with renewed vigor. A master of the hunt, he seemed to savor the thrill of the chase with almost unholy pleasure. Holly shuddered. He struck her as the sort of man who would take delight in toying with his quarry once it was cornered.

"I'd ask you to join us, Papa," she said hastily, "but the baron was just making his farewells. "Wasn't he, Elspeth?"

"On the contrary." Montfort's smooth rejoinder stifled Elspeth's murmured agreement and drew a glare from Holly. His dark eyes glittered with mischief as he lounged back on the bench, hooking one lean leg over its elaborately carved arm as if he, and not her flustered father, were the host. He took a lazy sip of wine, emptying his goblet. "My minstrel was just performing a *chanson* I composed as a tribute to the ample charms of the future Lady Montfort." His gaze hovered at the level of her bodice, paying its own lascivious tribute to her "charms."

Holly grit her teeth behind a gracious smile. "Before your minstrel proceeds with his homage, my lord, might I entice you to partake of some more wine?"

"Why, I'd be delighted."

Before Elspeth could rise to serve him, Holly closed fingers numb with anger around the delicate handle of the silver ewer. Eugene held out his goblet with a flourish. Tipping the ewer three inches past his cup, she poured a waterfall of steaming wine into his lap.

"God's breath, woman!" He sprang to his feet, trying vainly to pull the clinging velvet of his hose away from his skin.

"How clumsy of me. 'Tis fortunate the wine had cooled somewhat." She gave his bulging codpiece a scathing look. "I doubt you'll suffer any permanent damage."

Her father's horrified scowl warned her she had gone too far this time. "You must forgive my daughter, sir. She's been troubled by a slight palsy since childhood." He hastened to add, "Nothing hereditary, of course," before flapping a fringed kerchief at the baron like a flag of truce.

Eugene shoved the offering away, his posture rigid with offended dignity. His eyes had lost their sparkle, going cold and flat like extinguished embers. For the first time, Holly paused to wonder if her rash impulse had not only discouraged an unwanted suitor but earned her a dangerous enemy.

"It appears I've overstayed my welcome. Good day, my lord," he said, drawing his cloak around his narrow shoulders. His eyes caressed Holly's face in unspoken challenge as he snapped open a silver brooch and secured his cloak with a vicious stab. "Till we meet again, my lady."

After he had departed, his minstrel dragging at his heels like a chastened pup, a shroud of appalled silence fell over the solar. Holly eased from her seat as if an economy of movement could somehow render her invisible.

"Sit!" her papa barked.

Holly sat. Elspeth edged toward the lancet window. If her father hadn't replaced the ancient wooden shutters with colored glass the previous spring, Holly was convinced her nurse would be perched on the ledge.

The earl paced to the hearth, bracing his splayed hands against its stone hood. He rocked lightly on his heels, as if even unmounted he could feel the rhythm of the countless steeds that had bandied his squat legs.

Holly considered bursting into tears, but quickly dismissed the notion. The merest hint of moisture in her limpid blue eyes had been known to drop both knaves and princes to their knees, but her father hadn't lived with her for eighteen years without learning to resist such ploys.

When she could bear his unspoken reproach no longer, she wailed, "He said I had ears like a rabbit!"

Those ears rang as her father swung around and

roared, "Montfort has the king's favor. He can say you have ears like a jackass if it so pleases him!"

"And we all know how he curried His Majesty's favor, don't we? By overtaxing his poor villeins. By purchasing rotten foodstuffs for their tables and barren seed for their fields. By outlawing their precious feast days and spending the profit to buy the king's ear."

Realizing too late that her ire was a match for his own, her papa raised a placating hand. "That does not mean he would make you a poor husband."

"He made that unfortunate heiress he married a rather poor husband. Especially if you recall that the child tumbled out a tower window only hours before my eighteenth birthday. Are you *that* eager to see me wed?"

He rubbed the top of his head, ruffling his sparse hair. "Aye, child, I am. Most girls your age are long wedded and bedded, with two or three babes at the hearth and another on the way. What are you waiting for, Holly? I've given you over a year to choose your mate. Yet you mock my patience just as you mock the blessing of beauty our good Lord gave you."

She rose from the bench, gathering the skirts of her brocaded cotehardie to sweep across the stone floor. "Blessing! 'Tis not a blessing, but a curse!" Contempt thickened her voice. " 'Holly, don't venture out in the sun. You'll taint your complexion.' 'Holly, don't forget your gloves lest you crack a fingernail.' 'Holly, don't laugh too loud. You'll strain your throat.' The men flock to Tewksbury to fawn and scrape over the musical timbre of my voice, yet no one listens to a word I'm saying. They praise the hue of my eyes, but never look *into* them. They see only my alabaster complexion!" She gave a strand of her hair an angry tug only to have it spring back into a flawless curl. "My raven tresses!" Framing her breasts in her hands, she hefted their generous weight. "My plump, tempting—" Remembering too late who she was addressing, she knotted her hands over her gold-linked girdle and inclined her head, blushing furiously.

The earl might have been tempted to laugh had his daughter's tirade not underscored his terrible dilemma. Holly serene was a sight to behold, but Holly in a fit of passion could drive sane men to madness. Not even fury could mar the angelic radiance of her profile. Her black hair tumbled down her slender back like a nimbus of storm clouds. His heart was seized by the familiar twin pangs of wonder and terror. Wonder that such an exquisite creature could have sprang from the loins of a homely little troll like himself. Terror that he would prove unworthy of such a charge.

He bowed his head, battling the pained bewilderment that still blamed Felicia for dying and leaving the precocious toddler to his care. Holly had passed directly from enchanting child with dimpled knees and tumbled curls to the willowy grace of a woman grown, suffering none of the gawkiness that so frequently plagued girls in their middle years.

Now she was rumored to be the fairest lady in all of England, all of Normandy, perhaps in all the world. Strangers came from leagues away in the vain hope of catching a glimpse of her, but he allowed only the wealthiest, most reputable noblemen the boon of an audience. 'Twas not concern for her complexion that kept her locked within the castle walls, but his deep and abiding fear of abduction. His secret conviction was that some man would carry her away and defile her innocence without troubling to obtain the rightful blessing of both he and his God.

The obsession gnawed at him until he awoke in the still, dark hours between dusk and dawn, reeking of stale sweat and quaking like an old man in his bed. He *was* an old man, he reminded himself without pity. Nearly fifty. His bones creaked in complaint when he mounted his destrier. Old wounds earned battling both Scots and Welsh in the king's defense throbbed a dirge at the approach of rain. He'd done as well as he knew how by his only daughter. 'Twas past time for him to relinquish the burden to another man. Before he grew too feeble to stand between her and the avaricious world clamoring outside the castle walls.

"I've arranged for a tournament," he said without preamble.

Holly jerked her head up. Tournaments were common enough affairs, she thought. An opportunity for knights and noblemen to flex their brawny arms and secretly compare the size of their swords. So why had a gauntlet of foreboding closed steely fingers around her heart?

"A tournament?" she said lightly. "And what shall be the prize this time? A kerchief perfumed with my favorite scent? The chance to drink mulled wine from the toe of my shoe? A nightingale's song from my swanlike throat?"

"You. You're to be the prize."

Holly felt the roses in her cheeks wither and die. She gazed down into her father's careworn face, finding his gravity more distressing than his anger. She towered over him by several inches, but the mantle of majesty he had worn to shield him from life's arrows since the death of his beloved wife added more than inches to his stature.

"But, Papa, I—"

"Silence!" He seemed to have lost all tolerance for her pleas. "I promised your mother on her deathbed that you would marry and marry you shall. Within the fortnight. If you've a quarrel with my judgment, you may retreat to a nunnery where they will teach you gratitude for the blessings God has bestowed upon you."

His bobbing gait was less sprightly than usual as he left Holly to contemplate the sentence he'd pronounced.

"A nunnery?" she echoed, drifting toward the window.

"No one would gawk at ye there, my lady." Elspeth emerged from her own self-imposed exile, her hawkish features softened by concern. "Ye could cover yer fine hair with a wimple and take a vow of silence so ye'd never have to sing at someone else's bidding."

Dire heaviness weighted Holly's heart. *A nunnery.* Forbidding stone walls more unscalable than those that imprisoned her now. Not a retreat, but a dungeon where all of her unspoken dreams of rolling meadows and azure skies would rot to dust.

Sinking to her knees in the stone seat, Holly unlatched the window, gazing beyond the iron grille to the outer bailey where the quadrangles of her father's lists lay like a lush green chessboard. Soon warriors bearing their family standards would come pouring into those grassy battlegrounds, each prepared to lay down his life for nothing more than a chance to offer her his name and protection. But would any one of them dare to offer her his heart?

What are you waiting for, Holly? her papa had asked.

Her gaze was drawn west toward the impenetrable tangle of forest and craggy dark peaks of the Welsh mountains. A fragrant breath of spring swept through her, sharpening her nameless yearning. Genuine tears pricked her eyelids.

"Oh, Elspeth. What *am* I waiting for?"

As Elspeth stroked the crown of her head, Holly longed to sniffle and wail. But she could only cry as she'd been taught, each tear trickling like a flawless diamond down the burnished pearl of her cheek.

"A comely wife is a pox upon her husband's fortunes," Sir Austyn of Gavenmore called over his shoulder as his destrier's blunt hooves tore grassy divots from turf dampened by a recent spring rain.

Arguing philosophy with his man-at-arms gave him an excuse to steal a glance over his shoulder, something he'd been compelled to do with increasing frequency since leaving behind the sheltering bracken of the Welsh forest. He could ill appreciate the beauty of the verdant countryside while expecting an English arrow to pierce his hauberk and embed itself in his back with every breath.

Carey drew alongside him, leading a string of pack horses and bearing the oaken staff from which the Gavenmore standard proudly rippled. A gust of wind molded its faded crimsons and greens to his face.

He slapped it away, snorting harder than his piebald gelding. "Fie on you, Austyn! Would you rather bed an ugly woman than a comely one?"

"Bedding and wedding are beasts with different backs. For the one, a man might tolerate fairness of form, but for the other, a plain girl of gentle disposition will prove a jewel in her husband's crown. After all, 'Favor is deceitful and beauty is vain, but a woman that fearest her lord, she shall be praised.'"

"Stop mangling the scriptures to bolster your cause. 'Tis 'a woman that fearest *the Lord.*'" Carey's voice dropped to a wary mutter. "Although if a Gavenmore is her lord, she'd do well to fear him."

Sawing at the reins to slow his horse to a walk, Austyn shot his companion a baleful glare. Over the past eight centuries, the notorious Gavenmore jealousy had provided fodder for scores of legends. His own grandfather had kept his grandmother imprisoned in a tower for ten years after she had dared to bestow a smile on a traveling jongleur. The fate of the unfortunate acrobat was never confirmed, although it was rumored in discreet whispers that his final performance was rope dancing of a more lethal nature for his appreciative host.

"I've never lifted a hand to a woman," he growled.

"You've never married one either." Carey was not intimidated by Austyn's thunderous glares. He'd tolerated them since boyhood and had yet to feel the lash of threatened lightning. "Suppose this Tewksbury wench is as fair as they claim?"

"Ha! No mortal woman could be as fair as they claim her to be. If she were why would her father be offering such an extravagant dowry? I'll wager she has teeth like a horse and ears like a hare." He added hopefully, "Coupled, of course, with the loyal disposition of a hunting hound."

Carey shrugged. "Perhaps she's exceedingly fair, but possessed of a shrewish temperament or a fickle nature."

Austyn felt himself pale beneath his beard. His gauntleted hands flexed on the leather reins as if to warn him of the monstrous deeds they might commit should his bride prove less than constant.

Let beauty be your doom.

The damning indictment of the faerie queen Rhiannon, falsely accused of faithlessness by his Gavenmore ancestor, tolled in his ears. As he spurred his horse into a canter through a meadow dotted with purple heartsease, his gaze lifted to the parapets of the castle drifting in a haze of clouds on the far horizon.

"Then God help us both," he whispered, more to himself than to his man-at-arms. "For I intend to win her."

CHAPTER 2

Holly paced the parapet walk outside her chamber. Greedy gusts of wind tore at her cloak and mocked the silver fillet she had slipped over her brow to tame her unruly hair. Her head felt swollen with unshed tears and the narrow band seemed to tighten with each step. She finally jerked it off and cast it into the night, letting her hair whip where it pleased.

She had fled to the parapet to escape the excited chatter of the ladies-in-waiting her papa had summoned to attend her at tomorrow's tournament. The former haven of her chamber now swarmed with a half dozen well-meaning aunts and a bevy of Tewksbury cousins, all flinching beneath the direction of Brother Nathanael at his most caustic.

The spring wind was balmy, but the wintry pearl of a moon suspended in the north sky better reflected her mood. Pale stars frosted the canopy of the sky, their radiance dimmed by the greedy glow of the campfires scattered around the castle walls.

The hillside was awash in a sea of colorful tents and fluttering pennons. Tomorrow at dawn, the drawbridge of Castle Tewksbury would be lowered, the portcullis raised, and the gates thrown wide to welcome all challengers, including the man who would claim her for both his prize and his bride before the day was done.

Holly shivered as the wind carried a snatch of song and drunken revelry to her ears. She knew little more of men than she had a year ago when they'd began to woo her. Other than her suitors, her father had kept her cut off from masculine company, refusing to expose her to the smitten stares of scullion and groom. Her suitors showed her only their prettiest faces, but she had glimpsed the hunger lurking beneath their masques of courtesy when they thought she was paying them no heed—a sideways glance, a lowered gaze, a wetting of the lips as if in anticipation of sating their appetites at some dark and mysterious feast.

She gripped the rough, familiar stone of the parapet to steady her hands. Tonight she'd only been cast from her chamber. Tomorrow she was to be exiled from the castle itself. She wished for the dubious comfort of blaming her father, but found she could not. Most marriages were arranged by ambitious fathers when their daughters were only babes. Her papa had given her ample opportunity to choose a husband, yet she had failed them both.

The scattered fires winked at her, mocking her swelling panic. A distant rumble of masculine laughter sent a chill of despair shooting down her spine. Tomorrow she would be forever bound before God and man to a stranger. Tonight might be her last precious taste of freedom.

Casting the candlelit window of her chamber a furtive glance, she drew up the hood of her cloak to shield her face and melted into the shadows of the outer stairs.

"Oof. You're standing in my ear."

"Sorry," Austyn said, bracing his booted foot against Carey's sleek head. "If you'd stop squirming, I might be able to get some purchase on the rope."

"You'd squirm, too," Carey gritted out between clenched teeth, "if you had a full-grown ox standing on your shoulders. And it wasn't you who took that nasty plunge off the raft and into the moat." He wrinkled his nose at his own pungent scent. "I've little doubt now what the earl's guards have been using it for. I found it far more offensive than defensive."

Austyn grunted in triumph as the far end of the rope sailed from his hands to hook itself over one of the sturdy stone teeth crowning the inner bailey wall. When he'd judged it competent to bear his weight, he began to shimmy up its length, leaving Carey to sink to his knees in the damp grass, panting for breath. The pale face and hair bequeathed to him a century ago by some rapacious Norse invader gleamed up at Austyn from the shadows.

"This is madness, you know," he offered earnestly when Austyn paused at the first slim arrow loop to assure himself that the raucous cacophony of drunken celebration and petty squabbling from the hillside encampment had muffled their trespass.

A high-pitched giggle, unmistakably feminine, wafted to his ears. The Englishmen were wenching as if each of them were to take a wife on the morrow, Austyn thought. A full-fledged siege would have probably escaped their lecherous attentions. Remembering Carey's supplicant posture just in time, he resisted the urge to spit in disgust.

"Madness it may be," he called down softly, "but I must judge this lady with mine own eyes."

"And if she is as fair as they say?"

Austyn had no answer for that but to continue climbing.

Carey scrambled to his feet, cupping a hand around his mouth to muffle his shout. "If you're caught looming over the fair maiden's bed without benefit of a priest's blessing, you'll be hanged, you know."

Austyn swung one leg over the wall before gathering the end of the rope to drop it down the other side. "Then you may help yourself to my armor, my arms, and that sprightly little mare you've had your eye on for so long."

Carey clasped a hand over his heart. "Sir, in truth, your ill estimation of my devotion wounds me sorely!"

"Then consider yourself fortunate." Austyn's

crooked grin belied the gravity of his words. "We Gavenmores usually kill those we love."

Leaving his friend with a jaunty salute, he swung away from the wall and dropped into nothingness.

Holly eased back the folds of her hood as she slipped into the walled sanctuary of her mother's garden. The budding canopy of elm and oak muted the masculine clamor of voices from outside the castle walls. Even though her heart was heavy, the magical iridescence of the air possessed the power to lighten her step. Her throat tingled as she drank in a nourishing breath of it.

Moonlight silvered the tender shoots prodding their way through the rich, black soil, demanding birth. Beads of dew trembled on the unfurling petals of sweet violet and primrose. Holly paused to bathe her finger in one of the plump droplets, tracing the curling edge of a leaf impatiently awaiting the kiss of dawn.

A wistful sigh escaped her. She had been forbidden the pleasures of sunlight for fear it would mar her creamy complexion, but here in this garden, she became a creature of moonlight. Here she found the solitude denied her by the flock of chattering magpies her papa had appointed as ladies-in-waiting.

As a little girl, she had skipped and jumped along the winding paths as any child would, trusting that the soft loam would cushion her knees without betraying her folly should she stumble.

She wished she could recapture the delicious glee of scampering through the garden, the sense of freedom gained from being rid of prying eyes and expectations. Realizing with a pang of loss that this was the last time she would know such freedom, she sank into the broad wooden saddle of the swing dangling from the branch of a young elm.

Dragging her bare toes in the grass, she began to hum a melancholy tune. Here she could sing, not the elaborate rounds taught by Brother Nathanael and favored by her papa to entertain her suitors, but modest melodies such as the ballad she'd overheard a Welsh scullion maid singing yestereve.

She warbled into song, defiantly savoring the simple pleasure of singing with no one to please but herself.

Austyn swiped a low hanging bough out of his face, swearing beneath his breath. He'd gained his way into the inner bailey only to find himself trapped in an enclosed garden with nary a door in sight. Vines thick with fresh blooms crept up weathered stone walls and dangled from overhanging limbs. A narrow path wended its way through a thicket choked with buds. He followed it, ducking to avoid a thorny arch drenched in shiny, julep-scented leaves.

The garden bore little resemblance to the tidy herb beds he could remember his mother tending, but instead seemed caught in the grip of some enchanted anarchy. He prided himself on scorning the superstitions that plagued most of his Welsh kin, but wouldn't have been overly startled to see a mischievous Booka scamper out from beneath a toadstool to cast a curse on him. 'Twas a pity he was already cursed.

"Asinine rubbish," he muttered, but took the precaution of signing a cross on his surcoat.

He was to be thankful for such prudence when the first mournful notes of the melody wafted to his ears.

At first he thought he must have imagined it. He stopped, cocking his head to listen. An icy finger of memory caressed the base of his spine, lifting his hackles. Without realizing it, he rested a hand on his sword hilt.

He knew the words of the ballad by heart. Had learned them when his mother had, in her rich contralto, sung him to sleep. 'Twas a rather grim lullaby about a lady coaxing her lover to rest his head on her breast and sleep. Not for a night, but for all eternity, because sharing death would be preferable to one of them betraying the other should they live. A keen blade of grief sliced Austyn's heart, but its bleeding was staunched by a tattered bandage of rage.

"Rhiannon," he whispered.

'Twas surely not the shade of his mother who mocked him, but that treacherous Welsh faerie. He would have died before confessing it to Carey or any other man, but he had felt her presence before, when walking his horse through a mist-shrouded glade at twilight or skirting the weed-choked boundaries of his mother's grave. She was all spirit and no substance—a brief cooling of the air, a flick of gossamer hair across his face, the taunting whisper of a lover's breath against his nape.

Perhaps he should have heeded Carey's warning, for this was madness indeed.

Leaving the path behind, he plunged through the

thicket, determined to find the witch who worked such dark magic. She sang not in a husky contralto, but in a lilting soprano tuned to flawless pitch. He froze, holding his breath, as the final note of the song trembled in the air, mocking him.

An eerie creak sounded to his left.

He drew his short sword, forgetting that it was he who had intruded upon this haunted glade. "Who goes there?"

His hoarse demand was answered by a faint squeak and a rustle of undergrowth. Hacking away at the slender branches of a rowan, he charged forward only to find himself alone in a moon-dappled clearing sheltered by a single elm. An abandoned swing turned this way and that, as if prodded by the vagaries of the wind.

A triumphant smile curved Austyn's lips. The high wall surrounding the garden blocked the wind. Other than those he'd disturbed, not even a leaf trembled. He touched his hand to the wooden seat of the swing. Faint warmth emanated to his callused palm. He straightened, pleased to have proved his prey was not faerie or ghost, but mortal.

Just how mortal was proved in the next moment when a frantic rustle of blooms was followed by a delicate sneeze. Sheathing his sword, he strode over to part the greenery. The blooms still quivered, but whoever had sought their asylum had fled, darting once more out of his reach. His smile faded. His quarry was proving to be more fleet of foot than he. He was the sort of hunter who preferred the roaring challenge of a charging boar to the subtleties of tracking a doe through the forest.

The crack of a twig betrayed movement at the edge of the glade. Already savoring his impending victory, Austyn moved to investigate. The creak of the swing behind him warned him an instant too late. He whipped around to discover the contraption rushing toward him with dizzying speed, a darkly bewinged creature mounted on its back. Its feet slammed into his chest, knocking him backward. He would have been knocked to the loam, bruising only his pride, had his head not struck the edge of a marble bench. Tendrils of lightning shot through his bewildered brain.

As consciousness sifted from his mind, he would have almost sworn he heard the mocking notes of a woman's laughter drifting on the windless air.

CHAPTER 3

꩜

Slipping from the swing, Holly gazed down at the giant she had felled, her heart thudding wildly in her throat. He sprawled in a puddle of moonlight, bearing more resemblance to some shaggy beast than a man. A fearsome beard shaded his jaw, climbing to mate with a dark froth of unkempt hair. She doubted she could have spanned his tendon-corded throat with both hands—although at the moment she would have liked to try.

She was torn between the desire to rest her foot triumphantly on his surcoat and scream for her father's guards or flee and pretend she had never left the haven of her chamber. She cast the stairs a longing glance.

The knight's utter absence of movement drew her gaze back to him. With his mighty arms flung outward in supplication and his thick, stubby lashes resting flush against his pallid cheeks, he looked as vulnerable as a sleeping babe. Or a sleeping bear, she amended. Clammy fingers of dread stifled her thundering pulse.

Suppose she had killed him?

The wretch deserved no less, she thought, for daring to invade her sanctuary and scaring her half out of her wits. She tried to pull herself away, but found she could not abandon him without assuring herself she had not caused him mortal injury. Dropping gingerly to her knees beside his still form, she forced herself to splay a trembling hand over his surcoat, noting that the coral oval of one of her fingernails had been torn to the quick.

"Nathanael will have my head," she muttered.

Her dismay was tempered with relief as her hand rose and fell in rhythm with the giant's steady breathing. She frowned, suddenly bewildered. The jarring impact of her feet striking his chest had convinced her the knight was wearing chain mail, yet she felt no betraying links beneath the faded linen of his surcoat. Casting a furtive glance over her shoulder as if expecting Brother Nathanael to spring out of the budding heliotropes, she slipped a shy hand inside both surcoat and tunic to discover a chest armored not with the cold artifice of steel, but with an extravagant expanse of warm muscle. Crisp whorls of hair tickled her questing fingertips.

She snatched her hand back, disturbed by the urge to explore further. Jerking up her hood, she prepared to flee, but a heartrending groan stopped her. Trapped in a vise of indecision, Holly wanted to groan, too. So the man wasn't dead. But what if he were dying? Did she dare leave him at the mercy of the cold damp seeping into his bones? Perhaps if she revived him, she could convince herself to flee before he came fully to his senses and decided to pursue whatever sinister purpose had brought him to the garden.

She leaned over him. Her hair brushed his nose, making it twitch. "Sir?" she whispered. "Oh, sir? I pray, sir, can you hear me?"

His lips parted in a gentle snore, as if he would be content to slumber forever, deaf to her pleas.

There was no help for it, Holly thought. She was going to have to touch him again.

Amazed that one being could radiate so much heat, she curled her hand around his throat, determined to shake him awake if necessary. His hair teased her knuckles. The unruly locks felt soft and clean, not coarse and tangled as she had expected. She peered curiously at his face, wondering what manner of features such a forbidding growth of hair obscured. Beguiled by the mystery, she drew her thumb along the edge of his beard, exploring the strong curve of the jaw beneath.

"Witch."

Before she could react to the hoarse mutter, a brawny forearm clamped around her waist. One powerful hand seized her nape, dragging her down until she sprawled in ungainly shock across the knight's chest.

Holly turned her face away, convinced he was going to snap her fragile neck like a twig.

"Witch," he whispered, this time the word more endearment than accusation.

Quivering with terror, Holly eased her head back around. She expected his eyes to be as dark as the rest of him. Her shock was doubled when she found herself gazing down into orbs of glacial blue lit not by flame, but smoldering frost. It wasn't the absence of threat in those eyes that paralyzed her. It was the pained brew of dread and anticipation simmering in their depths. With unspeakable tenderness, the knight's big hand drifted up from her nape to smooth back her hood, baring her face to the moonlight.

Holly resisted the urge to flinch. Not even when being displayed on a dais before a potential suitor and his gawking retinue had she felt so exposed.

At the sight of her face, a shudder rocked the powerful masculine frame beneath her. The unspoken confession of vulnerability robbed her of conscious will. This man wore no mask to shield her from his desire. Holly knew instinctively that in that moment, he was as defenseless as she. He slid his fingers beneath her hair to capture her nape with gentle mastery, drawing her mouth down to his.

Holly had been kissed before—shy pecks on the cheek, fervent kisses pressed to the back of her hand, and once even a moist kiss on the lips from Eugene de Legget that had earned him a resounding slap. But this man did not so much kiss her mouth as partake of it.

With Eugene, she had kept her lips clamped tight, but with this stranger, it seemed only natural that they part beneath the coaxing urgency of his own. The unfamiliar tickle of his mustache and the silken heat of his tongue dipping into her mouth was blunted by the irresistible tenderness with which he seemed to savor their mingled flavors. A small sound, half dismay, half delight, escaped her throat.

As if her involuntary moan had jarred him to his senses, he tangled a fist in her hair and dragged her face away from his. Smarting tears of loss sprang to Holly's eyes. The stranger studied her face anew, his eyes no longer unguarded, but narrowed and sheltered by their thicket of dark lashes. She could not help but recoil as he dropped that exacting gaze to her lips, which felt swollen and scorched by the ruthless moonlight and the faint, minty gusts of his breath. Her tongue darted out to soothe them.

Swearing a guttural oath, he shoved her off of him and staggered to a standing position, drawing the back of his hand across his mouth as if her kiss had poisoned him. Had it not been for the overt shaking of that hand, Holly might have gathered the crumbs of her pride and fled. She was torn by a compulsion to touch him, to gently wrap her fingers around his until their troubled glissando had eased.

She had seen men robbed of speech or driven to babble like idiots in her presence, but she had never seen a man sickened unto death at the mere sight of her. He looked less like he'd caught her feet in his chest than taken a lance to the gut.

As she rose from her undignified sprawl, he backed into the shadows beneath the elm until she could see little more than the wary gleam of his eyes.

From his tense posture, she half expected him to whip out a crucifix.

"For God's sake, woman, cover yourself," he snapped in lieu of rattling a necklace of garlic cloves at her.

An absurd shame flooded Holly's cheeks with heat. Feeling as if she'd been caught in one of those horrid dreams where she was locked outside the castle walls naked, she barely resisted the urge to shield her breasts with her hands. A furtive flick of her gaze assured her that her modest cloak was intact. She lifted a hand to her hood, then lowered it, defiantly flaunting her face to the moonlight's bold caress and the knight's steely glare.

His voice deepened to a resonant growl. "Heed my warning, lady. Leave me now or suffer the consequences."

A foreigner, Holly realized by his crude accent. One of those savage Welshman who so frequently plagued the western borders of Eugene's lands. She took a tentative step toward him. "Do you seek to do me harm, sir?"

She already suspected his answer. If he wished her ill, why would he have spared her the gravest harm a man could inflict upon a lone woman in a deserted garden? And why would he be warning her from his presence even now?

"What I seek to do has no bearing on what I'm driven to do."

Holly ducked beneath a low-hanging bough, breaching the dappled shadows beneath the elm. "Ah, a man who favors riddles! Perhaps you'd care to answer one for me."

Robbed of further retreat, he folded his imposing arms over his chest, erecting a more impenetrable defense. "Will you leave me if I do?"

His words stung more than Holly would have admitted. She was accustomed to men tumbling over one another in their eagerness to seek her company. His reticence was beginning to insult her.

"If you wish," she said coolly. They were nearly toe to toe now, and as she tipped her head back to meet his gaze, her senses quailed at the reminder of how very large a man he was. And how very dangerous it might be to bait him. "Why did you pursue me?" she asked softly. "And once you'd caught me, why did you let me go?"

For several nervous thuds of her heart, he was so still he might have been hewn of stone. Then a crooked smile transformed his face into a derisive mask. "I was to meet my lover here. I mistook you for her. When you fled at my approach, I thought you were she, simply indulging in a game we sometimes play."

Holly found it painfully easy to imagine the outcome of that game, regardless of who its winner might be. It seemed the tender enchantment of his kiss had been only an illusion. In truth, she had done nothing more than interrupt a sordid tryst. She inclined her head, caught unawares by a jarring blow of disappointment.

Holly must have imagined his pained grunt, for when she lifted her head, his face was once again impassive. He unfolded his arms as if he'd come to some irrevocable conclusion. "Do not look so melancholy, my lady. 'Tis early yet. Perhaps we can restore the bloom of cheer to your cheeks before my own lady arrives."

Holly took a step backward. "I think not, sir. I should prefer my bloom to wilt on the vine before I bestow it on a faithless knave such as yourself."

He pushed away from the tree trunk with unmistakable menace. "A faithless knave, am I? What of your own fidelity, that you would bestow your kisses so freely on a stranger?"

His words cut more deeply for their truth. Now it was she who was being stalked. She backed away from his towering form, stumbling over the hem of her cloak. 'Twas little wonder he thought her wanton. She'd done naught to discourage such reasoning. But not even her mortification could prevent her from striking a parting blow.

"I might yet bestow my kisses on a stranger, but you can be assured, sir, that I will never again bestow them on you."

Wishing desperately that she'd heeded his earlier warning, she spun around to flee only to be wrenched to a painful halt. Believing he'd seized her hair, she closed her eyes, panting with dread of the moment when he would hurl her to the ground and tear at her skirts with his ruthless hands.

"Betrayed by your crowning glory, eh? How fitting." The mocking voice came from a few feet behind her and Holly was abashed to realize the knight had pursued her only in her overwrought imagination.

She dared a glance upward. 'Twas not a mortal hand, but a gnarled finger of the elm that had snagged her. She tugged at the treacherous strand, but only succeeded in weaving it into an intractable snarl around the branch. She hung there, as defenseless as a rabbit in a snare at the knight's swift approach.

As his shadow enveloped her, she nervously licked her lips, then wished she hadn't. They still tasted of the foreign, but not unpleasant, flavor of his kiss—the cool mint of wintergreen wedded with the warm musk of hops.

Her mouth went dry as he drew a misericorde from his belt. The tiny but lethal blade was dwarfed by his tense fingers. She whimpered involuntarily.

"Christ, woman, would you stop whining? I've no intention of cutting your throat." He captured the skein of hair in his fist, relieving the painful pressure on her scalp.

As the dagger bit into the captive strand, a fresh moan of dismay escaped her. The knight froze, his breathing audible, and glared at her as if reconsidering his pledge.

Her attempt at a sheepish shrug was hampered by her tenuous position. "Forgive me, sir. 'Tis just that a blade has never touched my hair. Not since I was born."

He gave the dark mane that rippled well past her rump an arch glance. "What of a comb? Has a comb never profaned its hallowed state?"

"Why, of course! My nurse combs it five hundred strokes each night before I lay down upon my pillow."

He snorted. "And I had supposed you slept sitting up, so as not to jounce a precious tendril."

Holly might have wrinkled her nose at him had Nathanael not taught her that such childish indulgences could carve permanent pleats in her skin. "If you're quite done making sport of me, sir, I give you leave to proceed."

Instead of clumsily hacking at the mess as she expected such a ruffian to do, he took his time, severing each filament as if it had been spun from gold. His care shook her composure as none of his blustering had done.

When he was done, she fingered her scalp, half expecting to find a gaping bald spot. She couldn't resist shooting a covetous glance at the glossy black curl laid like a sacrificial offering across his palm.

He closed his fist around it and shook his head. One big, blunt finger drifted upward to caress the delicate arch of her jaw. "Leave me now, my lady, and I shall consider it a trophy of a battle contemplated, but never fought."

Mesmerized by the frosty glitter of his eyes, Holly hesitated, sensing it was the last warning he would bestow upon her. A peculiar mixture of fear and anticipation quickened her breath as she briefly wondered what fate she might endure at his hands should she fail to heed it.

His mask dropped, briefly, tantalizingly, showing her the indisputable truth. He wasn't afraid of her. He was afraid of what he might do to her should she be fool enough to linger.

Tearing her gaze away from his, she raced for the stairs without daring a single backward glance.

Had she done so, she might have seen the knight sink down on the bench in the moonlight, his massive body folding in on itself as if to protect his heart from a blow that had already done mortal damage.

.   .   .

"Men! Faithless, miserable wretches, the lot of them!"

Holly groaned in grudging satisfaction as she sank into the hot bath Elspeth had prepared for her. Steam wafted up from the myrrh-scented water, curling the tendrils of hair that had snaked loose from the heavy coil wound atop her head.

Elspeth drew a rough sponge over her shoulders, the motion failing to soothe her as it should. "Ye shouldn't have run off like that, my lady. Brother Nathanael almost called for the castle guard. 'Tisn't safe to be rambling alone with all those *men* lurking about."

Remembering the naked desire she had glimpsed so briefly on the knight's face, Holly snorted bitterly. "You speak the truth, Elspeth, for it seems one woman will do as well as any other in the dark."

She leaned her head back against the lip of the wooden tub while Elspeth sponged her breasts and belly. As her eyes drifted shut, she was besieged by an unbidden vision of the knight entangled in the pale, plump arms of his "lady."

"Lady indeed!" she muttered beneath her breath. "Probably a castle doxy. Or one of the serving wenches."

"Eh? Did ye speak, child?"

"No," she snapped without opening her eyes, then mumbled, "Probably has a wife tucked away somewhere as well. Rutting boar." Her eyes popped open. "Bear."

Elspeth cast her mistress's sullen face a puzzled look. The girl had flown into the chamber a short while ago as if pursued by some wild beast, eyes sparkling and cheeks riotous with color. Ignoring her attendants' cooed questions and breathless protests, she had herded them from the room, even daring to slam the door in her tutor's livid face. The ladies had prudently retired, but Brother Nathanael still hovered outside the bolted door, his pacing punctuated by sharp knocks and imperious demands for entry.

Elspeth hummed beneath her breath as she wrung out the sponge. In truth, the nurse much preferred this grumbling virago to the pale, subdued ghost of her mistress who had haunted the castle since learning of the tournament that was to take place on the morrow.

Her bewilderment returned when Holly snatched the sponge from her hands and began to scrub at her lips.

Sensing Elspeth's scrutiny, Holly sheepishly lowered the sponge, knowing her efforts were in vain. No matter how hard she scrubbed, the knight's taste still lingered. It was as if his kiss had invaded not only her mouth, but her soul as well. She wanted nothing so much as to throw her hands over her face and burst into tears.

She had been on the verge of surrendering to her father's machinations, but her encounter with the knight had reminded her of one thing. She must fight for her freedom. She would never become the docile ornament of a tyrant like Eugene, or worse yet, the chattel of some man who would leave her languishing by the hearth while he trysted with his doxy in a moonlit garden.

The chamber door came under the assault of a persistent fist. "I insist that you let me in, Holly. I've yet to prepare you for your song on the morrow. This

childish sulking ill becomes you." The last was punctuated by a frustrated kick to the unyielding door.

Holly gritted her teeth. When he had applied for
the position as priest of Tewksbury, Brother Nathanael had sworn to her father that he had left the abbey
on a pilgrimage to seek sustenance for his starving
soul. Holly suspected the abbot had booted out the
arrogant young monk after he'd exhibited the poor
judgment of pointing out that if he were God, he would
have designed both women and kittens to function
with far more efficiency.

"Go away, Nathanael." She was the only one who
dared to strip him of his title, knowing it pricked his
boundless vanity beyond bearing. "I'll sing for no man
tonight. Not even you."

A distinctly impious mutter penetrated the thick
oak of the door before his footsteps receded.

"Men!" Holly sprang to a standing position,
streaming water over the sides of the round tub. "The
rogues care for nothing but sweetness of voice, fairness of face, and bounteous breasts. Why do they
praise such trifles? Why does no one ever compliment
me on the sharpness of my wit? Or my gentle demeanor?" She hurled the sponge at the far wall. It
struck with a satisfying splat and dropped to the floor.

Bounding from the tub, she stormed across the
chamber, leaving Elspeth to trot behind her, wringing
a linen towel in her chapped hands. "Come now, my
lady. Ye'll take a chill."

Holly paused before a full-length looking glass,
turning this way and that to give her naked form a
critical perusal. There was simply no help for it, she
thought grimly. She was stunning from any angle. As

Elspeth timidly patted the droplets of moisture from her back, she wondered if there was any way for her to outwit both her tutor and her papa. If their plan was successful, tonight would be the last night she would slip between her sheets naked and alone.

She reached up to uncoil her hair, briefly touching the spot from where the knight had cut his trophy. He had taken such care that she could barely tell a curl was missing. She remembered the wisp of ebony lying across his callused palm, the tantalizing brush of his fingertip against her jaw. Who would have thought his graceless paws were capable of such subtlety?

Sighing wistfully, she inquired of her reflection, "Why are men such vexsome creatures?"

"I can't say, my lady," Elspeth replied, lifting one of Holly's arms to dry beneath it. "Not a moment's trouble have they given me."

Holly's gaze slowly shifted to Elspeth's reflection. Her nurse was but a few inches shorter than she, but her simian bearing made Holly's slim form tower over her. Holly had never given Elspeth's looks, or lack of them, much regard. She saw only the twinkle of affection in the woman's crossed eyes, heard only the note of concern in her hoarse croak, felt only the tenderness in the touch of her gnarled hands.

Compared to those gifts, bestowed so generously upon a little girl still pining for her mother, Elspeth's sparse mustache and the pronounced wart beside her nose had all faded to insignificance. Until that moment.

Still fingering a strand of her hair, Holly glanced once more between their reflections, a calculating smile burgeoning on her lips.

Elspeth grinned, revealing a row of blackened stumps. " 'Ye'd best earn a position in the castle, girl,' my papa always said, 'for only a blind man would take ye to wife.' " She giggled, a girlish sound, devoid of self-pity. "Called me his little gargoyle, he did. Threatened to make me sit on the thatch o' the cottage and frighten off wicked spirits."

Elspeth dropped the towel with a startled shriek as Holly enveloped her in a damp embrace, nearly lifting her off the floor. "Then your papa was a fool, for I think you're the most beautiful woman in all the world!"

As Holly pressed her smooth cheek to her nurse's mottled one, Elspeth squinted at their reflections, recognizing with dawning alarm the spark of mischief in her mistress's eyes.

chapter 4

A crisp fanfare rippled through the morning air.

Carey spat out the plume of the feathered quill he was nibbling, his gaze shifting to the castle on the hill. The metallic rumble of the drawbridge being lowered underscored the brassy invitation of the trumpet.

As if drawn by its siren lure, Austyn emerged from their faded tent into the dappled sunshine. Carey promptly sat on his parchment and tucked the quill behind his ear, fully expecting to be chided for not devoting his free time to polishing his master's chain mail or some other practical task. His first glimpse of Austyn's face banished all such concerns from his mind and brought him halfway to his feet.

Carey had been dodging retching, moaning Englishmen all morning, men sickened to pale husks of themselves by their overindulgence in ale, wenches, and revelry, but none of them bore the haunted look of the damned as Sir Austyn of Gavenmore did. To Carey's knowledge, his master had indulged in none of those vices. He had returned early to the tent, declining to discuss the outcome of his quest, and retired without a word. It appeared he had not slept, but had spent the night wrestling demons and losing.

The skin of his brow was pale, his eyes burning hollows. Yet the mouth beneath his dark mustache was set in sullen determination. Carey had seen that particular twist of his lips only once before, when he'd discovered a nine-year-old Austyn struggling to carry his mother's body down the narrow, winding stairs of Caer Gavenmore without bumping her limp head on the wall.

Carey held his breath without realizing it, anticipating the gruff command to prepare the horses so they could begin the long journey home.

Austyn strode past him without a word, heading toward the castle.

Scrambling to gather ink and parchment, Carey hastened after him, trotting to match his long strides. "We're staying?" he dared.

Carey's boldness earned him a brusque nod. "Aye. We can't keep living as we have forever—riding from tourney to tourney, fighting and clawing for every ounce of English gold they'll surrender to us. What if I should lose a purse, or worse yet, a limb? What if I were to die on the jousting field? What would happen to Caer Gavenmore then?" He shook his head.

"I'll not leave this place without that dowry. My father has been punished enough by that damned curse. I'll rot in hell before I'll see him robbed of his freedom and everything he holds dear." Austyn's resolution failed to soften the fierceness of his expression. A twitching acrobat flipped out of his path, forgoing his penny payment to seek less hazardous turf.

The acrobat wasn't the only one looking askance at Austyn. Their passage among the ranks of the English streaming up the hill earned him more than a few wary stares, nudges, and knowing mutters of "Gavenmore." The Welsh giant towered head and shoulders over even the tallest of them. His current demeanor only contributed to his air of menace. He looked like a man about to sell his soul to Satan without reaping any of the benefits.

Carey's curiosity mounted. "Was the lady truly so fair?"

Austyn shuddered, never breaking stride. " 'Twas like looking into the face of my own death."

"Eyes?"

"Two of them. So blue as to be almost violet."

"Brow?"

"Fair as virgin snow."

Carey unrolled his parchment, juggling ink and paper. "Nose?"

Austyn lifted a self-conscious finger to his own nose, battered from too many blows taken in a helm. "Straight."

Drawing the quill from behind his ear, Carey wiped a smudge of ink from his temple before starting to scribble. "Voice?"

"Drizzles over your ears like sun-warmed mead."

"Oh, that's good. That's very good. What of her hair?"

Austyn slipped a hand into his hauberk, drawing forth a sable curl that unrolled past his knees. Carey stopped writing, swallowing hard. "Sweet Christ, Austyn? Did you leave her any?"

Austyn's glare as he tucked the treasure away prompted Carey to blurt out, "Lips?"

A pained mist captured his master's eyes. "Soft. Yielding. Made a man want to sink between them and . . ." His voice faded on a groan.

Carey scribbled madly. This was even better than he had hoped. "Temperament?"

Austyn's resignation erupted into passion. "Such boldness! Such brazen vanity! Saucy wench hadn't a morsel of sense. Too foolish to shrink from an armed knight in a deserted garden, yet sniveled like an infant when I laid my blade to her precious hair."

Carey tucked the quill between his teeth and nibbled thoughtfully. "So you found her distasteful, eh? Perhaps your repugnance will protect you from—"

Austyn's fist closed in the front of his tunic, driving him back until his shoulders struck a handy oak. Carey quailed before the desperation in his master's face. "Distasteful? Repugnance? Would to God that it were so! I wanted to drag her to the ground beneath me and plow her like a fallow field. I wanted to drop to my knees, bathe her feet in my kisses and swear her my eternal fealty. I wanted to lock her away so no man but me would ever lay eyes on her again."

In his friend's eyes Carey caught a glimpse of the beast Austyn had struggled his entire life to tame. A tremor of foreboding shook him. Ignoring the curious gazes of the passersby, he whispered, " 'Tis not too late to turn back."

Austyn released him, absently smoothing the wrinkle he had made in his tunic. Even as a boy, the weight of responsibility had straightened his shoulders instead of bowing them. "That's where you're wrong, lad. 'Twas too late to turn back before I was born." He squatted to retrieve Carey's scattered quill and papers, noticing them for the first time. "And what's this?"

Carey rescued his precious notes, trying not to squirm. He'd been hoping to put off this moment for as long as he dared. "While you were gone last night, I passed the time with some bards brought by their masters from Normandy. It seems the tournament is to commence with a test of chivalry."

"Chivalry?" Austyn spat out the word like an epithet.

"Aye. After the earl's daughter opens the tournament with a song, her suitors are to engage in a brief contest of"—he dropped his voice to a mumble— "verse."

Austyn spun on his heel and marched back toward the tent.

Carey rushed after him. "Don't be so rash! 'Tis only the earl's ploy to separate the civilized from any unschooled savages who might attempt to win his daughter."

Austyn's long strides did not falter. "Then you can congratulate the man for me. This unschooled savage is going home to Wales. Being damned for all eternity is one thing, but being made an ass of is quite another."

Carey scampered ahead of him, waving the papers beneath Austyn's intractable nose. "I'll not let them make an ass of you. That's why I've been up all night writing these masterful tributes to the lady's beauty."

Austyn stopped dead, a scant inch away from trampling his man-at-arms. His nostrils flared like an angry bull's. "Very well." He stabbed a finger at the beaming Carey. "But if she dares to laugh at me, I won't kill her. I'll kill you."

Austyn's hackles prickled as they passed through the inner bailey of Castle Tewksbury to be swallowed by the yawning jaws of the great hall.

The sturdy weight of the hauberk worn beneath his surcoat soothed his raw nerves. He refused to leave his back unguarded in such a mob of armed English. No peace decreed by treaty or surrender could banish the centuries of distrust bred into his Welsh bones.

A retinue of extravagantly garbed knights led by a hooded lord jostled past Carey, sneering at his worn tunic and faded boots. Carey waved a fist at their backs. "Flee my wrath, will you? Be ye knights or damsels?"

Austyn clapped a restraining hand on his man's shoulder, itching to caress his own sword hilt. He refrained, knowing any hasty flare of his temper might result in bloodshed. Better to save his hostility for the battlefield of the tournament, where he could vent it with honor for a worthy prize.

Provided, of course, that he survived the humiliation of dueling with rhyme instead of steel. A flush of heat crept up the back of his neck as he envisioned the beauty from the garden, her dark head tossed in laughter, her eyes sparkling with merriment at his expense.

He shot Carey a glower, but his efforts were wasted. His man-at-arms was gazing around, as wide-eyed and open-mouthed as if the pearly gates of heaven had parted to grant him entry. Austyn rolled his eyes. Carey was only two summers younger than his own twenty-nine years, but at times Austyn felt decades older.

He resisted his own temptation to gawk. Castle Tewksbury was less a castle than a palace. Instead of a central hearth with a crude smokehole overhead, three pairs of stone-hooded fireplaces flanked the plastered walls. Crushed beneath his boots were not sweet herbs and stale rushes, but luxuriant Turkish rugs. Austyn could remember when Caer Gavenmore had been adorned with such treasures, before his mother died and they'd all been sold off to pay the taxes.

At the far end of the vaulted hall sat a raised dais draped in white samite. Behind the platform, an oriel window sifted the sunlight through panes of colored glass, casting jade and ruby masks over the expectant faces clustered beneath it.

Carey nudged him. "Looks like a bloody cathedral, doesn't it?"

"Aye." Austyn nodded grimly, eyeing the virginal hue of the draped dais. "A fitting altar for an angel."

He could not help but notice that the crafty earl had admitted no women, noble or peasant, into the hall. He doubtlessly wanted every scrap of male attention riveted on the tournament's prize. Austyn snorted cynically. The precaution was unnecessary. From what he had seen of the earl's daughter, she embodied the unfulfilled desires of every man born into the world since Adam. With such a glorious Eve displayed before them, any other female present would have paled like the moon before the radiance of the rising sun.

The scarlet curtain draped over the arched doorway at the side of the platform parted. Austyn's pulse quickened in anticipation even as his gut knotted with dread.

A squat man emerged. Had his saffron-colored surcoat not borne the Tewksbury coat of arms, Austyn might have taken the fellow for one of the mummers. 'Twas incomprehensible to him that the dwarfish creature could have spawned the willowy nymph Austyn had encountered in the garden. The man looked better suited to frolicking beneath a toadstool.

His host's identity was confirmed by a rousing cheer and a violent press to the fore as the challengers elbowed their way closer to the dais. They gave Austyn a wide enough berth, but he had to reach out and snatch Carey back by his tunic to keep him from being trampled. Austyn was content to linger on the fringes of the crush, knowing he would have a clear enough view over their heads.

Stepping up on the dais, the earl lifted his stubby arms. His hanging sleeves swept open like mink-lined wings. "Welcome! Welcome all to Castle Tewksbury!"

Austyn winced. All the majesty denied the earl in stature had been granted him in voice. Austyn's head still ached from the blow it had taken the night before and Tewksbury's bass cracked through it like thunder.

The earl acknowledged the cheering and stamping of feet with a regal nod. "Many of you have traveled far and endured great hardship to accept my invitation this day. Before we commence with the competition, I wish to provide you with a vision of inspiration."

Excitement rippled through the crowd, borne by whispers and murmurs of "The lady! He shows us the lady!"

Austyn tried to unclench his fists, but found he could not. He only prayed he could stop himself from rushing up on the dais to shield her from the ravenous gazes of the other men. The thought of them leering at her, secretly imagining all the things they hungered to do to her lithe body, all the things *he* hungered to do . . .

A tortured groan escaped him. Carey shot him a wary look, his frown deepening as he spotted the beads of sweat Austyn could feel inching down his brow.

". . . my wish that you should no longer suffer in suspense," the earl was saying, his voice little more than a roar of doom in Austyn's ears. "My beloved daughter has chosen to honor your noble endeavors in song."

As the earl took a seat on the dais, the clamor of approval that had greeted his proclamation was muted to a reverent hush. Carey bounced up and down on his tiptoes to see over the head of the man in front of him.

Austyn slipped a hand into his hauberk to finger the ethereal softness of his hard-won trophy; the exotic scent of myrrh drifted to his nostrils. The first fey notes of the Welsh lullaby echoed through his pounding head, but he could not have said if they were composed of reality or dream.

The curtain parted.

A woman stepped into view.

Carey tugged his sleeve. His puzzled voice rang like a gong in those first few heartbeats of stunned silence. "Forgive me for asking, sir, but just how dark was it in that garden?"

chapter 5

Austyn's ears, like those of every man in the great hall, had been tuned to hear the melodic warbling of an angel. Which explained his overwhelming urge to clap his hands over them when the woman on the dais opened her mouth and cheerfully croaked through blackened teeth:

Nary a lady had a knight wi' such a roamin'
    lance.
Slay the wenches he did,
And begged they for more,
Til his lady booted him out the door
With nary a second chance!

Austyn's hand slowly uncurled from his trophy. He knew he should be thanking God for his good fortune, but as the gossamer threads of hair slipped through his limp fingers, he swayed as if some incalculable loss had left his heart bleeding from shock.

"She could have been anyone," he murmured, dazed by the revelation. "A lady-in-waiting. The earl's sister. His mistress." Austyn shook his head to clear it of that intolerable vision. "I never thought to ask her name. I just assumed . . ."

Carey smiled weakly, making a transparent effort to swallow his own revulsion. " 'Tis fortunate you were mistaken. Why, she's just what you wanted! A nice plain little wife."

Austyn forced back a shudder as the woman launched into the chorus of the ditty with rousing enthusiasm and wretched pitch. "She's not plain. She's . . . hideous."

From the discordant buzz rising around them, he wasn't the only one present to reach that conclusion. Mutters of trickery and fraud were swarming through the hall like angry honeybees as the men exchanged nudges and suspicious glares. A timid mention of witchcraft led several challengers to cross themselves and back away from the dais.

'Twas only the heartfelt sigh of a richly garbed noble that kept the crowd from disintegrating into a dangerous mob. The man shook his head regretfully, the badly singed plume of his enormous hat drooping over one eye. "Aye, a wasting disease. She tried to warn me of it, but her beauty was still such that I refused to believe her."

This produced several fresh murmurs of "webbed

feet," "bouts of blindness," and an even more alarming whisper of "pox" that had the men crossing their knees instead of their breasts.

As the rumors sped through the great hall, the knowing nods gathered momentum. At last the men understood the reason for the earl's haste in seeking a husband for his daughter as well as his offer of such a generous dowry. He plainly hoped to marry her off before her appearance deteriorated further. Several of the challengers cast horrified glances at the dais, the prospect eluding even their superior imaginations.

The song mercifully reached its conclusion. After gaping at his daughter for several long, terse moments, the earl stepped forward. Austyn narrowed his eyes. More often than not, his own survival had depended on his ability to judge the mood of his opponent, and he would have almost sworn the earl's clenched fists were shaking not in mortification, but in fury.

His host's voice cracked like a whip, lashing the gossip to a halt. "We shall proceed with the contest of verse. Who will be the first to pay tribute to my daughter in poetry or song?"

The silence swelled and deepened. The empty space around the dais seemed to be spreading of its own accord. Some of the men fidgeted. Others tried to hide lutes behind their backs or tuck flutes down the front of their hose.

Austyn was rooted to the spot.

Carey hissed in his ear, "Was it not you who said 'a comely wife is a pox upon her husband's fortunes'? God has given you a chance to outwit destiny. Don't squander it."

Austyn glanced at the tempting specter of the door behind him, then back at the dais where the woman stood beaming at the crowd as if too dull-witted to comprehend the stir her appearance had caused. Her father was mopping his shiny brow with his sleeve and inching toward the curtain.

Austyn was robbed of his right to choose when Carey planted a shoulder firmly in his back and shoved. He half stumbled, half lurched forward, regaining his balance amongst a chorus of ugly titters.

Clearing his throat of its sudden obstruction, he squared his shoulders, rested one hand on his sword hilt and boldly announced, "I've come for the woman."

Holly was having little difficulty maintaining her beatific smile. She was already savoring dreams of victory. She'd seen audiences enthralled by her performances before, but she'd never seen one quite so aghast.

She might have feared for her ruse had not Lord Fairfax of the scorched hat plume unwittingly come to her defense by repeating those ridiculous fables she had told him. Her sole remaining concern was the muffled thumping coming from the upstairs wardrobe where she and Elspeth had locked Brother Nathanael. Even that was fading as the minutes wore on.

Aye, she confessed to herself, the back of her papa's neck *was* a deplorable shade of magenta, and he was bobbing on his heels like a rotund cauldron about to overboil, but he would forgive her in time. He always did. Her smile took on a dreamy quality as she anticipated the clever wiles she would employ to coax him out of his temper.

First, she would order his favorite supper prepared: fresh peacock stuffed with rosemary and dressed in its own feathers, tiny capers roasted to golden brown perfection, tender sweetmeats and confections drizzled with melted butter. Her own mouth began to water in anticipation.

Then she would don his favorite cotte—the violet one with the matching wimple trimmed in cloth of gold. She resisted the sudden urge to reach up and touch her hair. 'Twould grow in time and until it did, she had dozens of lovely wimples to cover it. She could only hope her eyelashes would grow as quickly.

Once her papa was settled on the brocaded bench before the hearth, she would kneel on a cushion at his feet, pluck a melody from her harp, and sing his favorite song—the one her mama had sang to soothe him after he'd returned from breaking a new stallion or battling the obstinate Welsh.

Oh, he would sulk and grumble a bit as was his custom, but after she'd finished singing, he would shake his head ruefully, chortle beneath his breath, and reach down to ruffle her . . . well, her wimple. Then he would confess how relieved he was to keep her by his side and the two of them would toast her ingenuity with a glass of mead and . . .

"I've come for the woman."

The graceless declaration jarred Holly from her pleasant fantasies. Her grin faded.

She blinked away her sunny haze to discover an unexpected thundercloud looming on the horizon. A cloud of alarming proportions that had scudded in from the west on a tempestuous wind. She would have never thought it possible, but her nemesis from the garden was even more intimidating by daylight than moonlight.

He towered over the other men, his long, unruly hair and bristly beard a startling contrast to their Roman-cropped heads and drooping mustaches. He looked less a different nationality than a different species of creature. He bore his weight on his lean hips with such ease that he seemed to swagger even when standing motionless.

Holly could hardly fathom that such a shaggy beast of a man could have tasted her lips with such beguiling tenderness. They still tingled at the memory.

Her initial shock surrendered to an irrational flare of anger. So the wretch fancied himself one of her suitors, did he? Yet he'd been trysting with another wench the very night before he planned to challenge her father for her hand. Worse yet, when his *lady* had been tardy, he had actually thought to sample Holly's favors, therefore betraying his potential bride with none other than herself! She scowled, slightly befuddled by the paradox.

"Come forward, sir," her father commanded.

Holly swallowed a fervent No!, the resulting squeak earning her a simmering glower from her papa that warned her he itched to strip away her disguise before the entire hall, but did not dare risk igniting such a scandal.

As the stranger lumbered forward, the crowd shrank out of his path, warily eyeing the hand welded to his sword hilt. He was trailed by a slender man, as fair as he was dark.

"Your name, sir?" her father demanded.

"Sir Austyn of Gavenmore."

At the name *Gavenmore,* speculation once more churned the crowd to a muttering froth. Holly mentally searched her limited store of gossip, but found no reference to an arrogant Welshman with boorish manners and a fickle heart.

"Have you come to pay tribute to my daughter?" her papa asked.

The knight hesitated, his gaze flicking to the floor, the smoke-stained rafters, his companion's battered boots, anywhere to avoid glancing directly at her. Holly supposed she couldn't blame him.

He finally drew in a breath that swelled his chest to daunting proportions. "I have."

An unbidden shiver raked Holly. Gavenmore imbued the simple words with grim destiny, making his claim seem both inevitable and irrevocable.

Her father waved a hand and said, "You may proceed," before sinking into his chair. The narrow look he shot Holly plainly said, *I hope you're satisfied, girl.*

Holly locked her hands in front of her to hide their sudden tremor, her only consolation being that the knight looked even more miserable than she felt. His companion shoved a crumpled sheaf of paper into his hand. As he squinted at it, a fierce scowl claimed what little was visible of his features.

After clearing his throat twice, he began to read, his voice barely audible. "She walks in dreams, my lady sweet—"

At a sniveling gust of laughter from the back of

the hall, he jerked his head up and dropped his hand
back to his sword hilt. Holly found herself holding her
breath with the rest of them, waiting for him to snatch
out his sword and begin to cleave off limbs and heads
like some fearsome berserk. His hand twitched once,
twice, then returned to grip the paper tightly enough
to blanch knuckles dusted with dark hair.

This time, perfect silence greeted his halting recitation.

> She walks in dreams, my lady sweet.
> With p-p-purple eyes and dainty feet.

He shot his companion such a tortured glance
that even Holly felt a pang of sympathy for him. The
blond man offered a wink of encouragement, all the
while taking great pains to sidle out of reach of those
brawny arms.

> She haunts my sleep, my lady fair.
> With snowy brow and curly—"

He dared a tentative glance at the dais. Holly
bared her walnut-stained teeth at him in what she
hoped would pass for a flirtatious smile. His hand
dipped absently into his hauberk as his gaze seemed
to fixate against its will on the uneven tufts of hair
afflicting her scalp.

"—hag," he finished. His companion winced.

Sudden coughing fits seized several of the lords
and knights. A man in the back of the hall escaped out
the door, his howls of laughter echoing in the bleak
silence.

"Hair," Gavenmore muttered, correcting himself through clenched teeth. He crumpled the paper in his fist, standing so rigidly he might have been carved from a block of stone.

His deliverance came from an unlikely quarter. The earl bounded to his feet, applauding with such enthusiasm that the other challengers had no choice but to join in or risk offending their host.

Amid a half-hearted chorus of "Huzzah's!" Holly's papa called out, "A noble performance, Sir Austyn of Gavenmore! What man among you is bold enough to challenge such an eloquent opponent?"

Silence descended once more, fraught with renewed twitching and longing glances toward the door.

"Very well, then," her papa said. "I pronounce Sir Austyn the victor of the contest of verse. Let us proceed to the lists, shall we? Perhaps some of you would prefer to test your mettle on the jousting field."

A mad dash for the door ensued. Holly suspected most of the men would be driving their horses across the drawbridge before the frozen behemoth in their midst so much as blinked an eye.

She started toward her father, but his frigid demeanor stopped her in her tracks. He disappeared through the curtain in a flash of saffron.

She had assumed he would cancel the joust. Now her lovely plan was going awry. All because some Welsh clod was too stubborn to admit defeat.

She pivoted to shoot the knight a baleful glare only to find the flagstones before the dais empty. It seemed her champion had gone skulking off with the rest of them. She had little time to savor her disdain before her papa's arm shot back through the curtain, seized her by the wrist, and jerked her after him.

Holly stumbled along behind her papa, her rump already stinging in anticipation. He had never so much as lifted a fist to box her ears, but she suspected this hoax had earned her a full-fledged thrashing. Ah, well, she thought philosophically, 'twas best to have the unpleasantness done with so she could concentrate on wriggling her way back into his favor.

But when he dragged her behind the relative privacy of a carved screen and whirled to face her, 'twas not the ruddy flush of anger that tinged his face, but the sallow pallor of fear. "Have you any idea what manner of man you've provoked?"

"Now, Papa, I know you fancy yourself possessed of a fearsome temper, but I've never been the least bit afraid—"

"I'm not talking about me," he bit off between clenched teeth. "I'm talking about Gavenmore."

Holly knew more about what manner of man Gavenmore was than she cared to reveal. She forced an airy laugh. "He's naught but a lowly knight. A boorish Welshman with appalling taste in verse."

Her papa tilted his head back to thrust his face next to hers. "Sir Austyn of Gavenmore is one of the most dangerous and powerful warriors in all of Wales. And one of the most unpredictable. If I dare to slight his honor or incite his rage, it might very well cause a renewal of the hostilities between England and Wales. If Gavenmore doesn't claim my head, then the king most surely will." Groaning, he spun around to pace the confined area. "I should have snatched you off the dais the moment you appeared in that ridiculous costume. It never occurred to me that some fool would actually offer for you. Now 'tis too late."

Holly could weather her papa's blustering better than his despair. "Shall I confess my deceit?" she offered in a small voice. "Issue a public apology?"

"And disgrace yourself before all of England? What decent man would want a shameless liar for a bride? You might as well shave off what little hair you've got left and doom yourself to a nunnery." He ruffled his own hair until it stood on end in a manner almost identical to Holly's and muttered, "I suppose even Gavenmore would be better than no husband at all."

Holly could not fully convey the violent depths of her disagreement so she simply smoothed her father's disheveled locks beneath her fingertips. "You needn't fret, Papa. The arrogant knave is probably halfway back to Wales by now. 'Twas but a momentary twinge of madness that prompted him to declare himself for me."

He batted her hand away, pinning her with an icy glare that chilled her to the marrow. "You'd best pray that you're right, girl, because Gavenmore has taken every purse in every joust he's entered in the past five years. If you're wrong, you may very well be his most extravagant prize."

The queen of Love and Beauty reigned over the tournament from her throne atop the wooden gallery, the irony of her title not wasted on her.

Holly wiggled on the hard seat to avoid the rolls of cloth Elspeth had crafted to pad her skirt. Her breasts were beginning to ache from being bound so tightly and the urge to claw at her freshly cropped head was becoming impossible to resist. The midday sun beat down on her tender skin. She licked the sweat from her upper lip only to get a mouthful of the soot she had used to darken the imperceptible hairs there to the shadow of a mustache.

Half of the challengers had already fled. Remaining were those lords and knights who had pledged fealty to her father and a stubborn handful reluctant to forfeit their honor to rumors of cowardice. They clustered at each end of the list, making half-hearted gestures toward donning their armor and outfitting their mounts for a joust they knew would never take place.

A parade of curious gawkers had also joined the crowd: peasants from the village, scampering children, castle servants, slatterns who'd emerged from the hillside encampment with tangled hair and eyes slitted from too little sleep and a dizzying variety of masculine attentions.

Their shrill laughter was echoed by the more subtle, but no less malicious, giggles of the ladies seated with Holly on the gallery. Her aunts and cousins huddled on benches at her back, giving her a broad berth lest her affliction be contagious and they should awake in the morn to discover their own eyelashes and hair lying in clumps upon their pillows.

She stole a glance at her papa's stony profile. He perched on the throne next to hers, his feet dangling a good six inches from the floor of the gallery. He had snubbed all of her feeble attempts at conversation since their earlier confrontation. Given no choice but to sit slumped miserably in her chair, Holly was beginning to wish this grim farce over and done with.

As the heralds took the field, gleaming trumpets in hand, she suspected she was about to get her wish. When not a single challenger accepted their brassy invitation to battle, she would be free to retire to her chamber and face her father's well-deserved wrath. She shifted in a vain attempt to relieve an unpleasant tingle in her bottom.

The heralds lifted the golden bells of their trumpets. A flourish of notes trilled through the hazy air.

Holly yawned and scratched her head, anticipating a lazy afternoon nap.

A lone rider materialized at the far end of the list. Before she even realized it, Holly was on her feet, gripping the gallery rail in her damp palms.

As the Welsh knight muscled his broad-flanked bay destrier through the scattering mob, her father muttered, "Can't say much for his taste in verse or women, but the lad has a hell of a head for horseflesh."

If Holly could have choked a word past her shuttered throat, she might have agreed. There was no question that Gavenmore cut a majestic figure on a horse. He sat the saddle as if he'd been born to it. The armor beneath his quilted surcoat was modest, simple chain mail enhanced by steel plates at his elbows and shins. A silver helm obscured his features, making him look even more forbidding.

Praying he hadn't seen her rise, Holly sank back into her seat, fighting an involuntary thrill of excitement. "I don't know why he troubles with a helm. It seems his head is hard enough to deflect any blow he might receive."

As the destrier pranced down the list toward the gallery, its rippling drape mirroring the dusky greens and crimsons of its master's surcoat, the agitated snatches of gossip from Holly's aunts and cousins became impossible to ignore.

"Aye, Gavenmore . . . so arrogant he brought only a single man-at-arms to the contest, but 'tis rumored there are a thousand Welshmen crouched in the forest awaiting his signal to attack."

Holly felt her papa stiffen.

". . . little more than a savage . . ."

". . . once incredibly wealthy . . ."

". . . stripped of their earldom when his father murdered his own wife."

"Murdered her? I heard he ate her!"

A muffled rejoinder, too low for even Holly's ears to catch, provoked a round of naughty titters from the women.

An icy ball of dread hardened in Holly's chest. Dear God, she thought, what manner of man *had* she provoked? She had precious little time to contemplate her recklessness, for horse and rider had reached the gallery.

Steadying the restless beast between his powerful thighs, Gavenmore raised a gauntleted fist, displaying the baleful length of his lance for her perusal.

Holly might have ducked had she not been paralyzed by trepidation. She gazed at the thick staff until her eyes crossed. She briefly considered throwing herself on it, but its deadly tip was blunted by a ceremonial coronal.

Her papa dug a less than paternal elbow into her ribs. "As your champion, he wishes a tribute. Have you no favor to offer him?"

"Um . . . uh . . . well . . ." Holly shot her costume a panicked look, knowing that if she tugged the wrong thing, her entire disguise was likely to unravel before their eyes.

The knight shifted impatiently in his stirrups. Perhaps 'twas not too late to discourage this brash suitor, Holly thought. She reached beneath the skirts of her cotehardie to peel off one of the stockings she'd pilfered from Elspeth. Sensing the downward shift of the knight's gaze beneath his slitted helm, she quickly dropped her skirt. There was little she could do to mask her slender ankles.

She tied the dingy, hole-pocked stocking around his lance in a pretty bow. Fluttering her pruned lashes at him, she lowered her voice to a provocative croak. "Fare thee well in the joust, sir. My heart rides with you."

His answering mutter was blessedly muffled by the helm. As he wheeled the horse around, Holly fully expected him to go cantering off toward Wales, or perhaps Baghdad. Instead, he halted at the edge of the gallery and shoved back the faceplate of his helm. His narrowed gaze deliberately glanced off of her, but searched the faces of the women behind her with peculiar intensity. A chorus of nervous twitters greeted his perusal.

Holly swiveled around, stabbed by an unfamiliar pang. Surely his garden assignation hadn't been with one of her sniveling Tewksbury cousins?

He slammed the faceplate shut with a clang of finality, leaving her to wonder if he had found what he sought.

As he trotted to the end of the sand- and straw-sprinkled list, the earl's marshal took the field, bellowing, "Challengers, take your places!"

Amid much ribbing and jibes from his cohorts, a blushing Lord Fairfax took up lance and shield and drove his dappled mount to the opposite end of the list from Gavenmore. Holly noted that he'd rescued his scorched plume from his hat and affixed it to his helm.

The earl stood and lifted both arms. His familiar benediction lacked its usual heartiness. "Fight with honor, gentlemen, and show mercy to your opponent."

Robust cheers and cries of excitement went up as the horses roared toward their inevitable confrontation. Gavenmore rode low over his mount's back, at one with the speed and thunder of the magnificent beast. Holly clenched the gallery rail, her heart racing in her parched throat with involuntary suspense.

Gavenmore lifted his lance. Lord Fairfax went tumbling head over heels off the back of his mount.

Holly squinted in confusion. As Fairfax clambered sheepishly to his feet, dusting off the plume of his fallen helm, the chorus of jeers and boos that greeted him confirmed her suspicions. Gavenmore's lance had never touched him. She doubted he'd even remained mounted long enough to feel its wind whistle past.

Dispatching the next challenger required even less of the knight's effort. Sir Henry of Sovermoth launched himself off his horse before Gavenmore could so much as raise his lance. Holly's horror mounted as she realized that not a single one of her former admirers was willing to risk his neck to rescue her from the Welshman's clutches now that her legendary beauty appeared to have deserted her.

Gavenmore was more exasperated by their cowardice than she was. After his third opponent managed to fall off his horse before the heralds could even sound the call to battle, he hurled his shield, tore off his helm, and plunged down from his own mount. Shaking off the restraining hand of his man-at-arms, he strode toward the center of the list, no less threatening without destrier or lance.

A terse silence fell over the crowd, broken only by the snap of his dark hair whipping in the wind. He slammed back the faceplate of his helm, condemning them all with his unflinching gaze.

Drawing his broadsword, he hefted it in the air with both hands. "English curs! Is there not one among you man enough to offer me a fair fight?"

As her papa slowly rose, Holly resisted the urge to jerk him back down. The shameful proceedings seemed to have sapped him of his ability to feign even feeble enthusiasm. "If there are no other challengers, I am forced to pronounce Sir Austyn the vic—"

An imperious voice rang out. "Stay your hand, my lord. I'm more than prepared to offer this Welsh savage a fair fight for the lady's hand."

A cloaked figure at the edge of the crowd eased back his elegant damask-trimmed hood. His mocking gaze was not fixed on Sir Austyn or her father, but on Holly. She rose, blinking the sunlight out of her eyes to find herself staring into the dark, malevolent eyes of Eugene de Legget, baron of Montfort.

CHAPTER 6

Eugene wove his way through the muttering crowd, his serpentine grace a jarring contrast to the leashed power of Gavenmore's stance. Betrayed by her trembling knees, Holly sank into her chair as Eugene climbed the steps to the gallery. Unlike every other man in the assembly, he looked her full in the face as he dropped to one knee at her feet and brought her icy hand to his lips.

"You sly little minx," he murmured beneath the guise of kissing her hand. "You might have fooled these dunderheads with your mummery, but I'll not be duped so easily. You've made my task all the easier. After I best this Welsh whelp, you shall have only the

role of my bride to play and only the stage of my bed
for your performance."

His tongue flicked out to lash her knuckles. Holly
snatched her hand back, wiping it on her skirt in deliberate insult. " 'Twould be a performance indeed, my
lord, for I'd be unable to summon even a trace of genuine sentiment for the duty."

Eugene's smile grew frigid, sending a chill of foreboding down her spine. As he backed away, bowing
with each step, she thought it ironic that she had
never before been more in need of a champion.

Her desperate gaze was drawn back to Gavenmore. He had been watching the odd exchange
through narrowed eyes, his sword still held ready in
his hands.

She almost jumped out of her skin when her father reached over to give her hand a benevolent pat.
"Should have known Montfort would deliver us from
this disaster. He'll make you a fine husband, child, see
if he doesn't."

Holly could only hope he took her feeble grunt as
one of assent. It took little imagination to envision a
future as Eugene's wife. Once age began to fade her
beauty and some pert thirteen-year-old with supple
breasts and an opulent dowry caught her husband's
lascivious eye, she had only a headlong tumble down
the castle garderobe to look forward to.

As the marshal introduced the new challenger,
three men-at-arms rushed out to gird Eugene in plates
of armor so bright they seemed to reflect the fires of
the forge that had molded them.

This time her father's blessing rang with righteous conviction. "Fight with honor, gentlemen, and show mercy to your opponent!"

As Eugene drew his burnished sword to face Gavenmore, Holly wished she hadn't pared her beautiful nails to the quick, giving her no choice but to nibble the tender skin of one knuckle.

The men circled each other like wolves warily scenting the blood of a fresh kill. Holly might have been more intrigued by the spectacle had she not known that the victor would have every right to make her his next morsel. Gavenmore outweighed Eugene by at least two stone, but de Legget's slender grace offset the advantage. He darted like quicksilver, parrying each of the knight's mighty swings until their blades clashed in a deadly symphony.

Holly winced as Gavenmore took a blow to the helm that would have staggered a lesser man. A roar of approval went up from the crowd. She scowled at them. Eugene wasn't particularly popular, but they'd have probably cheered Satan himself had he volunteered to trounce the Welshman and uphold the precious English honor not one of them had been willing to defend.

A downward slash of Eugene's blade drew a dark bloom of blood on the Welshman's hose. He gazed down at the wound in patent disbelief.

Eugene tipped back the faceplate of his helm. "Shall you yield?" he invited with a sneer. "I fear hacking you limb from limb might offend my bride's delicate sensibilities."

Holly didn't realize she was holding her breath until Gavenmore drew off his helm altogether and cast it away. His crooked smile was a dazzling flash of white against his swarthy beard. Shaking sweat from his eyes, he said, " 'Tis not the lady you should fear offending, sir, but me."

With that fair warning, he charged, roaring like an enraged bull. Holly would have been hard pressed to say who was subdued most effectively—Eugene or the crowd. Here at last was the savage berserk they had all feared. The knight's fierce press gave Montfort no choice but to squander his every move in retreat and his every swing in deflecting the giant's relentless blows.

The onlookers lapsed into dismayed silence, but when Gavenmore whacked Eugene on the ear in a flat-sided blow that would probably leave the baron's smug ears ringing for a fortnight, Holly jumped to her feet, cheering wildly. Realizing abruptly that everyone was gaping at her, including her ashen-faced papa, she sank sheepishly back down, wishing for the protective veil of her eyelashes.

The knight kept swinging. Eugene kept retreating. His shiny helm went sailing as he tripped over his own windmilling legs and fell to his back in the straw. His sword dropped from his hand, landing only inches from his fingertips.

Holly peeped through splayed fingers as Gavenmore pressed the tip of his broadsword to Eugene's bobbing Adam's apple, wondering if anyone had bothered to tell the Welshman that this was not to be a contest to the death.

"Shall you yield, sir?" His steely voice lacked the scorn Eugene had displayed in his own request.

After a moment of agonizing hesitation, Eugene lifted his gauntleted hands, palms exposed in the time-honored signal of surrender. "I yield." His voice was hoarse, as if he were choking on his own blood. Or his own pride.

A single cheer went up from the far end of the list. Holly saw Gavenmore's lone man-at-arms, jumping up and down and waving his battered hat in the air. At the knight's cryptic signal, he scurried back to the fence to fetch his master's mount.

Gavenmore turned his back on Eugene and started for the gallery to claim his prize, his rolling swagger betraying more weariness than Holly would have suspected.

Behind him she saw Eugene sit up on his elbows. Sunlight glinted off the lethal blade of his sword as he prepared to hurl it at Gavenmore's defenseless back.

Time slowed until it seemed Holly could count each sparkling mote of pollen drifting lazily in the air. The distant song of a lark was muffled by the dull roaring in her ears. She turned her head this way and that, horrified to realize that not a single soul was going to warn him. He had done nothing but fought valiantly and well, yet they were going to let him be slaughtered just for daring to be a foreigner in their midst.

Suddenly 'twas not his bearded face, but their own that seemed the cruel visages of strangers. Her father's hand twitched, then went still. He was the most honorable man she knew, yet he, too, was willing to sacrifice the Welshman for his own gain.

For a brief, tantalizing second, she allowed herself to entertain the notion. With one coldly calculated strike, she would be rid of both Eugene and the obstinate Welshman. Eugene's disgrace would disqualify him from claiming victory. And the Welshman would be dead, his big body stretched out in the straw much as it had been in the garden. The vitality fading from his limbs. His blood seeping into the thirsty sand. His crooked grin frozen forever in a pale mask of death.

Eugene drew back his arm.

Holly sprang to her feet.

Don't speak above a murmur, Holly. You'll strain your voice.

Holly almost looked behind her to see if Brother Nathanael had escaped his wardrobe prison, but realized the rebuke was only in her head. Using the full volume of that magnificent voice, she leaned over the gallery rail and screamed, "Gavenmore! Behind you!"

The knight whirled, throwing up his arm in instinctive reflex. Eugene's blade glanced off his steel gauntlet and thudded harmlessly to the ground. Gavenmore stared at the sword for a long moment, his face unreadable, then scooped it up and strode back toward the fallen man. Holly cringed, wondering if she had unwittingly signed Eugene's warrant of execution. If he so chose, Gavenmore would have every right to embed the blade in Montfort's treacherous heart.

Instead, he reversed the weapon and dropped it across Eugene's lap, hilt extended in invitation, as if to say the man presented no more challenge with the sword than without it. It was an insult more damning than any blow. "You are a craven coward, sir, and a disgrace to the honor of this tourney."

Although Eugene made no move to touch the sword, his entire body quivered with impotent rage.

"Enjoy your bride while you may, Gavenmore. She'll be a widow soon enough."

Shrugging off his enemy's threat, the knight once again turned his steps toward the gallery.

Holly stood mesmerized at his approach, no less captive to his will than she had been in that moment when the elm had snared her curls. Her stubborn knees refused to bend, refused to lower her to the chair where she at least might cower in comfort.

She earned a brief reprieve when a carrot-curled little girl scrambled beneath the ropes and danced into his path, clutching a chaplet of woven bluebells in her chubby fist. He paused to accept the offering, ducking his head in a shy bow that coaxed a trill of delight from the child. An unfamiliar hand squeezed Holly's thundering heart.

Then he was climbing the shallow steps to the gallery, each resolute footstep shuddering the wooden platform. Fortifying herself with a deep breath, Holly turned to face him, naked in the ugliness she had inflicted upon herself. A breathless silence reigned over the gallery, the lists, the spring day itself.

She forced herself to meet his gaze, then wished she hadn't. As he searched her eyes, a faint frown of bewilderment creased his brow. Holly quickly inclined her head. There had been nothing she or Elspeth could do to disguise the unusual hue of her eyes.

She expected him to boldly proclaim his victory. She expected him to demand of her papa the prize that was his due. What she did not expect was the ethereal brush of bluebell petals against her ears as he settled the chaplet of flowers on her brow, ringing the ugliness of her shorn head with the unspoiled beauty of a child's generosity.

A tremor of shame went through her as he dropped to one knee at her feet, bowed his shaggy head, and brought her hand to his lips. "My lady," he said, the simple words both tribute and vow.

CHAPTER 7

Holly slipped into the castle chapel, forsaking the warmth of the afternoon sun for a dank coolness preserved year round by stone walls six feet thick. She had retreated to this place to seek her own counsel, but was not surprised to find her papa standing over her mother's tomb, his hands splayed over the granite as if to draw strength from it.

She crept silently to his side. Her mother's carved effigy bore none of the warmth Holly remembered. Felicia de Chastel had not been the beauty her daughter was. Her charm was of the more subtle variety, her snub nose and cherubic mouth hinting at a delight in life impossible to recreate in stone, no matter how talented the artist.

"Papa?" Holly dared.

Her father's graceless fingers caressed the carved tendrils of his wife's hair. "I have failed her. I have failed you both."

His pain wounded Holly in ways she had not anticipated. "Of course, you haven't! Why if Mother were here, she'd probably be laughing right now, thinking this all a great jest."

"I'm glad she's dead." Holly recoiled from his stark words. "Better dead than forced to witness such a debacle. She warned me of your strong will, said I might have to take harsh measures to protect you from yourself. But I failed to heed her. From the moment she died, I let that will rule our lives. When you cried, I nearly wept myself. When you pouted and sulked, I gave in to your demands. Now my weakness has brought us all to ruin."

Like everyone else at Tewksbury, her father seemed to be having difficulty looking at her. Holly seized his dangling sleeve, desperate to evoke some familiar response from him. "Not ruin, Papa, surely. Perhaps if we go to this Sir Austyn, the both of us together, and explain . . . he seems a reasonable enough fellow."

The words sounded hollow, even to Holly. She was talking about a man who had chased her through a garden with drawn sword, accused her of witchcraft, kissed her with a tender hunger that still had the power to make her toes curl, then proceeded to alternately threaten to ravish her and chasten her for behaving the strumpet. Reasonable indeed!

"If he was very angry with us, might you not lock him away in the dungeon?" she inquired timidly, ignoring a twinge of guilt. "Just for a few years until his temper cools?"

Her papa's sleeve was torn from her fingers as he paced away from her. His voice echoed from the rafters like cracks of thunder portending a mighty storm. "Aye, let us go to him together, this Gavenmore, and explain how your fine jest has made a mockery of the both of us! We shall tell him that I intend to break my vow to deliver you as bride to the champion of the tournament and forever cast a shadow on the name of Tewksbury. And if he chooses to lay siege to the castle and take you by force, what then? Will he still honor you with marriage or will he seek to punish you for making such a jape of him?" Her father pivoted on his heel, flinging his shout in her bloodless face. "Aye, we shall go to him, you and I, and explain that it was no more than a cruel, childish prank that brought a proud and mighty warrior to his knees at your feet!"

Holly pressed her fingertips to her lips to still their trembling. His words had done nothing but echo her growing sense of shame. She shook her head helplessly. "Truly I meant no harm."

"You never do when it comes to seeking your own will. But you've sealed your fate this time. The Welshman will take you to wife just as I promised he would." His next words were spoken so softly that Holly suspected they weren't meant for her ears. "You could have had anyone. A man who would have adored you. A man who would have humbled himself just to kiss the hem of your gown."

If Holly could have choked the words past her raw

throat, she might have told him that she wanted no such man. That she knew in her most secret heart that she was nothing more than a vain, ornamental creature, praised only for outward things. That she could never give her heart to any man fool enough to adore her. But she sensed another blow would stagger him so she gathered her skirts and left him to his regrets.

When his daughter had drifted from the chapel, her profaned visage nearly unrecognizable, Bernard de Chastel did what he had not dared do in the thirteen years since his wife's death.

He shook his fist not at his wife's effigy, but at the vast and indifferent heavens beyond the chapel roof. "Damn you, Felicia! I've done everything I could for her. The rest is up to you!"

Cast from the solace of the chapel, Holly fled to the garden, fearing that after the wedding that was to take place that afternoon she would be forever denied its sanctuary.

The somnolent spring day mocked her agitation. A chubby bumblebee hummed its satisfaction over a primrose blossom. Butterflies flitted from violet to heliotrope, their lacy wings limned in sunlight. The sultry perfume of jasmine caressed her sharpened senses.

Despite the warmth of the air, the chapel's chill still clung to her. Even more intolerable than her father's bitter denouncement had been the revulsion she had glimpsed in his face, a revulsion that seemed less for her appearance than for her character.

Holly drew her fingers along the ropes of the swing. It swayed gently at her touch as she struggled to comprehend that her father refused to relent, that he had every intention of giving her to the hulking giant of a Welshman who hadn't given her a moment's peace since invading this garden.

The grass beside the bench was still crushed from his fall. She remembered how he had lain with arms outflung, seeming somehow both vulnerable and formidable all at once. She brushed her fingertips against her lips, still stung by the impossible tenderness of his kiss. A kiss meant not for her, but for another.

Resisting the harsh reminder, her eyes drifted shut, provoking the dreamy mists of memory and moonlight to recreate that peculiar moment.

A brutal hand clapped over her mouth. A wiry arm seized her waist.

Holly's first irrational thought was that Gavenmore had somehow divined her perfidy. That he had summoned his mysterious minions from the forest and they were even now scaling the castle walls to lay Tewksbury to ruin, beginning, as was fitting, with her.

At the hoarse whisper in her ear, both relief and repugnance flooded her. "You've done it now, haven't you, you haughty wench. I'd hazard your clever little scheme didn't work out quite the way you planned."

Holly might endure her father acting the voice of her conscience, but she did not have to tolerate such posturing from Eugene de Legget. She slammed her heel sharply into his shin.

He released her, exhaling with such force that she could scent stale blood, coppery and feral, on his breath.

She whirled to face him. He would have never dared lay hands on her before, but now he had naught to lose. His good name was ruined, his honor shredded to tatters by his own villainy. Even with a trickle of blood dried on his chin and his cheekbone swollen, his eyes glittered with such malice that Holly could summon no pity for him, but only scorn.

She dropped him a deep curtsy, inclining her head. With precious little hair to stop them, the chaplet of bluebells slid down over one eye. "Have you come to gaze once more upon my beauty, my lord? Did you bring your minstrel to sing praises to my lustrous hair? My pearly teeth?" She bared her stained teeth at him in a travesty of a smile.

His withering gaze raked her, lingering over her bound breasts and padded hips. "Gavenmore may lack the imagination to divine the treasures that lay beneath that ridiculous costume, but I do not." His eyes burned with unholy hunger. "I should have taken you the first time I saw you. Had I defiled his precious child, your father would have had no choice but to give you to me. Now it seems I've no choice but to bid you a good riddance."

Genuine curiosity prompted her. "Without revealing me?"

Eugene stroked his chin, his thoughtful smile more threatening than a scowl. "Oh, I entertained the notion of exposing you for the deceitful little bitch you are, but decided being wed to the Welshman would be a far more fitting punishment. Perhaps once you've bedded a beast like Gavenmore, you'll be more than eager to welcome a man between your pretty legs." He swept her a genteel bow. "Fare thee well, my lady. For now." He took his leave, his fresh limp granting him more dignity than he deserved.

Once you've bedded a beast like Gavenmore. . . . The crude words lingered in the air like a curse.

Holly shuddered. She had never considered the intimacies that marriage entailed. In truth, she wasn't quite clear on the precise nature of the inexplicable act that bound wife to husband. She owed her veneer of sophistication to nothing more than Brother Nathanael's obsession with poise.

Nathanael!

Her gaze flew to the tower that housed her chamber. In all the excitement, she had nearly forgotten the priest imprisoned in her wardrobe. The priest who would be summoned by her father in a matter of hours to hear her wedding vows. Provided, of course, that he hadn't run out of air in the tiny cell and was even now gasping his last.

Lifting her skirts, Holly raced for the outer stairs, her spirits buoyed by a stubborn surge of optimism. If she had ever had need of Nathanael's superior wisdom, it was now.

Holly tapped the priest's lax cheek while Elspeth flicked drops of water in his face. Upon tumbling from the wardrobe to discover Holly's transformed visage hovering over him, his reddened face had gone bone white and he had fainted dead away.

They had revived him long enough for Holly to breathlessly explain her scheme, but her sheepish confession of its blundered outcome had sent him into a fresh swoon.

Holly's gentle taps seemed to be having little effect. She gazed up at Elspeth from her kneeling position, a worried frown creasing her brow. "Perhaps a bit more."

Elspeth upended the ewer, dumping its chill contents in the priest's face. A concerned moue puckered the nurse's mouth, but satisfaction twinkled in her eyes. Elspeth had clashed with the haughty priest more than once over the proper raising of *her* lady.

At the impromptu baptism, Nathanael shot to a sitting position, coughing and sputtering. Waving away Holly's offer of assistance, he scrambled to his feet, launching into a gasping tirade as if his brief spell of unconsciousness had only whet the razor-sharp edge of his tongue.

"Oh, woe is me! What terrible sin have I committed to deserve such grief?" His homespun robes swished as he paced the chamber, scattering sheafs of Holly's fallen hair with each step. Droplets of water flew from the sandy hair ringing his tonsure. "A gem! I sculpted a flawless gem only to lose it to an unworthy savage. I molded a bride fit for a king only to have her cast into the grasping hands of a mercenary." He rolled his eyes heavenward. "Surely even God Himself envied such a magnificent paragon of womanhood and has sought in His infinite wisdom to punish me for daring to usurp His role as Creator. I am chastised, my Lord! I am humbled!" With a wail of despair, he sank down on a chest and buried his face in his hands.

Holly exchanged a dubious look with Elspeth. From the priest's incessant harping, neither of them would have guessed he was fond of her, much less thought her "a magnificent paragon of womanhood."

Holly could not help but find his abrupt embrace of humility suspect, especially when he persisted in accusing God of being jealous of him.

"Nathanael?" She approached his penitent form.

"Brother Nathanael to you," he snapped, his tone recovering its waspish note. This time his sharp eyes did not shy from her, but studied her critically. "So how did you manage to create such a vision of ugliness?"

Holly spread her skirt and pivoted for his perusal, unable to resist a twinge of pride for her efforts. " 'Twasn't difficult. We simply rid me of all the virtues my suitors persisted in praising. My raven tresses. My lush lashes. My bounteous breasts."

"At least your wit is intact. And how do you plan to maintain this charade when your husband takes you to his bed?"

Holly dropped her skirt, her pride deflated by the reminder. " 'Tis why I sought you out," she admitted timidly. "I've no mother, you see, and I've little idea what's to be expected of me."

This time it was Elspeth and Nathanael who exchanged a glance, compatriots in their naïveté. Realizing that she was questioning a virgin and an avowed celibate about the carnal intimacies of the marriage bed, Holly felt a pang of doubt.

But Nathanael knew everything, she assured herself. Purely by virtue of his calling, he was nearly as omniscient as God. Hadn't he told her so a hundred times?

He did not disappoint her. Straightening upon the chest as if it were a throne of judgment, he cleared his throat with a stentorian whinny. "Your sole duty, my child, will be to submit to your husband's will."

"Aye, submit," Elspeth echoed, her chins jiggling in agreement.

The priest frowned at the nurse. "God has fashioned man so that he has upon his person a divine instrument, if you will. A mighty and holy lance."

Holly's eyes widened as she remembered the thick length of staff the Welsh knight had proffered to her during the tourney.

"Aye, and he'll want to poke it in ye, he will," Elspeth contributed eagerly. "And there'll be blood. Buckets of it. But ye'll take pleasure in the letting of it."

Holly was beginning to feel quite faint. 'Twas a pity Elspeth had wasted all the water on Nathanael. She feared she might yet have need of it.

"Silence, woman," Nathanael commanded the nurse. Elspeth subsided with a visible pout. "Of course she won't take pleasure in it. 'Tis a woman's place to suffer submission to atone for her sin in the garden."

Holly started guiltily. Was the priest truly so omniscient as to have learned of her sin in the garden? Did he know that she had surrendered to the knight's carnal kiss with nary even a pretense of struggle?

"Had she not partaken of the apple proffered by the serpent," he intoned, "mankind might still exist in a state of grace."

Holly sighed in relief to realize Nathanael was talking about Eve's sin, not her own.

Her nurse winked at her. "Ye must endure it, child, else he can't put his babe up inside of ye."

Holly's horror welled anew. A baby! A baby who

would bind her to the Welshman forever. She shuddered, envisioning a litter of furry little cubs with curved claws and upturned snouts. What manner of God would have concocted such a hellish punishment?

Her desperation drove her to pace just as Nathanael had. She was more than willing to accept reproof for her own sins, but would be damned indeed before she'd suffer punishment for a distant ancestress with an infernal weakness for the cunning of serpents.

After several moments of violent contemplation, she whirled around to face them both. "I'll wed this Welshman. I have little choice. But I have no intention of becoming a wife to him." Holly loathed humbling herself before her mentor, but she forced herself to kneel at Nathanael's feet and seize his hand. " 'Tis imperative that I remain so repulsive this Gavenmore can hardly bear to look upon me, much less lay with me. Will you help me?"

" 'Tis not too late to flee," Carey said as he and Austyn trailed an aged maidservant through the inner bailey of Castle Tewksbury. "We don't even have to go back to Gavenmore. We can go adventuring, you and I. Why, there are lords aplenty willing to empty their purses to purchase a pair of skilled sword arms such as ours."

Austyn cocked an eyebrow at him. "Suffering pangs of conscience, are you? Was it not you who compelled me to petition for the woman? You who claimed there was no surer way to break the curse than to wed this Lady Ivy?"

"Holly," Carey corrected absently. "But given time

to contemplate the reality of waking up each morning to that . . . that . . . face . . ."

He subsided into doleful silence, heightening Austyn's impression that he was marching to the gallows instead of the altar. As they followed the crone who had summoned him to meet his bride, the sun dipped behind a black-bellied cloud, mirroring the resigned gloom of his mood. A cooling breeze teased his brow. 'Twas in just such a moment that he might have once felt Rhiannon's mocking presence, but on this afternoon the air was empty, devoid of any derision but his own for himself.

Perhaps Carey was right. Perhaps in his union with this woman he could finally lay to rest all of his ghosts. Odd that he felt no peace in their absence, but only a peculiar emptiness.

Austyn's determined steps did not falter until they neared a stone wall. The crone pushed aside a curtain of ivy to reveal an iron gate, a gate that would have been nearly invisible in the shadows of night. A sense of bleak irony assailed him as he ducked beneath a stone portal to enter a wild tangle of a garden that lost little of its enchantment by daylight.

"You'd have thought she'd have wanted to be wed at night," Carey muttered. "In the dark."

Austyn elbowed him. "Stifle yourself. 'Tis hardly the girl's fault she is ill-favored."

The earl had mercifully banished all revelers from the ceremony, leaving only himself and a tonsured priest standing before the marble bench to witness their vows. Tewksbury looked even smaller than Austyn remembered, as if the prospect of losing his daughter had somehow diminished him. The maidservant did not depart at completing her errand, but stepped back to hover in the shade of a rowan tree, drawing out a kerchief to muffle her bleating sniffles.

Resisting the urge to steal a yearning glance at the abandoned swing, Austyn dutifully took his place at his bride's side. As the sun peeped out from behind the cloud to illuminate her beaming countenance, his gloom plummeted to dread. Since the tourney he had comforted himself with the secret hope that his perceptions had been flawed. They had been. She was far uglier than he had imagined.

"Lady Ivy," he choked out in greeting.

"Holly," she gently corrected.

At the priest's invitation, she shyly ducked her head to recite her vows; Austyn struggled to hide his relief.

He could not help staring at the top of her head, fascinated by the dull tufts of hair that adorned it. He fought the absurd desire to run his palm over her hair, to determine if it felt like the fleece of a shorn lamb it resembled. He would have thought she'd have chosen to shield herself with wimple or veil, but the chaplet of bluebells remained her only crown. The fragile blooms had gone limp, as if she possessed the power to wither everything she came into contact with.

Austyn cast a wry glance downward, fearing that particular attribute might bode ill for his hopes of an heir. The snug fit of his hose assured him that her mere presence didn't wreak such mischief. Since his encounter with the dark-haired beauty in this very spot, his loins had been afflicted with a most awkward, but perversely pleasurable *sensitivity*.

His gaze drifted to the swing. He might barter

both his name and his pride to wed this woman, but he would have bartered his very soul to make the mysterious beauty his wife. He was not a man given to rape, but had he known he was to enjoy only a handful of fleeting moments in her arms instead of a lifetime, he might have loved her until the dawn, ravishing her with such tender care that she would truly come to believe the surrender her own.

"Are you prepared to recite your vows, sir?" the priest asked, interrupting his dangerous musings.

"I am." Ignoring a pang of regret more akin to grief, Austyn did so, rendering them without pause or intonation until he reached the final and most solemn promise. "I worship thee . . . I worship thee with . . ."

Both the earl and the priest scowled at him. Carey poked him in the back. The maidservant honked into her kerchief and nodded her encouragement, her crossed eyes bleary with tears. Only his bride kept her eyes downcast.

He cleared his throat and tried again, reminding himself that he owed this woman his life. When the others would have allowed him to fall to Montfort's treachery, 'twas she who had warned him. "I worship thee with my . . ."

His hesitance shamed him. If he could not feign affection for this woman, he could at least summon a measure of compassion. Some malicious soul had obviously considered it a fine jest to spread rumors of her beauty throughout the land. And did whoever garbed her for the wedding not realize the graceful lines of her cotte only made a mockery of her awkwardness? The garment hung limp over her shapeless chest, clinging instead to the chunky width of her hips. Its emerald hue tinted her blotched complexion a sickly green.

At his prolonged silence, she lifted her head, transfixing him with her gaze. She might have the lashless look of a rabbit, but there was no denying the girl had lovely eyes.

Prodded by a startling surge of protectiveness, he gently gathered her hands in his, gazed deep into those eyes and said, "I worship thee with my body."

CHAPTER 8

The knight's husky promise coupled with his possessive touch sent a jolt of silken lightning through Holly.
A rush of dismay followed. She'd learned from hazardous experience on the very patch of grass beneath
their feet how hard and unrelenting the muscled
length of his body could be. Given Elspeth's dire de-
scription of the marriage act, she sincerely doubted
she would survive such a homage.

As if to test Gavenmore's resolve, Nathanael said,
"You may honor your bride with a kiss." The priest's
lips twitched with mischief. Why the rascal was enjoying himself! Holly thought, shooting him a glare.

The knight leaned down to shrink the considerable distance between their heights, closing his eyes when his lips were still a full two feet from her face.

An inopportune frisson of anticipation danced down Holly's spine. *I might yet bestow my kisses on a stranger, but you can be assured, sir, that I will never again bestow them on you.* Mocked by the memory of her own words, she puckered her lips, terrified they would betray her by melting beneath his persuasion.

Her caution proved unnecessary. His lips brushed her brow in the most chaste of pecks. Attributing the stinging of her cheeks to the nettles with which Nathanael had brushed them, she bobbed a bumbling curtsy. "You do me honor, sir."

His expression was grave, but not unkind. "I am your husband now. You may call me Austyn and I shall call you Ivy."

"You may if you like," she said, but he was already turning away to discuss the dispensation of her dowry with her papa. Bewildered by the unfamiliar sensation of being snubbed, she added faintly, "but it's not my name."

Holly was dismayed to learn that her husband wanted to depart Tewksbury within the hour. She had hoped to spend her wedding night beneath the canopy of her papa's protection. He might not heed her cries for mercy, she thought spitefully, but he would at least have to suffer hearing them.

Austyn was dismayed to learn that his wife expected both her nurse and her priest to accompany them. He could stomach the nurse, although he thought his bride a bit old for such indulgences, but the priest was another matter. Even mounted on a humble donkey for the journey, a distinct sneer curled the man's upper lip. There hadn't been a priest at Gavenmore for over two decades, a lack that suited Austyn well. What use had the damned for vain promises of God's mercy?

As Carey led their animals into the outer bailey beneath the earl's watchful eye, Austyn's bride announced, "I shall require a litter."

Austyn exchanged a droll look with his man-at-arms. Her papa had doubtlessly carted her about the countryside in a curtained litter to avert ridicule, but no man would dare mock her now that she was his wife. Not without risking both his teeth and his life.

"I fear that will be impossible," he patiently explained. "There is no one to carry a litter. Only my man and I." The image of such a frivolous contraption jolting over the craggy hills and dense forests of his homeland almost made him smile.

Holly rolled her eyes skyward, wondering how long her husband was going to persist in his stubborn pretense that the nearby woods weren't teeming with hordes of Welshmen just itching to rush out and cut their throats at the first sign of treachery.

"How would you have me travel then?" she asked, enunciating each word precisely, as if addressing a child.

"On horseback, of course," he replied, echoing her condescending tone.

Holly cast the horses a dubious look. Grazing beside the monstrous steeds that belonged to Sir Austyn and his man were four pack animals, their panniers swollen with her father's gold. She could hardly explain that her papa had only allowed her to travel chaperoned by armed escort in the stifling confines of a litter to ward off the lustful gazes of potential abductors. She had hoped for the privacy of such a conveyance where she might unbind her throbbing breasts for a few precious hours.

She shot her papa a pleading glance. He turned his bulbous nose skyward, informing her plainly that there would be no help from that quarter.

She forced a disdainful sniff. "I do not ride."

Gavenmore folded his arms over his chest. "Then you may ride with me."

Holly started for the nearest pack horse. "I shall learn."

Even more alarming than the prospect of mounting a horse for the first time was the prospect of spending hours cuddled against her husband's imposing chest. Of feeling his wintergreen-scented breath tease her naked nape or worse yet, being forced to embrace him from behind while the sensitive peaks of her poor, tortured breasts strained against their bindings. Such proximity would make it nigh impossible to sustain her disguise. Or her virtue.

She gingerly approached the smallest of the mounts. Compared with Gavenmore's fire-belching dragon of a destrier, the sorrel looked tiny, but as Holly drew nearer, its barreled chest seemed to swell to intimidating proportions.

She stretched out a hand toward the reins, wishing she had an apple or a carrot instead of only the succulent temptation of her fingers. "Here, horsie," she crooned. "Nice horsie."

The snort that came from behind her was definitely not equine in nature.

As she seized the reins, the horse tossed its snowy mane with a whicker of warning and took several prancing steps away from her. Hindered by her cumbersome skirts, Holly stumbled after it, refusing to surrender her hard-won grip.

An unladylike grunt escaped her as she grabbed the leather pommel and sought to heave herself into the saddle. The horse reared, spilling her into the dirt and giving her reason to be thankful for her cushioned backside. Ignoring the suspicious noises from behind her, she climbed to her feet, brushing off her rump.

She approached the horse again, squaring her jaw in determination. There hadn't been a male born she couldn't charm or outwit and that included this cantankerous gelding. Anticipating his prancing retreat, she seized the pommel and threw herself headlong over his back.

The horse moved nary an inch. Holly landed draped over the saddle on her stomach, giving her a startling view of the horse's underbelly. No wonder both charm and wit had failed her. The horse wasn't a gelding, but a mare—a conniving female like herself. She caught the chaplet of bluebells before it could be trampled beneath the beast's fickle hooves.

She had anticipated Nathanael's dry applause. What she had not anticipated were the strong hands that closed around her waist, lifting her until she perched sideways on the saddle, her skirts flowing prettily over the mare's flanks. As those hands lingered against the relative slenderness of her waist, she forgot to breathe.

Gavenmore frowned up at her, his eyes narrowed to frosty slits. "You're lighter than you look, my lady. No heavier than a thistle."

Scrambling away from his touch with such haste she almost tumbled off the other side of the horse, Holly clung to the pommel and her wits with equal desperation. " 'Tis only your superior strength that makes it seem so, sir."

Gavenmore looked less than convinced by her flattery, but it seemed to appease him for the moment.

Holly perched rigidly on the saddle while her belongings were divided among the remaining horses. She had packed little, bringing only the gowns Elspeth had spent the afternoon frantically altering. After all, if her aim was to repulse her husband, what use had she for golden fillets to adorn the cream of her brow? Embroidered girdles to emphasize the slimness of her waist? Ivory combs to tame the raven silk of her hair? Amethyst brooches to complement the color of her eyes? She sighed wistfully.

Her one concession to vanity was the tiny bottle of myrrh she'd tucked into her stocking, her one concession to sentimentality the gilded hand mirror her mother had given her on her fifth birthday.

The stab of regret she felt for abandoning her treasures was blunted by a keener grief as her father approached to bid her farewell.

He grasped her ankle. She leaned down, bracing herself for a hissed rebuke, a final denouncement of the folly that had brought them to this grim pass.

He pressed his mouth to her ear, his majestic voice reduced to a conspiratory rumble. "Don't rely solely on your disguise to repel him, girl. Just be your-self."

With that enigmatic advice, he slapped her mount on the rump, sending it into a smart trot. Holly had to snatch at both pommel and reins to keep her seat, but she could not resist stealing a last longing glance over her shoulder at her papa. As he lifted his squat arm in a salute, she would have given even her precious bottle of myrrh to know if it was his old familiar twinkle, the glimmer of tears, or perhaps a bit of both reflected in his misty eyes.

Holly scowled at her husband's back, envying the ease with which he sat his massive mount. Instead of flopping aimlessly in the saddle with each spine-jarring jolt of the horse's hooves, he rode with fluid grace, at one with the beast's loping stride like some legendary centaur of old. She frowned, trying to remember from Nathanael's teachings if centaurs were given to ravishing nymphs. Or was it satyrs?

Stealing a look around to make sure no one was watching, she slipped a leg over the sorrel's back to ride astride. No one commented upon her change of position.

Holly was so accustomed to being ogled that having everyone avoid her eyes seemed a curious sort of freedom. Elspeth stared straight ahead, convinced the Welshman would behead them all and leave their bodies rotting in the forest if he discovered their trickery. Gavenmore and his man presumably could not bear the sight of her.

Only Nathanael spared her a furtive glance, tapping the underside of his chin to remind her to tilt her face toward the remaining rays of the afternoon sun. He had assured her that all men found skin tinted by sunlight coarse and repugnant. Holly obediently tipped her head back. She was willing to do almost anything to avoid the future necessity of torturing her tender skin with nettles. She soaked up the unfamiliar sensation of warmth on her face with a surprising thirst.

As the sun sank and the moon rose, lacing the meadows with a filigree of dew, Holly's exhaustion grew. The tingling of her rump had long ago subsided to numbness. Her bound breasts ached with every plodding step of her mount. Yet Gavenmore showed no sign of halting their party for the night. When her eyelids grew too heavy to support, she slumped over the pommel, unable to summon even a ghost of pride to care if she tumbled off on her cropped little head.

Gavenmore and the man she had heard him address as Carey had slowed until her horse's nose was practically nudging their mounts' rumps. She heard Carey's mutter through a fog of stupor.

"God's blood, Austyn, are we going to ride all night?"

Her husband's answer was lower pitched, mercifully inaudible.

". . . best to throw up her skirts and have done with it." Holly knew his man's grim reply should have caused her alarm, but was too weary to remember why. ". . . all women . . . the same in the dark . . ."

"That's where you're wrong, lad. I know at least one woman I would never mistake for another. Not in a thousand years. Not even if I were blind."

Holly sighed, the unrequited hunger in her husband's voice stirring her own melancholy. Her papa had raised her to be little more than an exquisite trophy, not the sort of woman who could inspire ardor in a man like Gavenmore. As she nodded her way back into fitful sleep, she felt a reluctant pang of envy for the woman bold enough to lay claim to her husband's volatile heart.

A rueful smile touched Austyn's lips as he gazed up at his sleeping bride in the moonlight. Although her mount had been rooting beneath the bracken for nearly a half hour, she still slumped over the pommel, the shriveled chaplet of bluebells drooping over the tip of her nose.

A combination of admiration and guilt assailed him. She had warned him that she did not ride, yet sheer determination had kept her seated during the punishing trek he'd forced upon them all. 'Twas not even her frailty that had prompted him to call a halt, but the fear her aged maidservant might teeter off her mount and break a bone.

He reached up to pry her stiff fingers from the reins. Perhaps it wasn't determination that had sealed her grip, he thought ruefully, but fear. Perhaps she dreaded sharing his tent as much as he dreaded sharing hers. Ah, well, there was little help for that now. While Austyn had tended the other horses, Carey had pitched the tent in the heart of the pine copse, then retreated a discreet distance to make camp with her servants.

As Austyn drew her limp body from the saddle, he noted with amusement that somewhere along the grueling journey she had chosen to straddle the horse, proving herself not only determined, but sensible. Perhaps his homely little bride had more to commend her than he realized. God knew his superstitious folk could use a hearty dose of common sense.

He folded her into the cup of his outstretched arms, marveling once again at her scant weight. The spongy breadth of her hips and bottom did not encumber him as it should have. As he started for the tent, she nuzzled her cheek into the hollow beneath his chin. Austyn scowled to find himself seized once again by that inexplicable urge to protect, to shelter, and defend what was his own.

His grip tightened from protective to possessive as the cowled priest emerged from the shaggy boughs and planted himself in their path.

"Good eve, sir." The pious intent of the man's clasped hands was belied by the shrewd glint in his eyes. "I've come to hear my mistress's eventide prayers. 'Tis a nightly ritual that gives her much comfort."

Never one to be intimidated by the posturing of priests, Austyn nodded down at the cozy bundle in his arms. "As you can see, your *mistress* is quite comfortable as she is." He continued forward, forcing the priest to scramble out of his way. Just before reaching the tent, he turned and said mildly, "Don't trouble yourself after tonight, Brother. I'm her husband now. I'll give her all the comfort she requires at eventide."

Austyn ducked into the tent only to find himself the victim of another ambush. Damn Carey and his poet's soul anyway! His man-at-arms had used the scant time allotted him to transform the modest tent into a sensual bower fit for a sultan bent on deflowering a harem of twittering brides.

A single torch spilled forth a buttery puddle of light that stopped just short of illuminating the makeshift bed. Austyn wryly suspected Carey had created the effect less to achieve an air of mystery than to spare him the sight of his naked bride.

As he knelt to deposit her on the crimson drape cushioned by a generous layer of pine needles, he nearly groaned to discover his friend had gone to the trouble of scattering petals of wild heartsease across the cool samite. Their heady aroma mocked him. His heart had known little ease since pledging itself against his will to the beauty in the garden.

Had she been the woman in his arms this night, the tent would indeed have been an enchanted bower of delight until the dawn. He would have called a halt to their journey hours ago and loved her for the first time while the setting rays of the sun played pink and gold against the tent walls. He would have plucked the fragile petals of heartsease from her sweat-dampened skin with his teeth, tasting and caressing every succulent inch of the flesh beneath.

He would have captured her breathless cries of pleasure with his mouth, muffled them with his tongue. He would have wedged himself within her virgin's body, thrusting deep and hard until he coaxed from her beautiful lips a vow that no other man would ever—

Austyn bit off a savage oath. What more potent reminder did he need that the sensual spell that enslaved him would have inevitably led to his destruction? Not even in his fantasies could he be free of the jealousy that gnawed his soul. As if sensing the sudden violence of his grip, his bride stirred in his arms, a fretful spasm passing over her puckish face.

Ruthlessly ignoring the demanding throb of his arousal, he laid her on the silken nest. Her lips parted in a drowsy sigh of contentment. Puzzled, Austyn leaned forward, sniffing the air. How was it that her breath could be so sweet when her teeth were so foul? He ran his tongue over the straight, blunt edge of his own teeth, wondering if she would be offended by a gift of a carved twig with which to clean them.

She looked terribly defenseless with her sparse lashes shadowing her blotched cheeks, her small fists curled as if to ward off some unseen attack. Their bitten-to-the-quick nails stirred his conscience, yet he could not resist the peculiar temptation of her hair. He stretched out his hand, then drew it back, surprised to find it unsteady.

"She's your wife, you fool," he muttered. "You have every right to touch her."

Touch her he did, running his palm over the close-cropped contours of her skull only to learn that her hair felt less like the shorn fleece of a lamb than the downy fluff of a baby duck. Oddly charmed by the discovery, he chuckled, rubbing a feathery lock between thumb and forefinger.

A faint whimper of distress warned him. He slowly lowered his gaze to find his bride gaping up at him, trembling like a fawn beneath his guilty hand.

CHAPTER 9

Holly had already surmised that her new husband was a dangerous man, but until she saw his unguarded smile, she had no idea how dangerous. The shallow furrows carved into his brow crinkled in boyish delight. Even the coarse bristles of his mustache seemed to soften with the motion. She fought an imprudent urge to reach up and touch them. To run her fingertips over their foreign texture until she could summon the courage to seek the smooth warmth of the lips beneath.

His smile faded as he gazed down into her eyes, his expression shifting to mirror her own bewildered yearning. Then his face hardened just as it had in the garden, and he snatched her up by the shoulders, giving her a slight shake.

Believing her treachery discovered, Holly slammed her eyes shut, trying not to imagine the worst he could do to her.

"Have you a sister?"

Her eyes flew open. Caught off guard by the peculiar question, she blurted out, "No."

"A cousin then? Or an aunt? Any womanfolk who might share the uncommon hue of your eyes?"

"An aunt? A cousin?"

Still dazed by sleep and the delicious sensation of being tucked against a strong masculine chest and borne like a babe from horse to bed, it took Holly a muddled moment to fathom what he was asking. When it occurred to her that he must be seeking the identity of the irksome woman who had disturbed his tryst, a rush of mingled relief and alarm made her stiffen in his grasp.

"Oh, aye! I've hordes of cousins and dozens of aunts! Nieces, too, every one of them with purple eyes. 'Tis a trait as common as dirt among the de Chastels."

He arched one shaggy eyebrow, restoring his rugged face to its forbidding aspect. "I saw no such woman at the tourney."

Irritated that she had given him the answer he sought, yet still he dared to contradict her, she retorted, "Perhaps the brilliance of my father's gold blinded you."

He released her to rub his bewhiskered jaw. "Perhaps. Or perhaps I was fool enough to stare too long into the face of the sun."

He settled back on his heels, his imposing bulk

making the confined space seem even more cramped. Holly drew her knees to her chest, reaching up out of nervous habit to twirl a sleek curl only to be rudely reminded that she'd left it and all of its mates on her bedchamber floor at Tewksbury. As her fingertips brushed her shorn head, she frowned in confusion. Had she been dreaming or had Gavenmore been fondling the repulsive mess when she awoke?

She lowered her eyes, fearing it might not be their lavender hue that betrayed her, but the flicker of uncertainty in their depths.

Austyn was disturbed by his bride's shy withdrawal. She looked no less defenseless awake than she had asleep. Her whitened knuckles gripped her curled knees as if to erect an impenetrable bastion. Not for the first time, he wondered what manner of father would give his daughter into the hands of a stranger. A stranger who might not hesitate to lay siege to her fragile defenses, "throw up her skirts and have done with it" as Carey had so bluntly suggested.

A thread of dark temptation snared his conscience, holding it briefly at bay. He had taken this woman to wife, had he not? Why should he not sate his whetted appetite between her willing thighs? If nothing else, she could grant him a brief surge of relief from the lust that tortured him. Perhaps if he kept his eyes closed when he reached for her, he could dare to dream . . .

Austyn had believed himself exorcised of all his ghosts, yet the woman from the garden still haunted him. He could almost feel the taunting softness of her hair as it wrapped around his knuckles, scent the exotic spice of myrrh on her fair skin, taste the yielding softness of her lips as they shyly bloomed beneath his coaxing. An anguished groan escaped him.

Holly jerked her head up at the sound. Her husband's eyes were pressed shut as if he suffered some mortal pain.

Ignoring a spasm of envy for his dark thicket of lashes, she tugged his sleeve, daring to use his Christian name for the first time. "Sir Austyn? Are you ill? Does your wound pain you?"

The instant he opened his eyes, Holly knew that it was not he who was at risk, but herself. The joust with Eugene had been only a pallid shadow of the battle being fought behind the deceptive winter of those eyes. Eyes lit not by frost, but by a flame so hot it burned blue, scorching her with the realization that if the conflict was not decided in her favor, she might lose more than just her disguise.

He rose to his feet above her, blocking the torchlight. Holly found it ironic that the shadows should be both her ally and her enemy. When he reached to pry apart her rigid knees, he wouldn't see the padding sewn into her skirts. Nor would he see the tears sliding soundlessly down her cheeks.

She dared not beg tenderness or patience from him. If he granted her such a boon as to temper his lust with kisses and caresses, it would only be a matter of moments before his seeking hands exposed her deceit and turned brutal and punishing. All she could do was quiver in his shadow, waiting for him to fall on her like a bear on a fresh haunch of venison.

The passionless timbre of his voice startled her so badly she nearly sobbed with relief. "I have wed you under false pretenses, my lady."

As his words sank in, her relief shifted to panic. She realized dismally that she had stripped herself of all weapons that might have leavened his fury with mercy. She had no silky eyelashes to flutter, no sable curls to toss, no creamy cheeks to frame her tears of remorse.

She snatched at his leg, hugging it in supplication. The calf muscles sheathed beneath his hose felt as steely and resolute as the rest of him.

The frantic torrent of words gushed from her. " 'Twas never my intention to deceive you, sir, truly it was not. 'Twas only that one harmless little falsehood led to another and before I knew it, even I had lost sight of the truth." She turned her pleading face to his, hoping the shadows would not obscure the luminous sheen of tears in her eyes. "Punish me if you must, sir, but I beg you to spare Nathanael and Elspeth your wrath. 'Tis true that Nathanael's prideful spirit might benefit from a sound thrashing, but Elspeth is an old woman, too frail to endure the hardship of a beating."

Austyn tried to disengage his bride's clawlike grip, but met with such resistance he was forced to stop for fear of injuring her fingers. He gave his leg a shake, but still she clung.

"What on earth are you babbling about, woman?" he demanded, adding the tenacity of a rabid hedgehog to her list of intriguing attributes. He lurched away from her, forcing her to release him or be dragged across the tent floor.

She popped to a kneeling position. "Babbling? Was I babbling?"

"Profusely. Do you honestly believe I count thrashing priests and old women among my sins?"

"Sins? My sins?" she parroted. A winsome grin lit her face. "Oh! We were discussing *your* sins!"

Austyn scowled. When she grinned like that, she was so ugly she was almost comely.

"And which sin might you be atoning for this night, sir? Shall I hazard a guess? You do not truly fancy me. You sought only to win me for my dowry." Her ripple of merry laughter surprised him. "You and every other challenger at the tourney."

Austyn moved to shove back the tent flap, gazing into the inky darkness. "Would that my transgression were so easily shriven."

Holly's relieved mirth faded. "What is this terrible crime even God cannot forgive?" she asked softly.

A web of moon shadow laced her husband's profile. "I made my vows to you when my heart was already pledged to another."

Holly struggled to recapture her relief, but her breathless laugh sounded strangely dissonant. "Perhaps you are unfamiliar with the customs of courtly love, sir. 'Tis not seemly for a man to swear devotion to his own wife." She could hardly afford to regale him with the numerous tributes and pledges of devotion she had received and discarded from married men. "If you were wed to your beloved, then what would be the covert thrill of flaunting her ribbons on your lance in a tournament? Or penning a pretty verse to honor your chaste affections for her?"

His bearded jaw clenched, informing Holly that his affections for this mysterious woman were less than chaste. He drew a small object from his surcoat, his pained expression rousing Holly's curiosity. Was it a tribute from his lady fair? Some treasured memento

of their love? Surely the uncouth brute wasn't so senti-
mental as to carry such a token next to his heart.

"Forgive me, my lady," he said hoarsely, "but I
cannot be a husband to you this night. Whatever the
customs of the English, I'm not the sort of man to lay
with one woman while thinking of another."

The words slipped out before Holly could stop
them. "Not even if she's your wife?" Sweet Christ,
what was she doing? Encouraging him to bed her?

Slipping the object back into his surcoat, he
looked straight at her, his gaze both steadfast and
wary. "*Especially* not if she's my wife." With that cryptic promise, he ducked into the night, leaving her
alone.

Holly fell back on the pallet, her body going bone-
less with a conflicting rush of emotions. Austyn's de-
sertion should have alleviated her fears, yet tangled
through her relief was a disturbing thread of discon-
tent. She had believed her deception exposed only to
discover her husband was also hiding secrets. His
blunt confession mocked her own petty deceit, making
her feel more wretched than ever.

She threw herself to her stomach. The cool samite
failed to ease the fever in her nettle-stung cheeks.
Fearing her husband might yet make peace with his
conscience and return, she dared not draw off her
gown to sleep naked as she longed to do. A feathery
petal of heartsease tickled her nose. She plucked it
irritably away, holding it up to the torchlight.

It seemed her husband's heart was pledged to another just as his impassioned kiss in the garden had
been intended for another. A foreign spasm tore
through her stomach. Holly was at a loss to identify it.

Since she'd been old enough to stretch out her chubby little hands in supplication, every heart had been hers for the asking.

She rolled restlessly to her back, finding no recourse but to attribute the incessant gnawing in her belly to hunger. She gazed blindly up at the tent ceiling, barely realizing that her tense fingers were ripping the tender bloom of heartsease to shreds.

CHAPTER 10

"Elspeth!"

At the piercing shriek, Austyn shot straight up out of a troubled sleep. Leaping to his feet in a crouch, he wrenched his sword from its sheath, prepared to defend the nearby tent from a horde of slavering Englishmen or some other terrible foe more likely to have emitted that unearthly cry.

"Elspeth!"

His sword arm went limp with relief as he realized the cry had come from within the tent. 'Twas not some bloodthirsty banshee come to claim their unshriven souls, but only his wife bellowing for her maid.

Carey and the priest came stumbling out from the

pines into the misty dawn, the priest gripping a crucifix as if to ward off some supernatural threat, Carey fumbling to notch an arrow in his bow.

Austyn nudged the bow to a less lethal angle before he could skewer one of them. "Stand down, Carey. We're not under attack from the English."

Carey ran a hand through his disheveled hair, still gasping for breath. "The English? I thought a pack of mad dogs had fallen upon you."

The priest shuddered, his gaze darting wildly from bush to bush. "Dogs? I thought it was demons."

"Elspeth!"

No amount of reassurance could stop them all from blanching at the renewed vigor of that scream. Austyn's hand dropped instinctively to his sword hilt.

Carey stumbled backward with an involuntary cry as Austyn's wife popped her head out of the tent. With the tent flaps hugged close around her throat, her homely face appeared curiously disembodied.

"Could I trouble you to summon my nurse, sir?" she inquired sweetly, blinking up at Austyn as if she hadn't just startled a decade off his life. "I require her assistance to dress for the day."

" 'Twould be an honor, my lady," Austyn gritted out between clenched teeth. In truth, he would have summoned Beelzebub himself to stop her infernal squawking.

He was spared the task as the stooped maid came bustling out from the trees, gripping something he assumed to be a bundle of clothing under her cloak. At the sight of Austyn guarding the tent, hand on sword hilt, an alarmed squeak escaped her and she almost dropped her burden.

She bobbed an ungainly curtsy, chins quivering. "If it wouldn't trouble ye overmuch, might I pass, sir? I thought I heard the musical sound of my lady's voice bidding me—"

A slender arm shot out from the tent, jerking her inside.

Carey gaped at the place where she had stood before noticing the folded cloak at their feet. He nudged it with a bare toe, shaking his head sadly. Carey's crestfallen realization that Austyn had not shared the bower of delight he had so lovingly prepared didn't goad Austyn's temper nearly as much as the smirk of triumph that appeared on the priest's narrow face.

Holly arched her back, preening like a satisfied cat as she massaged her unbound breasts with the flat of her palms. Morning sun filtered through the tent wall, caressing her naked flesh in tingling fingers of warmth.

"Oh, Elspeth," she moaned. "I don't know if I can bear it another day."

Holly would have liked nothing better than to sleep away the morning, but the temptation of stealing a few unfettered moments with her nurse standing guard had proved too strong.

Elspeth's wry nod toward the rumpled pallet dampened Holly's innocent pleasure. "One look at ye with yer wee belly all tucked in and the rest of ye all tucked out and I'll vow that husband of yers won't leave ye to sleep alone another night."

As if invoked by Elspeth's words, Austyn's imposing shadow fell across the tent wall. Holly crossed her arms over her naked breasts, besieged by sudden, painful shyness. Her husband had been pacing around the tent in impatient vigil for over an hour, halting every few circuits to growl out a reminder of the passing time.

Admitting with a pang of resentment that her brief liberation had come to an end, Holly spread her arms, inviting Elspeth to mummify the natural exuberance of her breasts. When that was done, Elspeth fetched the pot of cold ashes she had smuggled from the fire and rubbed them in her mistress's hair, dulling its ebony gloss. Elspeth held the hand mirror while Holly added the finishing touch to her disguise by drawing a fingerful of ashes across her upper lip. Holly hoped such subterfuge would become unnecessary once the sun had coarsened her skin.

From outside the tent, a masculine throat cleared with the force of a thunderclap. The mirror slipped from Elspeth's trembling hand, striking the edge of the iron pot.

Austyn's voice reverberated with exaggerated patience. "If you care to eat while we take down the tent, my lady, you'd best finish your primping posthaste."

Fearing he might yet storm their citadel or tear the tent down around their heads, Holly hissed, "Quick, Elspeth. My gown!"

Holly snatched the narrow tube of her chemise down over her hips while Elspeth dropped the cotte over her head. She batted the smothering bulk of its padded skirts away from her face, then clawed her way out of the drooping bodice. The overtunic was a subtle shade of apricot that had once warmed her natural blush to peach. Sighing wistfully at the memory, she yanked the skirt this way and that around her hips, then twisted to peer over her shoulder for a troubled look at her backside.

Elspeth wrung her gnarled hands. " 'Tis a mite crooked, my lady. I had very little time."

" 'Twill have to do," Holly replied, snatching up the mirror.

She was less concerned by the fit of her skirt than by the need to break her fast. Not only was that odd pang in the pit of her belly still troubling her, but she had deduced without Nathanael's help that if she could eat enough to fatten herself up, there would be no need for padded skirts to maintain her disguise.

She surveyed herself critically in the hand mirror, noting with dismay that its glass had cracked in the fall. A thin schism divided her ravaged reflection into two halves.

Austyn's shadow loomed once more against the tent wall. Holly laid aside the mirror, defiantly dabbed a drop of myrrh oil in the hollow of her throat, and called out with calculated malice, "Coming, my lord."

Austyn struggled not to recoil as his bride swept out of the tent. The bright morning sunlight showed her even less mercy than the mellow afternoon sun. Pity tempered his irritation at being kept waiting. It must be a terrible blow to her that the eternity she'd spent preening had yielded no more pleasing results.

He was mystified to note that, on the contrary, she looked excessively pleased with herself. The smile she shot him was almost coy. "Did you make mention of food, sir? I'm ravenous. I feared perhaps you were trying to starve me."

"Of course not. 'Twas simply so late when we halted . . ." Austyn trailed off, already regretting his confession of the previous night. He'd been reluctant to divulge his secret, but feared it might wound her tender feelings if she believed her appearance alone had dissuaded him from bedding her.

She tilted her pert little snout in the air, sniffing eagerly at the aroma of roasting meat. " 'Tis never too late to indulge the appetite, sir. Nor too early." Hefting her skirts to reveal a pair of slender ankles that should have been too delicate to support her bulk, she trotted briskly in the direction of the food.

Austyn studied the saucy sway of her hips, bedeviled by a sense of unease. He would have almost sworn that unsightly bulge was on her right flank yesterday. He was distracted from that thought by the twitching of his nostrils. 'Twas not the scent of roasting hare that tantalized them, but a more elusive fragrance ribboning through the air. He shook his head, dismissing the absurdity. It seemed his wits had all but deserted him since the day he had first heard the name of Tewksbury.

Austyn was to rue that day anew as he and Carey leaned against opposing trees, glumly watching his bride pack away her third cold meat pie. She sat on a low stump, her knees spread wide so that her skirt might catch any morsel that escaped her avid attentions. Thus far it had gathered only the sparsest of crumbs. Austyn was beginning to understand how she'd managed to achieve such an impressive girth on such a delicate frame.

The hare Carey had shot and roasted had long since been reduced to a pathetic skeleton. Austyn tilted his head in reluctant fascination as he watched her eat. He was loathe to admit it, but her gluttony did possess a certain sensual elegance. She ate with the decadent abandon of someone either blissfully oblivious or blatantly scornful of the critical scrutiny of others. His gaze was drawn to her puckered lips as she sucked the grease from each finger in turn with mesmerizing thoroughness.

"Good God," Carey said, snapping him out of his reverie as she delved face first into another pie. "I've never seen such piggery. She eats like a horse."

"I feared she was going to eat my horse. 'Tis fortunate we shall reach Caer Gavenmore by nightfall or we'd all starve."

"Or be eaten," Carey muttered darkly.

The possibility of meeting such a fate seemed less unkind to Austyn once their journey got under way and the hours in his wife's company crawled past. After traveling only a few leagues, Austyn began to suspect that a vindictive Booka had wiggled its way into the tent during the night and replaced his long-suffering bride of yesterday with an insufferable harpy.

When she wasn't whining, she was complaining about the unseasonal heat. When she wasn't complaining about the heat, she was demanding they stop for another meal. Or a drink of water from a fresh running stream. Or a moment of privacy in the bushes. When she wasn't making impossible demands, she was bemoaning the godforsaken ruts in the narrow path. Or the bumpiness of the worsening

terrain. Or the increasing bleakness of the Welsh landscape.

Her incessant bleating not only was setting Austyn's teeth on edge but was kindling everyone else's
temper as well. When he inadvertently called her "Ivy"
after her third rendition of "How much farther have
we to travel?" the entire party, including her mousy
nurse, swiveled in their saddles and shrieked "Holly!"
at him.

He had subsided, scowling fiercely. His own comfort in the saddle was severely impeded by the perpetual state of arousal provoked by the hint of myrrh that
still haunted the breeze. He had thought Rhiannon
banished from his life, but perhaps the vindictive witch
had simply devised a more diabolical means of torture.

As they wended their way up a steep, rocky hillside, Carey drew his mount alongside Austyn's.
"Wretched little tyrant, isn't she? 'Tis no mystery now
why her father sought to rid himself of her company.
You should ride straight back to Tewksbury and demand more gold."

Austyn forced a shrug that was far more light-
hearted than he felt. He was beginning to fear he'd
made a terrible mistake. "The shaping of character is a
delicate task. Her father probably coddled her every
whim to console her for the curse of her looks."

Carey shot a dark glance over his shoulder. " 'Tis
a pity he got naught for his efforts but an ugly brat."

"Perhaps maturity will mellow her temper."

"If you don't strangle her first." All it took was a
wry flick of Austyn's gaze to make Carey blanch. "Oh,
Christ, Austyn, I'm sorry. I wasn't thinking."

Austyn smiled to reassure him. "Don't apologize.

As well you know, it takes more than a bit of nagging to tempt a Gavenmore to murder."

"Sir Austyn? Sir Austyn, I say, are we nearing the end of our journey yet? 'Twill be nigh on to noontide soon and I'm growing quite faint with hunger."

At the sound of the querulous voice, Austyn's smile tightened to a wince. "Mayhaps I spoke prematurely . . ."

Holly had never been so miserable in her entire life.

The mountainous terrain made any semblance of comfort impossible. Her persistent squirming only succeeded in wadding up a lump of cloth that seemed to take malicious pleasure in poking her in the spine with each torturous clop of the horse's hooves. She had obediently kept her face bared to the sun as the hours passed; now each lick of the afternoon breeze stung her cheeks with tongues of flame.

Her gluttonous attempts to plump herself up had done nothing but bloat her belly and make her drowsy. Yet the food had failed to sate the empty ache in the pit of her stomach, and with her nerves plucked like lyre strings, she found sleep to be even more unattainable than comfort.

She had spent half the journey poised on tenterhooks, expecting a horde of murderous Welshmen to spring out from behind every knoll, and the other half nursing the even grimmer suspicion that Gavenmore possessed no such reinforcements. That her papa had surrendered her without so much as a whimper for naught.

No one had dared speak to her since Nathanael

had urged his donkey to her side shortly after the noontide meal. "Splendid strategy, my child," he had murmured up at her, his long legs flopping over the animal's flanks. "A man finds nothing so repugnant as a shrewish wife."

Holly had fixed him with her haughtiest glare. "I haven't the faintest idea what you're talking about."

Try as she might, she could not keep her gaze off the broad, forbidding planes of her husband's back. He had been the very soul of patience with her, yet she feared his tolerance would not last. Especially not if he discovered her deception. As they passed beneath a gnarled arch of branches, the portal to a forested slope, Elspeth's dire prophecy of being murdered and left to rot beneath a blanket of lichen seemed less absurd than it had in the rolling meadows of England.

Holly's gaze darted from tree to tree, seeking escape from her own sinister musings. The Welsh landscape was as foreign as the circumstances she'd unwittingly thrust upon herself. Ancient oaks towered over their heads, bearing little resemblance to the sprightly birches and elms of Tewksbury. Their ponderous canopy faded the sun's rays, creating an eternal twilight of damp shadows and ferny hollows. A carpet of moss blunted their horses' hoofsteps to a sibilant hush.

Holly's imagination rapidly succumbed to the forest's dark enchantment. Instead of the throaty warble of some unknown bird, she heard the sly giggling of faeries mocking her predicament. The musical cadences of a waterfall tumbling over stone became the piping of some goatish Pan luring a maiden to her

ruin. The twisted trunks of blackthorn and alder
leered at her like faces frozen in anguish, the captive
spirits of other travelers foolish enough to profane this
hallowed forest.

Her panic surged as the slope steepened and she
realized how far she'd fallen behind the others. They
were already crossing the murky cauldron of a brook
that lay in their path. Wishing she'd had the foresight
to sneak her leg over the mare's neck while they were
still on level ground, Holly hastened her horse forward, tangling her hands in both reins and mane to
keep her tenuous seat.

As the mare splashed into the swirling water, its
front legs disappearing from hoof to fetlock, a gauzy
thread brushed Holly's naked nape. Terror seized her.
Icy gooseflesh erupted on her skin. She dropped the
reins and twisted in the saddle, screaming and batting
wildly at her head and shoulders.

The startled horse reared, dumping her rump
first into the chill water. Holly could not have said if it
was the jarring thump of her landing or the icy shock
of the water rushing up her skirt that restored her to
sanity. One moment she was screaming hysterically;
the next she was gaping dumbly up at the innocuous
twig she had believed to be the skittering claw of
some venomous spider and the willow leaf she had
feared was its lair.

The expectant silence swelled. Holly turned her
head to find the others frozen on the slope, gawking at
her as if she'd fallen not off a horse, but out of the sky.

She might have overlooked the grin Carey attempted to hide behind his discreetly raised gauntlet.
She might have tolerated Nathanael's snickering or

even the fact that Elspeth—her loyal, beloved Elspeth
—had compressed her lips so hard she was turning a
mottled shade of red from lack of air. What she could
not endure was the absence of both amusement and
reproach in her husband's eyes. They reflected only a
wary pity that made her feel even more foolish than
she was.

Her ragged fingernails dug into the muddy
stream bottom as homesickness crashed over her in
waves of misery. She wanted nothing more than to be
nestled back in her bed at Tewksbury. She wanted her
hair, her eyelashes, her flawless complexion. She
wanted her papa. And most defeating of all, she
wanted her mama. It was a primal yearning, subdued
for so many years that she had forgotten its power to
close her throat and bring tears welling to her eyes.

As she suppressed a crude sniffle, waiting for that
first tear to brim over and spill down her cheek like a
priceless pearl, it occurred to her that she no longer
need practice the art of weeping prettily. There were
no suitors poised to dry her tears, no tutor who would
dare chasten her for reddening her nose, no papa to
chide her for giving free and selfish reign to her un-
happiness.

With that liberating realization, Holly Felicia Bernadette de Chastel, lady of Gavenmore and the fairest
woman in all of England, tipped back her head and let
loose with an earsplitting wail.

CHAPTER 11

"Good Lord, man, can't you make her stop?"

Even if Austyn had a reply for Carey's plea, which he did not, Carey would have had to pry his hands away from his ears to hear it. Austyn and his companions sat paralyzed on their mounts, gaping at his bride with varying degrees of horror and disbelief. The horses shifted restlessly, desperate to bolt.

Austyn could hardly blame them. He was tempted to do the same. He had entertained the naive hope that his new wife might be a helpmeet, someone who would share his cares and responsibilities, thereby lessening them. But it seemed he had only earned himself another burden. And a deafening one at that.

She had thrown back her head and was bawling like a newborn calf. Fat tears streamed down her face. Austyn would have wagered it impossible that human skin could flush brighter than her sunburned cheeks, yet her nose had deepened to a ripe cherry red. She resembled nothing so much as a homely little troll having one hell of a temper tantrum.

Her childish display should have enraged him, but Austyn could not dismiss the plaintive note in her wailing. 'Twas as if she'd hoarded a lifetime of misery for just such a moment.

"For bloody's sake, Austyn, do something," Carey pleaded. "Comfort her. Offer her a kerchief. Go pat her on the . . . on the"—he fumbled for an appropriate body part—"shoulder."

Austyn was more than ready to take action. He swung one leg over his horse, dismounting with unmistakable resolve. "Take the others and ride ahead. Don't turn back no matter what you may hear."

The priest and nurse broke into a dismayed clamor.

"Oh, please, kind sir," Elspeth said, appearing dangerously near tears herself. "Ye mustn't be too harsh on her. My mistress is quite delicate."

Austyn cocked a skeptical eyebrow. Her *delicate* mistress was presently beating at the brook with both fists, sending great gouts of water spraying into the air.

"What she means to say," the priest shot Austyn's gauntleted fists a nervous look, "is that our lady's constitution is such that she might not survive a beating; therefore, we implore you—"

"Enough!" Austyn roared.

They all recoiled, even Carey.

"The only person I'm going to beat around here is the next one who dares accuse me of beating someone. Now go as I bid you." He turned to Carey. "If either of them tries to turn back, put an arrow through them."

Carey and the nurse scrambled to obey him, driving their mounts up the steep slope toward the ridge. Only the priest hung back, shooting a pensive look over his shoulder. Austyn glowered after him. The man's proprietary attitude toward *his* wife was beginning to gall his temper.

Determining that her howls showed little sign of ceasing without intervention, Austyn drew off his boots and gauntlets, waded straight into the brook and squatted down a few feet away from her, resting his elbows on his knees. The cool water lapped at his hose.

Holly had squinched her eyes shut and drew breath for a fresh howl when she sensed someone nearby. Not just any old someone, she realized, sniffing a wintry breath of mint through her clogged nose. Her husband.

Her exhalation dwindled to a strangled hiccup as she peered through puffy eyelids at the curious sight of Sir Austyn of Gavenmore squatting placidly in the middle of a rushing brook.

He smiled encouragingly at her. "Feel better, Ivy?"

His unruffled composure insulted her beyond bearing. Her misery flamed to rage. "My name is Holly, you dolt! *Holly!* Are you so stupid you can't remember your own wife's name?"

Too incensed to ponder the consequences, she hurled the contents of her hand, which happened to be a fat gobbet of mud, directly at his smug face.

Holly was immediately surprised to realize that she did feel better. Immensely better. 'Twas as if she'd just shoved the crushing weight of a stone gargoyle off her chest. But her recovery came at a very inopportune moment. She might have muffled her giggle at the sight of her husband's forbidding visage spattered with mud, but his confounded expression as he blinked the stuff from his eyes undid her entirely. She pointed at him, her sobs rising to shrieks of laughter.

He erupted from the water, striding toward her with lethal intent. Although alarmed to realize a fifteen stone Welshman with murder glittering in his eyes was a more substantial threat than an imaginary gargoyle, Holly was as helpless to stop laughing as she'd been to stop crying.

She skittered backward like a freshwater crab, fully expecting him to throttle her as she deserved.

Instead, he swept her up into the cradle of his arms. Her weighted skirts streamed water and she was forced to coil her arms around his neck or risk plunging right back into the brook.

Her shock grew as he sank down on a flat-topped rock on the bank, his implacable grip binding her to his lap. She thought to wiggle away, terrified he would discover the sodden lumps of cloth padding her skirt, but quickly realized that squirming only increased such a risk. She had no choice but to relax against his chest, his lap a cozier perch than she cared to admit.

In stoic silence, he retrieved a dry kerchief from his tunic and dipped it in the brook. Holly expected him to wipe the silt from his own brow, but instead he bathed her face with surprising tenderness. She closed her swollen eyes with an involuntary moan of pleasure, the cool water a heavenly ablution to her sun-scalded cheeks.

When she opened them, Austyn was drawing a leafy herb from a small leather bag. He held the pinch of green to her lips.

She drew back, eyeing his offering with a suspicion she didn't bother to hide. "Is it poison?"

His crooked smile didn't quite reach his eyes. "Poison's a bit subtle for the Gavenmore tastes." He bit off a leaf of the herb, chewing with obvious relish. "Try it," he challenged, brushing the stalk against her parted lips.

Holly would have tried hemlock itself to put a halt to his disturbing teasing. She snapped off a leaf, barely missing his fingertips. As she chewed, a foreign tingling besieged her mouth. Foreign, yet hauntingly familiar. As familiar as the scent of this man's breath on her throat. As familiar as the tickle of his mustache against her upper lip. As familiar as the taste of his kiss, the beguiling contrast of warm tongue and cool mint.

Plunged into confusion by the memory, Holly dropped her gaze to his lips, wondering again what manner of face lay beneath the mask of his beard.

" 'Tis wintergreen. For purifying the breath and teeth."

His matter-of-fact words snapped her back to reality. She was not the same woman he had kissed in the garden. Her teeth were no longer the snowy steeds of Eugene's ode, but a herd of mottled nags.

She clamped her lips together, driven to mute shyness by her appearance for the first time in her memory.

"So your name is Holly, eh?" he asked, wiping the mud from his own face with the damp kerchief.

"Aye. 'Tis whispered that I was conceived beneath the hollyhocks in the castle garden."

Austyn grinned at his wife's prim bluntness. It seemed he hadn't been the only man to succumb to the garden's enchantment. "From your prickly disposition, I thought it might have been the holly bushes."

She shot him a sullen glance. "Better to be spawned from thorns than hewn from unfeeling oak."

The beauty of her eyes startled him to silence. It was like tipping over a moss-encrusted rock to find a diamond beneath. He doubted she even realized it, but she had kept one arm draped around his neck for balance and was now toying with his hair, twirling first one strand, then another, about her slender fingers. The intimacy of the act sent a strange shiver across his nape.

"Why do you find me unfeeling? Because I didn't drag you out of the water, bend you over my knee, and give you the sound thrashing you deserve? Or is it simply because I haven't granted you the attention you're so desperately craving?"

She stared straight ahead, her delicate jaw set at a mutinous angle. "You are a most churlish man. I care nothing for your attention."

"And you are a most dishonest girl." Something odd flickered in her eyes. "Now why don't you tell me what made you so wretchedly unhappy?"

She bowed her head. Austyn almost wished she

hadn't. With her face hidden, he had only her naked nape to contemplate. Unlike the blotchy skin of her cheeks, her nape was pale cream dusted with baby fine hair. He was distracted by the overwhelming desire to feather his lips across it. He shook off the disturbing urge, making a mental note to order some fine silks for wimples and veils.

"I was unhappy because I wanted my mother," she confessed softly.

Austyn frowned. He could hardly fault her for grieving at being wrenched so abruptly from her mother's arms. "I saw no sign of the countess yesterday. Was she ill?"

"No. She was dead. She's been dead since I was five." Holly fixed him with those stunning eyes again. "So you must find me utterly ridiculous to be carrying on so over nothing more than a ghost."

Austyn found her much less ridiculous than he would have conceded. "Do you remember her?"

"Not as well as I'd like. Sometimes it seems as if time were melting my memories."

"Time hasn't been so kind to me. My mother's been dead for almost twenty years yet I remember everything about her. Her voice. Her smile. The angle at which she tilted her head when she was singing." He lowered his eyes before they could betray the full measure of his bitterness. "Would to God that I could forget."

Holly continued to weave her fingers through his hair, her touch dangerously near a caress. "She was unkind to you?"

There were some delusions Austyn could not allow himself, no matter the solace they would give. He met Holly's gaze squarely. "Never."

He would have found her pity abhorrent and her compassion suspect, but he could hardly resist the offhand grace with which she drew the kerchief from his hand and dabbed a missed speck of mud from his temple. He found himself gazing not at her ravaged hair or sparse lashes, but at the pursed temptation of her lips.

He had believed there to be no surer cure for his unabated ardor than his bride's presence on his lap, but at the tenderness of the wifely gesture, his loins surged as if galvanized by a jolt of lightning.

Austyn scrambled to his feet, catching her elbow before she could tumble back into the brook.

Fearing his conflicting urges would attract her notice, he started toward the horses at a brisk stride, hauling her along beside him. "Let us dawdle no longer, my lady. We must make haste if we are to reach Caer Gavenmore before nightfall."

"Very good, sir," she replied, the haughty bite restored to her voice. "Perhaps we shall yet reach your keep before I waste away to skin and bones for lack of sustenance."

If anyone was surprised when Austyn and Holly emerged from their private parley with Holly mounted behind her husband and the mare plodding after them on a rope, they were wise enough to keep their opinions to themselves. Since twilight was fast approaching and they'd left the shelter of the forest for a windswept slope, no one thought it unusual that Nathanael would draw up his cowl to shield his face.

Holly discovered that her husband's broad back provided shelter from any number of unpleasantries. Since she rode sidesaddle behind him, her arms secured around his lean waist, she no longer had to fret about revealing her padded skirts. Her papa had forbidden her the pleasures of hunting, hawking, or simply cantering across the countryside, and the rustic charm of the breeze ruffling her cropped hair was impossible to resist. She found she could even allow herself to doze by resting her cheek against Austyn's back.

She awoke to discover the soothing rocking of the horse had ceased. She sniffed the air, intrigued by its metallic bite. They must be nearer to a river than she realized. The sun had dropped, tinging the air with a violet haze and mellowing both shadow and substance to muted shades of gray.

She leaned around Austyn's shoulder for a clearer view, realizing that it was not the river's ripe tang that had jarred her from sleep, but the tension flaying her husband's body. His dark hair whipped in the wind, revealing an expression as remote as the crag of stone on which they stood.

She followed his gaze to a jagged promontory jutting out over the silvery belt of water. She widened her eyes, then blinked rapidly. Surely only a dream could conjure such a majestic vision! She might have sought to rub the stardust of sleep from her eyes had Elspeth's astounded expression not echoed her own.

A castle crowned the promontory, separated from thin air by a vast curtain wall of mortared sandstone. Crennelated towers flanked its mighty ramparts with a lithe grace that belied their defensive purpose.

"Your home?" she croaked, her throat inexplicably dry.

"Aye," he replied grimly. "And yours as well, my lady."

Holly swallowed, dumbfounded anew. 'Twas hardly the crude fortress she had expected.

"My God," Nathanael breathed, too awestruck to repent or even notice his lapse into blasphemy. " 'Tis one of the concentric castles the king's father ordered built a generation ago in the vain hope of taming the muleheaded Welsh savages—" He subsided beneath Austyn's level gaze, possessed by a sudden compulsion to polish his crucifix with the hem of his cloak.

Holly could not fathom how a lowly knight had come to possess such a wonder. Snatches of gossip from the tournament floated back to her ears on wings of malice—*once incredibly wealthy . . . stripped of their earldom . . . murder.*

"Hie!" Austyn cried without warning, driving the destrier into a gallop with a dig of his golden spurs.

Holly clung to his waist, petty gossip forgotten in her consuming desire to remain mounted. The others were forced to break into a jarring canter to match their pace. She would have almost sworn 'twas not eagerness that spurred her husband toward home, but the resolve to have done with something distasteful.

Unexpected exhilaration seized her as they thundered through the gathering twilight. Perhaps 'twas only the intoxicating hint of mist in the air or the stirring cadence of the beast's gait, but Holly found it difficult to imagine being anywhere else but pressed to her husband's back, her hands locked over the cool steel links of his hauberk. With Austyn to shelter her, she could turn her face to the wind without fear.

They descended the slope, approaching the promontory from the landward side. The wind stung tears from Holly's eyes, but she blinked them away, reluctant to tear her gaze from Caer Gavenmore, perched like a celestial palace on a cloud of limestone.

Halfway around the promontory, she realized something was wrong. Terribly wrong. Rather than circling to protect its treasure, the massive curtain wall tapered into rubble at the fore of the castle, leaving it defenseless to attack. Half a tower jutted in ghostly silhouette against the darkening sky.

It seemed the castle was not an impregnable fortress after all, but a dreamer's folly, abandoned long before completion. Holly's heart wept at its wasted beauty.

Austyn slowed their party to a walk as they traversed the long hill toward the hollow maw that should have housed an iron gate. A lopsided half of a gatehouse watched them pass over a drawbridge that spanned a parched moat, its empty windows gaping like sightless eyes. Chilled by its abandoned air, Holly tightened her grip on Austyn's waist without realizing it.

'Twas only fitting that the first thing she should see after they passed into what should have been the inner bailey had the outer bailey been completed was a grave. A mantle of weeds and ivy choked the stony cairn. Austyn did not spare it even a glance, but Holly twisted to stare, curious as to who might have been buried in such a prominent spot, yet denied eternal slumber in the family chapel.

She longed to ask Austyn, but his rigid posture made him seem as forbidding as their surroundings. He bore little resemblance to the man who had cradled her on his lap and tenderly sponged the tears from her face.

She was gathering her courage to ask him anyway when an arrow whizzed past her ear and something slammed her to the ground with the force of a catapulted stone.

CHAPTER 12

Holly snatched in a wheezing breath, her mind too foggy to determine if she'd been impaled by a falling timber or trampled by a herd of elk. Stars twinkled in her vision, fading slowly to a firmament of patchy grass. Only then did she realize the massive object pinning her face down to the ground was her husband's body. It was a testament to both his keenly honed reflexes and his judgment that he had executed such a maneuver without crushing her fragile bones to dust.

The beguiling mint of his breath singed her nape. Her first desperate instinct was to squirm out from under him. That urge was stifled by the implacable press of his lean hips against her backside. It was then that she realized her skirts had twisted in the fall and there was nothing to separate his loins from the naked swell of her rump but her delicate chemise and the thin skein of his hose. Her eyes widened with shock. Not only did Austyn not wear a padded codpiece; he had no need of one. She pressed her cheek to the cool grass, afraid to so much as breathe.

She flinched as a quavering roar descended from one of the towers above them. "Goddamned leeches! Cursed whore-mongering tax collectors! You can trot right back to your bastard whore's son of a king and tell him I'll not contribute a ha'penny to fatten his English coffers. This is Welsh land, and Welsh land it shall remain as long as this old man has a gust of breath left in his body!"

Austyn lifted his head and called out, "Stay your arrows and your tongue, old man! I—"

Another arrow whistled past. Austyn pressed his mouth to Holly's ear, warming it with his breath. "Stay down. No matter what happens, stay flat on your belly."

Had it not been such an absurd fancy, Holly would have almost sworn his lips brushed her nape in the ghost of a caress before he sprang to his feet in one lithe motion. She barely resisted the urge to jerk him back down. For his protection or her own, she could not have said. She felt naked without his body shielding hers, but he looked even more vulnerable as he strode boldly to the center of the courtyard, offering his heart as an unguarded target to the bowman in the tower.

"Father, it's Austyn," he shouted in an irrefutable

tone of authority. "I've come home." He jerked one of the gold-laden panniers from the pack horse Nathanael was cowering behind and held it triumphantly aloft. "And I've brought enough gold so that you'll never have to fear Edward's tax collectors again!"

The courtyard hung on tenterhooks of silence. Holly held her breath, surprised by the depth of her fear that the next arrow would make a widow of her.

But from the tower came only a sheepish "Harrumph," then the clatter of retreating footsteps. Nathanael crept out from behind the pack horse while Carey helped Elspeth up from her kneeling position. Austyn lowered the pannier to the ground, the sudden slump of his shoulders betraying his relief.

"Does your father greet all of his guests with such enthusiasm?" Holly could not resist asking as she climbed to her feet. Nathanael shot her a frantic glance, and Holly wrestled her rebellious skirts into submission before Austyn could turn around.

"Just be thankful I hid the oil for boiling before I left." Austyn ran a hand wearily over his beard.

They appeared to be standing in the main courtyard of an ancient stone keep ringed by wattle-and-daub cottages and outbuildings. The master architect of the concentric castle had plainly hoped to preserve the keep as the bustling heart of his creation. Now it slumbered beneath the same tragic spell of unfulfilled promise that enslaved the entire promontory.

Full dark had descended and bats flitted from merlon to parapet. At least she didn't have to fret about them getting tangled in her hair, Holly thought ruefully, edging a few steps nearer to Austyn.

An iron-studded door creaked open to reveal a

hesitant huddle of castle denizens. Several of them gripped torches in whitened fists. As they crept forth from the keep, shuffling their feet in unison like some timid dragon with twenty-four legs and twelve swiveling heads, torchlight flickered over their faces, revealing expressions of chilling dread.

Holly took an involuntary step away from her husband, shying away from his grim profile. How was she to survive being wedded to a man who evoked such terror in his own retainers? A frisson of primal fear danced down her spine.

A man whose scalp was as hairless and pink as a newborn's rump separated himself from the quivering mass. "Welcome home, master. It seems your journey was a successful one."

Austyn clapped him on the shoulder without eliciting so much as a flinch. "Aye, Emrys. I've brought you a new mistress. 'Tis far past time, wouldn't you say?"

Holly's confusion mounted. The servants clustered around Austyn, almost as if seeking his protection. Each of them seemed only too eager to touch him or offer some word of welcome or encouragement. She was the one receiving the fearful looks, the poorly concealed glances of dread. Why they weren't afraid of Austyn, she realized with a start. They were afraid of her!

Her suspicion was confirmed when Austyn reached to draw her out of the shadows. Several of his minions took hasty steps backward, stumbling over their own feet. One old fellow even dared to wiggle two fingers at her in the universal sign to ward away evil.

As the ruthless torchlight struck her face, nearly

blinding her, Holly resisted the urge to shield its desolate condition with her hands. Instead, she forced herself to stand straight and tall, bracing herself for the repugnance they were sure to express at her appearance. Austyn slipped one brawny arm around her waist.

A collective gasp went up.

"Oh, my," breathed a female voice. "She's precious!"

"Aye," said a man, drawing off his feathered cap in tribute. "I've never seen a more perfect lady. Why she's like a little doll!"

Holly could only blink in shock, utterly mystified by their reaction. Austyn was nudged away as they swarmed around her, touching her hacked-off hair, her mud-spattered gown, her blistered nose with coos of awe and delight. The old man who had shaken his fingers at her even dropped to his knees to bestow a kiss upon the damp hem of her skirt. Nathanael and Elspeth gaped in openmouthed astonishment.

Holly had graciously accepted more than her share of adulation in her short life, but she'd never been worshiped with such childlike rapture. She could not comprehend their curious behavior. Were they all blind?

She shot Austyn a baffled glance. His cheeks were taut with what might have been chagrin, but his eyes sparkled with some secret amusement. "May I present to all of you my bride and the new mistress of Gavenmore—Lady"—he hesitated, glancing about as if to ensure the area was free of potential missiles—"Holly."

The teasing intimacy of his smile coaxed an unbidden flip from Holly's heart. A bemused ripple of laughter escaped her.

"Gwyneth? Gwyneth, is that you?"

At the plaintive query, a shadow passed over Austyn's face, fading his smile. A tense hush claimed the courtyard. The servants parted as a wasted figure crept out of one of the corner towers and made his way toward Holly. The blustering bravado their assailant had exhibited upon their arrival seemed to have melted away.

He lifted a trembling hand to touch her cheek. "Gwyneth?" he repeated. "Is that you?"

Holly found herself gazing into gray-lashed eyes that might have been twins of Austyn's had their frosty flame not been extinguished by shadows of the past. A mane of silver hair framed the man's furrowed face.

Austyn rested a hand on his shoulder. "Nay, Father, 'tis not Gwyneth. 'Tis my bride."

"A bride," the man echoed wistfully, aged beyond his years by his shrunken posture and the quavering note in his voice. Holly realized in that moment that Austyn's father was not just eccentric; he was mad.

Austyn's wary gaze rested not on his father, but on Holly's face. He plainly feared she would slap the impertinent stranger away with some scathing rebuke.

She caught the old man's chilled hand, warming the frail parchment of his skin between her palms. "My name is Holly, sir," she said, bestowing a gentle smile on him. "If you will allow me to call you 'Father,' perhaps in time you'll come to think of me as your own daughter."

This time when Holly met Austyn's gaze over his father's stooped shoulder, the mysterious regard in her husband's eyes wrenched her heart with a violence that was almost painful.

"Aye, our master is a sly one, he is. Frighting us all half to death by running off to woo the most beautiful damsel in all of Britain. Why I'd box his ears as I did when he was a lad if he didn't outweigh me by five stone. Still might if he gives me cause!"

Holly followed Winifred, wife of Emrys Ab-Madoc, through the shadowy warren of passageways that would eventually lead to her chamber, reluctant to point out that the tiny woman would have to stand on a stool to box Austyn's chin, much less his ears. The faded flax of her hair would have betrayed her as Carey's mother even had Holly not witnessed her kissing and pinching the bowman's cheeks with equal vigor, inciting a blush of lurid pink from his fair skin. The woman chirped like a sparrow, but bobbed along the narrow vaulted corridors like a plump gray pigeon.

Holly was thankful for her prattling company. Elspeth and Nathanael had lingered by the kitchen fire to partake of a hearty stew, the mere sight of which had turned Holly's bloated stomach and she much preferred Winifred's chatter to the chattering of her own teeth as she contemplated her future as Austyn's wife.

"Our family has served Gavenmore for generations. My Emrys is the master's steward, but I'm the one that carries the keys." A faint clanking as they climbed a winding stone staircase confirmed her boast.

"What of Sir Austyn's father?" Holly asked. "I can't

help but notice 'tis not the father, but the son, you call your master."

Winifred shook her head sadly and tapped her forefinger against her temple. "The old master ain't been right in the noggin since his lady died. I suspect he never will be. He spends half his days cursing the king and the other half searching the castle for his beloved Gwyneth."

"How tragic," Holly replied, thinking how easy it would have been for her own papa to succumb to the madness of grief.

Caer Gavenmore itself seemed to have fallen under the same dark spell of mourning. Holly had grown accustomed to flitting through the spacious corridors and airy chambers of Castle Tewksbury with their glass-fitted windows and generous embrasures. The shuttered windows and cramped arrow loops of this ancient keep loomed out of the shadows like malevolent eyes. Cobwebs frosted the hanging sconces, drifting like tattered veils stirred by an invisible sigh.

Carey's mother carried a tallow candle to light their way over the uneven flagstones, but each time it wavered, Holly held her breath, fearing the next chill draft would cast them into darkness. To her intense relief, Winifred sheltered the flame with her cupped hand as they bustled past a curving stairwell that wended upward into darkness.

A woman's moan, low and poignant with some unspeakable anguish, pierced the musty air. Holly hesitated, every meager hair on her head tingling with alarm.

Winifred threw a cheery smile over her shoulder, assuring Holly that her imagination was once more triumphing over her common sense. Holly pressed a palm to her galloping heart and forced her feet into motion, eagerly awaiting Winifred's explanation that the unearthly keening was simply the wind whistling through some narrow crack in the mortar.

"Don't mind the noise, child. 'Tis only the master's grandmother."

"His grandmother? She's still alive?" Holly cast a nervous glance back at the stairwell, scrambling to calculate the woman's age. She adored classical literature, but Nathanael had pronounced her paltry brain unfit for the masculine science of mathematics.

Winifred waved an airy hand. "Of course not. The poor dear threw herself out the tower window after her husband locked her away for flirting with a minstrel." She shot Holly a knowing wink. "Some say 'twas despondency that drove her to it, but I say 'twas more likely boredom. After all, ten years is a long time to endure your own company."

Holly was still pondering that grim revelation when they rounded a corner to be assailed by the deafening clatter of chains. She clapped her hands over her ears, removing them only when the clamor died to a ghostly echo.

She swallowed a congealed lump of fear, searching Winifred's serene countenance hopefully. "A loose chain on the drawbridge? Bats in the belfry?"

Winifred shook her head, clucking her tongue dolefully. "That would be the bride of the master's great-great-great grandfather."

Holly didn't have to be Pythagoras to calculate the mathematical odds of that particular Gavenmore lady still being alive. "I don't suppose the woman died in her sleep of natural causes," she said in a small voice.

"I'd say not. Old Caradawg of Gavenmore had her burned at the stake in the castle courtyard." Winifred's voice lowered to a conspiratorial whisper. "He claimed she was a witch, but 'twas rumored the careless chit simply showed a bit of ankle while climbing into her litter. Ah, here we are! I sent the maidservants ahead to ready your chamber."

The woman threw open a massive oaken door and backed Holly inside. Chucking her fondly beneath the chin, she said, "Don't mind the White Lady, dear. She doesn't usually trouble anyone unless the moon is full."

With those dubious words of comfort, Winifred shut the door in Holly's face. Holly stood staring at the door for several dumbfounded minutes, afraid to turn around for fear some ghoul would be waiting to greet her, its skeletal fingers dripping clods of grave dirt. She'd always heard the Welsh were a superstitious lot. Now she understood why.

"Steady, girl," she whispered before forcing herself to face the chamber.

A plump apricot of a moon peeped coyly through the arrow loop on the opposite wall. Holly clapped a hand over her mouth to muffle a shriek. She wasn't sure which would frighten her more—a nocturnal visit from the "White Lady of Gavenmore" or one of her husband's homicidal ancestors.

Rushlight flickered over the mundane cheer of the chamber, mocking her fears. A basin of steaming water rested next to a linen towel on a low-slung chest. Her scant belongings had been piled in one corner.

The paintings on the plastered ceiling were chipped and faded, but here and there Holly could make out pastoral scenes of scampering pups and idly grazing sheep. The four-poster bed draped in pleated silk made her sigh with yearning. 'Twas as if every comfort had been deliberately designed to lure the weary traveler to rest.

Holly longed to succumb. And why shouldn't she? she asked herself. After all, her husband had made it plain that he did not seek to share her bed. That he preferred the ephemeral memory of his lady fair to the carnal knowledge of his wife. She had seen his eyes caress the mysterious memento of that liaison with a hunger that made the affections offered by her own admirers seem only pale echoes of passion. Austyn might treat her with amused tolerance, even kindness, but it was the phantom of his ladylove who haunted his heart and his bed.

Fighting an absurd wave of melancholy, Holly jerked the cotte and chemise over her head and began to unwrap her breasts, defiantly inviting the night air to caress them. After spicing the basin of water with a few precious droplets of myrrh oil, she rinsed the ash from her hair, bathed her face and body, then fished out her hand mirror to give her reflection a perusal in the cracked glass.

She would have almost sworn the glossy silk of her hair was beginning to curl at the tips. She ran her tongue along the edge of her teeth. The stains were definitely fading. She would have to send Elspeth and Nathanael foraging in the forest for more walnuts on the morrow. She laid aside the mirror with a sigh. She was beginning to feel as divided as her reflection—

relieved to have escaped her husband's amorous demands yet insulted by his lack of regard for her.

"What did you expect, pudding head?" Holly inquired of herself as she smothered the rushes, then padded across a plush bearskin rug to the bed. "That he would lift your ugly little mask, discover your true inner beauty, and declare his undying love for you?"

A self-effacing giggle escaped her as she slid naked between the scratchy linen sheets, luxuriating in the forgotten pleasure of feeling like herself again. She snuggled into the feather pillow, refusing to give voice to her most secret fear—that Austyn might lift her mask and find nothing at all beneath.

The following morning Holly marched toward the grassy bluff where Emrys had told her she would find Austyn, determined to confront her husband about Winifred's grisly tales.

At least her mouth no longer tasted as if she'd been licking the hearthstones, she thought. Upon waking to discover the painful pinkness of her skin had subsided to a burnished russet certain to repulse any man who favored a lady over a milkmaid, she had declined to paint a mustache of ashes on her upper lip.

Holly topped the crest of the bluff to discover a man kneeling on the bank of a crystalline pool. He wore no surcoat or tunic. The day was already warm and a glistening sheen of sweat bronzed the well-defined slabs of muscle and sinew in his shoulders and back. Holly felt tiny beads of sweat bud along her own brow at the sight. She fanned herself with her hand, feeling oddly breathless.

She must have made some small sound for the man began to rise and turn. Realizing too late that this man wore no beard or mustache, and flustered at the prospect of being caught ogling a stranger, she blurted out, "Forgive me, sir. I was told I could find Sir Austyn . . ."

Her voice faded to a wordless sigh as the man wiped the mask of soap lather from his face and she discovered her entire life had been nothing but a cruel and vicious lie.

CHAPTER 13

Holly's earliest memory was of the adoring moons of her parents' faces hovering over her crib.

"Just 'ook at Mama's b-o-o-oootiful baby," her mother would croon, reaching down to finger a silky curl.

"Her is Papa's pwecious wittle angel," her father would lisp in reply, tickling the satiny skin beneath Holly's chin until she rewarded him with a delighted chortle.

Soon they were joined by others, an entire galaxy of pale moons gazing raptly down at her, all eager to pinch her rosy cheeks, tweak the tip of her upturned nose, poke the chubby perfection of her downy belly.

Her mother had refused to swaddle her as was the custom, pronouncing it an affront to God's artistry to tuck away such exquisite little arms and legs.

At the conclusion of each such rite of worship, her mother would turn and solemnly inquire of their guests, "Isn't our Holly simply the fairest creature God ever created?"

Her audience would intone their awestruck agreement, their eyes glazing over with adoration as they leaned over the crib, clucking and cooing in the fervent hope of coaxing a smile from Holly's rosebud mouth.

"Liars," Holly muttered, backing away from the man on the bluff. "Every one of them. Wretched, heartless liars!"

The sparkling frost of his eyes narrowed in bewilderment. "My lady? What is it? Is something the matter?" He lowered the linen towel, revealing a muscular chest shaded by damp whorls of hair. Holly could remember only too well the crisp feel of them beneath her fingertips. He took a step toward her.

She splayed a hand to ward him away and he stopped, seeming to sense that any sudden movement on his part might result in dire consequences. Such as her throwing herself over the edge of the bluff into the roiling river.

Holly's suitors had lied to her. Her papa had lied to her. Even her beloved mama had lied to her. She could never be the fairest creature God had ever created as long as Sir Austyn of Gavenmore lived.

His was not the fey comeliness of Eugene de Legget or even the boyish charm of his fair-haired man-at-arms. His was a purely masculine beauty, as dark and compelling as the visage of one of God's own angels cast from the portals of heaven for daring to supplant his Master's affections in the heart of every mortal female who laid eyes on him.

His scruffy growth of beard was gone, no longer defending her from a rugged jaw mellowed by the hint of a devilish dimple in one cheek. Gone as well the bristling mustache that had shielded her from the sulky curve of lips chiseled by a master artist for the delights of kissing and other sensual pleasures Holly could only pretend to imagine.

In her pathetic naïveté, she had thought him closer to her father's age than her own, but the dripping misericorde in his hand had shaved decades from his age. He could not have wounded her any more deeply had he plunged its blade into her thundering heart.

Her pallor must have reflected her shock for the quizzical concern in his eyes deepened. "Are you ill, my lady?"

Aye, she was ill! Sickened by her own stupidity. Sickened by the lurching betrayal of her heart. Sick with a fury she knew was as absurd as it was unjust. She wanted to fling herself at the sun-gilded planes of the bastard's chest and beat at him with her fists. She wanted to snatch down the bodice of her gown, revealing her breasts in all of their splendor, and shout "Ha!"

She wanted to cup the damp, freshly shaven planes of his cheeks between her palms and draw his mouth, that exquisite mouth with its beguiling promise of both damnation and deliverance, down to hers for a long, thirsty draught.

To keep herself from doing anything that might expose her folly, she turned her back on him in one violent motion. But even clenching her eyes shut so tightly they ached could not blind her to the image of him standing at the edge of that bluff, the dusky sable of his hair framed by the azure sky and caressed by the breeze blowing off the river.

Remorse flooded Austyn as he gazed down at his wife's narrow shoulders. He'd never seen anything so rigid, yet so brittle. 'Twas as if the merest nudge of his fingertip would cause her to crumble and scatter on the wind. What an utter churl he had been! It should have occurred to him before he shaved that his accursed fairness of face would only make her more conscious of her lack.

He slipped behind her, the ashen vulnerability of her nape rebuking him. He brushed a hand over her shoulder, but she shied away from his touch.

Austyn's fingers curled helplessly in on themselves. "Forgive me, my lady. 'Twas never my intention to wound you."

She wheeled on him. For a dazzling instant, the glistening violet of her eyes against the apricot flush of her skin blinded Austyn to her lank hair and mottled teeth. "Then what was your intention, sir? To burn me at the stake in the castle courtyard? To swab my spattered remains off the cobblestones beneath the north tower?"

He reached to rub his beard, then lowered his hand when it encountered only smooth jaw. "So Winnie's been regaling you with the Gavenmore history, eh?"

"Only the family propensity for either murdering

their wives or driving them to suicide. How long will it be before *my* restless spirit is wandering the corridors of Caer Gavenmore, rattling a dried chaplet of bluebells and wailing a warning to the next Gavenmore bride?"

Austyn shuddered at the image. He knew better than anyone how *haunting* Holly's caterwauling could be. "You've no need to fret about your own well-being. All of those unfortunate incidents were crimes of—" He stopped abruptly, realizing his casual words contained jagged barbs that might shred her feelings anew.

But it was too late. Without the mask of his beard to shield his thoughts, his treacherous face had revealed him.

"Passion?" she asked softly. "Jealousy?" She met his gaze squarely, the luminous oases of her eyes now dry and barren. "Then I am relieved, sir, to know there is to be neither between us."

Turning from him, she started down the hill toward the castle, her affronted dignity a fragile shield. Austyn watched her go, his heart plagued by an odd pang at the endearing awkwardness of her waddle.

He was too awash in regret to hear Carey come rustling up the path from the river, a string of fish dangling from one hand. "I say, fellow, have you seen Sir Aus—" The fish flopped from his fingers to the grass. *"Good God, man, what have you done?"*

"Proved myself an utter clod," Austyn replied absently, laying aside the misericorde and towel to rescue his tunic from a nearby rock. "Trampled my wife's delicate heart into the dirt."

"And it's not even noontide yet. But I was talking about the beard." Carey wiped a missed streak of soap lather from Austyn's cheek. "Why I'd forgotten how comely you were or I might have wed you myself!

Austyn cuffed him lightly on the chin. "My face was never good for naught but attracting the very sort of women I sought to avoid."

Carey sighed wistfully. "Ah! Beautiful women. Exquisite feminine creatures with soft, creamy hands and lush, rosy lips eager to . . ." He shook himself out of his reverie.

Austyn buckled a crimson surcoat over his tunic. "Now that I've a wife and am protected from such dangerous temptations, I thought it safe to shave."

Carey snorted. "God pity the harlot that incurs the wrath of your bride. The little minx would doubtlessly snatch her even balder than—" He lowered his eyes. "Sorry."

Austyn picked up the memento he had carried next to his heart since that night in the moonlit garden, studying it with troubled eyes. "My wife is a most curious girl. She doesn't seem the jealous sort. 'Tis almost as if she doesn't deem herself worthy of fidelity." Still haunted by her fleeing image, he closed his hand, crushing the forgotten treasure heedlessly in his fist. "When I told her my heart was pledged to another—"

"You told her such a thing? Have you lost your wits, man? Women despise candor."

Austyn scowled. "To lie would have been a dishonor to her. And had I not told her the truth, she might have thought I found her"—it was his turn to lower his eyes—"distasteful."

"Ah, but now you wish to make amends?"

What Austyn wished for was his beard to hide the flush he could feel creeping toward his clenched jaw. In matters of the heart, he had no choice but to bow to Carey's superior wisdom. To avoid any entanglements that might inadvertently cost him his soul, Austyn had chosen to bargain for the majority of his pleasures. He'd learned to bring a woman to shuddering ecstasy when he'd been little more than a lad, but knew nothing of wooing one. His coin had always been persuasion enough.

"I'll not praise her virtues in honeyed verse if that's what you're thinking," he growled. "I'd rather she gut me with my own sword than repeat that debacle."

Carey absently picked up the misericorde, tapping its hilt against his pursed lips as he contemplated how best to display his sophistication. "Women, particularly new brides, love to receive gifts. And they adore any excuse to fuss over their menfolk. Offer the girl some tokens of your affection. Give her a bit of mending to do."

"Mending? But I've nothing that requires it. Your mother does all—" Yelping, Austyn jumped back as Carey jabbed the misericorde toward his side, splitting the seam of his surcoat and barely missing his ribs. He shot his man-at-arms a disbelieving glare. "What are you trying to do? Give her the pleasure of stitching up my hide?"

"Only as a last resort. I'm sure you can scrape up some more garments to go on the pile." Carey clapped him on the shoulder. "Take heart, man. The girl has probably had little enough wooing in her life. I wager 'twill take but a handful of pretty trinkets to win back her favor."

Holly glared at Austyn's offerings, fuming with impotent anger.

After fleeing the bluff and the regal stranger masquerading as her husband, she had spent hours restlessly prowling the castle, giving only the shadowy stairwell that wended its way to the haunted tower a wide berth. Twice she had thought she heard shuffling steps behind her, but had whirled around to find herself alone. Perhaps 'twas only rats, she had thought bitterly, or the shambling specter of her own idiocy.

She had retreated to her chamber after noontide to find a silver tray resting on the chest. A silver tray containing an array of exquisite offerings: a tiny replica of a misericorde no bigger than her smallest finger, its wooden blade carved to a delicate point; a pewter box brimming with fresh cut herbs, their wintry aroma making her nostrils tingle; a silken veil so gossamer it might have been woven from nothing more substantial than the dreams of wistful spiders.

Holly picked up each item in turn, surveying them with brutal candor. "A veil to spare my lord the sight of my face. Herbs to sweeten the foulness of my breath. And a pick to clean my rotten teeth. How thoughtful."

A knock sounded on the door. Holly marched over to it, wielding the tiny toothpick like the most lethal of daggers. She was only too eager to plunge it into her husband's churlish heart.

Winifred stood on the threshold, teetering beneath a mound of garments. She staggered over to the bed, dropping her burden with a grunt of relief. "From the master, my lady. He remembered your papa boasting that you were proficient in needlework."

"Proficient?" Holly echoed acidly. 'Twas rumored throughout England that she could sew a man's flapping tongue to his chin before he'd finished declaring his eternal devotion to her. "Thank you, Winifred," she said stiffly, ushering the tiny woman out the door.

She wheeled around to shoot the innocuous-looking pile of garments a baleful glare, thankful to have been given yet another gust of irritation to fan the embers of her rage.

"Of all the masculine arrogance! Why the sheer vanity of it boggles the mind! He must think it the most esteemed privilege for me to prick my fingertips raw in his exalted service!"

She snatched a crimson surcoat from the top of the pile, wringing it between her hands as if it were Austyn's thick neck. An achingly familiar aroma wafted to her nose. She buried her face in the garment, breathing deeply of an intoxicating hint of leather, horse, and crisp minty musk.

A despairing moan escaped her. She sank to her knees on the bearskin rug, still clutching the garment.

How Nathanael would laugh if she allowed him to discover her predicament! she thought. How many times had he sneered his approval while she scoffed in the crestfallen face of some poor man whose only transgression was to allow his heart to be drawn into her snare by a flutter of her silky lashes or a provocative pout?

Yet she had allowed herself to be beguiled by

nothing more than the hint of an unlikely dimple in a man's stern jaw, the wry quirk of his chiseled lips.

A dry sob, half laughter, half grief, broke from her lips. She was lying to herself even now. In truth, she had began to feel the first stirrings of infatuation for Sir Austyn as early as the tournament, when his valor on the jousting field had proved him a man of honor. She had behaved as the most abominable brat on the journey to Gavenmore, yet instead of punishing her as she deserved, he had rewarded her with patience and compassion.

He had forfeited both his freedom and the hope of a future with a woman he truly loved to wed a stranger and protect a father too tormented by grief to ever fully appreciate the sacrifice his son had made. Oddly enough, even Austyn's fidelity to that faceless wraith of a lover stirred Holly almost as much as it pained her.

She rubbed the worn samite of the surcoat against her cheek, realizing that she was trapped in a web of her own deceit. Once she might have captured the heart of a virile man like Austyn with nothing more than a crook of one elegant fingernail. But now her fingernails were shredded to the quick and Austyn's heart was bound to another. Her father had warned her too late of the grim consequences of forever seeking her own way.

"Oh, Papa," she whispered. "What have I done?"

Don't rely solely on your disguise to repel him, girl. Just be yourself.

Her father's enigmatic advice rose unbidden in her mind. A wild hope flowered in her heart. If she could repel Austyn with her shrewish temper, might she not also win his favor with the sweetness of her demeanor? Then for once in her life, she would be assured that someone loved her for something other than her fairness of form.

And once she'd won her husband's favor, she would be free to confess her trifling deception. Freshly dazzled by the promise of her beauty, he would gather her into his arms and seal his pledge of eternal devotion with the tenderest of kisses.

Holly sighed, enchanted by the blissful vision. It took several dazed moments for the bright crimson of the surcoat to come back into focus. When it did, she jumped to her feet, giving the garment a brisk snap. If she was going to be the sweetest, most attentive wife a Gavenmore had ever been blessed with, there was much work to be done.

She tossed a handful of wintergreen into her mouth before throwing open the door. "Elspeth!" she bellowed, chewing vigorously. "Elspeth, fetch my sewing box this very instant!"

CHAPTER 14

Austyn dragged his gaze away from the stairs winding down into the great hall long enough to slide his rook across the length of the carved board to protect his queen.

"Ha! Checkmate!" his father crowed, seizing Austyn's hapless king in his fist. "How many times have I warned you, son, not to leave your liege unguarded while you trot after the skirts of some woman? She may appear delicate, but the treacherous bitch can look after herself."

'Twas almost worth letting the old man best him to witness his glee, but Austyn was not in the mood to endure one of his father's rambling lectures on the evils of the fair sex. Yet he knew there was only one other topic compelling enough to keep his father from sliding back into brooding silence.

Austyn leaned back on the bench, stretching his long legs. "You would have bested me anyway, Father. Your king's strategy was far superior to mine."

'Twas all the distraction Austyn had need of. Rhys of Gavenmore launched into a fevered recitation of the triumphs of his beloved Welsh kings—Llewelyn ap Gruffydd, Llewelyn the Great, even the mighty Arthur, a warrior so elusive that none of them truly knew if he had been flesh and bone or just a noble phantom forged from dreams of glory. From there, his father rushed on to castigate the English cur Edward.

Which Edward was irrelevant. In his father's twisted imagination, the first Edward still sat the throne. The Edward whose visit to this very keep in the autumn of 1304 had brought them all to ruin. The Edward who died three short years later after stripping them of their earldom, their vassals, and all other Gavenmore holdings, leaving them nothing but a crumbling ruin on a barren promontory overlooking the river Wye and the fading echo of a woman's laughter.

Austyn ruthlessly blocked out his father's prattling, a trick he'd been forced to learn long ago to preserve his own capricious sanity. His temper was growing more irritable by the minute. He glowered at the stairs, longing for nothing so much as a glimpse of his homely little bride. If she did not choose to join them for the eventide meal, he would have to assume his gifts had failed to soothe her wounded feelings.

Carey crouched with his back to the circular stone

hearth in the middle of the hall, idly plucking the strings of a lute. Brother Nathanael had tucked himself in the corner and sat cracking walnuts into a wooden bowl. A curious pursuit for a priest, Austyn thought, puzzled by the hint of rancor around the man's mouth. The persistent *crack-crack* sound was beginning to fray Austyn's tightly strung nerves even more than his father's droning or Carey's discordant plucking.

He drummed his fingers on the table, disturbing a furred film of dust. After growing up in the splendor of Castle Tewksbury, he feared Holly must find the ancient keep little more than a hovel.

Crack-crack.

A stale layer of rushes carpeted the flagstones. A haze of smoke from the crude rushlights drifted over the hall, too cloying to be sucked out of the circular smoke hole cut in the vaulted roof above the hearth.

Crack-crack.

Austyn flexed his hands, fearing that if one more denuded walnut skittered into that bowl, he was going to rush over and crack the priest's skull.

Brother Nathanael was spared that grim fate by the appearance of his mistress on the stairs. Austyn came to his feet without realizing it. His father's blustering tirade subsided on a fretful note.

Lady Holly descended the stairs with regal grace, her broad hips swaying, her features obscured by a fall of gauzy silk. The train of her gown rippled behind her, rescued from the grimy taint of the stone steps by her nurse's loyal hands. Her mincing steps did not betray her until she misjudged the last step and trusted her dainty foot to thin air.

Austyn rushed forward to catch her before she could topple forward, frowning to realize the veil must make vision difficult, if not impossible, in the murky light. He cupped her bare elbows through her slashed sleeves, marveling at their silken texture. No matter how fair the face, he'd yet to meet a woman with comely elbows.

"Good eve, my lady. Shall we sup together?"

A smile warmed her voice. "If you wish it so, my lord."

She turned away from the table, forcing Austyn to capture her shoulders and gently guide her in the right direction. He fought a ridiculous impulse to lift the veil and steal a peek at that downy nape of hers. As they approached the table, his father retreated to huddle against the faded tapestry, still clutching his captured king.

Holly nodded at Carey as she slid onto the bench. "Good eve, Winifred. I hope my tardiness has not allowed the food to cool."

Carey opened his mouth, but Winifred mercifully bustled in at that moment, bearing a tray of trenchers. The bowls of coarse brown bread overflowed with steaming portions of mutton and leeks. "The master's favorite, my lady," she said, slapping a trencher down between Austyn and Holly. "I hope it pleases you."

"I'm certain it will, Winnie," Holly replied mildly. "It takes very little to please me. I hope you'll find it the least taxing of your duties."

Austyn stared at his wife in patent disbelief while the others gathered at the far end of the trestle table. Yesterday she'd been nigh on impossible to please. He was beginning to resent the veil. He missed judging

Holly's mood from the imperious angle at which she tilted her nose. Missed witnessing the first sparks of violet fire in those extraordinary eyes. When her groping fingers closed around the salt cellar, bringing it to her lips for a drink, he flipped the veil away from her face, growling beneath his breath.

She exchanged salt cellar for goblet, her eyes dewy with surprise. "Does my costume displease you, sir? I thought only to honor your generosity."

Austyn recoiled, his eyes watering. Her breath positively reeked of wintergreen, the crisp blast of mint overwhelming even the pungent aroma of the leeks. It disgruntled him further to learn that he preferred the sweet, faintly floral, scent of her natural breath.

"Aye, it pleases me," he lied. "That veil belonged to my grandmother."

A fetching giggle escaped her. "I do hope you asked her leave before you borrowed it. I'd rather she not drift into my chamber at midnight, wailing and bemoaning its loss."

Austyn's lips twitched, but he scowled to keep from smiling. No woman had ever dared mock the family ghosts before.

But nor had any woman dared to share his trencher without an invitation, to soothe his mood with bright chatter about the rustic charms of Caer Gavenmore, to feed him tender bits of mutton from her fingertips. Oddly enough, it was Holly's hands with their rein-chapped palms and bitten-to-the-quick fingernails that stirred him most. They fluttered about him like two delicate-boned birds, beguiling him with their grace, enticing him with their unspoken desire to please.

They stilled when Brother Nathanael's shadow fell over them. "I sought you earlier, my child, but Elspeth said you were napping."

"Then I was." Holly slanted an inscrutable look up at the priest, before bestowing an amused smile on Austyn. "He calls me 'child,' forgetting that he is only a few years older than I."

Brother Nathanael flushed as Austyn himself might have done beneath her blithe mockery. He indicated the bowl tucked beneath his arm. "I spent the morning foraging in the forest for walnuts, my lady. Your favorites."

"No, thank you, Brother," she replied sweetly. "I seem to have lost my taste for them."

The priest set the bowl on the table, his walnut-stained fingernails more ragged than Holly's. " 'Twould benefit you greatly to partake of these. I've never seen a meat so tender, so succulent." He reached to urge a walnut into her hand.

Austyn's arm shot out, sweeping the bowl into the floor. "She doesn't want them, dammit! Are you deaf?"

As the echo of his roar faded, Austyn felt the weight of shocked gazes bearing down on him. His father cowered against the tapestry as if he might weave himself into its threads. More damning than the shock was the bald concern reflected on the faces of Emrys, Winifred, and Carey. A concern not for their own well-being as it should have been, but for his.

"Forgive me, sir. I should not have troubled you." The priest retreated with a stiff bow, crushing walnut bits beneath his sandaled feet.

Holly was the only one who appeared bemused rather than offended by Austyn's outburst. "Don't mind Nathanael. He's only feeling slighted because he's been denied the privilege of hearing my prayers today."

Austyn steadied his hands around his goblet, as confounded as the rest of them by his unexpected surge of temper. "And what would you pray for, my lady? A more reasonable husband?"

She grazed his jaw with the backs of her fingers, jarring him with her tenderness. "Why I'd pray for you, sir."

He gazed into her eyes, their quizzical brightness robbed now of all mockery, and wondered if she knew how prophetic her words might prove to be. She might very well be the last hope of salvation for the noble name of Gavenmore. The final prospect of redemption for his own jaded soul.

"Pretty lady."

At first Austyn feared the hoarse croak had come from his own lips. But he looked up to discover his father had crept out from his hiding place to hover shyly at Holly's shoulder.

"Pretty lady," the old man repeated, brushing his gnarled fingers over the silk of her veil.

"Why, thank you, Father." Holly tossed a smile over her shoulder before whispering to Austyn, "He should take care on the stairs. The poor dear's eyesight must be failing him."

This time Austyn failed to smother his grin. Perhaps his father, like himself, was intrigued not by his bride's beauty but by her unabashed lack of it.

Holly rose, giving Elspeth a cryptic signal. The

nurse approached to present Austyn with a folded garment.

"If my efforts please you, husband," Holly said, her hands folded demurely over her plump little belly, "perhaps on the morrow I might assume more of my wifely duties."

Austyn watched her climb the stairs, wishing he could keep his lecherous mind off the one wifely duty he had assured her she would not be expected to perform. He barely noticed when his father tiptoed after her, skulking in Elspeth's shadow.

"Let's have a look at her handiwork, man," Carey said, he and his parents crowding eagerly around Austyn. "What did I tell you? Give a woman a chance to fuss over you and you'll soon have her purring like a kitten in your lap."

Carey's mother whacked him with a wooden spoon. "What do you know of women? I see no ladies rubbing up against *your* ankles."

To spare his man-at-arms further indignity, Austyn hefted the garment. His surcoat unfurled before him like a crisp crimson banner.

As Carey examined the seam, his smirk of triumph faded to a baffled frown. "I don't understand. She hasn't mended it at all. Why I can still put my fist through the tear." He did so to prove his point.

The surcoat began to quiver, then to emit gruff choking noises. While they exchanged alarmed glances, Austyn turned the garment, displaying its back for all of them to see.

Sewn across the broad shoulders of the garment in delicate stitches that must have taken exquisite

workmanship and an even greater surfeit of patience
was an intricate border of glossy green ivy.

Austyn chuckled ruefully as he wiped his streaming eyes. "It never occurred to me that our definitions
of *needlework* might vary to such a degree. God, if I'd
have known having a wife was going to be so damned
amusing, I'd have sought one long ago!"

Hugging the garment to his chest, he threw back
his head and roared with laughter.

The others might have joined in had they not
been stunned to silence by a shock even more keen
than that they'd felt upon witnessing Austyn giving
vent to that infamous Gavenmore temper he kept under such rigid control. They'd seen rare flares of rage
before, but it had been twenty long years since they'd
heard the music of their master's unbridled mirth.

CHAPTER 15

From that day forward, Sir Austyn was rarely seen in any other surcoat but the crimson one with the delicate chain of ivy emblazoned so boldly upon its shoulders. To Winnie's chagrin, he refused to let her mend the torn seam, preferring to expose the tunic beneath rather than risk offending his bride.

His extravagant praise of Holly's handiwork was so convincing that within a week, a majority of his tunics, his surcoats, and even his stockings, sported frivolous chains of daisies, plump bouquets of posies, and tiny pink butterflies flitting from hem to cuff. He finally begged Carey to help him hide the surcoat he wore in battle, fearing his industrious wife might embroider a meadow of hollyhocks on its padded chest while he slept.

Faced with the daunting challenge of becoming mistress of her husband's castle, Holly came to the humbling realization that she had been trained to be a bride, not a wife. She could sing a complicated round of "Sumer is Icumen In" in perfect pitch and dance a sprightly carol with nary a stumble, yet she was helpless to master the intricacies of baking a loaf of bread over the kitchen fire. Her flaming puddings fizzled. Her mulled wine soured. Her cream curdled.

Winifred took to keeping a bucket of well water by the hearth to extinguish the daily blazes ignited by her efforts. Emrys trailed behind her in the garden, digging up the hemlock and nightshade she inadvertently planted among the neat rows of sage and thyme.

Rather than reproving her for her incompetence, Austyn greeted all of her domestic tragedies with profound interest and a fond tweak of her nose.

After soaking several pairs of her husband's hose in a vat of boiling water, shrinking them to the size of sausage casings, she earned a disbelieving bark of laughter from Carey upon informing him with a yearning sigh, "Your master must truly be a saint. He has no temper to speak of, does he?"

It was Winifred, desperate for a reprieve, who finally shoved a wooden bucket and a handful of rags into Holly's eager hands. Delighted to find something she could excel at, Holly devoted those first golden days of summer to restoring Caer Gavenmore to its former grandeur. She polished the brass torch holders until they gleamed, tore the cobwebs from every corner, and swept the flagstones clean.

'Twas a full fortnight before she screwed up the courage to attack the shadowy landing at the foot of the stairs winding up to the haunted tower. Her task brightened considerably after she broke out the rotted shutters that had sealed the gloom for nearly fifty years, flooding the landing with sunlight and sweetening the stale air with summer's breath. She batted her way through a dervish of dust motes, then dropped to her knees to scrub the wooden planking, thinking how her papa would chuckle if he could see his "wittle angel" now.

Her days were no longer filled with trivial amusements and desultory boredom, but with hard work and satisfying results. Instead of tossing restlessly in her bed at night, plagued by nameless yearning, she slept deeply, dreaming of the day when she would coax her husband to surrender his heart. She no longer felt like a canary trapped in a gilded cage, but like a graceful curlew gliding high over the river Wye at sunset, free to pursue its dreams.

Austyn was warming to her as slowly but undeniably as the black Welsh soil was warming to the summer sun. His boyish grins had grown more frequent, his silences less brooding. And even more promising, she'd not seen him slip his hand into his tunic to finger that elusive token of his lady's love for nearly a sennight.

Charming a man without twirling a spiral curl around a crimson fingernail or puckering her rouged lips in an inviting moue had proved an even greater challenge than molding beeswax candles that did not go limp at the first kiss of flame. Yet Holly had em-

braced the challenge, savoring each tiny victory—
each fleeting glimpse of the dimple that softened the
rugged angle of her husband's jaw—as a herald of a
more lasting triumph.

She sank back on her haunches to rub a trickle of
sweat from her brow. Exertion had warmed her, only
making the icy prickle at her nape more pronounced.
She swiveled to peer at the yawning mouth of the stairwell. No amount of sunshine could banish the miasma
of despondency that seemed to come rippling down
the narrow stairs like a pool of tears.

Holly rose to her feet, sternly reminding herself
that her disquiet was only a childish fancy. She'd already banished one of the legendary ghosts of Caer
Gavenmore, proving the eerie rattling in the south corridor to be nothing more than the mischievous bobbing of an iron candelabra designed to be raised and
lowered on chains for ease of lighting. She crept
toward the stairwell, refusing to be cowed by a growing sense of unease.

Resting her foot gingerly on the first step, she
peered upward into the shadows, knowing a door must
be hidden just beyond the curve of the wall. Her spine
tingled as a faint scraping sound reached her—like the
desperate scrabbling of fingernails on wood.

"Mice," she muttered.

She climbed another step, brushing aside a veil of
cobwebs. A musty breath of air, as fragile as a
woman's sigh, struck her face, making her flinch.

"Naught but a stray draft," she pronounced,
clenching her teeth to keep them from chattering.

As her foot came down upon the third step, a low-pitched dirge swelled around her, rising to a lamentation so keen it sliced Holly's tender heart to the quick. Clapping her hands over her ears to block out its sorrowful warning of broken promises and shattered hopes, she fled, kicking over the bucket as she went.

Austyn was in the solar, poring over a parchment scroll yellowed by age and neglect, when Holly went flying past the doorway, her face so pale she might have been one of the Gavenmore haunts. He rose from his chair, then forced himself back down.

He was getting as addled as his father, he thought, tempted to trail after his young bride like one of his own hounds besotted by a leg of mutton. He scowled at the mildewed plans for the completion of an outer curtain wall. His bride's unflagging exuberance must be wearing off on him. Not a stone had been lifted toward finishing Caer Gavenmore since that cold, rainy autumn of 1304, yet here he sat, daring to dream of castles in the clouds.

His restless gaze drifted to the door. Perhaps he'd do well to follow Holly and see what nonsense she was about today. He'd been reviewing the accounts with Emrys only yesterday morning when a shrill cacophony that sounded as if every demon in Christendom had been summoned down upon their heads had sent them all careening toward the south corridor. They had arrived to find Holly riding up and down on a rusted candelabra, squealing with glee at each dizzying ascent to the rafters.

Austyn had plucked her down the moment she came into arm's reach, choking his heart from his throat to deliver a stern lecture on the dangers of such reckless behavior. Her nose tilted at an unrepentant angle, she had vowed to take more care before offering the gentle suggestion that she might not have had to exorcise the ghost of his great-great-great grandfather's bride had the malicious old rogue not burned her at the stake.

Snapping the scroll shut, Austyn rose to his feet. He was not a man given to stealth, but it wasn't as if he were following Holly just to study the beguiling habit she had of tucking her little pink tongue between her teeth when she was concentrating on some arduous task. Or to puzzle over the hint of gloss the morning sunlight evoked in her drab hair, as shimmering and elusive as a raven's wing.

Suppose she took a notion to ride the bucket down the castle well? Or curl up for a nap in the bowl of the catapult? Reassuring himself that a husbandly concern for his wife's well-being could hardly constitute spying, Austyn slipped from the solar, looking both ways before following in the path of Holly's rapid footsteps.

Some instinctive yearning for refuge drove Holly to the castle chapel. She dropped to her knees before the dusty altar and folded her trembling hands, offering up a wordless prayer for the restless soul of Austyn's grandmother. Apparently, the poor woman's plunge from the north tower window had failed to restore the freedom her vindictive husband had denied her.

Holly started violently as a hand came down upon

her shoulder. "Praying for the soul of your pagan husband, my child?"

"Good Lord, Nate," she swore, scrambling to her feet to find the priest lurking behind her. "You frightened the devil out of me. What are you doing here?"

All it took was an acerbic roll of his eyes to make her realize the idiocy of her question. "I should have known you didn't come to seek me out. Why I'd almost suspect you've been avoiding me."

With his lean, wiry body blocking her retreat, all Holly could do was incline her head to avoid his eyes. "Please don't lecture me. I've no need of any more guilt to burden my soul."

"I've seen little enough evidence of a troubled conscience in the past fortnight. On the contrary, your behavior has been quite . . . shameless."

Holly lifted her head, unable to hide her hurt at the injustice of his accusation. Her retort died as the beams of sunlight slanting through the lancet windows revealed his haggard condition. His robes were rumpled, the hair around his tonsure disheveled. Shadows dwelt beneath his dark eyes.

She reached instinctively for his arm, distressed anew by the sharp angles of his bones beneath the nubby wool. "Have you been ill, Nathanael? You look terrible."

"Ah, but you don't, do you, child?" His benevolent smile chilled her. "Your lashes are growing. Your hair is beginning to curl. Your very teeth grow brighter with each besotted smile you bestow upon your lord." His gaze flicked to her bodice, lingering just long enough to make her face heat. " 'Twill be only a matter of time, I suppose, before even your tender young breasts begin to bud."

Holly withdrew her hand. "Don't be ridiculous. My new duties have consumed my attention. I haven't had time to darken my teeth or crop my lashes or . . . or—"

" 'Thou shalt not bear false witness!' " Nathanael thundered. "So cease your lying before you've more than just your unholy lust for a Welsh pagan to repent!"

Holly's first instinct to quail beneath his attack was supplanted by a stronger urge to lash out, to hurt him as he was hurting her. "What would you know of lust, *Brother*? Or of love for that matter? Of the tender devotion that can bind a woman to a man? A wife to her husband?" Holly had never meant to reveal so much, but the truth spilled over like a brimming teardrop, leaving her heart exposed and raw.

"Ah, 'tis worse than I feared. You fancy yourself in love with the churl when all you really desire is to feel his greedy hands pawing your naked flesh. To submit to the indignities of his animal lust!"

Holly's hand shot out, wiping the sneer from Nathanael's face with a single open-palmed blow. The color bled from his cheeks, leaving only the brand of her handprint. His eyes clouded with dazed hurt. His hands hung limp at his sides. The crumbling of his pious armor made him appear not only vulnerable but terribly young.

"Oh, Nathanael," Holly whispered, besieged by pity and remorse. She lifted a hand to his cheek as if the caress of her fingertips could somehow erase the damage they'd done. "Please forgive me. I'm so terribly sorry."

Neither one of them saw the man who slipped from the back of the chapel like an angel banished from the presence of God.

CHAPTER 16

Austyn rode.

The thunder of a man's rebuke. Fierce, impassioned words, pitched too low for his ears to decipher. A woman's response, her plea unintelligible, but trembling with fervent conviction. The unmistakable crack of a hand striking human flesh.

He had rushed forward then, prepared to do battle for his lady's sake, only to discover Holly, *his* Holly, with her palm pressed tenderly to a man's cheek. *His* Holly, begging prettily for a man's forgiveness. A man of God perhaps, but first and always, a man.

A veil of darkness had descended over his eyes.

And he had flung himself on the bare back of his horse and rode.

Austyn rode until the silent bellow of rage trapped in his lungs subsided to ragged pants. He rode until his fists unclenched from their primal need to do harm. Until they surrendered the seductive temptation to smash and maim and utterly destroy the wall of sanity he'd labored upon for a lifetime, one heavy stone at a time. A wall so thick and so high that it was already completed before he realized too late that he had enclosed himself inside.

He rode until he could do nothing but slide off his winded mount and drop to his knees in the tall, coarse grass at the edge of the river.

The rising wind whipped his hair into a frenzy, stung his burning eyes, sang a mournful refrain over the rushing in his ears. Gray clouds scudded in from the west, bringing with them a wistful hint of the sea that had birthed them. Austyn remembered laying on this very bluff as a small boy, his head pillowed by his mother's skirts as she recited from memory one of the epic poems he adored. Tales of battle. Tales of valor. Tales of honor.

She had raked his hair from his brow and smiled down at him, her eyes alight with love. "Someday, my son, you'll be such a man as these. A knight. A hero. The pride of the Gavenmores."

Austyn doubled over, sickened by the memory. Sickened by the poison festering in his soul. He had thought Holly—his funny, homely little Holly—to be the one who would purge him of it. 'Twas utterly ludicrous that she would be capable of provoking even a shadow of the debilitating jealousy that had scarred the hearts of the Gavenmore men for generations.

He pressed a hand to his heart, feeling beneath his tunic the outline of the token bequeathed to him so grudgingly by the beauty he'd encountered in the Tewksbury garden. Now *there* was a woman to incite madness in the heart of a man! he thought. *There* was a woman worth surrendering his soul for! But when he closed his eyes to conjure her face before him, her exquisite features melted, reforming into a puckish grin and a pair of animated violet eyes. Her mane of sable curls vanished, disintegrating into springy tufts that bobbed like a nest of baby snakes, yet felt surprisingly silky to his touch.

Austyn groaned. What in God's name was he to do now? Rush back to the castle, drag that snide priest from the chapel by his cowl, and demand to know the nature of the man's impassioned quarrel with his wife? Corner Holly and bully her into a confession of wrongdoing?

He came to his feet, setting his lips in a grim line of determination. He wouldn't give that treacherous witch Rhiannon the satisfaction of doing either. 'Twas but a single stone of the wall around him that Holly had crumbled with her clumsy affections and artless attempts to please him. It could be easily enough repaired with the mortar of indifference. And what man would dare to judge him for refusing to count the terrible cost of that indifference?

As Austyn swung himself astride the horse and drove it back toward the castle, the first cold beads of rain struck his face like a baptism of his mother's tears.

. . .

Thunder rumbled over the black mountains like the purring of a giant cat. A cool breeze drifted through the oriel window of the solar, carrying with it the gentle pattering of the rain on the balcony. 'Twas the seventh day of rain and the gloom and damp were beginning to sorely vex Holly's nerves. She paced the cozy chamber, the defiant crackling of the fire on the hearth only heightening her restlessness.

Carey sat sharpening his arrows on the windowsill while Emrys, Winifred, and Elspeth played a muffled game of dice in the corner. Two yellow hounds drowsed before the fire. They lifted their broad heads to give Holly a doleful look as she swept past.

She stopped abruptly before the table, planting her palms firmly on its freshly polished surface. "Sir, I have strewn the floor of the great hall with new rushes and dried herbs—sweet-smelling tansy and lavender, basil and winter savory, even a sprinkling of wintergreen."

Her boast earned her only a taciturn grunt from the man behind the table. A man nearly buried behind a mound of ledgers and scrolls. A man who'd barely spoken to her for a sennight and who only endured her company when he could devise no escape from it.

Holly wracked her brain for more achievements to recite. "I've scrubbed the rust from all the manacles in the dungeon."

"Very industrious of you," he said, refusing to grant her even the boon of a glance. His voice was as cool and distant as the silvery web of lightning arcing over the river.

Elspeth crooked a sympathetic eyebrow. Winifred

and Emrys stared fixedly at the dice. Carey scowled at Austyn's back.

Holly straightened, her back rigid. If she could no longer please her husband, perhaps she could anger him. Any stamp of emotion upon the impassive beauty of his countenance would be a welcome variation.

She reached up to tug a lengthening curl, her eyes narrowing with a hint of temper only Elspeth recognized. "I've asked Winifred to prepare pickled lamprey for your supper tonight."

Nothing. Not even the threat of pickled eel could induce a shadow of his crooked grin, a petulant twitch of his chiseled lips. Lips that had once praised even her smallest effort with extravagant charity.

Holly folded her arms over her chest and tapped her foot on the floor. "I fear I accidentally spiced your porridge with hemlock this morn. You should succumb to the throes of a convulsive death by nightfall."

"That's very nice," he murmured. Snapping a ledger closed, he rose in one crisp motion, directing his words at Carey. "I'm off to the north fields to see how long the rain will delay the haying. I shall return at eventide." He brushed past her as if she were invisible, leaving her standing empty-handed and hollow hearted before the table.

Carey unfolded himself from the windowsill. "My lady, you mustn't take his brooding to heart. The Gavenmore lords have always been prone to black moods. They harden their hearts and—"

Holly lifted a hand to silence him, forcing a tremulous smile. "I fear that one must first possess a heart before one can harden it."

Terrified that Carey's compassion would entice

her hurt and frustration to spill over into tears, she turned and fled blindly from the solar.

Holly wandered the castle like a restless wraith, pondering how she was going to endure the next thirty years of Austyn's indifference. Had he treated her with such callous apathy from the beginning, she might have been left the comfort of blaming her unsightly appearance or her churlish behavior. She might have resigned herself to a marriage between two strangers who were destined to remain thus until death parted them.

But Austyn had given her a taunting glimpse of something more. Of stories shared before the fire after an exhausting, but exhilarating, day of labor. Of a crooked smile and a deep rumble of laughter, made all the more precious because they were bestowed with such rarity. Of a strong masculine hand that reached to rumple her butchered hair as if it were yet a cascade of sumptuous curls. He had given her all that, then snatched it away without even a clue as to what terrible transgression she had committed to lose his favor.

Had she known what sin to confess, she might even have humbled her pride to seek Nathanael's ear. The priest had apologized for their quarrel, vowing that it was only concern for her soul that had prompted his outburst, but relations between them remained strained and guarded. He spent most of his days poring over the musty Gavenmore histories he had discovered in a chapel vault.

As Holly passed an arrow loop, a watery swath of

sunlight informed her the rain had ceased at last. Too late, it seemed, to dispel the gloom of her spirit. Each time she rounded a corner, her pathetic attempts to prove herself a fit wife for Austyn mocked her: the fresh coat of whitewash covering the cracked plaster of the buttery walls, the pungent aroma of the herbs crunched beneath her shoes, the tubs of scarlet poppies perched along the battlements. She had left her cheerful stamp on every chamber of the keep, abandoning only the north tower to its cobwebs and ghosts.

Holly could bear it no longer. She snatched up a woolen shawl and fled the castle by an outside staircase. Escaping the enclosed courtyard, she trudged through the wet grass of the inner bailey, paying more heed to the clouds scudding across the sun than to the shy footfalls behind her.

"Gwyneth."

Holly sighed wearily. She was not in the mood to be mistaken for anyone's wife, dead or otherwise. "No, Father Rhys," she said, glancing back over her shoulder at him. "I'm not Gwyneth. I'm Holly." She could not quite banish the wistful note from her voice. "Austyn's Holly."

He shook his head. "Gwyneth," he repeated with stern conviction, pointing at the knoll just beyond her.

A phantom of a shiver caressed her nape. The breeze teased gooseflesh to her arms as she drifted toward the stone cairn nearly smothered by a blanket of ivy and weeds.

She stopped at the edge of the unmarked grave. "Gwyneth?" she whispered, hugging the shawl tight about her.

The wind bore the echo of Austyn's baritone, its gruff timbre softened by an edge of yearning. *I remember everything about her. Her voice. Her smile. The angle at which she tilted her head when she was singing.*

Gwyneth. Rhys's wife. Austyn's beloved mother. Holly swallowed around the lump that rose unbidden to her throat.

She glanced back at the keep, frowning in bewilderment. She could understand why the castle had fallen to neglect without a mistress to maintain it, but she could not fathom the disgrace of this untended grave. Her own mother's tomb was kept dusted and polished, lit day and night by costly beeswax tapers, decorated with armfuls of fragrant yellow jonquils each spring on the anniversary of her death.

A stray beam of sunlight slanted full across Holly's face, warming her for the first time in days. Perhaps 'twas not too late to win her husband's favor, she thought. Perhaps she had sought to impress him with trivial domestic accomplishments when all he really required was a simple gesture of her devotion. A gift from the heart.

Turning, she clasped the old man's gnarled hands in her own. "Father Rhys, would you care to help me?"

He nodded eagerly, the slant of his smile tugging at her heart with its familiarity. A gust of wind parted the lingering clouds as they both fell to their knees and began clawing the ivy away from the cairn.

Holly sank back on her haunches to rub a smudge of soil from her cheek. Dirt encrusted the abbreviated crescents of her fingernails. Her lower back ached.

The wind had chapped her face. She grinned, as delighted as she was exhausted by her afternoon's labor.

Her shawl lay abandoned on the grass beside her. A tangle of weeds and ivy was heaped a few feet away, begging the touch of a torch. A profusion of transplanted anemones crowded boldly around the neatly piled stones of the cairn. As Holly gently poked the last plant in the dirt, Austyn's father marched over the crest of the hill, cradling a freshly cut armful of red hyacinths. They were to be Holly's special gift to her husband—a fragrant blanket to guard Gwyneth of Gavenmore's eternal slumber.

Between one step and the next, the old man's eager smile faded. His feet faltered. The flowers fell from his arms in a crimson shower.

Holly turned to gaze behind her, shading her eyes against the lowering sun. The earth beneath her knees vibrated with the thunder of approaching hoofbeats. Her heart began to race, beating in time to the frantic rhythm.

Austyn slid off his destrier before it could come to a complete halt, stalking toward her with deadly grace. She came to her feet in instinctive defense. 'Twould seem her efforts to coax a response from her husband had succeeded beyond her wildest hopes. He was in nothing less than a murderous rage.

He stopped less than a foot from her, his broad chest heaving, his nostrils flaring with each ragged breath. "How dare you? Is there no corner of my life you won't scrub or sweep or befoul with your childish attentions, your ridiculous flowers?"

A bellow of rage would have been less wounding than his low snarl of contempt. He was gazing at her as if she were a vile thing—a profanation of the holy ground on which they stood.

Holly could do nothing but summon the queenly composure Nathanael had taught her. Clasping her hands in front of her, she tipped back her head and said, "I sought only to please you. Your father told me his beloved Gwyneth was buried here."

"Gwyneth," he spat. As if seeking a fresh target for his fury, he stormed past her and grabbed his father by the front of his tunic. "Did you tell her, old man? Did you tell her what your *beloved* Gwyneth did? Did you tell her what *you* did to your *beloved* Gwyneth?"

At seeing a helpless creature so abused, Holly's fear was supplanted by reckless anger. She snatched at Austyn's arm, tugging the rigid muscles with all of her strength. "Stop it! You're frightening him!"

Austyn freed his father and wheeled on her. For one terrible moment, Holly thought he would strike her. She recoiled, not in anticipation of physical harm, but of the irreparable damage such a careless blow would do her heart. At her blatant flinch, shame flickered in his eyes, so intense as to be almost self-loathing.

Holly reached for him, this time in tenderness, but he jerked his arm out of her reach and strode back to the cairn. Dropping to his knees, he dragged off his gauntlets, then began to tear up the tender anemones with his bare hands, hurling the ripe gobbets of earth as far as they would go.

Holly felt as if her heart was being wrenched from her chest with each snap of the fragile roots. She came to kneel on the opposite side of the grave, not bothering to wipe away the tears trickling steadily down her cheeks.

"I don't understand how you could defile her memory," she said softly. "She was your mother."

Austyn's eyes blazed cold blue fire as he threw back his head and roared, "She was a faithless whore!"

CHAPTER 17

"Aye, a more treacherous harlot never lived! As cunning as Eve. As wanton as Jezebel. Enticing decent, God-fearing men to her bed like bees to a honey pot."

It took Holly a dazed moment to realize the damning denouncement had come not from Austyn, but from his father. The old man waved his arms for emphasis as he strode toward the grave, all traces of uncertainty banished from his step. The fire had been restored to his rheumy eyes. Sanity flirted with their depths, somehow more dangerous than the vague madness that kept him occupied most of the time. Having never heard him utter more than two words at a time, Holly could only gape.

"A weak, willful woman my Gwyneth was, given over to sins of the flesh. She could never be satisfied with only one mortal man to quench her insatiable lusts. Nor with two. Nor with . . ."

'Twas as if the floodgates of silence had parted to loose a river of virulence. As he ranted on, Holly became aware that his impromptu sermon was collecting an audience. Emrys, Carey, and a white-faced Winifred clustered at the garden gate. Nathanael watched from the chapel door. Other castle inhabitants came creeping out from the brewery, the mews, the smithy, their curiosity overcoming their trepidation. Holly kept her eyes averted from Austyn, fearing he would judge her just another leering witness to his anguish.

'Twas Carey who came forward and gently took the old man by the arm. Holly suspected it was not the first time he had done so. Nor would it be the last.

"Come, sir," Carey said. " 'Tis time for your evening meal. Pickled lamprey, you know. Your favorite." The others retreated as abruptly as they'd appeared, as if Carey's simple act of kindness had shamed them.

Rhys of Gavenmore pointed a condemning finger heavenward as he marched alongside the man-at-arms. "Strumpets, every last one of them! Panting for a man's rigid staff like bitches in heat. Only too eager to spread their thighs and milk him of every last drop of God-given vigor—"

A door thudded shut, mercifully cutting off the vivid recital. If Holly could not look at her husband before, she certainly couldn't look at him now.

"I've never seen you blush before. 'Tis quite becoming."

Austyn's quiet words confused her. They gazed at

each other over the chasm of his mother's grave. Unnerved by his steady perusal, Holly ducked her head, worrying her bottom lip between her teeth. Since he'd began to stare *through* her instead of *at* her, she'd grown rather careless about mangling her appearance.

"I've never seen you throw flowers before, sir. 'Twas quite unbecoming."

"I should have warned you. All the Gavenmore men are cursed with"—he hesitated, as if uncertain how much to reveal—"unpredictable tempers. By Gavenmore standards, that was but a mild tantrum."

"Then I should hate to see a severe one."

"As would I." Austyn rose and wandered to the crest of the hill. He stood with hands on hips, gazing over the crumbling curtain wall to the swollen river. The bruised lavender of twilight framed his rugged profile.

"My father's Welsh loyalties weren't always as pure as he pretends them to be," he said. "When he heard the English king Edward was attempting to ensure peace with his contentious neighbors by building several castles along Welsh rivers and strategic byways, he volunteered Gavenmore as a site. He knew the king would bestow extravagant rewards of land and wealth to each lord who swore his fealty to such an undertaking."

"Nathanael taught me of such castles." She did not add that Nathanael had also taught her that Edward's dream had never been fully realized. That the Welsh continued to stage sporadic rebellions against the sovereignty of Edward's son to this very day.

A wistful smile played around Austyn's lips. " 'Twas a magical time to a boy of nine. The place swarmed day and night with master builders, carpenters, diggers. Carey and I managed to get ourselves into some abominable mischief. You can imagine our excitement when we learned that Edward himself was to honor us with a royal visit. We'd never seen a real king before."

Austyn's expression darkened. " 'Twas a rainy autumn eve when he and his entourage arrived. Edward was getting on in years, but he was still a virile man. I was a rather plump lad, but he lifted me as if I weighed no more than a feather."

Holly could not help but smile at the image. There was certainly no hint of lingering baby fat on Austyn's well-honed physique.

"They sat up late into the night—my father, my mother, and this English king. Laughing, talking, jesting with one another. The king was charmed to distraction by my mother's singing."

Holly shivered as the ghostly echo of some long forgotten melody seemed to play across her nerves.

" 'Twas almost midnight when they retired. My father awoke later to find the bed beside him empty."

Suddenly, Holly didn't want him to go on. Would have done anything to stop him. Even thrown her arms around his neck and smothered his words with her mouth. But she was paralyzed, her limbs weighted by dread of what was to come.

All emotion fled Austyn's voice, leaving it cold and distant. "He searched the castle for his Gwyneth, just as he still does. But that night he found her. In the king's bed."

"What did he do?" Holly whispered.

Austyn shrugged. "What could he do? 'Twas not

uncommon for an ambitious lord to permit his liege the pleasure of his wife's favors. He simply closed the door and returned to his own bed.

"At dawn the next morning, he bid Edward a gracious farewell, swearing his eternal fealty. Then he climbed the stairs and strangled my mother to death."

The stark beauty of Austyn's profile was stripped of humanity, so impenetrable it might have been carved upon a tomb. "I found them there on that bed, on the same rumpled sheets where she had lain with another man. Father was cradling her lifeless body in his arms, rocking back and forth and weeping. He kept kissing her face, begging her to wake up. All the while her limp neck was swollen and purple with the marks of his fingers, her face black with death."

Holly clapped a trembling hand over her mouth, appalled that she had come to Rhys's defense. Had allowed him to follow her about the castle like a harmless puppy. Had gently clasped his frail hands in her own, those very hands that had squeezed the life from Austyn's mother.

"When Edward heard of her death," Austyn continued, "he withdrew his builders and his favor. He stripped my father of his title and all his holdings, drove all of his finest fighting men to desert him until only the most loyal of his peasants remained."

Holly understood now why she'd witnessed no squires or knights training in the list. Why the castle was guarded not by skilled men-at-arms, but by farmers and bakers and beekeepers.

"Edward's son continues to hound us, seeking to tax us until we have no choice but to surrender even this barren rock. All because of the treachery of a woman. Because she betrayed us." Holly heard in his bitter whisper the echo of a wounded child, a child forced too soon to bear the somber responsibilities of manhood. "Abandoned us."

"Abandoned *you?*" She shot to her feet, her compassion smothered beneath a maelstrom of churning emotions. "I think not, sir, for 'tis you who have abandoned her."

CHAPTER 18

Austyn would not have been surprised had he been forced to endure his wife's pity. Or had she shrank from him in disgust. Or bowed her head in shame at his family's disgrace. But he was flabbergasted by the petite virago who leaped to her feet to challenge him. He'd faced less daunting opponents on the jousting field. Had she been a cat, he had little doubt she would have been hissing and spitting in his dumbfounded face.

"Abandoned you?" she repeated. "The way I see it, the poor woman had very little choice in the matter."

The sheer volume of her attack jolted Austyn out of his brooding. He raised his voice to match hers.

"She could have chosen to remain in her husband's bed! To honor her wedding vows!"

"And your father could have chosen not to choke her to death! I can't help but notice that he didn't strangle his precious king."

Austyn fell back a step at the well-placed blow. Every soul at Caer Gavenmore had been tiptoeing around the subject of his mother's death for decades. The incident had stained all of their lives the color of blood, yet no one dared to speak of it. Until Holly. Ugly, courageous little Holly.

She was without mercy, his Holly. "Was your father's crime a less terrible transgression than your mother's infidelity? You coddle him as if he were an invalid, yet deny her even a humble flower to honor her memory. She has only cold rocks to mark her resting place."

Austyn strode over to Holly and snatched her up by the shoulders, dragging her rigid body against his own. "Every one of which was placed there by my hand!"

Her violet eyes blazed with a passion that surpassed his own. Instead of hanging limp in his harsh embrace, she clung to his arms, refusing to be cowed. Her fierce expression betrayed not even a hint of a flinch. Austyn could not have said how much that pleased him.

"How generous of you," she said, softening her voice to a scathing rebuke. "Tell me, did you truly hate your own mother so much?"

"I adored her!" The declaration, pent up inside of him for twenty years, burst from his chest with the force of an explosion. He dropped his gaze to Holly's lips, suddenly so soft, so inviting, and whispered, "I adored her."

Holly was only too willing to bear the brunt of Austyn's anger, but the bewildered yearning in his eyes threatened to dissolve her. She wanted to melt into his arms. To draw his head gently down to her breast and . . .

She remembered with a painful shock that his head would not encounter the nurturing softness of her breasts, but the stiff strips of her bindings. Panicked by the realization, she pushed against his chest. For a dizzying heartbeat, he held her as if he would refuse to let her go, then his arms fell away without protest.

She backed away from him lest she fall prone to some other, even more dangerous, temptation. "So your mother was not the harlot your father painted her to be?"

Austyn's frown reflected his conflicted memories. "She was a beauty, aye, but she was also modest, devout. She could bear no more children after me, so she knew I was to be her only son and my father's only heir. She taught me to read and write, encouraged me to develop the manly skills that would make me worthy of becoming a knight and lord of these lands. She taught me to pray." His dark thicket of lashes swept down to veil his eyes. "I haven't prayed since she died."

Holly gathered up her shawl and wrapped it around her shoulders. "Then perhaps 'tis time you did."

She turned, determined to leave him to make peace with his memories.

"Holly?"

She paused. "Sir?"

He shook his head with a wry wonderment that squeezed the remnant of her breath from her chest. "You're enough to tempt me to trust my heart to a woman's care."

Holly had no answer for him that would not condemn her for the wretched liar she was. She could only hasten her steps toward the castle.

When she dared to steal a look back by the light of the rising moon, Austyn was kneeling beside his mother's grave, his big, blunt hands gently patting the earth around the bowed stem of an anemone.

Holly was lost. Running headlong through a shadow-laced forest, blinded by mist and tears. No, she realized. She wasn't lost. Someone was lost to her. Someone dear. Gnarled branches whipped at her face, clawed at her gown, seeking to stop her from finding who she sought.

Her frantic flight ended when she slammed into an iron-banded door. She beat upon it until her fists were bloody, but still it would not yield. She sank into a despairing heap, weeping and pleading for mercy from her faceless captor on the opposite side of that door. Her hot, salty tears ignited a tiny flame at the hem of her gown. She beat it out with her hand, but another sprang into its place, then another, until her entire skirt was ablaze.

A shadow fell over her, extinguishing not only the flames but her last hope of redemption. A man's face emerged from the darkness, harsh with contempt and accusation. 'Twas a face she had once caressed in tenderness, a face she had adored with both her lips and her heart.

The worst of it was that she loved that face still, loved him. Reached to draw him into her embrace even as his powerful hands closed around her throat.

Holly sat straight up in the four-poster bed, her heart thundering in her ears. The moon had dipped below the arrow loop, abandoning her to the cloying darkness. She touched her quaking fingertips to her cheeks, surprised to find them damp with tears.

Casting aside the tangled sheets, she fumbled to light the tallow stub at her bedside. Its feeble flicker did not completely exorcise the ghosts of those other Gavenmore brides, but it at least drove them back to the shadows writhing along the plastered walls. She could not say if they had come to warn her or if her dream was nothing more than the tormented ramblings of her own conscience.

She slipped from the bed and padded over to the chest. Dropping to her knees, she picked up her mother's hand mirror and slowly turned it to capture her reflection. Relief slowed her heartbeat to a dull thud. She had feared the poison of her own guile might have transformed her into something even more monstrous than her disguise. She watched her brow crinkle in a bewildered frown as she realized she was instead gazing into the face of a stranger.

Her features had lost their haughty cast. The tension around her mouth had softened. The yearning in her eyes deepened them to misty violet pools. She lifted a hand to her sun-burnished throat, gliding it downward until her splayed fingers encountered the tingling swell of her unbound breasts. A sigh escaped her parted lips. 'Twas no longer the face of the fairest lady in all of England reflected in the mirror. 'Twas the wistful face of a woman in love with her husband.

She laid the mirror aside, no longer able to bear the transparency of her reflection. Did she dare go to Austyn now? Confess all and cast herself upon his mercy? Would he turn her away from his bed? His heart? His life? Would he believe she betrayed him, just as his mother had betrayed his father?

Perhaps 'twould be better if she did not trust her plea to the inconstancy of words. If she simply slipped into his bed in the darkness. Burrowed against the crisp fur of his chest and coaxed his big, warm body to cover hers. The vision left her breathless, terrified, exhilarated.

Surely with his heart softened in the aftermath of their lovemaking, he would forgive her deceit.

But what would she have proven? she asked herself. That she could beguile a man with her touch? Bewitch him with the velvety softness of her skin? Charm him with the sumptuous plumpness of her breasts? She'd been confident of those powers before she wed Austyn. The faceless lover he still pined for had surely offered him no less.

You're enough to tempt me to trust my heart to a woman's care.

In truth, Austyn's hoarse confession, wrung from his throat in the bloody aftermath of battle, meant more to her than any honeyed words he might whisper in the dark. If she crept beneath his sheets with shadows for her shield and beauty as her sword, she might never know if he would have succumbed to that temptation. If he would have dared to trust his heart to a stocky, flat-chested, crop-curled little minx who adored him.

One day, Holly vowed to herself. She would give him one more day. If she could coax from him some gesture of affection for the woman he had married, then tomorrow night she would go to him. She would scoff at the warnings of those other Gavenmore brides and take the risk of laying her heart at his feet.

Her resolve strengthened, Holly danced back to the bed, feeling as lithe as a Welsh faerie without her padding to hinder her.

"Good morn, Winnie," Holly called out as she passed the woman bent over a laundry tub in the courtyard. "I'm off to gather some wildflowers from the river-bank."

"And a good day to you, Lady Holly." Winifred straightened to rub her lower back, envying the spryness of her young mistress's step.

Holly swung the basket draped over her arm in cheery rhythm, humming beneath her breath a melody ripe with hope. The azure sky sprouted blossoms of cloud as white and fluffy as chrysanthemums. 'Twas as if the rain had baptized the earth, then sent the sun to shine full upon it to fulfill the promise of its salvation.

The crisp sparkle in the air had coaxed most of the castle residents to turn their talents to chores that could be undertaken away from the gloom of the keep, such as gathering honey from the castle hives or trimming the hooves of a placid donkey. They offered Holly jovial greetings and shy smiles as she passed.

The twin yellow hounds capered at her heels for several steps before being lured away by the aroma of ham being cured over an open fire.

Holly was relieved to find Rhys of Gavenmore nowhere in sight. She had no desire to sort out her conflicting feelings about Austyn's father on such a delicious day.

She waved at Carey as she passed the list, laughing merrily when her distraction forced his arrow to miss the target painted on a moldy hay bale. He shook his fist at her in mock anger, then blew her a teasing kiss.

Holly's steps slowed as she passed the grave of Austyn's mother. Much of the earth surrounding it still bore the raw scars of warfare, but at uneven intervals, scraggly anemone plants had been rescued and embedded in the dirt in clumsy splashes of crimson and purple.

Holly's throat tightened as she saw scratched upon a large, flat rock in an unsteady hand the words *Gwyneth of Gavenmore, Beloved Mother.*

The moment was nearly spoiled when Nathanael came flapping after her like an overgrown crow, a sheaf of papers rolled in his fist.

She hastened her steps, starting down the hillside toward the river. "I've no need of your pleas for atonement this morning, Nate. I chose to share my prayers with God in the privacy of my chamber and I can promise you that my soul is as shiny as a new coin." Or it soon would be, she amended silently, after she confessed her duplicity to Austyn.

Nathanael slid after her, his sandals finding little purchase in the rocky soil. "You must listen to me,

Holly. 'Tis not your soul that concerns me. 'Tis you. You're in danger. Terrible danger."

"I'm in danger of rolling down this hill and breaking my neck if you don't cease trodding upon my heels. Do you know what a challenge it is to toddle about in these skirts?"

Her gentle scorn failed to deter him. He shook open the papers. They rustled with a life of their own in the sinuous breeze. "In my extensive study of the Gavenmore history, I've come upon irrefutable evidence that your husband may very well be cursed."

Holly sighed. "Cursed, eh? Eternally damned and all that rot? Tell me, does he sprout horns and cloven feet during the full moon? Cavort with demons and sacrifice maidens to his lust on a bloodstained altar?"

"Worse. Listen to this. These were purported to be the words of the faerie queen Rhiannon after she was falsely accused of infidelity by one of Austyn's forebears." He stumbled over the uneven turf as he read, " 'Let love be your mortal weakness and beauty your eternal doom.' "

That those melodramatic words could actually cast a chill over the glorious summer day only exasperated Holly further. "For God's sake, Nathanael, you're a priest! Surely you haven't come to believe in pagan curses."

"The curse may not be a pagan one. 'Tis written this Rhiannon called the very wrath of God down upon the unfortunate fellow's head."

"Then I give you leave to wave a crucifix over Austyn while he naps." Holly wiggled her fingers. "Or sprinkle some Holy Water in his porridge."

The priest skidded to a halt, as if realizing his surrender would be more effective than open pursuit. "Don't you think it odd that so many of the Gavenmore brides have met gruesome ends at their husband's hands?"

Holly stopped and stood with hands on hips for a long moment. Then she turned and marched back to Nathanael, stabbing a finger at his chest. "You may believe whatever superstitious nonsense you like, Brother, but I'll tell you what I believe. That there's no curse that cannot be broken by the blessing of true love."

She left him standing there, his expression forlorn, his robes tossed by the wind. As the ancient scrolls crumbled in his grip, he whispered, "God go with you, Holly, and may He in His infinite mercy prove you right."

The river was sluggish and calm today, but Austyn's wife, it seemed, was not. He watched from beneath the sprawling branches of an elm as she waded through thigh-high weeds, snipping and snatching to fill a basket with a colorful profusion of wildflowers, muttering beneath her breath all the while.

Austyn grinned. She was so funny, so charming, so damnably bold. Graceless and yet so full of grace it made his eyes sting just to look at her.

Yestereve in the fading twilight with her eyes sparking violet fire and her mouth taut with challenge, she had been almost comely. Sunlight banished that illusion without remorse. She waddled about like a brown little butternut with legs, pausing only to swipe a stray grasshopper from her listless hair. Austyn shook his head, chuckling with amazement that he could still want her so badly. To be his wife. To bear his children. To warm his bed.

She had given him a glimpse of a different kind of beauty yesterday. A beauty comprised of courage and brutal honesty. A beauty unselfish enough to restore to him his loving memories of a mother he'd spent the last twenty years despising. A beauty that had little to do with a creamy complexion or a cascade of sable curls that required five-hundred strokes of the comb at bedtime.

Austyn reached into his tunic, drawing forth his memento from its hiding place. He recognized it for what it was now—a token of his empty infatuation with a woman he had never truly known. A woman who would have doubtlessly proved to be his damnation just as Holly had proved to be his deliverance.

Tucking it carelessly back into his tunic, he started down the riverbank toward his wife with eager strides.

Holly was popping the heads off a cluster of marigolds with spiteful satisfaction when a wry voice behind her said, "I hope you're not pretending I'm one of those flowers."

She looked up from her kneeling position, her heart doubling its rate. Austyn was leaning against the trunk of a willow, garbed all in black except for his crimson surcoat. The sun-bronzed skin around his eyes had crinkled in a slanted grin. That frivolous dimple flirted with his jaw. He was so devastatingly handsome that she had to look away.

She nervously ripped one of the marigolds to shreds. "In truth, I was pretending they were a certain pesky priest I know."

Austyn's tones were carefully measured. "And have you and the young Brother Nathanael been quarreling again?"

"Brother indeed! He nags me like the older brother I never wished I had. The man is insufferable. He thinks that just because he was once my tutor, he is entitled to instruct me for the rest of my life."

"And what did your Brother Nathanael teach you?"

Holly glanced up, startled by Austyn's sudden nearness, the odd light in his eyes—half resignation, half amusement. Before she could reply, his callused palms were cupping her forearms, guiding her to a standing position. The basket slipped from her arm, spilling her floral treasures over their feet in a fragrant shower of crimson and gold. Even in her unwieldy disguise, Holly felt very small next to him, as frail and delicate as one of the wood hyacinths huddled around the trunk of the willow.

Her voice sounded faint to her own ears, as if it were coming from leagues away. "He taught me to chew each bite of food fifty times."

Austyn crooked an eyebrow and Holly blushed, remembering how she had wolfed down the cold meat pies on the journey from Tewksbury.

"He taught me never to speak above a polite murmur." Her husband's expressive eyebrow shot higher.

Holly knew she was revealing too much too soon, but she could hardly think with Austyn's warm hands gliding up her arms, seeking the naked flesh beneath her slashed sleeves.

"Have I ever told you what entrancing elbows you have, my lady?" he murmured against her ear.

Her voice was fading faster than her reason. "Nathanael taught me to rub cut lemons on them," she whispered. "And he taught me never to speak with my mouth occupied by anything other than my tongue."

Austyn leaned forward until his lips were a heated breath away from hers. "What about your husband's tongue?"

His lips brushed hers then, as feathery and beguiling as a butterfly's wing. Holly moaned softly, eager for more. He rewarded her with a fiercer, sweeter press, molding her lips beneath his own as if he might sculpt their malleable contours anew for his pleasure. It seemed only fitting that they should part to beckon him inside. His tongue accepted her shy invitation, its rough satin stroking deep to claim her yielding mouth with exacting mastery.

When Holly swirled her tongue to joust in kind, he captured her nape in the cup of his palm, a growl of pained delight rumbling deep in his throat. He kissed her until she could not speak at all. Or breathe. Or stand without the bracing support of his arms wrapped around her lower back. 'Twas different from his kiss in the garden somehow. Less tentative. More possessive. Less a culmination than a prelude to a more exquisite rapture. When he finally drew away, she was clinging to him, utterly overwhelmed by the desire that had risen between them, hot and fragile.

His eyes sparkled with pure devilment, yet she could feel his massive body battling a tremor, as if the earth beneath his feet was no steadier than the earth beneath her own. "Tonight, my lady," he whispered against her brow, " 'twill be your husband who teaches you."

With that husky vow, he brushed his lips across the bridge of her nose, then turned to go, leaving her limp, trembling, damp with wanting. It was through a haze of bliss that she saw the wisp of ebony tumble from his tunic and blow across the grass.

"Sir?" she called after him, pointing at the grass. "You dropped something."

A sadness too brief to be reckoned passed over his face before he shook his head. " 'Tis nothing of any import."

He had barely crested the hill before Holly was scrabbling through the tall grass on hands and knees. She let out a muffled whoop of triumph as her questing fingers found what they sought. 'Twas a brooch woven of black thread so fine as to be almost gossamer. She held the curious object up to the sun, mystified.

She tugged first one thread, then another. Her heart began to pound faster as the brooch unraveled, leaving her holding what had once been a single glossy curl. A curl severed by the unsteady hand of a surly knight who had mocked its owner for her vanity, yet sought to preserve this one memento of it with a care that bordered on obsession. Holly lifted the shimmering tendril to her cheek, having nearly forgotten what it felt like to have her face caressed by such bounty.

Astonishment paralyzed her. It seemed she had been the only rival for her husband's affections all along—Lady Holly of Tewksbury, that shallow, selfish girl who had branded him a crude barbarian because he dared to speak with a different accent from her own. She had fled his company like a frightened rabbit rather than linger in that moonlit garden and face her own desires.

Holly's spirit soared. She could only imagine the wonder that would light Austyn's face when she revealed that he had been wed to the woman of his dreams all these weeks. With her husband's kiss as a pledge of his present affections and the brooch as proof of his past devotion, her heart brimmed with hope for the future. A future she simply could not wait until tonight to begin.

As she scrambled to gather her scattered flowers, her happiness overflowed in wordless melody. When her humming could no longer contain her joy, she broke into song, absently crooning the haunting ballad that had first summoned Sir Austyn of Gavenmore to her side.

Austyn marched along beside the unfinished curtain wall, struggling to convince his ravenous body that his sweet wife deserved more than a boisterous tumble among the weeds of a riverbank. She deserved a fluffy feather mattress on a luxuriant four-poster draped in pleated silk. She deserved silver goblets brimming with spiced wine to ease her maidenly shyness. She deserved scented tapers to cast flickering light over their entwined limbs.

Austyn groaned aloud. It seemed his truculent body was not to be persuaded. It clamored more insistently and with far more cunning than his besotted brain. After all, what need had husband and wife of silk and feathers when the bounty of God's green earth was spread beneath them? He could lay her gently down upon his surcoat, sprinkle her naked flesh with fragrant petals of hyacinth and heartsease.

What need had he of wine to ease her shyness when he possessed the skill to intoxicate her with pleasure, to coax her to shed her inhibitions with nothing more than a nimble stroke of his fingertips?

And were not tapers but a pale reflection of the splendor of God's sun? Did he dare affront the Lord himself by implying 'twould be preferable to bed his bride in the wan glow of beeswax than partake of her innocence beneath the benevolent rays of the sun?

Austyn made an abrupt about-face, marching back toward the river.

He was nearly to the top of the hill when the first haunting notes of the melody came wafting to his ears on a jasmine-scented breeze. His steps faltered as the warm summer day went as cold and black as the deepest winter night.

CHAPTER 19

Holly had just tossed the last flower in her basket when a dark figure came sliding over the hill. She shaded her eyes against the sun, fearing Nathanael had hunted her down to plague her further with his proclamations of impending doom. A tremulous smile softened her lips as she recognized her husband's imposing shoulders and mane of dark hair. It seemed he was as eager to begin their future as she was.

Her smile died as she caught a glimpse of his burning eyes, the only hint of life in a face as still as death. She took an involuntary step backward. Austyn kept coming, the lumbering grace that had once seemed so endearing now a terrible and relentless thing. She backed away from him, driven by some primitive instinct for survival. She stumbled, sliding the last few feet down the muddy bank into the shallows fringing the river.

The current sucked greedily at her skirts, yet she continued to retreat until the chill water swirled around her ankles, her calves, her trembling knees. Her cowardice did not deter him. He plunged in after her, closing the distance between them in two splashing strides. Tangling his fist in her scant hair, he jerked her head back, baring her face to his merciless scrutiny much as he had that long ago night in the garden.

Fear seized her as he searched her features. His eyes seared her tender skin, scorching away the layers of her deceit with the flame of truth. Open fury would have been preferable to his icy composure. His silence terrified her more than any bellow of rage.

"Please," she whispered, tears welling in her eyes.

Unmoved by her entreaty, he captured her jaw and forced apart her lips. Lips he had kissed only moments before with aching gentleness. His thumb penetrated her mouth, scrubbing at her chattering teeth with rough efficiency.

When he had examined the results, he freed her hair to study his other hand, finally wiping the dull film of ash coating his palm on his surcoat as if it were the vilest filth.

Holly hugged herself, trying to still the shudders that wracked her body. "Please, Austyn, I never meant to deceive you. I was going to tell you. I swear I was. If you'll just let me explain—"

Her fractured litany was cut short as he seized

her in his powerful hands and shoved her head beneath the river's surface. Dank water rushed into her mouth and nose, strangling her hopes. Believing he intended to drown her, Holly's soul died a tiny death, but her body refused to give up the fight. She was still clawing and pummeling when he jerked her from the water.

Even as her desperate lungs struggled for air, she saw reflected in the smoldering chasm of his eyes a cap of sodden curls as black and glossy as the wing of a raven.

By the time he drew the misericorde from the chain at his waist, Holly had grown wise enough to know he had no intention of killing her. Killing her would have been quick and merciful and not a drop of mercy lingered in this man's soul. She choked back her pleas, knowing they would be to no avail, but not even her tattered pride could staunch the tears flowing in a river of regret down her cheeks.

He shredded the padded fabric of her skirts, cutting them adrift and leaving her shivering in her thin chemise. The dagger made even quicker work of her bodice, cutting its laces to expose the crude linen of her bindings. Holly stood as rigidly as a statue while the cold blade skated over the fluttering pulse in the hollow of her throat in a mocking caress. Then with a single downward slash, Austyn—her kind, loving, patient husband—severed her bindings, baring her naked breasts to the uncompromising sunlight and the dawning hell in his gaze.

Holly's pride crumbled. With a sob of anguish, she sought to cover herself, but Austyn caught her wrists and forced her arms apart, his eyes drinking their fill of her as if it were their sacred right. Trembling with humiliation, she searched the unearthly beauty of his face for a crumb of compassion that might have escaped the ravening beast feasting on his humanity.

When her search yielded nothing, she bit back her sobs to try again. "Austyn, you must grant me the boon of an audience. 'Twas never my intention to anger you. Or hurt you. I sought only to—"

"Cease your babbling, woman!" he roared.

Austyn felt the tremor that wracked Holly's body at his rebuke, but the part of him that might have felt shame for his bullying had been seared to a crisp by her betrayal. She was no better than his mother, he thought bitterly, his grandmother, all the beautiful women through the ages who had brought ruin to his family and his name.

He gazed down at the pale, exquisite globes of her breasts, struggling to fathom that she was the same creature he had once pitied for her ugliness. Her generous breasts were crowned with circles of the softest peach and tipped with ripe nipples that pebbled beneath the brutal caress of his eyes. Not in desire, he knew instinctively, but in fear.

Her chemise clung to every swell and hollow of her slender body, rendered almost sheer by the treacherous kiss of the water. He lowered his gaze, allowing it to linger with deliberate insolence on the teasing hint of shadow at the juncture of her thighs. She moaned, a soft, broken sound that enticed rather than convicted him.

Austyn tightened his grip on her wrists as he battled a mingled lust and fury so desperate it made a mockery of every constraint he'd exerted over his temper since boyhood. He wanted to drag her to the riverbank, force her to her knees in the weeds, and do things to her that a man would do to no decent woman. Things he wouldn't even do to a whore.

But how long would it be before fury overcame his lust? How long before he fastened his hands around her fragile throat and began to crush the life from . . . ?

Austyn started as a single tear splashed the back of his hand. He lifted his gaze to Holly's pleading eyes. Violet eyes that would soon be fringed by lush sable lashes. His wife's eyes.

When Austyn grabbed her arm and began to drag her toward the castle, Holly had no choice but to stumble along behind him, desperately clutching the tatters of her bodice over her naked breasts. Mortification scorched her cheeks as they passed a pair of shepherd lads who could only gape at the curious sight of their master hauling a scantily garbed stranger over a break in the curtain wall.

As they approached his mother's grave, Austyn's steps never faltered. He dragged her right across its rocky surface, crushing the tender anemones beneath his boots.

His relentless strides carried them past other inhabitants of Caer Gavenmore, their puzzled faces nothing more than a blur to Holly until the first astounded cry went up.

"Good Lord, 'tis Lady Holly!"

Then with the grim clarity of a nightmare, it all came into focus. Their appalled cries as they realized the exquisitely beautiful wraith stumbling along behind Austyn was indeed their mistress, their apprehensive glances at his resolute face, the chill burn of their stares on her face, her exposed body.

A withered old man shouted, "What is this dark enchantment? Mayhap she is a witch!"

They began to recoil from her after that, some in fear of her, others in fear of Austyn's wrath. Worse than their unspoken condemnation was the bewildered hurt Holly glimpsed on Winifred's round face. She ducked her head for the first time, shamed by her own deceit.

The hounds capered after them, barking at their heels. Emrys and Carey came running from the list to seek the source of the commotion, swords in hand. Carey slid to a halt, his jaw dropping in naked shock. His father followed suit, his own ruddy face darkening with dread.

As their grim procession neared the chapel, a man slipped from its doors to plant himself firmly in their path. Holly began to mumble a spasmodic litany of curses and prayer. At first she feared Austyn would just run right over Nathanael, forcing her to trample him, too, but her husband stopped several paces away, drawing her in front of him like a shield. He slipped one arm around her waist, the mock tenderness of his embrace an affront she could hardly bear.

"Stand aside, priest," Austyn commanded, "unless you care to hear your own last rites."

Nathanael's eyes were dark and hollow, but his voice rang with a conviction Holly had never heard in any of his Candlemas masses or Ascension prayers. "I'll not stand aside and allow you to mistreat this lady."

"She's no lady. She's my wife. Or have you forgotten that you were the one who united us in unholy wedlock?"

" 'Tis not I but you, sir, who seem to have forgotten your vows." Nathanael stood his ground, staunch as always in his pious arrogance.

"You test my patience, *Brother*." Austyn snarled, his arm tightening around Holly's waist until it nearly cut off her air. "Are you truly concerned with my wife's well-being or are you just protecting your lover?"

Holly's was not the only gasp to go up at such blasphemy. Could Austyn truly believe such a terrible thing of her? And why not? she wondered wildly. She'd given him little enough proof of her fidelity.

Nathanael's gaze dropped from Austyn's face to her own. Holly's mumbles escalated to a frantic murmur of, "Oh, God, Nathanael, don't do it. Not now. Oh, please, not now," as she saw humility in his eyes for the first time, coupled with the dangerous knowledge of what she had always known, but denied, even to herself. The crowd held its breath in anticipation of his reply.

"She is not my lover," he said softly.

Holly breathed a sigh of relief.

"But I do love her!"

Groaning with despair, Holly collapsed over Austyn's arm.

" 'Tis God's truth!" Nathanael shouted. "I love her! She's bright and beautiful and talented and charming and you, Sir Austyn of Gavenmore, are not fit to lick the soles of her slippers!"

Holly slowly straightened, bracing herself for Austyn's reaction. When it finally came, it was far worse than anything her feeble imagination could have conjured. He threw back his head and laughed. 'Twas a black sound that rolled through the courtyard in mirthless waves even as he set Holly firmly behind him and pried Carey's sword from his hand.

Nathanael's courage faltered as Austyn stalked toward him, broadsword in hand. The bell of his voice tolled with a smidgen less zeal. "I'm not afraid of you, so you needn't think I am." He took two steps backward to match each of Austyn's, but Austyn just kept coming. He fumbled for an appropriate scripture. " 'F-f-fear not them which kill the body, but are not able to kill the soul, but rather fear him which is able to destroy soul and body in hell.' "

Holly winced as he stumbled over his own robes and sat down abruptly on the cobblestones. Austyn's shadow fell over him like a messenger of death. Holly knew what she had to do. Knew even as she flung herself forward that it was both the worst thing she could do and the only thing she could do. She had no choice but to reward Nathanael's foolish gallantry by striving to save both men's souls.

Austyn was already drawing back the sword when she fell across Nathanael's body, still clutching her bodice, but spreading her free arm in a protective gesture as old as Eve. Nathanael poked at her, but she refused to budge.

She glared up at her husband, allowing him to witness the birth of the first spark of defiance in her eyes. "Need I remind you that I saved your life once, sir? I ask in return the life of this humble priest."

For a chilling moment as the gleaming blade hung

poised above them, she thought he would drive it home through her breast, bidding them both a gleeful fare thee well.

Then his lips quirked in a crooked grin more sneer than smile. "Humble indeed. How touching! Would that I could ever hope to inspire such devotion in a woman's heart!"

He reached down, grabbed her wrist, and hurled her aside with one hand. She stumbled to her knees as his fist struck Nathanael's jaw with a resounding crack. The priest melted into a limp puddle on the cobblestones.

Through a haze of shock and relief, Holly became aware that Carey knelt beside her, his deft hands gently assessing her for injury. She might have told him that only her heart was bruised had Austyn's voice not cracked like a whip in their ears.

"Move away from her."

Her husband stood over them, every trace of grim humor stripped from his face. The crowd was deathly silent, the tension so hot and thick even a broadsword could not slice it.

"She fell," Carey said. "I was simply seeking to—"

"Take your hands away from her."

Carey gazed up at him disbelievingly.

"Now," Austyn said, touching the tip of Carey's own sword to his friend's throat. Holly's agony multiplied a thousand fold to be the cause of such.

His mouth taut with resentment, Carey rose to his feet, surrendering her to her husband's mercy.

When Austyn withdrew his gaze from her in that moment, Holly somehow sensed that he had done so for the last time. 'Twas far worse than when he had recoiled from her in the garden at Tewksbury or avoided glancing at her homely visage during the tournament. Worse even than enduring his icy loathing at her betrayal. This was a dissolution of every bond, both holy and earthly, a separation more absolute than death. Grief pierced her heart, loosing a fresh flow of tears.

"Whore! Jezebel!" The triumphant cry rose from the sky, borne on the wings of insanity. "May God punish the harlot who dares to tempt the righteous man!" Rhys of Gavenmore stood on the parapet with arms outstretched, calling the wrath of God down upon her poor, damp, rumpled head.

Holly had had enough. This time when Austyn reached for her, she resisted. His grip was no longer tinged with violence, but was as implacable as an iron manacle clamped around her wrist. Ignoring her spirited struggles, he marched her into the castle, past a sobbing Elspeth, and up the first set of winding stairs to a landing drenched in sunshine.

When Holly saw where he meant to take her, she began to fight in earnest, hammering at his broad back with her fists, clawing at the sun-bronzed skin of his arms. He remained as impervious to her blows as a stone golem. Her curses rose to frantic screams as panic seized her, so dark and consuming it verged on madness. By the time they'd reached the ancient oak door, she was begging, despising herself, but begging all the same, promising anything if he would not lock her away in that terrible place.

He shoved open the door and dragged her inside. Shadows masked his expression. Where before she had struggled to escape him, now she clung to him, pleading with him not to go, not to leave her alone. Tearing her arms from his neck, he thrust her away from him.

Holly stumbled and fell, but was already lurching back to the door when it slammed in her face. A bolt fell into place with the finality of a death knell. Bracing herself with splayed hands, Holly slid down the door, no longer able to summon the will to hammer and scream and plead. All she could do was hug her knees to her chest and pray that if she curled herself into a small enough ball, she would disappear altogether.

PART II

And, like another Helen,
fir'd another Troy . . .
Could swell the soul to rage,
or kindle soft desire.
JOHN DRYDEN

None but the brave deserves the fair.
JOHN DRYDEN

chapter 20

'Twas a dark eternity before Holly emerged from that shadowy netherworld between madness and stupor. She knew a vague surprise to find herself still alive. 'Twas inconceivable to her that her battered heart could go on beating as if nothing had happened. As if Austyn still loved her.

She uncurled her stiff limbs. Dried tearstains had hardened the tender skin of her face. She did not mind, preferring its expressionless mask to any vain twitch of sorrow or hope. She found the numbness a blissful relief, especially when she realized it had crept all the way to her bones.

She rose to face the chamber. She would not have

been surprised had Austyn abandoned her to total darkness, but freshets of moonlight streamed through the cracks in the wooden shutters hanging askew from their hinges.

The circular tower defied her expectations. She found no horde of rats nibbling on a fresh carcass. No bleached bones rising to dance a clattering jig. Not even a chorus of Gavenmore brides wailing their mockery at her for failing to heed their warnings. She had anticipated the spartan horrors of a dungeon, but instead found herself in the most luxuriously appointed chamber in the entire castle.

Decades of neglect had left their stain of decay, yet the room still possessed the faded elegance of an elderly woman who clung to her velvets and silks to maintain her fragile illusion of beauty. The thick fall of cobwebs only added to its unearthly air, billowing from the rafters of the vaulted ceiling like veils of ermine.

Holly drifted farther into the chamber, her footsteps muffled by the heavy tapestries surrounding the walls. A massive four-poster bed crowned a gilded pedestal in the center of the room. Not even the moth-eaten condition of its hangings could disguise their brocaded splendor. Tattered velvet ribbons hung from each of the thick, carved bedposts. Holly reached to caress one absently, wondering at its purpose. A magnificent chest resting on four carved claws perched at the foot of the bed.

She ran a finger over its dust-furred surface. A pot of dry, crumbled rouge lay beside a silver comb and an empty scent bottle, reminding Holly with stark clarity that another woman had once occupied this opulent prison. A woman accused of infidelity by her husband, then cut off from his company with ruthless finality, leaving her only these mocking mementos of his former affections.

She lifted the lid of a squat silver box, half expecting to find a severed finger or some other such horror. Her breath caught as the grudging moonlight sparkled over a king's ransom of gold and gems. She buried her fingers in the tangled treasure, sifting through an emerald-studded fillet, a diamond brooch, a ruby-encrusted pendant on a gold chain thicker than her smallest finger. Why in God's name hadn't Austyn sold them to sate Edward's greedy tax collectors? she wondered. Surely it wasn't out of respect for his poor dead grandmother.

Dropping the jewels as if they were a nest of snakes, she went to the window and tore open the shutters. No stingy arrow loop here, but a generous rectangular window framed by stone window seats. 'Twould have to be a large window, she thought bitterly, large enough for a woman to hurl herself out of.

Wind battered Holly, scorching the barren dryness of her eyes. The dizzying height offered her a panoramic view of the surrounding countryside bathed in a silvery quilt of moonlight, but little more than a slice of the solitary courtyard below. She gazed down at the cobblestones, wondering if any trace of blood remained to stain their pitted surface.

A sigh grazed her nape, faint yet audible enough to make the fine fleece there stand erect. She closed her eyes, fearful the ghostly echo would awaken her from her benumbed state. The sigh escalated into a bereft moan that mirrored her suppressed grief so exactly she feared the sound had come from her own throat.

The shutters began to flap wildly on their hinges. Holly backed away from the window, stricken by terror. The moan rose to a piercing wail, a keening protestation of wronged innocence. Her heel caught the edge of the hooded hearth and she fell hard on her backside. She clapped her hands over her ears, but the lamentation swelled until it vibrated the very marrow of her bones to aching life.

Tearing her hands away from her ears, she screamed, "Stop it, damn you! Stop it, I say!"

The shutters slammed shut. The howling ceased as abruptly as it had began, leaving her in silence. Quaking like a dormouse, she searched the shadows, fearing an even more dire visitation.

The shutters swung open with a creak. A dank gust of breath stirred her hair. She swiveled to stare into the fireplace, finding nothing but cold ashes and the tiny skeleton of some unfortunate rodent.

A shrill whistle assailed her ears, escalating to a tormented shriek as a musty draft poured from the gaping jaws of the fireplace.

"The wind," Holly whispered in dull astonishment. " 'Tis only the wind whistling down the chimney flue."

An abashed giggle escaped her, then another. She cupped a hand over her mouth, but the torrent of mirth refused to subside. Soon she was laughing aloud, laughing until her sides ached and tears streamed down her cheeks.

She was utterly alone now. Without Austyn. Without even the ghost of his grandmother to share her exile. Holly doubled over, gasping for breath, never even realizing when her laughter deepened into broken sobs.

Carey found Austyn standing atop the battlements on a completed section of curtain wall, gazing over the molten pewter of the river by moonlight. The balmy wind whipped the dark veil of his hair from his face, revealing features as soulless and foreign as an infidel's. He bore little resemblance to the man Carey had called friend through sunny days and stormy battles and none at all to the bright-eyed boy with the ready smile and rollicking laugh he remembered from childhood.

"The priest is secured," Carey said softly, folding himself into a sitting position between two merlons. "but I cannot coax her nurse to stop weeping. I fear the woman's tears will flood the hall before she's done."

"Let them," Austyn replied, his face betraying not even a flicker of pity. "My father?"

"Sleeping at last. He was quite excited. It took several spoonfuls of mead to calm him."

They were both silent for several moments before Carey dared to ask, "Did she tell you why?"

Austyn gave a harsh bark of laughter. "Shouldn't the question be 'Did I bother to ask?' "

Carey already knew the answer to that. "What will you do with her?"

"Why? Do *you* want her?" At first, Carey feared his friend did not speak in jest, then a humorless smile quirked Austyn's lips. "What are my choices? Had he not gone to such pains to be rid of her, I could send her back to her father. Given her talent for mummery, I could sell her to a band of passing troubadours. Or I could just keep her locked in the north tower until her hair grays and her pearly little teeth fall out one by one."

"And if she chooses to escape captivity as your grandmother did?"

Austyn shrugged. "Then I shall once again be without a wife. 'Twould be almost a pity though." His voice softened to a musing purr, his eyes taking on a speculative gleam Carey did not recognize. "Do you know that she promised me anything if I would not lock her away? Pleaded quite prettily for her freedom, she did. Fires the imagination, does it not? The temptation of having a beauty like that on her knees before you, eager to do your bidding . . ."

"Stop it!" Carey jumped to his feet, no longer able to bear Austyn's taunting. "She's still your wife, man, not some Londontown whore. Have you no shame?"

Austyn's icy indifference shattered with a roar. "Aye, I have shame! I burn with it. Shame for being such a fool! Shame for being so blinded by her charms that I couldn't see through her ridiculous disguise! Shame that I was ready to offer the deceitful little creature my love." Austyn turned away, gripping a stone merlon until his knuckles whitened.

Carey reached for his friend's shoulder, then let his hand fall back to his side, sensing his comfort would be neither welcomed nor accepted. "You were no more fool than the rest of us," he said.

When Carey's soft footfalls had faded, Austyn threw back his head, savoring the roar of the wind in his ears. He had hoped its savage clamor might drown out the haunting echoes of Holly's pleas, her pathetic screams as she begged him not to leave her, to stay by her side even if he would extract a terrible price for doing so. He could still feel the weight of her fragile arms clinging to his neck, the plush softness of her breasts pressed to his chest.

He gritted his teeth against the primal urge to howl with loss. He wanted to go to her. To batter down the door that stood between them with his bare fists. To draw her beneath him and rut her like a ravening beast, as if to prove to them both that that was all he ever would be. All any Gavenmore man could be.

He had not shared his darkest shame with Carey —that he had locked away his wife not to punish her, but to protect her from himself.

He searched the indigo sky, finding in its star-tossed sweep no warmth, but only a frigid beauty that chilled him to the marrow.

"You heartless bitch," he whispered hoarsely, unable to say if he was cursing Rhiannon or his wife.

At a muffled thump outside the door, Holly awoke from a stupor nearer to death than slumber. She did not remember crawling to the bed or curling up on the tattered ermine coverlet. She unfurled her stiff limbs, sneezing as her movements stirred up a cloud of dust.

The sound came again, the unmistakable thud of someone fumbling with the bolt. Holly sat straight up. Some cynical demon had already convinced her that Austyn would pack up his household and ride away without a backward glance, leaving her to starve. But as the door swung open, her heart lurched with a hope she despised, but could not help.

Her pulse ceased its expectant thundering when a crown of flaxen braids appeared, but her disappointment was quickly squelched by joy at the sight of Winifred's familiar face. She jumped down from the bed and ran over to her.

"Oh, Winnie, you cannot know how glad I am to see you. I knew you wouldn't desert me."

Winnie's plump cheeks had been robbed of their ruddy glow. Puffs of flesh hid her eyes as she rested the tray she carried on a table and turned back toward the door.

Holly could not believe she was going to go. Without a glance. Without a word.

She trailed behind the mute woman, her desperation swelling. "Please, Winnie. Has Austyn forbade you to speak to me? Are you afraid he'll punish you if you do? If you could just convince him to come here. To grant me a few meager moments of his time so that I might explain . . ." Winnie reached for the door handle. Holly clutched her arm, starved for the warmth of a human touch. "If Austyn refuses to come, then send Carey. Austyn will listen to Carey. I know he will!"

"Have you lost your wits, girl?" Winifred hissed, jerking her arm from Holly's grip. Holly recoiled from the wounded virulence in her eyes. "Do you seek to have my son cast into the dungeon with that rash young priest of yours?"

Holly felt a flare of shame that she hadn't even paused to consider Nathanael's plight. For all she knew, Austyn might have returned to the courtyard and whacked off his inflated head.

"Of course not," she replied. "I would never wish Carey harm. He has been naught but a friend to me."

"Aye, and I see how you repay him. How you've repaid us all."

Kind-hearted Winifred's derision was even harder to bear than Austyn's. Holly's lower lip began to quiver; her eyes welled with tears.

As Winifred stared at Holly's rumpled chemise, her matted curls, her grubby, tear-streaked cheeks, the woman's broad face slowly crumpled in horror. "Oh, God," she whispered, "you're so beautiful." Staggering over to a stool, she sank down and buried her face in her hands.

Holly crept near to her, longing to pat her shuddering shoulder, but fearful of being rejected. She dropped to one knee at the woman's feet. "Please don't cry, Winnie. I never meant to make you cry."

"Don't you know what a terrible thing it is you've done?" Winifred lifted her head; her Welsh accent was thickened by grief. "We thought you were different. That you might be the one to finally break the curse." At last Holly understood their open-armed welcome of Austyn's new bride, their unabashed delight in her ugliness. "And now 'tis happening all over again. The lies. The jealousy. The accusations. Half of them calling you a shape-shifting witch and begging the master to burn you at the stake. The other half blaming him for locking you away."

"What do you think? Do you think I'm a witch? A monster?" Holly could not have said why Winnie's reply was so vital to her.

Winifred studied her from beneath her damp lashes, then shook her head. "I think you're a foolish girl who's played a nasty trick on a man as much son to me as my own. Don't ask me to help you. For I won't."

Holly straightened as Winifred brushed past her. "I still love him," she said defiantly before the door could close.

"Then may God have pity on your soul," Winifred murmured before shutting the door and dropping the bolt into place.

Winifred came twice a day after that, bearing hearty meals of stew and fresh baked bread, ewers of steaming water for bathing, and crisp linen sheets, but never again did Holly shed a tear or utter a single plea for help. She sent most of the trays back untouched and left the clean sheets piled on the chest, preferring to curl up each night on top of the moth-eaten coverlet.

When Winifred stiffly told her, "The master wants to know if you require anything else for your comfort —extra blankets or perhaps a fire to warm you at night," Holly burst into peals of merry laughter, their shrill edge sending the woman fleeing from the tower.

For Holly knew that no measure of blankets could warm her. No fire could banish the chill from her soul. She might have been deprived of the company of Austyn's grandmother, but she still felt a keen kinship with the woman. She finally understood that 'twas not being falsely accused that had driven her to that window or the tedium of her own company. 'Twas the anguish of being torn from the arms of the man she loved. Knowing she would never again see his crooked smile or watch the way his eyes warmed when they beheld her.

But there the similarities ended. For Austyn's grandmother had been innocent of wrongdoing and Holly knew herself to be guilty, guilty of a cruel deception. If Austyn left her there for a month or a century, she would be no less deserving of her punishment.

She roamed the tower in her frayed chemise as the minutes melted into hours, the hours into days. The wind wailed its melancholy refrain and she found herself standing more often than not at the tower window, gazing down at the courtyard below with an emotion akin to yearning.

Nearly a fortnight had passed when she began to envision her body there, pale and broken on the cobblestones, and to wonder what Austyn's reaction would be when he discovered it. Would he cradle her across his lap and repent his harshness as his father had done, or would he be relieved to be rid of her so tidily, sparing him the embarrassment of seeking an annulment from the king?

Holly stepped up on the window seat, then onto the narrow sill, bracing her palms against the cut stones that framed the opening. The warm wind pummeled her, molding the thin garment to her shivering body, bearing on its wings the ripe scents of summer and life and freedom. She lifted her eyes from the cobblestones and gazed across the Welsh countryside, drinking in its rugged beauty. A beauty so wild and sweet it hurt her eyes to look upon it, yet so compelling she could not bear to look away and forsake all of its unspoken promises for the morrow.

Holly's knees collapsed. She crawled back on the window seat, clamping a hand over her mouth, ill with the thought of what she might have done had the bullying wind not snapped her out of her haze of despair. Feeling as if she'd just awakened from an enchanted sleep, she gazed around the tower, seeing it with crystalline clarity for the first time. Her father might have pronounced her selfish and wayward, but he would not have wished such a heartless penance upon her. Despite what her husband might have chosen to believe, she was guilty of idiocy, not adultery.

The wind whined down the chimney flue, no longer a comfort but an irritant. Holly sprang off the window seat, snatched the wad of pristine sheets from the chest and stuffed them up the flue. Her stomach growled its approval. Marching over to the table, she grabbed an untouched loaf of bread, then sank down cross-legged on the floor. As she tore off fat hunks of bread and tossed them in her mouth, she felt a blazing surge of something in her belly. Something even more dangerous and wonderful than hunger.

Anger.

When Winifred came to deliver supper and fresh water for bathing to the tower that night, Holly informed her that she required only two things: pen and paper. Although fearing the girl would scribble some maudlin, tear-smeared missive Sir Austyn would refuse to read, Winnie dutifully delivered both items the following morning.

When she returned at twilight, Holly presented

her with a ten-page list of articles she required from the master for her comfort. The words *master* and *comfort* were underlined with a scathing flourish.

Winnie and two wide-eyed maidservants trundled in the next morning, staggering beneath their assorted burdens of tub, towels, sheets, embroidery frame, thread, fragrant oils, fresh apples, harp, beeswax tapers, broom, bedclothes, books, and various other treasures that would make Holly's captivity tolerable, if not pleasant.

The girls continued to gape at her, even as Winifred shooed them out and shut the door in their faces. Winnie awkwardly cleared her throat. "The master wishes to know if you require any lemons to rub on your elbows, or perhaps a Nubian slave to comb your hair five hundred strokes before bedtime."

Holly snapped a crisp bite from a fat red apple. "Tell him that given the current length of my hair, two hundred and fifty strokes should be sufficient."

When Winifred had gone, Holly surveyed her plunder with a calculating eye. She had chosen few items that could not be used as a weapon against her husband. She'd already pillaged the chest at the foot of the bed for her armor—brocaded cottes woven of samite and cloth of gold, twin cloaks lined with the softest sable, sendal chemises so sheer they appeared more suited to a harem than a noblewoman's bedchamber. Most were in need of only minor repairs and a healthy airing.

Holly carried cloaks, thread, and needle to the window seat and curled up in the sunshine. A devilish smile played around her lips. If Austyn thought he was going to just lock her away and forget her existence, he had sorely underestimated his opponent. 'Twas here while she prepared for battle that she would wield her most lethal weapon of all.

Tipping back her head, Holly began to sing.

CHAPTER 21

Holly sang.

She sang while she swiped the dust from the furniture and swept the timber floor. She sang while she replaced the moth-eaten coverlet with the wedded cloaks, creating an inviting nest of plush sable. She sang while Winifred and the maidservants carried in buckets of steaming water for her bath. She sang while she soaked her weary muscles in the tub and afterward, while she rubbed oil of myrrh into her neglected skin, restoring its pearly glow. She sang while she combed her flourishing curls and each night when she lay down upon her pillow, she sang herself softly to sleep.

She sang cheery May songs and wistful ballads. She sang stirring Crusade anthems and complex rounds, alternating the parts of the different singers. She sang children's rhymes and bawdy ditties. She sang liturgical chants, spinning songs, lays, and laments. And one evening at sunset, she stood at the window of the tower and warbled a hymn so full-throated and magnificent that even Nathanael in his dungeon cell lifted his eyes heavenward, seeking a choir of celestial angels.

Austyn suffered no such delusions. 'Twas no heavenly visitation, this scourge of melody, but a demonic infestation. Each note pricked his tortured flesh like a tine of Lucifer's pitchfork. There was nowhere he could flee to escape the compelling sorcery of Holly's voice. He could ride to the ends of the earth and still it would pursue him.

He did not know if she sang in *her* sleep, but by God, she sang in *his*. In his fevered dreams, she sang only for him while he coaxed her to a climax of flawless rhythm and perfect pitch.

'Twas not her soaring hymns that disturbed him most, but the simple lullabies she sang at night when her voice had grown weary with just a hint of a husky croak. 'Twas then that he found her most beguiling. 'Twas then that he had to brutally remind himself that the sirens had sought only to lure Ulysses to certain doom.

Then one twilight eve when he thought he was going to have to beg Carey to tie him to one of the pillars in the courtyard just as Ulysses had been bound to his own mast, the singing ceased. Just like that. No hint of hoarseness. No fading. It simply ceased.

The silence was more terrible than anyone had anticipated. A pall of dejection descended like a black cloud over the castle. When Austyn strode into the great hall, all conversation lurched to a halt and he felt the gazes of everyone in the hall settle on him. He'd grown accustomed to their weight in the past month. Grown accustomed to Carey's furtive glances, Winnie's nervous stares, Emrys's unspoken question of, "What monstrous thing will he do next?" Gone were the days when they had looked upon him with pride and admiration instead of fear.

Most damning of all were the swollen eyes and perpetually reddened nose of his wife's nurse. Austyn suspected the old woman would have fled for help long ago if she hadn't feared to leave her mistress at his mercy.

Even his father, who had not uttered a single word since his harangue from the parapet, blinked up at him with the wide, frightened eyes of a child. With his soul so recently stripped of melody, Austyn felt naked and raw beneath their probing scrutiny. Suddenly, he could bear it no more.

"What ails the lot of you?" he bellowed, whirling around to glare at them. "Are you never going to smile again? Laugh again? Speak above a godforsaken whisper?"

With a heart-wrenching sob, Elspeth threw her apron over her face and burst into tears. But not before Austyn had caught a glimpse of himself through her eyes—a towering brute, more ogre than man.

The deafening hush only made the music of Holly's voice clearer, more seductive. She beckoned him with her crystalline silence, driving him to stride blindly toward the stairs, determined to confront the enchantress who had bewitched him into such a beast.

Austyn's treads slowed as he neared the north tower. The silence was no longer pristine, but haunted by the echoes of Holly's screams and pleas as he had dragged her up the winding stairs beneath his feet. 'Twas as if the ancient stones had absorbed her piteous cries. His wrists and forearms still bore the fading marks of her scratches, but he feared the deeper scars of her betrayal and his abandonment would never heal.

His hands shook as he lifted the heavy bolt from its iron brackets. He had no idea what he might find. Each time Winifred had dolefully displayed an untouched tray for his inspection, he had hardened his heart to images of Holly's vibrant flesh wasting from her bones.

The door creaked open beneath the coaxing of his hand. A cobweb drifted across his face; he swiped it away, fighting a shudder. The chamber was bathed in the gathering shadows of dusk. Fading light drifted through the open window.

There was no sign of Holly. A chill of dread caressed Austyn's spine as the abrupt cessation of song took on a more sinister cast. He stood transfixed by the gaping maw of that window. The window Carey had begged him to fix an iron grate over. The window overlooking the enclosed courtyard he had forbade anyone to enter. The one man fool enough to scale the wall and try to steal a glimpse of his captive bride had been exiled from Caer Gavenmore with naught but the tunic on his back.

Austyn took a hesitant step. Then he was hurling himself toward the void, leaning out just as a honeyed voice behind him said, "I wouldn't give you the satisfaction."

Sparrows twittered and hopped on the cobblestones below, mocking him with their serenity. Austyn slowly turned as a woman brushed aside a veil of webs and emerged from the shadows around the bed.

"Sorry to disappoint you so sorely," she said, "but I've not made a widower of you yet."

He folded his arms over his chest, much as he had done the first time they met. "A pity. I thought perhaps you had sang yourself to death."

The lit taper Holly carried cast a flickering halo around her, giving Austyn his first true look at her since she'd stood trembling and debased by his brutal perusal in the river.

She was slender, aye, but hardly wasted. Her breasts swelled against the brocaded bodice of her cotehardie as if seeking to overflow it. Her skin had lost its sun-burnished hue, but its translucence only made her look more fragile, more alluring. He fought the urge, but his gaze drifted to her face of its own volition.

If she'd thought to ruin her appearance by cropping her hair, she'd sorely miscalculated. The dark cap of curls framing her face only enhanced its heart-shaped purity. The missed meals had sculpted beguiling hollows beneath her cheekbones. If anything, she was more beautiful than she'd been in the garden at Tewksbury. She'd been naught but a shallow girl then. Now her violet eyes sparkled with the complex depths of a woman.

Austyn narrowed his eyes, seeking any hint of the awkward, charming girl he had called wife for a few idyllic weeks. He found nothing of her in the exotic creature standing before him. 'Twas her loss that both wounded and enraged him beyond bearing.

"Why?" he asked hoarsely. "Did you and your father think it a fine jest to play upon an ignorant Welshman?"

She rested the taper on a stone corbel jutting from the wall, but lingered near enough to remain bathed in its lambent light. " 'Twas never meant as a jest at all. My father sought to wed me to a stranger. I believed I had no other choice than to try and stop him. Have you never felt powerless?"

Powerless to resist you, Austyn thought, but he would have died before uttering the words. "Powerless? With your father's wealth at your disposal? Your own beauty a sword to drive into any man's heart?"

"You see where beauty has gotten me. It has been naught but a curse since the day I was born." She widened her eyes in mock innocence. "And you, of all men, should understand curses."

Austyn scowled at her, admiring her boldness against his will.

"I sought only to repel my suitors," she continued. "How was I to know you'd be so pigheaded as to pursue me despite my ugliness? Or so greedy, I might add?"

"Greedy?"

She tilted her delicate chin to a defiant angle. "Aye, greedy! You dare to cast shadows on my own motives while yours were none too pure. You sought not a wife, but a fat purse to swell your coffers. As I see it, sir, you are no better than I."

'Twas all Holly could do to stand her ground when Austyn came swaggering toward her. She had spent the lonely days and interminable nights plotting schemes to summon him to her, not what to do with him once he arrived. As he entered the spill of candlelight, she bit back an involuntary gasp.

He was dressed all in black with the shadow of a new beard darkening his cheeks. He looked younger, more gaunt, yet somehow larger and infinitely less manageable.

He circled her like a wary raptor, his eyes narrowed to frosty slits. "You've had ample time to concoct such a cunning tale. Why should I believe you? How do I know your father didn't seek to marry you off to some unsuspecting jape because you'd been ruined?" His gaze flicked to her taut belly, then back to her eyes. "How do I know that even as we speak your womb doesn't thicken with another man's babe?"

Holly choked back her outrage and managed a sneer of her own. "And I suppose you believe this imaginary lover of mine followed me here to Gavenmore in the guise of a priest?"

At the murderous flare of his eyes, Holly feared her sarcasm might cost both she and Nathanael their heads. But Austyn swung away from her, flexing his fingers as if to keep them from curling around her throat.

Mustering her courage, Holly moved to stand within his view. If her beauty was his only weakness, then she would exploit it to her full advantage.

"Since you're determined to believe me a harlot, regardless of the truth," she said softly, "what will you do with me, Austyn? Will you beat me?" Taking a terrible chance, she reached for his hand. He flinched at her touch, but did not pull away. She cradled his knuckles in the cup of her palm, gently folding each finger until they formed a mighty fist. " 'Tis well within your rights as my husband. Or will you burn me at the stake, laughing as my tender flesh melts in the flames?"

She surrendered his hand to splay her palms against his chest with reckless abandon, whispering over the erratic thunder of his heart. "Or will you simply turn around and leave me here? Walk away and bolt the door behind you as your grandfather did. Forget you ever saw my face, heard my voice, kissed my lips . . ."

His ravenous gaze caressed her face. Holly moistened her lips, nearly breathless with hope.

Austyn tore away from her with a harsh laugh. "Is that what Winifred told you? She always did have a gift for glossing over the more sordid aspects of the family history."

Holly's confidence faltered. "What do you mean?"

With one fleet step, he jumped up on the pedestal supporting the bed. Holly would not have recognized the cynical quirk of his lips as a smile were it not accompanied by a diabolical flash of his dimple.

"Oh, my grandfather did imprison my grandmother in this tower for ten years. But he never forgot her. On the contrary, legend has it that he returned to rape her nightly. With unflagging enthusiasm." Austyn reached out to finger one of the frayed ribbons still attached to the bedpost, shooting her a naughty glance from beneath his dark lashes. " 'Tis whispered he was quite imaginative in his . . . punishments." The ribbon slipped through Austyn's deft fingers. "Twas only after he bored of the sport and sought solace in the arms of another that she hurled herself to her death."

A shiver of shameful anticipation coursed down Holly's spine as Austyn stepped off the pedestal. She took an involuntary step backward, wondering too late what manner of predator she had engaged.

He strode right past her, making for the door.

"Austyn?" she said.

He turned, the sensual curves of his mouth robbed of any hint of humor.

"I'm innocent."

He sketched her a mocking bow. "That, my lady, remains to be seen."

As the bolt thudded into place, Holly groped blindly for the nearest stool. Even as she pressed her fingertips to her lips to still their trembling, she felt a spark of triumph. For she had seen the indisputable truth in her husband's eyes. He would return to her.

One night passed. Then three more. By the end of a sennight, Holly's hopes were beginning to wane. Perhaps, she feared, her goading had only driven Austyn further from her embrace. Perhaps he, like his grandfather, had chosen to seek his pleasures in the arms of another.

Her eyes clouded at the image, her throat tightening with a sense of loss as keen and poignant as anything she had endured since her mother's death. She tried to sing, but found the melodies would not come. Even the most soulful of ballads failed to convey the depth of her yearning.

As a sennight melted into a fortnight, she ceased to don the elaborate cottes each day, ceased struggling to arrange her unruly curls into some semblance of elegance.

Late one night, she curled up on the window seat in her chemise and watched a summer storm batter its way across the sky. The far horizon vanished as black clouds billowed toward the castle. Thunder rumbled and jagged forks of lightning crackled over the roiling cauldron of the river. Holly hugged her knees, paralyzed by the inevitability of the approaching maelstrom. 'Twas a kindred spirit, prowling the sky with a hunger as wild and restless as her own.

'Twas only when the wind began to drive sheets of rain against her skin that she rose to latch the shutters, unable to bear the elusive scent of freedom. She paced the tower, lighting every taper to cast a fragile pall of brightness over the gloom.

The wind hammered the shutters with angry fists. Holly curled up on the bed and struggled to focus her torn attentions on an illuminated manuscript detailing the spiritual ecstasies of Mechtild of Magdeburg, bride of Christ. Perhaps Austyn had sent it so that she might prepare her own wicked soul for its future in the nunnery, she thought bitterly.

Between one sullen growl of thunder and the next, the door crashed open and Holly jerked up her head to meet the smoldering eyes of her earthly husband.

chapter 22

Austyn had envisioned Holly in many guises in the past fortnight: haughty lady sneering down at her patrician nose at him; malicious harpy berating him for his greed; bewitching temptress taunting him with a flutter of her burgeoning lashes and a flick of her moist, pink tongue. But as he gazed at her curled on the bed of sable like a small, contented cat, he realized each of those women were only illusions contrived to distract him from who she really was.

His wife.

The thin chemise had puddled around her hips, baring her slender legs. 'Twas impossible for a man to look upon such legs and not envision them wrapped around his waist. As if Holly had divined his thoughts, she tugged the chemise down to shield them from his gaze. Her modesty pricked his conscience, stirring his conflicting desires to protect and possess.

He tore down the veil of webs that separated them with a savage swipe. "Rather enjoying playing the captive princess, aren't you, sweeting? Would you like me to fan you with peacock feathers or pop grapes in your mouth?" His sarcasm betrayed him, battering him with images of Holly's succulent lips parting to receive whatever he would give her.

Holly moved to a sitting position, warily eyeing the savage stranger she had once called "husband." His hair was unkempt, his eyes red-rimmed and wild, as if he hadn't slept since their last encounter. He'd been seething with icy anger then, but now an edge of desperation sharpened his expression. Holly longed to reach out to him, but did not dare. She knew with a conviction beyond faith that if she drove him to abandon her this night, he would never return.

She hid her distress behind a mask of scorn. "If you think I take any pleasure in my captivity, then you're sorely mistaken. I'd gladly trade my lavish cell to lay in a meadow of fresh cut hay or feel the cool rain beat on my face. But I suppose you wouldn't understand that, being the sort of man who locks up a lady and allows a murderer free roam of his castle."

Austyn's faint flinch told her she had struck well and deep. "You, my lady, committed your treachery willfully. My father had no choice."

Had Holly not been convinced that Austyn believed every word he was saying, she would have given vent to the hysterical laugh that welled in her throat. "Ah, the dreaded curse of the Gavenmores! Refresh my memory. Was it cast by a temperamental mermaid offended by some clumsy fisherman?" She wiggled her graceful fingers at him. "Or some fat little Booka infuriated because one of your ancestors stepped on his toadstool?"

A becoming flush crawled up Austyn's throat. Holly doubted that anyone had ever dared to question the veracity of the Gavenmore curse. At least not to his face. " 'Twas neither," he strangled out. " 'Twas the faerie queen Rhiannon, a cruel and heartless witch."

"A heartless witch falsely accused of infidelity." Holly twined a curl around her finger, pursing her lips in a thoughtful pout. "If a man refuses to trust a woman he claims to love, then tell me, husband, who between them is the faithless one? Has it never occurred to you that your father might be cursed with nothing more than a savage temper? Perhaps 'twas his own wretched jealousy that drove your mother into the arms of another man."

"Enough!" Austyn roared. "You know naught of what you speak. Perhaps you seek only to justify your own infidelity."

Holly sat up on her knees, eager for any opportunity to defend herself. "If you believed that, Nathanael would be dead instead of rotting away in your dungeon. You are a knight, sir. 'Twas I who wronged you; therefore, honor should demand that you free him."

Austyn's caustic smile never reached his eyes. "See how prettily she pleads for her lover's freedom."

"He is not my lover!" Holly yelled, pushed beyond endurance by her husband's stubbornness. "I am innocent!"

Austyn's voice softened to a velvety rasp. "There's only one way to find out, isn't there?"

A fearful hope quickened in Holly's heart. If her husband required proof of her innocence, then she was only too willing to provide it. As he stalked toward the bed pedestal, she scrambled off the other side, provoking him to pursue her with deliberate insolence.

"Did you think Nathanael my only lover? How naive of you! There were scores of others. Dozens! Hundreds!" She ran to the window and wrenched open the shutters. A violent gust of wind and rain extinguished every taper, whipped the webs into a dancing frenzy. Holly refused to cower from Austyn's inevitable approach. "They visit me here in my bed every night." She gave her riotous curls a shake. "I just lower my hair and up they climb!"

Wrapping a muscular arm around her waist, Austyn drove her against the sill, parting her legs with the breadth of his hips. Cold raindrops pelted her back in stark contrast to the rigid heat pressed to the vulnerable hollow between her thighs. He tangled his free hand in her curls, bending her head back until his lips hovered above hers, a sigh away from possession. Each desperate catch of his breath throbbed in her ears.

If only he would kiss her, Holly thought frantically, she might be able to reach the man she had married.

"Why do you hesitate?" she whispered hoarsely. "Is it the curse you fear?"

"The curse has no power over me."

"Why not?"

Holly's world narrowed to the feral gleam of his

eyes in the darkness, the note of savage despair in his voice. "Because I would have to love you first."

She knew then that he wasn't going to kiss her. Knew it even as he wrapped an arm around her hips and lifted her to the bed. Knew it as he laid her beneath him on the plush sable, shoved up her chemise, baring her to the waist, and nudged her knees apart.

She reached for him, desiring nothing more than to caress his bearded jaw, thread her fingers through his hair, wrap him in her embrace. But he caught both of her wrists in one hand, his grip a gentle manacle that sought not to bind her in cruelty, but to deprive him of a tenderness that might destroy them both. Shivering with reaction, Holly braced herself for the worst.

Her entire body convulsed as if seared by lightning as one of his deft fingers parted the fleecy down between her thighs.

She turned her face to the pillow, aflame with shyness at his perverse gallantry. He might deny her the kisses and caresses of lovemaking, but he would not brutalize her. Broken gasps escaped from between her clenched teeth as he probed the tender cleft, his big, blunt finger burrowing deeper with each stroke, making her ready to receive him. Devastating tingles of pleasure spread from his touch. When his one finger was joined by another, she could not resist the foreign urge to arch against his hand.

Austyn knew he'd erred the instant his hand breached Holly's silky nether curls. He'd had every intention of bedding her urgently and crudely, as if she were nothing more than a jaded harlot he had laid down his coin for, but the feel of her delicate body shivering beneath his own had stirred some lingering remnant of decency in his soul.

When his finger sought to prime her for his possession, he bit back a groan to discover the fragile cup of her womb already overflowed with nectar for him. 'Twas a bitter sweetness he had not entreated and did not deserve.

It tempted him to graze his thumb across the sensitive nub buried in her own sable pelt. Tempted him to suckle her magnificent breasts through the gossamer sendal of the chemise until she writhed with pleasure beneath him. Tempted him to part the tender petals of her lips with his tongue. But how long would it be before that tongue betrayed him? Before he began to murmur hot, hoarse words against her mouth, the curve of her throat, the satiny cream of her belly? Words of tenderness. Words of love. Words of doom.

His reckless musings cost him dearly. Holly's hand escaped his and twined around his nape, scorching him like a red-hot brand.

Ruthlessly quenching every longing but his most primal one, Austyn unfastened his hose, linked his fingers through hers and pressed her hands back on each side of her head.

Holly clung to Austyn's strong hands, all she knew of substance in a shadowy universe of torrential rain, crashing thunder, and howling winds. When terror threatened to overwhelm her, she reminded herself that this was no stranger looming over her, but her Austyn—big and warm and smelling of mint and the musk of his need.

A flash of lightning illuminated the tower. Their gazes locked for a brief eternity, then he drove himself between her splayed legs with a guttural groan, cleaving the fragile barrier of her innocence.

Holly's fingers arched along with her back as a bright lance of pain consumed her. Austyn's hand could have ravished her for hours and not prepared her for this fulsome weight inside of her. He seemed overwhelming to her, so massive she did not know how her slight body could contain him. Yet somehow it did, adjusting magically to welcome the length and breadth of him into her melting core.

As the pain subsided, she squeezed his hands until their palms were mated as tightly as their bodies. He ground his hips against her own, wedging himself as deep in her throbbing sheath as she could take him, then withdrawing to do it again. His hands held her captive to his will while his body bludgeoned her with waves of dark pleasure until she could hardly recognize the sound of her own voice, entreating him with broken moans and hoarse whimpers for some shimmering reprieve he alone could deliver.

His only reply other than the harsh rasp of his breathing was to double the intensity and rhythm of his earthy siege. She gasped with pure delight as every muscle of his powerful body went as rigid as the part of him buried to the hilt in her. Lightning sizzled through the tower, gifting her with a glimpse of the savage beauty of his features as he threw back his head in exultation, breaking his silence at last to roar her name in an incantation of pure ecstasy.

He collapsed against her, burying his face against her throat. Holly slipped her hand from beneath his limp one, thinking only to curl her fingers in the damp silk of his hair. He rolled off of her with nary a word, adjusted his hose, and went striding from the tower as if a legion of demons nipped at his heels.

Holly lay there in the dark with her bare legs sprawled apart, her chemise crumpled around her waist, her tender body still overflowing with the scalding bounty of her husband's seed and murmured, "Oh, my."

Austyn's steps grew heavy as he descended the winding stairs to the great hall. The cavernous chamber was deserted, the dying embers of the fire in the central hearth its only light. A tankard of ale and an abandoned goblet sat on the table. The storm's threat had subsided to a distant rumble of thunder and the muted patter of rain on the battlements.

At the discordant strum of fingers against lute strings, Austyn nearly jumped out of his skin.

"What ails you, man? Guilty conscience?"

Austyn scowled into the shadows fringing the hall, finally making out the luster of Carey's fair hair. " 'Tis fortunate I'm unarmed. I might have mistaken you for a Viking raider and whacked off your pretty head."

Carey plucked a few saucy notes in reply, then tilted his head to study him. "That didn't take nearly as long as I thought it would."

For a searing moment, Austyn hated his friend for knowing him so well. It took little more than his heightened color to betray him to Carey. He strode over to the table, poured a strong splash of ale in the goblet and drank it down in one swallow. "I didn't rape her, if that's what you're thinking."

"Would I imply such? I have no doubt that she

simply succumbed to your gallant charms. What did you do? Growl some poetry at her?"

Austyn clenched his teeth to suppress a growl. "There is no need of such nonsense between us. She is my wife. I had every right to determine if she had lain with another man before me."

Carey's tone was as light as his fingers dancing over the strings. "And had she?"

"No," Austyn replied, despising his own sullen tone.

"But that didn't stop you, did it?"

Nor could Austyn stop himself from reliving that moment when he'd primed himself with Holly's copious balm and breached the taut cocoon of her body. She'd fit him like a silken gauntlet. Even as guilt assailed him at the memory of her muffled whimper, his insatiable body stirred to life.

He slammed the goblet on the table, paying it no heed when it overturned. "What would you have had me do? Withdraw and apologize? Say 'Forgive me, my lady, for piercing your maidenhead. I can promise you 'twill never happen again.'" He paced over to the stairs, sank down on the lowest step, and rested his aching head in his hands. "God forgive me, Carey, I used her like a common whore," he confessed hoarsely. "I kissed neither her lips nor her breasts. I offered her not a word of kindness or solace. I swear I did not deliberately seek to hurt her. I left no bruises to mar her beautiful skin." He raked his fingers through his hair, lifting his despairing gaze to Carey's face. "At least none you can see."

Carey only strummed a thoughtful chord.

Austyn shook his head. "I had such tender courtesies plotted for my wife's seduction before I discovered her treachery. Scented tapers and spiced wine. Gentle kisses and honeyed words. Yet I offered her none of those tonight."

The lute fell silent. "And she accepted your brutish attentions with open . . . um, arms?"

Austyn nodded.

"Then perhaps you should ask yourself why."

As Carey rose and strolled from the hall, his fingers plucking a pensive melody, Austyn stared into the glowing embers on the hearth. He had bedded Holly without grace or tenderness, fearing that if he allowed his hands to explore the extravagant curves of her breasts or given his thirsty lips leave to sip the honeyed nectar of her mouth, his soul would be eternally lost.

Yet as he buried his face in hands still scented with the wedded spices of musk and myrrh, he felt more damned than ever before.

CHAPTER 23

❧

Holly was drowsing in the sunshine of the window seat the following morning when she saw the donkey appear in the distance. She had slept late, overcome with a delicious languor that had yet to subside. As she recognized the robed figure astride the donkey, she sat up on her knees, wincing as her tender muscles twinged in protest.

Even from her dizzying perch, the dejected slump of the rider's shoulders was evident. Nathanael must know what his freedom had cost her. Even if Austyn hadn't been so vindictive as to enlighten him, the priest was bright enough to realize that if her husband still harbored the faintest suspicion that he'd been her lover, he would have been carried away from Caer Gavenmore on a burial litter, not a donkey.

As she watched, he slowed the animal and glanced back over his shoulder.

She lifted her hand in a farewell salute, murmuring, "God go with you, brother."

Nathanael did not return her wave, but stared up at the tower for a long time before plodding on. Troubled by mingled affection and regret, Holly watched him fade to a tiny speck on a vast canvas of moor and mountains still damp from last night's storm.

"Austyn should never have sent him alone," she muttered to herself. "The man has a wretched sense of direction. He'll probably ride straight into the sea or incite some hot-headed Scot to martyr him."

She had little time to fret over Nathanael's fate for the dull clatter of the bolt being lifted warned her invasion was imminent. She lifted her chin, unable to stifle the expectant flutter of the pulse in her throat.

'Twas not her husband, but Winifred and a flock of tittering maidservants who entered, each one of them bearing an urn of steaming water. Winnie kept her head bowed, more reticent even than before, but Holly noted that poppies once again blossomed in her cheeks. Her mouth was compressed to a stiff line, as if she might burst into giggles herself at the slightest provocation.

Her darting gaze managed to ricochet off everything in the tower except Holly's face and the bed. "The master thought you might enjoy a hot bath this morning." She nodded down at the crisp bundle in her arms. "And some fresh sheets."

The girls ceased pouring water into the tub long

enough to nudge each other and steal sly glances at the rumpled bed. Winnie gave the one nearest to her a warning swat to her generous backside.

Holly stood to greet them, inclining her head as if her chemise was a mantle of ermine and her disheveled curls a crown. If they thought she was going to blush and stammer with shame over the long overdue consummation of her marriage, they were sorely mistaken.

However, she could not quite banish the note of irony that crept into her voice. "How very considerate of him. Do convey my most humble gratitude for his largesse."

"He thought ye might enjoy a bit o' my company as well, my lady."

At the familiar croak, a warm rush of tears blurred Holly's vision. Elspeth emerged from behind Winnie, her wizened little hobgoblin face one of the dearest sights Holly had ever seen. As the nurse scampered into Holly's arms, sobbing joyfully, Winnie and her disciples tactfully withdrew. The hollow thump of the bolt falling into place jarred Holly and Elspeth from their tender reunion, reminding them that Elspeth now shared her mistress's captivity.

Elspeth blotted Holly's cheeks with a license born of long habit before wiping her own eyes. "Oh, my lady, ye cannot know how afrighted I was for ye. With Sir Austyn stalking 'bout the castle like a madman, ne'er sleeping nor eating for days at a time. All of us tiptoeing 'round him, a-whispering 'neath our breaths, lest he turn his temper on us. When he came for ye last night, I thought to stop him, I vow I did. I would have thrown myself on his blade if need be, but Master Carey clapped a hand over my mouth and held it there until 'twas too late."

Holly narrowed her eyes thoughtfully. It seemed Nathanael had not been her sole champion at Caer Gavenmore. Even Winnie had appeared secretly pleased that their union had been consummated. Perhaps the woman had not yet given up hope that Holly might be her master's salvation.

Elspeth shot the decadent disarray of the bed a wide-eyed glance. A shudder rocked her bony shoulders. "Oh, child, was he a terrible beast to you?"

Holly hoped her impish smile would quiet her nurse's fears. "Quite ferocious. But most bears are when they've been cornered in their own dens." She drew herself from Elspeth's embrace and wandered to the tub, leaning over to trail her fingers in the steaming water. "I'd almost dare to venture my beast is suffering rather human qualms of remorse this morn. He frees Nathanael. Sends you to nurse my wounded feelings. Provides a luxurious bath to soothe my . . . um . . . spirits." Holly turned to the bed, beset by misty images of the wondrous act that had taken place there in the darkness. A tingling ribbon of delight curled through her belly. "And clean sheets so that I might whisk away all memory of his debauchery."

"He rode out before dawn," Elspeth volunteered, "his face so fierce I'll wager he's not coming back. And a good riddance to him, I say, for daring to lay a finger on my lady!"

"Oh, he'll be back," Holly said softly, but with grave certainty.

She only wondered what his tormented conscience would expect to find. His wife pale and weeping in the window seat, her skin scrubbed raw of his touch, her red-rimmed eyes shadowed by reproach? Or perhaps cowering in the bed with the pristine sheets drawn up over her head?

A slow, dangerous smile curved Holly's lips. "Elspeth, darling, would you mind helping me with a bit of laundry while you're here?"

'Twas near nightfall when Sir Austyn of Gavenmore returned to his castle in utter defeat. He had battled his way through steep, stony gorges, forded streams and rivers swollen by the previous night's rain, and driven his steed over countless leagues of windswept moor. Where once he had sought only the challenges of war to test his mettle, now he sought that most elusive of all prizes: peace.

His quest had been fruitless. The perfume released by the wildflowers crushed beneath his mount's hooves was but a wan imitation of the fragrant bouquet of Holly's skin. The wind tousled his hair, sifting through the damp locks at his nape just as Holly's fingertips had sought to do. The whisper of the breeze in his ears echoed her soft, broken gasps as the silken petals of her untried body had flowered to receive him.

He could not know if they were gasps of pleasure or pain since he had taken neither the time nor the care to find out.

Biting back a fierce oath, Austyn drove the destrier over a crumbling section of curtain wall. Both he and the animal were lathered with sweat and near to trembling with exhaustion. He had hoped he might ride his insatiable appetite for Holly out of his blood, but he feared there was only one way to do that. Desolation tinged his dark hunger. He wondered if his grandfather had dreaded climbing those stairs as much as he did, had known even as he did so that each step carried him nearer to damnation.

Austyn walked the horse past his mother's grave, refusing to honor it with so much as a glance. He could not help but remember the days when he had returned to Caer Gavenmore in triumph, when not even the specter of his father's madness could spoil his pride at returning victor from some tournament or bloody skirmish in which he'd been allowed the privilege of proving his worth in battle. His people would line the courtyard, waving green and crimson kerchiefs and cheering his victory as if it were their own.

A ghost of a cheer reached his ears. Austyn jerked up his head, wondering if impending madness had somehow given substance to his memories. But, no, there it was again—a lusty roar of approval, underscored by a smattering of applause. The sound baffled him. There had been little cause for celebration at Caer Gavenmore since Holly's unmasking and none worthy of such glee since the night he'd brought his ill-favored little bride home to present to his people. His brow clouded at the memory.

He glanced up at the battlements, but all he could see over the roof of the abandoned gatehouse was a thin slice of ivory dangling from a corner merlon. Odd, he thought, narrowing his eyes against the fading light. He could not remember there being a gargoyle perched on that particular embrasure. His eyes widened with astonishment as the gargoyle in question spotted him and went scampering over the parapet to disappear behind a stone chimney.

Besieged by curiosity, he hastened his mount's steps toward the inner bailey. An excited crowd milled beneath the battlements. As they spotted him, their cheers swelled to a roar of acclaim.

A burly beekeeper clapped him on the thigh as he passed. "The purest honey is always worth waitin' for, sir."

An ancient beldame bobbed him a girlish curtsy and crooned, "I'd be pleased if ye'd offer Master Longstaff my regards."

Austyn didn't have the faintest idea who this Longstaff fellow was, nor did he appreciate the rogue getting his castle into such an uproar.

As he dismounted, a freckled lad trotted up to relieve him of his mount. "Might I have a strip of it when ye cut it down, sir? My ma says if I sleep with it 'neath my pillow 'twill increase my p-p-pot'ncy."

Utterly baffled, Austyn followed the direction of the boy's pointing finger and rapt gaze to a square of ivory fluttering like a pennon from the highest rampart. The cheers died to a wary, but expectant, silence.

'Twas not a pennon, Austyn realized with a nasty shock, but a rumpled bedsheet, its fine linen stained with the unmistakable evidence of his wife's innocence. He swayed as every drop of blood drained from his face, then rushed back to suffuse it with a blazing heat.

Austyn had been a knight for ten years—long enough to know that the harmless looking sheet flapping in the breeze was not a flag of surrender, but an open declaration of war.

ChApTER 24

🖎

Austyn took the winding steps to the tower three at a
time. He briefly entertained the notion of shattering
the bolt with a kick, but decided not to waste his violence on such trifles. He did allow himself the gratifi-
cation of hurling the wooden bar aside and sending
the door crashing open into the wall. 'Twas only then
that he realized he had been fool enough to march
unarmed and unarmored into his enemy's camp.

Holly had girded her own exquisite loins with a
flowing emerald cotte shot through with shimmering
threads of cloth of gold. A plump ruby glimmered like
a teardrop of blood in the pale hollow of her throat. A
diamond-studded pomander ball dangled from the

woven girdle resting on her slim hips. She had cast a
net of thinly beaten gold over her lustrous curls, but
they resisted capture, preferring to coil and frolic in
saucy rebellion.

She stood before the window, so beautiful and
brimming with grace that it was all Austyn could do to
keep from falling to his knees at her feet and surrendering his heart and soul to her dominion.

Her impeccable poise made him painfully conscious of his own sweat-dampened tunic and disheveled locks. With his fists clenched and his chest
heaving with thwarted fury, he must appear little more
than a savage to her. He'd certainly done nothing to
supplant that notion last night. She probably thought
all Welshmen rutted their wives like stags mounting a
doe in season.

Both angered and shamed by his lack, Austyn
averted his gaze from her, taking in the slender beeswax tapers, the feast spread for two on a linen-draped
table before the hearth, the round tub emitting enticing little curlicues of steam over its rim, the delicate
harp propped against a nest of pillows on the floor.

The opulent bed, its pristine sheets and sable coverlet folded back in brazen invitation.

His eyes narrowed as he realized his wife must
have enlisted some very powerful allies indeed. 'Twas
as if his possession had somehow elevated her from
princess to queen and she was demonstrating no
qualms whatsoever about ruling *his* castle from a
locked tower.

"Good evening, sir," she said, her voice as melodious as a hymn. "I've taken the liberty of having supper
prepared and a bath drawn for you."

Austyn could not help but think how he might have welcomed such tender attentions from the wife he had once believed Holly to be. "I'm not hungry," he growled. He could hardly claim not to be dirty with the same conviction.

"A pity. I had Winifred prepare all of your favorites. Not a pickled lamprey in sight. I wanted to assure you that your efforts to please me did not go unappreciated." At first Austyn thought the minx bold enough to remind him that he had made little effort to please her during his last visit, seeking only his own crude satisfaction, but her beatific expression lacked any trace of cunning. "After all, you were kind enough to free Nathanael and send Elspeth to spend the day with me."

He pointed a finger skyward. "That wouldn't be the same Elspeth I just saw cavorting about the ramparts."

A maddening smile played around Holly's lips. She glided to the table and seated herself, the pomander ball jingling against her shapely thigh. "I'm surprised you didn't have Carey draw his bow and shoot her."

"Had I known what mischief she was about, I might have considered it." Austyn folded himself warily into the opposite chair. "Of course, I'm sure you knew naught of her mission. As you hasten to remind me at every opportunity, you are, above all things, innocent."

She poured mead into two goblets and handed him one, refusing to allow so much as a blush to betray her. It galled him that she could still look as pure and serene as a violet-eyed Madonna. "Not this time, I fear. A confession is forthcoming and since you've sent my priest away, I am thrust into the unenviable position of casting myself upon *your* mercy."

He arched his eyebrow in a skeptical invitation to proceed.

She took a dainty sip of the mead. "It has occurred to me, sir, that you might attempt to rid yourself of me by having our marriage annulled and sending me back to my papa in disgrace."

Austyn caught himself staring as her luscious tongue darted out to dash a golden drop of mead from her lower lip. "Why would I do that? So you can gather more hearts to break?"

She shot him a reproachful look from beneath lashes that seemed to be growing even as he watched, but continued as if he hadn't spoken. "As I see it, you can accomplish such an end in one of two ways—by claiming our marriage unconsummated or by swearing that I was no virgin when I came to your bed. 'Tis why I chose that perfectly honorable, if rather barbaric, custom to display proof of my chastity to your people."

Austyn leaned back in his chair to survey his wife through narrowed eyes. He had to admire her shrewdness, but in doing so, he discovered his horror of loving her was nearly equaled by his horror of liking her.

He twirled the stem of his goblet between two fingers. "Had I known you craved an audience, my lady, we could have invited them into our bedchamber. Then you wouldn't have been forced to enjoy their accolades from afar."

"I heard the cheers. 'Tis gratifying to know that

not every man at Caer Gavenmore equates beauty with harlotry."

Austyn started to protest, but knew his words would ring hollow when compared with his deeds. In truth, Holly appeared more angel than harlot. His clumsy pawings might have robbed her of her virginity, but innocence still shimmered around her like a novice's veil. Disturbed by the image, he slammed the goblet down on the table and rose from his chair.

As Austyn paced behind her, Holly's nape prickled. In truth, she had welcomed his decision to decline a bath, for he smelled of sunshine and freshly cut hay and all the sweet summer aromas she'd been denied for too long. She longed to nuzzle her lips against the crisp froth of hair at the throat of his tunic, to lick the salty tang of sweat from his bearded jaw.

When he strode back into her line of vision, a helpless scowl had claimed his features. " 'Tis not that I believe you inclined to infidelity purely by virtue of your appearance. 'Tis only that I find you a . . . a . . ." He seemed to be having difficulty looking directly at her. ". . . a disappointment. You're hardly the woman I bargained for as a wife."

Holly lifted the goblet to her lips to hide how deeply his words wounded. Her entire education had been devoted to molding her into an engaging mate for her future husband. She could not help but wonder if he had found her as keen a disappointment in his bed. A treacherous lump welled in her throat.

She washed it down with a swallow of mead. "We seemed to suit well enough before you discovered my trickery."

"That's because I thought you were . . ."

"Someone else?" she gently provided.

He slammed a palm on the table, rattling the dishes. His eyes blazed with a frigid fire. "Aye! Someone else! A plain, ordinary girl who would entice no man to challenge her husband for possession of her. A lady a knight could trust the care of his people and his castle to when he was summoned to battle without being tormented every second he was away from her with visions of her succumbing to the seduction of some lusty rogue." The sharp edge of Austyn's voice was blunted by a yearning more piercing to Holly's heart than all of his ranting. "A woman I'd always know would be waiting to welcome me when I returned. A devout wife and mother to my children."

Knowing that he had examined her and found her unfit for such a virtuous task as motherhood cut Holly to the quick. 'Twas hardly the first time someone had addressed her as if she had no feelings. As if her beauty were a shell of pretty armor that somehow made her impervious to their slights. But only with Austyn did she discover how fragile that shell could be.

She rose from the chair to face him, praying he would attribute the uncommon sheen of her eyes to the flickering candlelight. "If my beauty renders me unfit to be your wife, then what did you seek to make of me last night? Your paramour? Do the whores of the Gavenmore men fare any better than their wives?"

"They tend to live a hell of a lot longer." Austyn's restless strides carried him to the window where he stood gazing out into the deepening night. "As I see it, you should be begging me to send you back to your father. *Especially* after last night."

She forced a brittle laugh. "Don't be ridiculous, sir. I'm not some mewling child bride ready to flee back to papa because her husband chose to assert his carnal rights."

He turned to face her. "But an annulment would grant you freedom. Freedom from this tower. Freedom from my demands."

Holly was wise enough to know that if Austyn exiled her from his life, she would never be free of this tower. It would enclose her heart, stone by stone, until it smothered her.

She drifted toward him, cocking her head to gaze her fill, but not daring to touch. "Are your demands so unreasonable, my lord? Loyalty? Truth? Fidelity?"

"Those aren't the demands I spoke of and you know it." His voice was harsh, but his hands as they clasped her shoulders flirted with gentleness. "Shall I send you back to Tewksbury or would you rather remain imprisoned in this tower at the mercy of my every whim, forced to endure what my grandmother endured night after night after night?"

Holly met his desperate gaze boldly. "I am not your grandmother. Nor are you your grandfather. You may bluster and growl all you like, but I haven't the faintest fear that you're going to rape me. Or strangle me," she added out of spite for the hurt his candid words had caused her.

A disbelieving bark of laughter escaped him. "Do you honestly believe if you had denied me last night, I would have begged your pardon and taken my leave?"

"Aye, 'tis exactly what I believe. Which is why I'm denying you tonight." Her words tumbled like pebbles into a bottomless well of silence.

Austyn released her shoulders and backed away from her, as if realizing too late that he had stumbled not into an enemy camp, but into a trap. His heel came up against the edge of the harp; it collapsed with a discordant thunk.

He drove a hand through his hair as his bemused gaze raked the chamber. "Are you trying to tell me that had I partaken of your delicious supper, allowed you to recline at my feet and enchant me with a lullaby, then given you leave to strip my weary body and bathe me from head to toe with those exquisite hands of yours, you still had absolutely no intention of taking me to your bed?"

"None whatsoever."

"Why you shameless little . . ." He took a menacing step toward her.

"No," she said firmly.

He did not curb his dangerous charge until a mere inch of air sizzled between their bodies. To keep from shrinking in his shadow, Holly forced herself to remember the husband who had cradled her across his lap while he sponged her tears away. The warrior who had spared Eugene de Legget's life when vengeance demanded he take it. The knight who had leashed his mighty strength to cup her nape in his broad palm and stolen her mouth's virginity with nothing more than the gentle persuasion of his tongue. If she had miscalculated that man's honor, the price would be very dear indeed.

She could almost see the unholy war being fought behind the glittering palisades of Austyn's eyes. A war between temptation and honor. Lust and mercy. Passion and compassion.

Just when she feared his dark desires might emerge the sole victor, he stroked the backs of his fingers down her cheek with a bewitching tenderness she had thought never to feel from him again. "You've chosen your weapons well, woman. Now I shall choose mine."

With that cryptic warning, he turned on his heel and left her.

When the bolt had fallen into place, Holly sank down on the window seat, trembling like a reed in the wind. Austyn might never return to her, but by proving to him that he wasn't the monster his grandfather had been, she had at least sent him on his way with his soul intact. She touched her fingertips to her tingling cheek, wishing wistfully that she could say the same of her heart.

Sleep eluded Holly. She squirmed and tossed in a bed that seemed to have swelled to twice its normal size since she had shared it with her husband, however briefly, the night before. The feather mattress threatened to swallow her whole. The coverlet and sheets tugged at her ankles until she kicked them away. Even the flimsy chemise sought to bind her, twisting its way around her throat in a perverse noose. She finally dragged it off and cast it to the floor, preferring to sleep as she had since childhood.

But the caress of the cool night air against her naked breasts only served to remind her that she was child no more.

Sleep came to her in fitful spurts and fevered dreams. She awoke from a sojourn into wrenching loneliness to find a dark shape poised above her. Her rational mind warned her that she should be afraid, but some more primitive instinct welcomed this shadowy manifestation of her longings.

Her womb quickened with expectancy as he descended on her, a swaggering satyr—half angel, half demon—in the darkness.

He would not kiss her mouth.

This loving Austyn forged from stardust and shadows brushed his lips against her temple, traced the delicate shell of each ear with his tongue, nibbled the curve of her jaw, then coasted lower to nuzzle his lips against the throbbing pulse in her throat. She sighed her delight.

His delectable wooing enticed her to touch him, but she curled her hands into fists, fearing that if she succumbed to the temptation, he would melt back into the mists of yearning from which she had summoned him.

A shudder of pleasure convulsed her as his cunning tongue flicked out to lash one of her nipples. She arched her back, unable to resist the accomplished devilment of his mouth. The generous globes of her breasts had been both leered at and praised, but they'd never been debauched with such reverence. He licked and nipped and teased until she'd dropped every defense, then suckled her hard and deep, coaxing a surge of hot, thick nectar from between her thighs.

He would not kiss her mouth.

He rained tender kisses on the quivering skin of her belly. His tongue delved into her navel in a sinuous swirl, as if to warn her there was no secret hollow of her body he would not brand with his touch. He did not have to use his powerful hands to urge her legs apart. At the tingling scrape of his beard against the downy skin at the inner curve of her knee, her thighs melted into acquiescence, shyly inviting him to sate his darkest appetites in a sweet, forbidden feast.

Holly would never forget the first sensuous tickle of his mustache. Her fingernails drew tiny pearls of blood from her palms as she fought the desire to curl her fingers in the coarse silk of his hair. At her soft whimper of mortification, his tongue both soothed her and maddened her, flicking her swollen flesh with devilish skill to whip her into a frenzy of incoherent pleasure, then lowering to lap gently at the bounty of his ministrations.

He would not kiss her mouth.

He drove her to the very brink of ecstasy once, twice, three times, but her choked pleas for deliverance only seemed to prolong the taut circles of his tongue. Just when she thought she would surely perish from want if he did not fill that melting hollow aching for his attention, he added his deft hands to her sensual agony, ravishing her tenderly, but with exquisite thoroughness, with his longest finger, then with his broad, spatulate thumb.

Holly writhed, desperate to wrap her arms and legs around him. Besieged by thick, throbbing waves of pleasure, she reached up and grasped the velvet ribbons dangling from the bedposts, placing herself in willing bondage to save herself from drowning in a sea of rapture. 'Twas then that he reached beneath her with his other hand and gently stroked the tip of a single finger down the fragile, cloistered valley between her buttocks.

That touch, so primal, so provocative, shuddered her to the soul. A low moan tore from her throat, so feral she did not recognize it as her own.

His voice was woven of the darkness itself, both hoarse and silken. "Would you deny me now, my lady? Shall I beg your pardon and take my leave?"

He had ceased to touch her, but even the kiss of his breath scorched her eager flesh. She could feel the flames roiling off his artful tongue, his big, graceful fingers, as they awaited her breathless leave to probe and stroke and possess. He had chosen his weapons with the diabolical skill of a mortal enemy, but Holly still had enough faith in him to know he would abide by her wishes. If she denied him, he would abandon her without so much as a growl of protest, leaving him bereft of release and herself teetering on the precipice of some wondrous discovery.

Gripping the velvet ribbons so tightly they cut into her palms, she uttered the one choked word that would seal both of their fates.

"Stay."

He stayed. His fingers plundered every vulnerable cleft they could reach while his mouth suckled her with devastating tenderness. Holly cried out as ecstasy pulsed through her in surge after indescribable surge.

Before the last of those shivery frissons could cease to wrack her womb, he was sliding his turgid staff past the quivering petals of her sex, stroking deep with a dreamy, deliberate cadence that bore little resemblance to what had passed between them the night before. That had been a brief, roaring conflagration; this was a slow burn that threatened to incinerate her very soul. 'Twas as if he had all night, all eternity, to claim her for his own.

He would not kiss her mouth.

His brutal tenderness made Holly want to claw at his back, to beat at his muscled shoulders with her fists. She turned her face to the pillow with a hoarse sob, helpless to do anything but lay beneath him with her legs sprawled wide and her throbbing core up-tilted for his pleasuring. Pleasure her he did, reaching to fondle and stroke the tiny nubbin sheltered by the damp nest where their bodies were joined until cry after cry of surrender was wrung from her throat. 'Twas as if he sought to turn her into the very thing he feared the most—a piteous, mewling creature ruled by her darkest, most sensual, impulses.

She lost track of the number of times he urged her to that dark peak and hurtled her over its edge. 'Twas a sweet infinity before his surging rhythm and straining muscles told her he had joined her in the fall. He came and went in equal silence, leaving Holly sweat-drenched and shivering in the empty bed.

Yestereve her husband had fled her company as if to linger would be to forfeit his soul, but this night he had torn away a jagged fragment of her soul and taken it with him.

Without ever once kissing her mouth.

There was but one door leading to the walled court-yard below the north tower. Austyn battered it open with his fist and staggered into the blessed chill of the Welsh night. He collapsed against the stone wall, tilting his face to the sky to let the misty air bathe his fevered flesh.

Holly might have been a fool to toss down the gauntlet of her denial, but he had proved himself an even greater fool by taking it up.

He could not have said what had possessed him to believe he could touch her in every manner, both sacred and profane, in which a husband could touch a wife, yet remain untouched himself. She had wooed him with nothing more than her soft sigh of welcome when she had discovered him standing over her bed. Yet he had forced himself to maintain his maddening charade of restraint until the bittersweet end, clenching his teeth against a roar of ecstasy that would have betrayed him for the fraud he was.

Austyn groaned. How in God's name was he to keep Holly at arm's length when he could still scent her on his beard, taste her on his lips? Never before had any woman, plain or comely, bought with coin or offered freely, so cut his heart to the quick. He feared her bewitching surrender in this initial battle might very well cost him the war.

"Are you satisfied, Rhiannon? Is this how it begins?"

His hoarse query was not greeted by the echo of mocking feminine laughter he expected, but by the muffled notes of his wife's weeping.

Austyn gazed at the darkened tower window for a tortured moment, then buried his face in his hands, unwittingly blinding himself to the stooped figure who cast himself from the shadows and went scrambling over the wall.

CHAPTER 25

꩜

Holly's days soon settled into a predictable routine.
She lacked for no luxury but freedom.

Her invisible jailer sent Winifred to deliver armfuls of freshly cut flowers—late-blooming jasmine and
morning glory, wood hyacinths and blood-red roses
that sent the haunting fragrance of the waning summer wafting through the tower.

As she tossed them out the window in a shower of
lavender and crimson, Holly compressed her lips to a
bitter line and wondered what his offerings would be
in winter when the fecund earth slumbered beneath a
shroud of snow. Perhaps he would have tired of her by

then and would be bestowing his floral tributes on a more appreciative lover.

Her harp was joined by a newly strung lute and a carved flute flawlessly molded to the contours of her lips. Illuminated manuscripts followed—rare pieces of music suited only to the ripe soprano of a woman's voice.

The instruments sat in forlorn silence; the manuscripts remained untouched.

He was even so generous as to send Elspeth to keep her company during the languid hours of daylight. Dear Elspeth who possessed the gift of chattering cheerfully about nothing at all, but could not quite hide her troubled glances at the smudges of exhaustion beneath her mistress's eyes.

Perversely enough, Holly thought the interminable days of captivity might have driven her mad were it not for the tempestuous liberties allowed her in the darkness of night.

For after she'd sent Elspeth on her way and extinguished the candles, Austyn would slip into her bed to cast his tender sorcery over her body. He had ceased being her husband to become a phantom lover in the darkness, stealing another precious splinter of her soul with each nocturnal visit.

He would not kiss her mouth or allow her to caress him in tenderness. He broke his fierce silence only to whisper what wicked magic he was going to work until it took little more than the husky rasp of his voice in her ear to bring her to the brink of fulfillment. Had there been even a hint of brutality in his attentions, Holly might have brought herself to hate him, but his accomplished hands cherished her flesh as if it were his own private altar. She'd never known such unbridled ecstasy. Or such misery.

He left no fragile hollow of her body unexplored, storming the last remaining bastion of her innocence with such wrenching tenderness that even as she buried her face in the mattress to muffle her sobs, her body was wracked by shudders of dark, exquisite rapture.

'Twas that night, when he withdrew from her without so much as a grunt of satisfaction, donned his hose, and padded heavily to the door, that she broke her own stubborn silence.

"Are you going to leave nothing of me, sir?" she cried, clenching her teeth against a belated chill of shame. "Have I given you cause to hate me so much?"

He hesitated for no more than a heartbeat. Then the door shut and the bolt fell gently in place, sealing her in with only her fading hopes for company.

Elspeth shot her mistress an apprehensive glance as Holly paced the tower, the slashed sleeves of her cotehardie rippling with each stride. She paused each time she passed the window, as if compelled to watch the daylight die. Her exquisite features were cast in bitterness and her eyes had a wild look that had never boded well for anyone, least of all herself.

"I care naught for the gleam in yer eye, child," Elspeth said, laying aside her sewing. " 'Tis the same gleam ye had when yer papa forbade ye a pony when ye were only six. Ye hid yerself in that tinker's cart and ran away during a snowstorm. 'Twas nearly two days later when yer poor papa found ye curled in the hollow o' that elm like an innocent sprite. Drove him half out o' his wits with worry, ye did, but all he could do was smother yer grubby little face with kisses."

A brief, wistful smile softened Holly's lips. "Perhaps if he had thrashed my naughty little rump instead, I wouldn't now find myself in such a predicament."

The door swung open and Winifred poked her round face inside. " 'Tis time to go, Elspeth."

The nurse hesitated, reluctant to leave her mistress in such bleak solitude. Holly's pallor and glittering eyes made her look both fragile and dangerous, as if she were possessed by some exotic fever that might burn both her and anyone she touched to ashes.

"Sleep well," Holly said gently.

Elspeth cast Winifred a helpless look, but the Welshwoman shook her head, her fretful expression mirroring Elspeth's own. They had spoken bluntly about Holly's plight, but were at a loss as to how to break this cycle of destruction. 'Twas as if their master and mistress were locked in some dark dance of the soul, both determined to carry it to its grim conclusion.

Having nothing else to offer Holly, Elspeth gave her a fervent hug. "God keep ye until the morrow, my child," she whispered, wishing she could shake off her chill of foreboding.

When Elspeth had gone, Holly glided about the chamber, the jagged edge smoothed off of her restlessness by a growing sense of purpose. Instead of pinching the flame from each taper as she usually did, she retrieved the candles she'd been hoarding for days and lit every feathery wick until the tower was bathed in a luminous glow.

If Austyn would come to her, then let him come to her in light. She would no longer offer him a shield of darkness to hide his heart behind. She would face him boldly in the candlelight, even if doing so made her blush to remember what had passed between them in the shadows.

She would have the truth from him. And if he vowed to her upon his honor as a knight that he could never love her, she would humble herself before him for the last time and entreat him to return her to Tewksbury. A spasm of anguish gripped her heart, but she squelched it without mercy.

As in the nights before, there was little she could do but wait. She drifted to the window, breathing deeply of the bittersweet incense of the flowers decaying on the cobblestones below, never feeling the sly caress of the eyes that watched from the gathering darkness.

Tonight would be the night he would keep himself from her.

Austyn strode up the moonlit hill, knowing himself a liar even as he made the vow. She burned like a molten fever in his blood. He was as helpless to resist her as the tides were to resist the siren tug of the moon.

The stones of the unfinished curtain wall gaped like ivory teeth in the jaws of night. He vaulted over a low section, welcoming the shadows and the sweet anonymity they would bring. 'Twas only in darkness that he dared reveal himself to her.

He slipped past the deserted chapel and into the inner bailey, skirting the rushlights like the predator he could feel himself becoming. He had nearly reached the refuge of an outer staircase when a fair-haired figure disengaged from the shadows and sauntered into his path.

Austyn halted and rested his hands on his hips. "You might not have as much leisure to act as my conscience were you to seek a wife of your own."

The cocky flash of Carey's smile should have warned him. "Now why would I go to the trouble when I was hoping you'd grant me a tumble on yours?"

At the furtive creak of the door opening and closing behind her, Holly squared her shoulders, girding herself to do final battle for the man she loved. She drew in a bracing breath as she turned. It escaped in an exclamation of surprise at the sight of the man huddled against the door.

"Father Rhys?"

Her father-in-law was the first man aside from her husband allowed entry to the tower since her captivity had began. Alarm tinged her bewilderment as she remembered his thundering denouncement from the parapets on the day Austyn had discovered her ruse.

He touched a finger to his lips to beg her silence, looking bashful and almost childlike. "Father forbade me to come. But I slipped away while he was with his doxy."

Holly's confusion mounted. "Your *father* forbade you? I don't understand."

"He said you were wicked, but I don't believe him." Tears puddled in his pale blue eyes—eyes so like Austyn's that it hurt Holly just to gaze into them. They only served to remind her of all the darkness had robbed her of. "I miss you, Mama. I miss you terribly."

Comprehension dawned. In all of her empathy for the woman who had inhabited this tower prison before her, Holly had never once cast a thought for the woman's child. A small boy forbidden his mother's love by a cruel and vengeful father. For the first time since learning how Rhys of Gavenmore had murdered his own wife in a jealous rage, Holly felt a twinge of pity for the man.

Sympathy gentled her voice. "I'm sure your mama missed you, too, sir. Very much. But I am not her."

He cocked his head to the side, as if listening to an echo of a long forgotten melody. "I hear the two of you, you know. When Father thinks I'm sleeping, I sneak into the courtyard and listen." Cunning crept in to banish the shyness from his expression. "I hear you moaning and panting. Sometimes you scream as if he's hurting you, but then you beg him to hurt you more. You fancy the lewd things he does to you, don't you? Perhaps you are wicked after all."

Holly clapped a hand over her mouth to smother a gasp of horror. 'Twas distressing enough to imagine a small boy hearing such noises between his parents, but even more appalling to realize he must have been eavesdropping on her and Austyn from the beginning.

He made her feel violated in a way that his son never had.

He advanced on her, his voice swelling from the plaintive tones of a child to the dangerous vigor of manhood. "Perhaps you're nothing but a deceitful harlot." He raked her with a lascivious gaze. "How many men have you welcomed between those milky thighs of yours, Gwyneth? A dozen? A legion?"

"I am not Gwyneth! Nor am I your mother." Only too aware of the yawning chasm behind her, Holly sidled away from the window, realizing too late that she was backing toward the bed. "I am Holly, Father Rhys. Don't you remember me? You helped me carry tubs of poppies up to the battlements. We planted flowers on Gwyneth's grave together." When her frantic words failed to halt his pursuit, she cried out, "I'm your son's wife, for God's sake! Austyn's wife!"

Even to her own ears, her avowal lacked conviction. In truth, Austyn had not claimed her as his wife since that dark day by the river. How was she to convince this madman she was more than just a contemptible harlot if she could not even convince herself? Hadn't Austyn proved her as weak and wicked a creature as Rhys described, panting with eagerness to abandon her body and soul to torrid nights of carnal revelry?

Blinking back tears, she groped behind her for a weapon. A discordant twang provoked her hopes even as the backs of her knees struck the bed pedestal.

"Lift your skirts, love," he snarled, the endearment a profanity on his lips, "and we shall see if you find me as robust a satisfaction as you found the king when you enticed him to your bed."

He took his eyes off of her to fumble with his hose, his palsied hands betraying his delusion of youth. Holly swung the lute in a wide circle, aiming for his head.

The instrument shattered against his temple. He staggered backward, shooting her such a wounded look that it might have been comical under less dire circumstances. But before Holly could celebrate her triumph, he shook off the blow and rushed her. He tore at the rich damask of her cotte with a strength born of madness, leaving her only one weapon with which to do battle.

Austyn could not think of a single reason why his man-at-arms would seek to provoke him to murder. Especially with himself as the most likely victim.

He stared at Carey through narrowed eyes. "Have you lost your wits?"

Carey hiked one shoulder in a lazy shrug and began to circle him, affecting a swagger that was a creditable imitation of Austyn's own. "I haven't lost my wits, man. I've come to them. And I must say 'tis really not like you to be so selfish."

"Selfish?"

"Aye! Or greedy either. You've never begrudged me a taste of choice pheasant or a sip of your finest wine. So why should you be so grasping as to hoard a treasure like Holly all for yourself?" He elbowed Austyn in the ribs, shooting him a leering wink. " 'Twouldn't be the first time we'd shared a woman."

A scarlet curtain of rage unfurled over Austyn's eyes. He snatched Carey up by the tunic and slammed him against the nearest wall. "How dare you? You're not talking about some ha'penny whore. You're talking about my wife!"

Carey looked far more nonchalant than he should have with Austyn's brawny forearm pressed against his windpipe. "Then you'll have to forgive my insolence for 'twas my impression that a man doesn't lock his *wife* in a tower. Nor does he creep into her bed by night to steal her favors like a thief."

"She brought that on herself. She should never have betrayed me!"

Carey's gray eyes glittered with challenge. "Aye, and if you snap my fool neck this very minute, you'll find a way to blame that on her, too, won't you? After all, isn't that what wicked women such as your mother and Holly delight in? Setting husband against king? Brother against brother? Friend against friend?"

Austyn sucked in a breath through clenched teeth, glowering down into the flushed face of a man who had been more brother to him than friend. A man willing to risk his life to make him see reason. The harsh rasp of their mingled breathing slowly dwindled.

The taut fabric of their silence was torn by a sound Austyn had heard only once before. A sound so terrible he wanted to drop to his knees like the terrified nine-year-old he had been and clamp his hands over his ears.

A full-throated scream stifled in mid-note with brutal efficiency.

CHAPTER 26

As Rhys's gnarled hands closed around her throat to mangle the life from her, Holly thought ruefully that at least there would be less of a mess for Austyn to mop up than if his father had hurled her out the window. By this time tomorrow night, she'd be just another Gavenmore ghost.

'Twas a pity she did not believe in ghosts. If she did, at least her spirit might have lingered to watch over Austyn and wreak mischievous havoc if he dared bring home some plain, docile bride to replace her. She would sing off-key in their bedchamber and shove tubs of poppies off the battlements on the woman's dowdy head. Holly might have giggled at the vision

had she been able to suck any air into her tortured
lungs.

The tower was dimming around her. 'Twould be
full dark soon. Holly welcomed the gathering shadows. Austyn always came in the dark. 'Twas the one
place where his touch promised love even if his lips
would not. A single tear slipped from her eye. A tear of
longing. A tear of regret. But she refused to surrender
her hope. For Austyn would never abandon her to face
the dark alone.

Jesus, God in heaven, it was happening all over again.

Austyn's knees had buckled at that ghastly cry
and for a heartbeat of hesitation, 'twas only Carey's
grip that kept him standing. They exchanged a frantic
glance before Austyn tore himself from his friend's
grasp and went racing for the castle.

He could hear Carey at his heels as he thundered
past the stark white faces in the great hall and shoved
his way through the men who had already started up
the first set of stairs.

Please, God, he prayed, *don't let me be too late. Not
this time.*

He reached the landing beneath the north tower
in less than a dozen steps, yet felt as if he were wading
through a silence as thick and viscous as death. He
flew up the narrow, winding stairs, numbed to the
sparks of pain that exploded through his brain when
his shoulder slammed against the door.

He stumbled into the tower only to be engulfed by
a swell of desolation so intense it threatened to sub-
merge him.

Images came to him in fragments: the splinters of the lute scattered across the floor; his father straddling a woman; her slender fingers hanging limp over the side of the bed, just as his mother's neck had hung limp when he had carried her down the stairs to bury her.

'Twas the stubborn twitch of those fingertips that jerked Austyn from past to present. Crossing the chamber in two strides, he caught the back of his father's tunic and hurled him off the bed. He snatched Holly up in his arms, terrified he would find her beautiful face blackened by death.

Her wheezing gasp was the sweetest melody he'd ever heard from her lips. "Breathe deep, love," he begged, his own voice the hoarse rasp of a stranger. "Oh, please breathe. Breathe for me."

He rocked her in his arms, supporting her head with his palm until her nostrils lost their pinched look and her face faded from purple to white. His father's fingerprints marred the pale palette of her throat.

Rhys had collapsed in a flaccid heap, his lower lip quivering, his rheumy eyes puddling with tears. Blood trickled from a gash on his temple. "I'm sorry, Mama," he whispered plaintively. The anguished timbre of his voice deepened as he buried his face in his hands. "Oh, dear God, Gwyneth, I'm so sorry."

Not a drop of pity would have lingered in Austyn's heart had he not possessed the grim knowledge that he might yet be gazing into his own future. He would have risen to deal with his father then and there, but his arms refused to relinquish Holly's precious weight.

A blessed hiccup drew his hungry gaze back to her face. A hint of rose had bloomed in her cheeks.

Her eyes fluttered open and she blinked up at him earnestly. "Am I a ghost, sir?"

Austyn tightened his embrace, shivering as he contemplated how close she'd come to achieving such a spectral state. He buried his mouth in the softness of her curls. "No, love, although I suspect you might be an angel."

She snuggled deeper into his arms. " 'Tis just as well I s'pose," she whispered in an endearing croak. "I should have been a very naughty ghost. I was going to sew the legs of your hose together and rip all the seams out of your surcoats."

Her eyes flew open. She glanced down, as if just remembering that Rhys's attack had torn her cotte. The damask had parted to offer a teasing glimpse of one creamy breast. Her gaze shot to the door to find Carey standing in the doorway, an anxious crowd hovering behind him.

Trembling like a child in his arms, she snatched the shredded bodice together to shield her nakedness and turned her pleading eyes on Austyn. "Oh, please don't be angry at Carey. 'Twasn't his fault. I enticed him to look at me. I swear I did."

Her teeth began to chatter with delayed reaction. Tears welled in those extraordinary eyes, spilling over to scorch Austyn's skin like droplets of boiling oil. His massive body shuddered as he felt the invisible wall around his heart collapse. How ironic that he should labor on it for twenty years only to discover too late that it had been forged not from stone, but ice! It had taken nothing more than the bittersweet warmth of Holly's tears to melt it to a heap of useless rubble, leaving his heart raw and exposed.

He had to do no more than cast Carey an agonized glance. His man-at-arms gently shepherded his
father and the others from the tower, leaving Austyn
and his wife to their privacy.

Austyn ran his hands briskly over Holly's icy
arms, seeking to warm them. "Aside from trying to
strangle you to death, did the wretch hurt you?"

Holly shook her head. "I shouldn't have hit him. I
know he's naught but a frail old man, but he said such
ugly things to me. When he began to untruss his
hose . . ." She bowed her head, leaving Austyn to
gaze helplessly down at the tender nape he had cov-
eted for so long. "He's been hiding in the courtyard
each night. Listening . . ." A fresh shudder rocked
her shoulders. Her voice was so soft, 'twas nearly inaudible. "He believed I was naught but a wanton harlot
who would welcome his attentions . . . because I welcomed yours."

Remorse staggered Austyn. Had he been standing, he would have fallen to his knees. 'Twas not his
father who had reduced this proud, beautiful girl to
cringing shame, he realized, but himself.

He tipped her delicate chin up, forcing her to
meet his gaze. "You're right. You shouldn't have hit
him. You should have hit me."

Holly's face was no less lustrous than the candlelight, but as Austyn gazed down at her parted lips, the
tears trembling on her dark lashes, he realized her
physical beauty had never been the true threat to him.
The passing seasons might mist her hair with silver
and etch seams in the satin of her skin, but 'twas the
beauty of her spirit that would never fade. The beauty

of her spirit that had shone through her ridiculous disguise to blind him with its radiance.

'Twas that beauty he had sought to deny by seeking the supple grace of her body only in darkness. That beauty he had feared as he had propped pillows beneath her stomach and guided her face away from him, as if he could pretend she was another woman. Any woman at all. But the shimmering melody of her pleasure, the arch of her slender spine, the milky nape where he had longed to press his kisses, had always belonged to Holly.

His Holly. Generous and stubborn and fiercely protective of those she loved. And brave. Braver than any warrior he had faced on the battlefield. Brave enough to bash a rapacious madman upside the head with a lute. Brave enough to defy her papa when he sought to force her to a fate not of her making. Brave enough to offer her body as a sacrifice to his own selfish lust.

His remorse was but a pale shadow of another emotion, an emotion he had believed buried forever when he had laid his mother to rest in the rich Welsh earth. An emotion both tender and tremulous, yet possessed of the power to topple kingdoms and tempt a man to risk his soul for just one night to savor its priceless wonders.

A blade of irony twisted in Austyn's gut. As long as he'd stubbornly clung to the notion that he could never love Holly, he'd been free to keep her for his wife.

Holly stiffened as her husband's arms slipped away from her. She hugged herself in a vain attempt to duplicate his warmth. "You're going now, aren't you? I made it too bright and you're going away."

But instead of seeking the door, he moved to the table to pour a stream of wine into a silver goblet with leisurely grace. He eyed the glowing tapers with satisfaction, then frowned. "Where are all the flowers? Aren't there supposed to be flowers in here?"

Holly winced with belated guilt. "They were making me sneeze," she lied, "so I had Winifred take them away."

Her bewilderment grew as he returned to the bed, slipping to his knees so that they faced each other on the turbulent sea of sable.

He lifted the goblet. "A toast to my bride."

His solemn expression touched a wistful chord in Holly's heart. Before she could give voice to her yearning, he was pressing the rim of the goblet to her lips. She drank deeply, savoring his honeyed homage as if her thirst for it could never be sated.

He drank in kind, then let the goblet roll from his fingertips to the floor. Cupping her face in his hands with a fierce tenderness that both beguiled and frightened her, he gazed deep into her eyes and said, "I worship thee with my body, Lady Holly of Tewksbury."

Austyn kissed her mouth.

At the first brush of his warm lips, Holly's teeth stopped chattering. Dazed by delight, she thought she might have died and gone to heaven after all. 'Twas a miracle this, a mingling of spirit and flesh more intimate than all the earthy pleasures they'd shared in darkness.

A veil of tears blurred her vision as she realized

what Austyn had just done. He had taken her to wife. Not some petulant stranger garbed in an outlandish disguise and a withered chaplet of bluebells, but she, Holly of Tewksbury, clothed in shredded damask, yet somehow as naked and vulnerable as Eve must have been when God first delivered her to Adam.

The ceremonial reverence of his kiss made her feel as fresh and pure as Eve before the fall. 'Twas as if his chivalrous gesture had restored both her lost innocence and her hope for the future. She wouldn't have been surprised had she glanced in a mirror to discover the ugly marks left by his father's fingers had faded away, washed clean by her husband's regard.

Her cry of joy was muffled by his mouth as she threw her arms around his neck, binding him to her heart as she had longed to do for so long.

Austyn would have been content to remain thus forever—rocking Holly in his arms, sipping tenderly at her lips, pausing only long enough to murmur hoarse regrets and broken endearments into the rumpled silk of her curls.

'Twas she who drew her mouth from his and began to nuzzle the sensitive skin at the base of his throat, she who slipped her hands beneath his tunic to sift her fingers through his chest hair.

'Twas Austyn's turn to gasp when those entrancing hands fluttered over his abdomen to seek the points of his hose.

He caught one of her wrists, bringing it to his lips to soften the impact of its brief bondage. "You don't have to do this," he murmured, unable to resist sampling the spot where the fragile tracing of veins pulsed beneath her skin. " 'Tis not what I want."

The gentle press of her belly against his loins proved him a flagrant liar. "Perhaps 'tis time you thought about what *I* want," she said. "I should warn you that my papa always claimed me a very spoiled girl."

Sensing that she needed to prove her own power after being rendered so powerless by his father's attack, Austyn favored her with a crooked grin. "Then far be it for me to deny you."

He sealed his pledge by guiding her hand back down to his hose and pressing her palm to the throbbing measure of his desire for her. A desire that had stubbornly refused to abate since the first moment he had laid eyes on her in the garden at Tewksbury. As she folded her lithe fingers around him, he threw back his head, gritting his teeth against a groan of ecstasy.

Austyn discovered with that single touch that he could deny her nothing. Not even when she fanned her hands over his shoulders, pushed him to his back, and began to undress him like a child. When he lay naked with only the plush sable to tickle his skin, he reached for her.

She drew away from him, her eyes sparkling like polished gemstones. "You may look, my lord, which is more than you allowed me, but you may not touch."

He cocked his head to the side, entranced by her boldness. "You wouldn't?"

A provocative smile spread across her face. "Watch me."

The extravagant candlelight made watching her an unparalleled pleasure. Sitting up on her knees, she drew both cotte and chemise over her head. As she shook out her tousled curls, Austyn found himself giving fervent thanks that her hair hadn't yet grown enough to shield those magnificent breasts from his gaze. His hands were already aching to caress her, to cherish each succulent swell and hollow of her flesh as he should have on their wedding night. He was only too eager to repay the debt he had incurred when he had robbed her of her virginity with such callousness.

But Holly had in mind a more diabolical reparation.

This time when he reached for her, she cast the velvet loops on the bedposts a glower of mock threat. "Restrain yourself, sir, or I shall be forced to restrain you."

He fell back among the pillows, his empty hands knotting into fists. "Dare I beg you for mercy, my lady?"

She grazed his lips with her own in a tantalizing caress just short of a kiss. "Don't waste your breath."

Austyn had never dreamed revenge could be so sweet. Especially when that revenge was exacted with such exquisite care from his own willing body. Holly nuzzled his fevered flesh, only to return to his mouth after each thrilling foray, as if to gorge herself on a feast she had been denied for too long. When her ripe lips strayed to the taut planes of his abdomen, his hands caught in the coverlet, bunching great wads of it between his fingers.

She glided up his body, the softness of her breasts teasing his chest, and brushed his mouth with a kiss as artless and bewitching as a virgin's. Austyn groaned his delight. But it seemed that reprieve was only a prelude to a more delicious torture. For those same innocent lips drifted back down his quivering body and parted like the petals of a flower to enfold him.

Austyn did not seize the velvet bonds. He seized the bedposts themselves, squeezing until he was sure they would crack off in his hands.

"Sweet God in heaven, have mercy, woman!" he choked out, arching off the bed in an instinctive thrust that doubled both his torment and his pleasure. He survived her generous assault without shattering only by plotting in scrupulous detail his own sensual retaliation.

When Holly once again laid those delectable lips against his own, he kissed her with savage abandon, thrusting deep and hard with his tongue.

He had taught her only too well. She tugged at his lower lip with her teeth before murmuring, "Would you deny me, husband? Shall I beg your pardon and take my leave?"

A lance of pain speared Austyn's heart. At the sudden somberness of his expression, the teasing light fled her face. She made no protest when he enveloped her in his arms and rolled her beneath him, molding her to his body as if God had fashioned them to fit that way.

"Stay," he whispered hoarsely, knowing it was the last time he would ever entreat her to do so.

As Austyn bore her back against the mattress, Holly breathed a sigh of utter delight to be allowed the once forbidden luxury of wrapping her legs around her husband's waist to coax him deep inside of her.

Austyn knew he had much to atone for, but this was both the sweetest and most excruciating penance he had ever endured. He cursed his own stubbornness for denying them the blessing of candlelight through all those dark nights. 'Twas sheer bliss to draw back and watch rapture flicker and dance across Holly's exquisite face. To watch her creamy cheeks flush with rose and her cherubic lips part in half-gasps, half-moans that inflamed him beyond bearing. To flick his gaze downward and witness the primal splendor of her body arching to welcome each of his bold thrusts.

She was a beauty, aye, but for this one last night, she was *his* beauty. His bride. Enchanted by the mask of pleasure mellowing her features, he slipped a single finger into the slick valley above where their bodies were joined and applied a most delicate friction until her gasps escalated to panting whimpers and her eyes fluttered back in her head.

Those first shivery pulsations gloved him in ecstasy. He drove himself hard against the mouth of her womb, muffling his roar of sweet agony against her lips as the love of a lifetime spilled from his loins in a searing cascade.

The pearly pall of dawn hung over the chamber when Holly awoke to find the bed beside her empty. Her spirits plummeted as she believed for one desolate moment that the preceding night had been only a night like all the others, when Austyn took his pleasure, then took his leave with equal disregard.

Biting back a wistful sigh, she reached toward the hollow in the mattress where his big, virile body should have lain. A trace of warmth still lingered in the rumpled sheets. Her sigh escaped in a joyous sob of relief.

Laughing aloud, she rolled into the hollow, tumbling and writhing with childish abandon, then buried her face in the pillow to breathe deep of Austyn's masculine spice.

As she flopped to her back and gazed up at the wooden canopy, the silken threads of memory wove a shimmering tapestry before her eyes. Instead of fleeing her company after that first sweet convulsion of ecstasy, Austyn had pillowed her head on his chest and stroked her damp curls away from her face, hoarsely begging her forgiveness for all the nights he had abandoned her and vowing to make amends.

She'd lost count of the number of times he had sealed his pledge during the fleeting hours between midnight and dawn. Equally precious to her were those moments when sated exhaustion had seized them both and she had snuggled against his warm chest, savoring the delectable sensation of feeling both safe and adored. If she rolled away, he would scowl and mumble, then wrap his arms around her waist and drag her tight against him, bumping his chin on her head. She would smile a small, secret smile to learn he was possessive even in slumber.

Then would come the first sleepy stirrings of his loins against her rump, and the wondrous cycle would begin again.

Holly's stomach gave a petulant growl. She sat up, wondering if Austyn had gone to seek some cheese and sausage so they might sate an appetite of a more mundane nature. The tapers had melted to squat nubs of wax. A faint chill clung to the air. She peeked over the edge of the bed to discover Austyn's hose were

missing, but his tunic still lay in a careless heap where
she had cast it the night before.

On a whim, she rose and tugged the garment over
her head, hugging it against her skin as if she could
absorb Austyn's essence through her pores. The
coarse wool made her tingle. She could not resist a
giddy twirl to admire the way it belled around her
calves.

She stumbled against the table.

And had to grab its edge to keep from falling
when she realized the tower door stood ajar, beckon-
ing her into the misty morning.

CHAPTER 27

Holly crept down the stairs, keeping her back pressed to the wall without realizing it. She picked her way gingerly over the handful of castle dwellers who had chosen to sleep on benches and blankets in the great hall. The main door was cracked ajar, inviting in a sliver of pallid light.

She slipped through the narrow breach and padded into the inner bailey, pausing at its boundary to search the sky as if seeing it for the first time.

The brooding vault delivered no vain promises of sunrise. 'Twas the sort of late summer day more easily mistaken for early autumn—the whisper of a cooling breeze blowing off the river, the skittering surprise of a leaf forsaken too soon, a glimpse of ruby in the verdant emerald crown of an oak. 'Twas a subtle reminder to savor the sighs of summer while they lasted, for winter's icy breath was drawing nigh.

Holly had forgotten how immense the world was. With no walls to enclose it, it sprawled in an unbroken vista of soaring peaks, vast moors, and impenetrable forest, all bound by the pewter thread of the river flowing through drifting veils of mist toward the mighty sea.

Her breath caught in her throat. She was seized by a shiver, a primal fear that such an unbridled wilderness would surely swallow her whole. She longed for the familiar walls of her tower cell, the cozy nest of her blankets. She might have gone creeping back into her hole like some timid mouse frightened by the castle cats had she not seen the man standing at the crest of the bluff overlooking the river.

The sight of her husband standing with one foot braced against a rock, his dark hair sifted by the caress of the wind, would have given her the courage to walk through the flames of hell itself.

Her fear lessened with each step that drew her nearer to him, until finally her invisible fetters fell away, making her limbs feel lighter than air. She wanted to run and skip and frolic across the dewy grass like a newborn colt. But Austyn's curious stillness stopped her. He seemed oblivious to her approach. His eyes were glazed, as if he could see beyond the bend of the mist-shrouded river to the distant sea.

Not wanting to startle him, Holly reached out a

hand and gently rested it against the curve of his lower back.

At the tentative touch, Austyn looked down to find Holly smiling up at him. Holly somehow managing to turn his graceless tunic into the robes of a queen. Holly with bare feet, tangled curls, puffy eyes, and lips still faintly swollen from the voluptuous kisses they'd bestowed and been granted during the night. She'd never looked more beautiful, which made what he was about to do both easier and far more difficult than anything he'd done before.

Holly knew the instant she saw the expression on Austyn's face that something was wrong. As her smile faded, he drew her into his arms and kissed her softly. There was something so wistful, so inexplicably sad, about that kiss, that instead of allaying her apprehension, it only worsened it.

He caressed her shoulders with wrenching gentleness. "I'm sending you home."

She took a step away from him, as if distance would provide a shield against further blows. "I *am* home."

"But you're not safe. You'll never be safe at Caer Gavenmore." Anguish flickered across his face as he cupped her throat, gently fitting his fingertips to the faint necklace of bruises gifted to her by his father's hands. "What happened last night only proved that."

"I'm not afraid of your father. You're strong enough to protect me from him."

Austyn's shell of calm determination shattered. "But who will protect you from me!"

Holly flattened her palms against the beguiling warmth of his chest and gazed up into his haunted face, praying her eyes reflected the tenderness and trust brimming from her heart. "I'm not afraid of you either."

"Then you're a merry fool!" A tiny crack shot through Holly's heart as he caught her wrists and pushed her hands away from him as he had done so many times before. Sinking to a sitting position on the rock, he drove his fingers through his hair. "Have I not already proved that my love is capable of bringing you naught but disaster and death? Oh, 'twould start out innocently enough. You'd get a speck of ash in your eye from sitting too near the hearth and I'd accuse you of winking at Carey. The next thing you know," he drew a finger across his throat, "you'd both be lying dead on the flagstones and I'd be left to finish my supper alone."

Holly didn't know whether to laugh or cry. Only yesterday she had planned to entreat Austyn to return her to Tewksbury this very morn if he could not love her, and now he was determined to send her away because he did.

He buried his head in his hands. "How am I to make you understand? This jealousy is like a crippling sickness that flows through my veins. It poisons everything I touch and twists love into something monstrous and hurtful." He lifted his dark-lashed eyes, letting her see for the first time the full extent of his despair. His voice lowered to a defeated whisper. "I can't even look at you without thinking about losing you."

A tremulous sob of laughter escaped her. "But you won't lose me if you grant me leave to stay here by your side. I would never willingly abandon you."

She knelt beside him, resting a hand on his knee. "To dare to love is to court hazard, is it not? 'Tis a risk I'm more than willing to take."

He cast the grave behind them a dark look. "My mother took such a risk and it cost her her life. I'll not imperil you so."

Holly was slowly coming to fear that there would be no swaying him. She had fought so hard, but it seemed her heart's blood had all been spilled for naught. The realization made her both furious and afraid. "So what you're truly trying to say is that no matter how much you claim to love me, you could never find me worthy of your trust."

Frustration sharpened his voice. " 'Tis not you I find lacking, but myself."

She curled her lips in a haughty sneer that would have done Nathanael proud. "And if this dreaded 'Curse of the Gavenmores' turns out to be naught but a lot of superstitious gibberish?"

Austyn sighed. "It matters naught if the curse is true, so long as I believe it to be."

Holly could not dispute his twisted reasoning. She swallowed her pride, bowed her head, and whispered, "You could keep me locked in the tower. If 'tis the only way . . ."

He tilted her chin up with one knuckle, his eyes smoldering with that same frosty fire that had first drawn her into his arms. "I'd wrap myself in chains and cast myself into the deepest dungeon in hell before I would cage you again."

Holly rose stiffly to her feet, savoring the fleeting sensation of towering over him. "Then I shall cage myself. If you want me removed from your household, sir, I suggest you order Carey to fetch the battering ram and catapult. For I'll not set one dainty foot outside that tower until you cease this nonsense." She whirled around and began to march toward the castle. "If this Rhiannon wants you so badly, she's going to have to fight me. The witch crosses my path and I'll pluck off her little faerie wings and give her a taste of 'mortal doom.' "

"If you won't go to save your own soul, then go to save mine."

Austyn's voice tolled in her ears like a death knell. Holly froze, allowing herself the brief luxury of hating him. Hating him for knowing her so well. For issuing the one challenge she did not have the armor or the weapons to resist. He could have cut her no more deeply had he slapped her across the face with his steel gauntlet.

She spun around to find him standing, his feet braced for battle. Her impotence made her want to lash out, to hurt him as he was hurting her. "If you were going to request such a noble sacrifice of me, perhaps you should not have risked getting me with child. What if you're sending me back to my father with the Gavenmore heir in my womb?"

Austyn's jaw clenched as he inclined his head. Whether at being reminded of the tender communion their bodies had shared or at the thought of bidding farewell to his unborn child, Holly could not say.

"If you should bear a male child, then keep it as far away from me as possible. I've naught to offer him but a birthright of damnation."

Holly set her chin defiantly and dashed a tear from her cheek. "I know 'tis not uncommon for a hus-

band and wife to reside in separate households, but
what if I am not content with this mock marriage you
propose? What if I choose to offer my hand to another?"

She knew it to be the cruelest blow she could
have dealt him. Austyn's reply when it came was soft
and edged with bitter resignation. "If you choose to
remarry, I shall lie before both God and king to see
that you're granted an annulment. There's no reason
you should spend the rest of your life paying for my
folly." He lifted his eyes to her face. "But you are, and
always will be, the wife of my heart."

'Twas as if his vow split her heart asunder. Holly
felt her face crumple into a mask of pain. "The only
folly I ever committed, sir, was loving you!"

With that impassioned cry, she turned and ran
blindly toward the castle, seeking the refuge of the
tower for the last time.

The cracked oval of the hand mirror reflected a flawless oval face. The dark brows were lightly winged,
the arch of the cheekbones high and pure enough to
survive for decades without betraying a trace of wear.
Only the violet eyes betrayed the hollow soul of the
mirror's owner.

Holly rouged her pursed lips to an inviting pink,
then ran her tongue over them, thinking absently that
rouge tasted much more pleasant than ashes. She adjusted the ruby at her throat and slipped a gold fillet
over her curls. Let her husband accuse her of thievery
if he dared! The woman who had once owned these
gems and trinkets bore more kinship to her than to

him. If he protested, she would simply claim them as payment for pleasures rendered.

Ruthlessly stamping down an urge to steal a last wistful glance at the rumpled bed, she drew a thin line of kohl beneath each eye to enhance their feverish glitter. *You mustn't cry anymore,* she chided herself sternly, *lest it smear and streak down your cheeks like a mummer's face paint.*

'Twas just as well Austyn was sending her away, she thought, touching the tip of her pinkie to the fragile depressions beneath her eyes. Another sennight in his contentious company would have doubtlessly worn irreversible creases into her skin. No woman could be expected to endure such dizzying flights of joy and despair without displaying the scars of it. And she hadn't spent all of those years avoiding the sun and anointing her skin with sheep fat just to end up as wizened as Elspeth.

As if the unkind thought had invoked her, a quavery voice behind Holly said, "My lady, Master Carey has prepared the horses."

Holly laid aside the mirror and swept her ermine-trimmed mantle in a graceful bell as she rose from the stool.

Elspeth could not contain a gasp. She had been present at Holly's birth and witnessed the cream-and-pink miracle that had slipped effortlessly from her mother's body with a perfectly rounded head and tiny, dark eyelashes as fine as feathers. She had gripped Holly's chubby little hand on her third birthday when a visiting Arabian prince had demanded the honor of her hand in marriage. The twelve-year-old lad had wept and stormed when her papa had refused, but

Holly had simply tossed her silky, black curls in disdain and toddled off to dig for worms in the garden.

Elspeth had studied Holly's beauty in all of its guises, but she'd never seen her mistress look quite so breathtaking. Or so brittle.

'Twas as if she were a princess sculpted from ice. The notion made Elspeth afraid for her. Ice might be hard, but 'twas also fragile—vulnerable to heat and apt to shatter under pressure.

"Would you please bear my train, Elspeth?" Holly asked, drawing on a pair of miniver-lined gloves. "I should so hate for it to get dusty in this tomb."

As Elspeth dutifully fell into step behind her, Holly set her shoulders to a haughty angle. She refused to crawl away from Gavenmore with her train between her legs. Her heart might be shattered, but she was determined to leave with her pride intact. Let her beauty be a slap in the face to Austyn and all of his faithless kinfolk, dead or alive!

Both the great hall and inner bailey were crowded with onlookers. A gasp went up at her appearance. Some, like Winifred, were openly weeping. Others did not bother to hide their relief. Perhaps now their precious master would be safe from the destructive wiles of comely women, Holly thought bitterly. She held her head high, long accustomed to the impolite stares of those less lovely than she.

Carey waited with the restless horses—a piebald gelding, a small bay, and a dainty gray palfrey perfectly suited to Holly's height. Carey's face was somber. 'Twas impossible to miss the reproachful look he cast the hill.

From the corner of her eye, Holly saw Austyn—a

shadow garbed in black standing beside his mother's grave. His very presence there was a silent testament to the righteousness of what he was doing.

Without so much as a disdainful glance in his direction, Holly accepted Carey's hand and mounted the palfrey sidesaddle, spreading her skirts in a pretty fan over the beast's flanks.

As Elspeth settled herself on the bay, Carey looked as if he would have desperately liked to say something, but Holly flared her nostrils with such aristocratic scorn that he did not dare.

She folded her gloved hands over the reins and announced with the aplomb of a young queen, "We may proceed."

Proceed they did, past the gawking spectators, past the crooked gatehouse, past the rubble of the abandoned curtain wall. Past the point on the road where one could look back and entertain the childish illusion that Caer Gavenmore was a celestial palace perched on a bed of clouds.

Holly no longer believed in castles in the clouds, nor in the princes who inhabited them. Under the guise of smoothing a rebellious curl, she lifted the back of her hand to her eye, leaving a single smear of kohl on the pristine silk of her glove.

ChAPTER 28

Holly huddled deeper into her mantle, wondering how it was possible that the world had succumbed to winter in August, forsaking both the indolent pleasures of summer and the crisp delights of autumn. A pall of gloom hung over the forest. The brisk wind took spiteful glee in rattling the leaves and hurling gusts of cold drizzle into her face.

They'd already wasted a day and a half of their journey crouched beneath a shelter of pine boughs, watching the rain unfurl in a dense gray curtain. They might have spent another interminable day doing the same had Carey not feared they would run low on provisions. So they had emerged from their sodden nest and plodded on toward Tewksbury, their spirits as glum as the weather.

Even Elspeth seemed to have lost her gift for chatter. After catching her rubbing her gnarled knuckles as if the dampness pained them, Holly had ignored the nurse's croaked protests and insisted she don the fur-lined gloves that had belonged to Austyn's grandmother.

Holly could no longer feel her own fingers on the reins. She only wished the hollow ache in her chest would subside to numbness. After years of fearing she was naught but a pretty shell, she had finally discovered she possessed a heart as vital and vulnerable as any other woman's only to have it ripped out by the roots.

'Twas just as well, she supposed. She would have no further need of it. It seemed she was destined to spend her life being worshipped from afar, never again to know the loving intimacy of her husband's touch.

You are, and always will be, the wife of my heart.

Austyn's pledge echoed through her mind in a bittersweet refrain. He had probably believed the words when he spoke them, but she was certain a few months of solitude would tarnish his noble intentions. Under the benevolent guise of setting her free, he would seek that annulment they'd discussed and woo some mild-tempered maiden with calf-brown eyes and a face like a horse to his marriage bed. Holly would bump into them at a tournament or Mayday celebration, smile graciously to hide her pain, and compliment the herd of coltish children frisking about their heels.

One of her hands fluttered to her abdomen, giving

silent testament to a hope she'd barely dared to acknowledge. Austyn had made it painfully clear that he had little interest in any child she might bear him, but she could not help but wonder if his resolve might not soften if she presented him with a squirming son. A precious little man-child with dark locks and the hint of a mischievous dimple in one chubby cheek. The dull ache in her chest sharpened to yearning anguish.

"Stop torturing yourself," she muttered beneath her breath, earning an uneasy look from both Elspeth and Carey.

The rain had nearly ceased. A canopy of branches spanned the narrow path, muting the feeble daylight to premature dusk. Holly's nape prickled. She glanced over her shoulder, hard pressed to shake off the sensation of malevolent eyes peering at them from the tangled bracken.

She swallowed hard to calm her nerves, remembering what a fool she'd made of herself when she'd succumbed to similar fancies on the journey to Gavenmore. This time there would be no Austyn to draw her into his lap and dry her tears. No Austyn to hoist her up on his mount and offer the comforting expanse of his back as a pillow.

She was not the only one affected by the sinister atmosphere of the forest. Carey's hand strayed to his shoulder to check the readiness of his bow. Elspeth lowered the hood of her cloak, her gaze darting from tree to tree. They all breathed a sigh of relief when the tunnel of foliage opened into a mist-shrouded glade.

Holly's sigh surged to a cry of astonishment as she saw a cowled figure standing at the edge of the clearing. Ignoring Carey's shout of warning, she threw herself off the palfrey and ran to meet him.

" 'Tis only Nate!" she called to Carey, smoothing away the priest's hood to reveal his familiar features.

Carey settled back on his mount, his face darkening with a scowl that would have done his master proud.

"Thank God you're well!" Nathanael exclaimed, enveloping her in a less than brotherly embrace.

Holly drew away from him, rather discomfited by the intimacy. "Of course, I'm well. But what are you doing out here in the middle of nowhere? Why aren't you at Tewksbury?"

Hectic patches of color brightened Nathanael's cheeks. "I was coming to rescue you from that tyrant." He shuddered. "You can't begin to imagine the dreadful fates I've envisioned you suffering at his hands."

Holly might have defended her husband, but she feared her own fair coloring would betray the variety of delicious torments she had suffered at Austyn's accomplished hands. She knew Nathanael would never believe her anyway. His pious fervor had been stirred into a frenzy by the prospect of a quest. In his estimation, a princess locked in a tower by a wicked ogre held no less allure than the search for the Holy Grail.

"How have you come so far? Is my father with you?" She searched the woods behind him, not realizing until that moment how much she longed to cast herself on her papa's neck and weep out her grief.

"We thought it best not to alarm your father unduly. Once we'd laid siege to Gavenmore and liberated you from the clutches of that villain, we were planning to—"

"We?" Holly interrupted, his smug expression sending a skitter of dread down her spine.

They slithered from the rustling undergrowth like a nest of vipers. Before Carey could slot arrow to bow, the tip of a rusty sword was pressed to his Adam's apple. Elspeth's cry of alarm was cut off mid-croak by the filthy hand clamped over her mouth. Between one breath and the next, Holly and her party were surrounded by a dozen men.

Holly had heard tales of these men before. They'd been spotted skulking at the borders of her father's land more than once. They were infamous for terrorizing their master's own villeins—robbing them of their pathetic earnings, beating old men and dragging their virgin daughters into the forest for a bit of brutal sport. They were slovenly and vicious, their eyes narrowed by an inbred appetite for depravity that made them seem more beast than human.

But somehow the man who stepped out from behind their ranks—his ebony surcoat and hose immaculate, every hair slicked back into flawless alignment, a genial smile pasted on his handsome features—made them look no more menacing than a band of bumbling pages.

"If 'tis not the damsel in distress herself! How very courteous of you to spare us the bother of rescuing you. I do find sieges to be most tiresome."

Holly had been clutching Nathanael's sleeve without realizing it. She pried her fingers loose, reluctant to exhibit any sign of weakness before this man. "Nathanael, what is *he* doing here?"

Nate's patronizing smile faltered. "Why, he saved my life. I lost my way in the wilderness. Were it not for the baron's kindness and hospitality, I might have perished."

Eugene de Legget snorted with contempt. "We found him wandering in circles, half-dazed with hunger and thirst, mumbling a rather tedious string of mea culpas beneath his breath. He was only a few feet from your father's border at the time."

"You never told me that," Nathanael said indignantly. "I thought I was still in Wales."

"Of course I told you. You were simply too delirious to remember." Eugene turned his oily charm on Holly. She was surprised he didn't ooze right out of his surcoat. "Once the good brother informed us of your grave predicament, we were only too willing to offer our assistance. I must confess you don't seem much the worse for wear." He reached out to finger a curl. "I like it. 'Tis rather . . . boyish."

His lips caressed the word, shedding an entirely new light on his penchant for maidens who'd yet to celebrate their thirteenth birthdays. Suppressing a shudder, Holly ducked out from beneath his hand. He shook his head at her rudeness.

She grabbed the front of Nathanael's robes. "Do these ruffians look capable of conducting a siege to you? I see no crossbows or battering rams. And where are the scaling ladders? The catapults? The archers?"

Nathanael blinked like a man reluctant to wake up from a pleasant dream for fear of discovering it had been a nightmare all along. "I—I do not know. I just assumed the baron knew what he was about. He promised we would save you."

"Aye, most likely by slipping into Gavenmore by

night and slitting the throats of its helpless inhabitants. How could you be so impossibly naive?"

Eugene *tsked* beneath his breath. "Don't be so hard on him, Holly. I found his innocence to be rather touching."

She faced de Legget, lowering herself to address him directly for the first time. "Then make good on your vow, my lord. Escort me to my father at once."

" 'Twould be my most humble pleasure, my lady."

The tension seeped from Holly's shoulders. Perhaps she had overestimated de Legget's villainy after all.

His lips puckered in an apologetic moue. "But I'm afraid 'twill be quite impossible." He reached to his braided belt and unsheathed a small silver dagger.

Holly took an instinctive step away from Nathanael, then another. As de Legget stalked her, two of his rogues seized the priest by the arms.

He squirmed in protest. "I say, sirs, unhand me this minute!"

Holly's back came up against a tree. Eugene twirled the knife in his deft fingers.

"If you harm a hair on her head . . ." Carey snarled.

Elspeth whimpered, her eyes bulging with terror.

Only Holly was silent, determined to stare Eugene down with all the scorn at her disposal. She forced herself not to recoil, not even when he pressed his hot mouth against her ear and whispered, "You won't be quite so haughty when I'm through with you, my lady, for I have every intention of bringing you to your knees. One way or another."

The dagger's blade grazed her cheek. From the corner of her eye, she saw Carey start to struggle. Saw the sword at his throat notch away a sliver of flesh, sending a rivulet of blood trickling into the neck of his tunic.

"You might bring me to my knees," she hissed. "But I won't be reduced to slithering on my belly as you do."

She bit back a cry of pain as he seized her hair, hacking away a single curl with icy detachment. Drawing a folded parchment from the velvet purse dangling from his belt, he sealed the curl inside.

"This should do to ensure the effectiveness of my demands. Were I not so chivalrous, I would throw in your tongue as well. I'm sure your husband has endured enough of its nagging to recognize it."

Holly swallowed her retort, for once in her life choosing discretion over valor. She almost wished she hadn't when one of his henchman seized her around the waist, crushing the breath from her with a burly forearm. She knew she really ought to be grateful she couldn't breathe. The toothless fellow smelled nearly as bad as he looked.

"Bring the horses," de Legget commanded. Two of his cohorts slunk off through the trees.

"I believed in you, sir," Nathanael said softly, looking as bewildered as a child by his rapid change of fortune.

Eugene slanted him a glance, as if just remembering his existence. Holly cared nothing for the look. A knot of foreboding tightened in her chest. As de Legget approached the priest, the dagger shimmering like quicksilver in his fluid hand, she bucked and clawed in a futile attempt to escape the giant.

The baron's heartfelt sigh would have melted winter frost. " 'Tis the most tragic failing of we mortals, don't you think, brother? That we so consistently disappoint each other. But you still have faith in your God, do you not?"

Nathanael nodded, his dark eyes somber. "Aye."

Eugene's tender smile spread. "Then give Him my regards." Grunting in satisfaction, he rammed the dagger into Nathanael's breast.

A scream of anguish ripped from Holly's throat. Carey went down beneath a sea of flailing arms and legs. The hand clamped over Elspeth's mouth could no longer muffle her squeals of horror.

As Nathanael collapsed, Holly managed to shake off her captor and stumble forward.

Even as a damning stain blossomed on the front of his robe, he stretched out a hand toward her. "Forgive me," he whispered, his eyes going so hazy and unfocused she could not have said if he entreated her or God. "Please forgive me."

Holly's fingertips grazed his; Eugene's henchman caught her around the waist, jerking her out of his reach. She wailed her frustration as Nathanael's eyes drifted shut and he rolled to his back.

Eugene reached down, coolly withdrew the dagger, and wiped the blade on the parchment still in his hand. "May God rest his pathetic soul."

Ignoring Holly's murderous glare, Eugene strolled over to where Carey lay pinned to the ground by four hulking men, his lower lip puffed to twice its normal size and one of his eyes already swollen shut.

"Do try not to kill him or break his legs." Eugene tucked the parchment into the waistband of Carey's hose. "Either eventuality would necessitate finding a new messenger and I really haven't the patience."

As Eugene grabbed Holly's elbow and jerked her toward the waiting horses, she winced at the sickening thud of fists on flesh and the sound of Carey's helpless grunts.

"You bastard," she spat, blinded by a hot torrent of tears as she stumbled past Nathanael's still form.

His fingers dug into her tender flesh. "Remind me to teach you to address me with more courtesy when I'm your husband."

"I already have a husband!"

His cold smile sent a shaft of pure terror through her soul. "Not for long, my lady. Not for long."

Holly soon learned that there were more grueling ways to travel than perched sidesaddle on a palfrey in the rain. Such as being trussed hands and feet and heaved like a sack of grain over the back of a monstrous destrier. Each thunderclap of a hoofbeat jarred her spine and set her teeth to rattling like dice. Cold gobbets of mud spattered her face. She shivered to imagine the effects of such torture on Elspeth's frail bones.

As the hours passed, her thoughts churned in rhythm to the horse's strides, stirring up a maddening maelstrom of grief and regret. If only her love had been strong enough to win Austyn's trust. If only she hadn't baited Eugene. If only she'd never enlisted Nathanael's help in her mad scheme. He might be safe at

Tewksbury this very moment, nagging the servants about their lack of piety and chiding her papa for hawking when he should have been attending Mass. A rush of warm tears blurred the flailing hooves.

She sought to dry her eyes by offering up a prayer for Nathanael's poor unshriven soul. But each time she closed them, 'twas not Nathanael's pallid face she saw, but Austyn's—Austyn sprawled in a puddle of his own blood, his dark lashes feathered against his cheeks. Austyn the hapless victim of another man's obsession. Was Eugene's treachery to be the fulfillment of the dreaded Gavenmore curse? Was her beauty truly to be her husband's doom?

Holly had no more time to ponder before her horse was snapped to a halt and she was dragged off its back by the clumsy paws of Eugene's personal giant. As he heaved her over his beefy shoulder, she caught a chilling glimpse of their destination.

She should have known Eugene would be too cunning to risk taking her to his own castle, where word of her captivity might spread to her papa's ears. He had chosen for his den a crumbling ruin of a watchtower so shrouded with ivy that from a distance 'twould be nearly indistinguishable from the surrounding trees. Here in this isolated glade, there would be no curious villeins, no prying servants, no chattering pages or squires to spread gossip or intervene in whatever diabolical revenge he had planned. Here she and Austyn would be completely at the mercy of de Legget and his henchmen.

Holly shuddered.

She knew Nathanael would have frowned upon appealing to the capricious mercies of a pagan faerie, but as she bounced along over the colossal shoulder, she pressed her eyes shut and whispered fiercely, "Please, Rhiannon, you may be a faerie, but if you've a woman's heart, keep him far, far away from this place."

CHAPTER 29

Sir Austyn of Gavenmore was a haunted man. He stood on the battlements of his ancestral home, blinking rain from his eyes to gaze toward the eastern horizon. His crimson surcoat was plastered to his skin. The frivolous border of ivy embroidered along its back weighted his shoulders like fetters of iron.

Rhiannon's revenge was naught but a mild scolding compared with his wife's retribution. The faerie queen's shade could only bedevil one place at a time. Holly's ghost was everywhere.

It waddled along the riverbank, strewing marigolds in his path. It patted anemones into place around his mother's grave, glancing up at him to reveal sparkling violet eyes and an impish nose smudged with dirt. He passed it on the stairs, lugging a tub of scarlet poppies up to the battlements.

Austyn reached out and brushed a raindrop from the withered petals of one of those poppies.

The first manifestation had occurred only hours after Carey had escorted Holly from the castle. Austyn had been in the solar with Winifred and Emrys, packing away his plans for completing the castle and calculating how much of Holly's dowry had already been spent on ordering slate and sandstone. He intended to return every penny to the earl as soon as he could recover it.

'Twould be only a matter of weeks, Austyn supposed, rolling a scroll into a neat tube with methodical hands, before the king's tax collectors would be pounding at the door, threatening to seize the castle and its meager lands if they could not pay. The prospect no longer distressed him as it once had. Without Holly, the keep was naught but an empty shell. A tomb for his dreams.

Ignoring Winifred's worried glance, he rested his aching brow in his hands. A discordant jangling drifted to his ears. He lifted his head, a crazy hope sputtering to life in his heart.

"Did you hear that?" he inquired of Emrys.

"Hear what, sir?"

Shoving his way past his puzzled steward, Austyn flew from the solar. He skidded to a halt in the south corridor, fully expecting to find the iron candelabrum bobbing up and down on its tarnished chains.

The candelabrum hung silent and still, its rusty music playing only in his head.

Austyn slid down the wall to a sitting position. 'Twas of little import that Holly's ghost had made itself invisible. He could still hear the echo of her merry laughter.

He crouched in that darkened corridor until nightfall, finally rising only to have his dazed steps carry him to the door of the north tower. When he realized where he was, he turned and resolutely sought the barren confines of his own bed. After tossing and thrashing for hours, he shot bolt upright from a fitful nightmare to the angelic strains of his wife's singing.

He bounded from the bed and pelted up the winding stairs. But when he threw open the door of the tower, hollow silence greeted him. Surrendering any pretense of sleep, Austyn spent the remainder of the night in the window seat, gazing at the bed and remembering how Holly had so generously shared both it and her warm, loving body with him. When Winnie discovered him there the following morning, he refused to allow her to tidy the chamber, fearing her efforts might banish the scent of myrrh that still clung to the rumpled sheets.

He understood why his grandfather had forbidden anyone to disturb the tower after his grandmother died. 'Twas as if the man never relinquished his hope that the woman who had once inhabited it might someday return.

Austyn's final glimpse of Holly had assured him that his hopes were no less vain than his grandfather's. He would never forget the proud set of her shoulders, the haughty cast of her features, the wounded look in her beautiful eyes. He had sent her away to protect her, yet she seemed to believe he had broken faith with her in some irredeemable manner.

After his fourth night in the window seat, Austyn decided 'twould be best to have Emrys brick up the tower door to ensure that never again would any Gavenmore man be tempted to punish a woman for his own sins. 'Twas only then that he remembered there would be no more Gavenmore men after him. The curse had not only robbed him of his wife, but of his children as well.

Austyn's hands clenched on the rain-slicked parapet as he imagined what magnificent sons Holly would have given him.

He had yet to give the order to seal the tower, for he knew that he would be walling up his heart as well, this time forever. Then there would be nothing left for him to do but spend the remainder of his days wandering the castle in search of his wife's ghost and rattling his own invisible chains.

Shaking the rain from his hair, Austyn turned away from the parapet, driven by loneliness to seek the one man who shared his exile.

Austyn slid his knight across the chessboard, then watched his father's pawn pick it off, feeling nary a sting of regret. Rhys had been almost placid since his attack on Holly. 'Twas as if the ugly spell of violence had exorcised some dark demon from his soul. Compassion had tempered Austyn's first urge to cast him into the dungeon. Instead, he had committed him to Emrys's reliable care, determined that his father would never again harm another woman.

Emrys poked at the fire he had built to ward off the damp while Winifred plucked and cleaned a chicken with efficient hands, striving to conceal her fretful glances at the door of the great hall, but failing miserably. Austyn's own concern was mounting. Carey should have returned more than two days ago. Perhaps he had chosen to linger at Tewksbury until the rain cleared, Austyn told himself. He refused to humor his own impulse to glance at the door between every move, not wanting to reveal his pathetic eagerness to hear news of Holly.

His father's muteness suited his own brooding temper so well that he flinched with surprise when Rhys snapped, "Check."

Stealing a glance at the door from beneath his lashes, Austyn slid his king out of the path of his father's bishop, carelessly leaving his queen unguarded.

Rhys captured her, cornering Austyn's king to cement his victory. "Checkmate."

"It seems the best man won," Austyn said, forcing a half-hearted smile as he began to rearrange the pieces for another game.

"I think we both know that's not true, son."

Austyn jerked his head up. His father's blue eyes were as clear as Austyn had seen them in years. The sight pained him. Reminded him of a time when his father had been his only hero. A time when they'd all been happy.

"I was in the courtyard," Rhys said softly.

Austyn lined up his pawns in a precise row, struggling to keep the anger from his tone. "Holly told me. 'Twas rather boorish of you, don't you think? Eavesdropping on your own son and his"—he clenched his teeth against a pang of anguish—"bride."

Rhys shook his head. "Not then. The night my mother jumped."

Austyn's hands stilled. This time when he met his father's gaze, he found he could not look away.

"I hadn't seen her since I was a small boy," Rhys said, "so I slipped up to the tower to visit her. I was the one who told her that Father was with his doxy. She started to cry. She hugged me very tightly and told me I was a good lad and she loved me with all of her heart. Then she sent me away." He stared at the chesspiece in his hand. "Perhaps if I had stayed . . . if I hadn't told her about Father's woman . . ."

Austyn was surprised to learn his barren heart still had any forgiveness to offer. He held up one of the smallest chessmen. " 'Twas never your fault. You were naught but a pawn in your father's game of jealousy and revenge."

"She loved me, you know. She was a loyal and devoted wife."

Austyn fought to keep his own bitterness at bay. " 'Tis fortunate you can remember your mother with such charity."

Rhys blinked at him. "Not my mother. *Your* mother. Gwyneth."

Austyn was baffled. 'Twas the first time he had heard his father speak well of his mother since her death. Perhaps Rhys had retreated to the past, to the golden days of summer before that fateful autumn had shattered their lives.

Rhys caressed the carved queen with his thumb,

his hand oddly steady. "She begged me not to send her."

Austyn frowned. "Send her where?"

His father gently placed the white queen on the square next to the black king. "Edward did not come to Gavenmore to bestow his blessing on the new castle. He came to inform me that he was withdrawing his support. That he'd decided the Welsh were a savage and ungrateful lot and their petty rebellions had convinced him his castle strongholds were naught but beautiful follies. Oh, he clucked his regret and praised me for my loyalty, but he refused to relent. Not even when I begged . . ."

Austyn became aware that Emrys had ceased stirring the fire. Winifred was gaping at his father, a bloody chicken bone clutched in one hand.

"I believed that I might yet sway him. Appeal to his sense of honor. When I saw how he fancied Gwyneth—"

Austyn came to his feet, overturning the chessboard. He heard the pieces scatter across the flagstones through the dull roaring in his ears. "You sent her? You sent your own wife to lay with another man?"

Tears began to trickle down Rhys's papery cheeks, but his voice was still the voice of a man, not the whine of a petulant child. "She cried so prettily and pleaded with me not to ask such a thing of her. I told her that if she truly loved me, she'd be eager to make such a small sacrifice for our common good. Then the next morning when Edward bade me a regretful farewell and I realized it had all been for naught . . ."

The roaring in Austyn's ears reached his lips. He snatched his father up by the shoulders, shaking him like a rag doll. "You murdered her for doing your bidding? You strangled her for sacrificing her virtue to further your own greedy ambitions?"

Through a crimson haze of rage, Austyn heard Winifred's shrill pleas, felt Emrys tugging frantically at his arm, but his eyes were locked with his father's in a mortal battle of wills. What Austyn saw in those pale blue orbs was not fear, but grim satisfaction. Rhys wanted his own son to kill him. He wanted his wife's death avenged, but lacked the courage to do it himself. A ponderous burden rolled off of Austyn's shoulders as he realized the sins of the father were no longer his own to bear.

His hands slowly unclenched. Rhys crumpled into the chair.

Austyn gazed down at his bowed head with genuine pity. "Sorry, old man. I'll not send you to hell. 'Tis a far greater punishment that you should live with what you've done."

Shaking off Emrys's hand, Austyn squared his shoulders and started for the stairs, eager to escape the hall and all of its haunts.

"And can you live with what you've done?"

His father's voice rang with an authority that froze Austyn in his tracks. Time swept backward. He was nine years old again, bracing himself to receive a scolding for carving his name into the wet mortar of the moat. He spun around, half expecting to find his father straddling the chair, his face flushed with the vigor of youth.

The old man had cocked his head to the side and was watching him like a bright-eyed bird. "You were only too eager to believe the worst of your mother."

"I was a child! I thought that she'd abandoned us!"

Holly's ghost tapped him on the shoulder. *Abandoned you? I think not, sir, for 'tis you who have abandoned her.*

Austyn whirled on Winifred, eliciting a gasp of alarm and a drifting blizzard of chicken feathers. "Did you hear that?"

"N-n-nay, sir. I heard nothing."

"Nor did I." Emrys exchanged a nervous glance with his wife.

His father laughed, a dry rasp that grated on Austyn's raw nerves. He was beginning to wish he'd killed the old rogue when he'd had the chance.

"Don't mock me," Austyn snapped. " 'Twas naught but that infernal witch Rhiannon. Her sole delight is in plaguing me witless."

His father nodded knowingly. "She used to badger me as well until I realized her taunts were only the echo of my conscience."

"I never knew you had one."

Austyn's sarcasm failed to ruffle Rhys. "Aye, 'twas my conscience that tortured me because I knew in my heart that your mother didn't betray me. I betrayed her. Nor did my mother disgrace the Gavenmore name. 'Twas your grandfather who shamed us all by imprisoning an innocent woman and depriving her of her only son while he committed adultery with a castle whore. Old Caradawg's young bride was probably equally blameless, burned at the stake because of her husband's wretched lack of faith in her fealty."

Holly's ghost twirled a curl around a graceful finger with saucy defiance. *If a man refuses to trust a woman he claims to love, then tell me, husband, who between them is the faithless one?*

"Cease your prattling, woman!" Austyn thundered, raking a hand through his hair.

Winifred sidled toward the kitchen, as if his sudden spell of madness might be infectious.

His father was right about one thing, he thought wildly. He ought to be steeped in shame for all the dreadful things he'd believed about his mother. But at the edge of his remorse danced a frantic hope.

"The curse . . ." he whispered.

"Rubbish, lad!" his father barked. " 'Twas never a curse, but a prophecy destined to fulfill itself by those superstitious enough to believe in it. Beauty never brought ruin to the Gavenmore men. The Gavenmore men brought ruin upon themselves and the women fool enough to love them."

I would never willingly abandon you, Holly whispered, her breath warm and sweet in his ear.

Austyn braced his hands on the table, feeling curiously light-headed. 'Twas of little import if the others heard her, for the truth rang in his heart like the tolling of a cathedral bell. 'Twas not Holly who had betrayed him, but he who had betrayed her by having more faith in an ancient curse than in the power of their love. If she sought solace in the arms of another man, 'twould be only because he had driven her to do so by his lack of trust.

Holly's ghost threw back its head and sang—a trilling hymn of joy and hope for the morrow.

With her song still chiming in his ears, Austyn snatched up a cloak and started across the hall.

Before he could reach the door, it flew open. He

flinched as a gust of wind and rain struck him full in the face. A man staggered into the hall, but had it not been for Winifred's agonized cry, Austyn might not have recognized him.

Carey's eyes were feverish slits in puffs of bruised flesh. His right cheekbone was split, his left arm hanging at an impossibly awkward angle. His other arm clutched his ribs through the tattered strips of soaked wool that had once been his tunic.

Austyn caught him before he could fall. "My God, man, what happened?"

He struggled to speak through his swollen lips, but the words were garbled. Grunting his frustration, he fumbled at the waistband of his hose with his intact arm, withdrawing a folded scrap of paper. Austyn mastered his panic long enough to entrust Carey to his parents' waiting arms, then tore open the battered parchment.

'Twas not the message or map outlined in the effeminate scrawl that made him want to howl with fear, nor even the ominous copper smudge staining the paper. 'Twas the solitary sable curl that coiled around Austyn's finger in velvety reproach.

CHAPTER 30

Holly paced her tower cell in crisp, restless strides.

Instead of a sumptuous four-poster with hangings of pleated silk, a moth-eaten blanket lay crumpled beneath the narrow window. In lieu of a cloth-lined tub, a basin of brackish water, intended for bathing *and* drinking, sat on the barren timber floor. On the crumbling hearth, a scrawny mouse nibbled at the chunk of stale brown bread that had served as Holly's breakfast and lunch and was to have been her supper as well. Her captor had denied her even the solace of Elspeth's company, whisking away the whimpering nurse immediately upon their arrival at his lair.

As a pale moon rose in the drab sky, her desperate gaze kept straying to the pair of rusty manacles affixed by iron plates to the wall opposite the window. She was thankful Eugene had not restrained her, but the expectant emptiness of those fetters drenched her in dread. She would have almost preferred they contain the skeletal remains of de Legget's last unfortunate prisoner.

Weary of pacing, she knelt and scraped at a patch of loose mortar she'd discovered behind the right manacle, paying no heed to the damage she was doing to fingernails that had yet to recover from her original assault against them.

"I do so hope you're enjoying your accommodations, my lady."

Holly snapped to her feet at the elegant drawl. Eugene was leaning against the doorframe, an amiable smile softening his perpetual sneer.

"From the priest's blithering," he said, "I determined that your chamber at Gavenmore was similarly appointed."

She dropped him a mocking curtsy. "Oh, no, sir. We only had moldy bread crusts twice a week and the rats were much larger there."

He stepped into the chamber, closing the door behind him. "A pity. I'll have to comb the dungeons and see what I can arrange."

Holly forced herself not to recoil from his approach. 'Twas the first visit he'd deigned to pay her since taking her hostage three days ago and she doubted his presence boded well for her future, bleak prospect though it was.

'Twas doubly hard not to flinch when he cupped the vulnerable column of her throat in his hands, caressing the faint smudges that still marred her skin. "I must say your husband has exquisite taste in jewelry. But had you consented to be my bride, I'd have draped you in diamonds and pearls rather than bruises."

Holly bit back her impassioned defense of Austyn, fearful such a show of devotion would only kindle Eugene's hatred toward him. She chose instead to divert it toward herself. "I would never consent to be your bride. Not even if you murdered my husband and every other man on earth."

He flexed his hands; 'twas all Holly could do to keep from clawing at them. She didn't think she could endure being strangled twice in one week.

They slowly eased their pressure, dropping to hang limp at his sides. "I hate to disappoint you, my dear, but my offer for your hand has been withdrawn. Surely you knew your charms would pale once you'd shared them so generously with that barbarian. You're no longer fit to be my bride."

"My, my, aren't we the fickle one? Upon our first meeting, when I was only twelve, was it not you who dropped to your knees, kissed the hilt of your sword, and swore your undying devotion?"

He blinked. "I was striving to look up your gown."

"An indulgence that still eludes you."

The nasty edge of his smile sharpened even as his voice softened. "Only for a very brief time."

Holly's confidence faltered. "But you just said I was no longer worthy of your attentions."

"I said I'd lost interest in wedding you. Bedding you is another matter entirely."

She took an involuntary step backward.

"There's no need to cringe, my dear. I can understand how that oaf's clumsy fumblings might have made you dread the act, but I can promise you I possess skills that will soon have you begging for my touch."

Holly resisted the urge to mock his arrogance as a misty image flashed in her mind: Austyn lowering his magnificent body to hers, making her his own with tender grace and irresistible mastery.

She drew herself up to her full height. "The only boon I shall entreat from you, sir, is my freedom."

Eugene's smile vanished. "On the contrary, my lady. If you persist in defying me, you'll be begging not for liberty, but for mercy."

As the door slammed and locked behind him, Holly's bravado dissipated. Betrayed by her wobbly knees, she sank to a sitting position and dragged the musty blanket around her shoulders. As the shadows of night came creeping over the unfamiliar window ledge, there were no lit tapers to hold them at bay and no Austyn to cradle her in his arms until her trembling ceased.

The knight drove his destrier through the ancient forest much as his ancestor had done over eight centuries before.

A treacherous net woven from moonlight and shadows dappled the mossy turf, but he nudged the horse's lathered flanks with his golden spurs, refusing to slow his perilous pace. The loyal beast snorted, its nostrils flaring with exertion, then strained its massive chest forward to seek another inch of speed. Once the lord who bore the title of Gavenmore would have had a powerful army of knights beneath his command, but Austyn had only his haste and his honor. He prayed they would stand him in good stead against an opponent as crafty and lacking in integrity as Eugene de Legget, the baron of Montfort.

Not once since he'd been handed Montfort's missive had he been tormented by visions of the woman he loved in another man's arms. Instead he was consumed with fears for her welfare—Was she hurt? Was she cold? Was she hungry? Was she afraid? 'Twas Holly's courage that frightened him the most. He knew only too well how her reckless defiance could incite a man to rage.

The destrier surged through a deep brook. The spray of frigid water failed to dampen Austyn's resolve, for unlike his hapless Gavenmore forebear, he was forging ahead to seek not his doom, but the woman who was both his destiny and his salvation.

As Holly sought to detach her stiff limbs from the chilly timber planks, she halfway wished she'd never succumbed to the temptation of sleep. Rubbing the cobwebs of slumber from her eyes, she rose and trundled to the window. For one wistful moment, she dared to believe she might see the sinuous thread of the river Wye unraveling between black mountain peaks.

Instead, a lush emerald carpet of treetops stretched toward every horizon. Summer had returned to England with a perverse vengeance and the brilliance of the morning sun stung Holly's eyes to near blindness. She was further tortured by the knowledge that just beyond the eastern ridge lay Tewksbury and her father.

Shaking off her lethargy, she leaned over the window ledge and gave one of the thick garlands of ivy that clung to the tower wall an experimental tug. It snapped off in her hand. Sighing with disappointment, she tossed it to the cobblestones below, earning a nasty look from one of Eugene's henchmen. Five of the brutes patrolled the boundaries of the isolated glade, clutching sharpened iron pikes in their beefy fists.

The creak of the door swinging open warned her she had company. The gleeful bounce in Eugene's step as he joined her made her more wary than before. "Languishing at the window, my dear? Pining away with hands clasped in supplication while you wait for your noble knight to come charging to your rescue?"

Holly burst into merry peals of laughter.

A flicker of unease marred her captor's smile. Holly felt a surge of triumph at having disarmed him, however briefly.

She favored him with a pitying look. "Forgive my mirth, sir, but after having spent a summer wed to that boorish clod of a Welshman, I find your romantic notions to be hopelessly naive. I can assure you that Gavenmore is as delighted to be rid of me as I am of him. He'll not waste a penny of his precious dowry to ransom me from your clutches."

"Ah, but I did not demand a penny of ransom. I simply requested an . . . audience." De Legget's sensual lips shaped the innocent word into an abomination.

"Then I fear you'll be equally disappointed," Holly forced herself to say lightly. "My husband is as stingy with his time as he is with his coin—especially where I'm concerned. Surely Nathanael told you of the impasse we reached when Gavenmore discovered my charade."

Eugene rested one hip against the sill and pursed his lips thoughtfully. "I seem to remember something about a minor confrontation. Lots of shouting and threats of violence. The peasants demanding you be burned at the stake. Gavenmore dragging you through the streets half-naked. What an enchanting spectacle! I am sorry I missed it."

Holly bowed her head, feigning a sulky pout. "He pronounced me a shrewish, deceitful witch and said I was unfit to bear his children." The barb of truth in those words still had the power to wound.

"Why those are the very qualities every mother should aspire to! You can't expect me to believe you couldn't flutter your lashes and charm your way back into his good graces." He cradled her chin between two fingers with chilling tenderness and turned her face to the light. "According to your doting priest, the Gavenmore men are known to possess a potentially mortal weakness for beautiful women."

Holly kept her lashes lowered, horrified to learn that Nathanael may have unwittingly laid in Eugene's fiendish hands the one weapon that could destroy both she and Austyn. The knowledge stripped her of all defenses save the truth. Or something near enough to it to mislead a mind as shrewd as Eugene's.

Shaking off his mocking caress, she paced across the tower, then whirled to face him, giving her bitterness free rein for the first time since Austyn had bid her farewell. "Aye, the Gavenmore men have a weakness for beauty. They consume it as other men consume bread or ale. Their appetites are insatiable. I'm sure Nathanael also told you that I was forced to trade my virtue for his freedom. My husband was only too eager to partake of my *beauty* night after night so long as it pleased him to do so."

"Lucky fellow," Eugene murmured, his insinuating glance lingering at her breasts.

"Yet now that he's grown bored of me, what does he do? He publicly repudiates me. He humiliates me by sending me to live in my father's household. Why he's probably seducing some comely serving wench even as we speak!" Holly felt a tear tremble from her lashes and chart a burning course down her cheek. "I swear to you the man cares naught for me!"

Her performance was so wrenching that even Holly might have come to believe it were it not for the jarring thunder of hoofbeats, shouts of alarm, and the bellow of pure rage that drifted up through the tower window.

"Montfort! What the hell have you done with my woman?"

chapter 31

Holly swallowed a despairing groan as Eugene snaked an arm around her waist and dragged her back to the window. The sight below was both better and far worse than any she might have imagined. Two of de Legget's henchmen lay crumpled on the cobblestones. The giant hunched over to the side in the grass, rubbing his lolling head.

Austyn sat his prancing destrier between the two remaining guards with nary a visible scratch. Nor did he look the least bit concerned that one of the ruffians had seized his reins and sword while the other held an iron pike poised at his back.

Holly's throat tightened with a helpless surge of

love. 'Twas so like Austyn to charge into peril for her sake without counting the consequences. She remembered how he had swaggered into Tewksbury with naught but a single man-at-arms and his irreproachable honor and walked away with the most extravagant prize of his jousting career—a bride.

His expression was stormy, from jealousy or concern she could not say. Perhaps he believed she had provoked Eugene's attack in a vindictive attempt to punish him, she thought wildly. Perhaps he would see this as yet another damning proof of the faithlessness of women.

"I've come for my wife."

I've come for the woman.

Before Holly could recognize the echo from the past, Eugene had seized the back of her gown and heaved her up on the window ledge. The window was much narrower than the one at Gavenmore, but there was ample room for her slight form. Her head swam as blue sky and green earth threatened to reverse.

"Would you care to come up," Eugene called out, "or shall I send her down?"

Austyn hesitated for an insulting moment. "I'll come up."

"Excellent. I'll have my men escort you."

The devilish note in Eugene's voice alerted Holly, but she did not dare betray herself. All she could do was bite back her scream of warning and wince in sympathy as the pike came down on the back of Austyn's head, sending him crashing off his mount to the cobblestones.

.   .   .

Austyn's lips curled in a dreamy smile. He was reclining in a meadow of purple heartsease, his head pillowed against the plush warmth of Holly's bosom. Her fragrant curls tickled his nose as she leaned over and began to plant tender kisses along his brow, crooning praise for his valor in those dulcet tones of hers.

"Wake up, you bumbling oaf!" A torrent of cold water struck him full in the face.

His eyes flew open to discover Holly looming over him, her charming little face puckered not in a kiss, but in a scowl. He also discovered she was holding an empty basin, he was sitting in a puddle of spreading water garbed only in his hose, his wrists were manacled to the wall behind him, and by the slant of the sun's rays pounding their way without mercy into his throbbing head, 'twas no longer morning, but early afternoon.

A dark crescent of a moon intercepted the sunbeams as Eugene de Legget bent over to peer into his face with solicitous concern. "I offered to rouse you myself, sir, but your wife begged to do the honors."

Austyn's gaze flicked from Eugene to Holly. Her glittering eyes flared in unspoken warning.

Austyn shook his head like a great shaggy mastiff, sending droplets of water flying everywhere. Holly recoiled, dropping the basin and screeching in outrage.

" 'Tis the only way that shrew could rouse any man," he pronounced, curling his upper lip in a smirk.

Holly planted her hands on her hips, smiling a smile of acid sweetness. "Oh, I doubt that most men are as difficult to rouse as you, sir. Nor so easily expended."

"Why should a man rouse himself to satisfy a

woman who'll do naught but lay beneath him like a cold herring?"

Eugene patted water from his brow with a kerchief, gazing from one to the other of them with unabashed fascination. "Would that be a live herring, sir, or a dead one?"

"Oh, dead, most certainly. At least a live one would have flopped a bit now and then."

Holly snorted with scorn and tossed her curls, her haughty beauty at its peak. "Not live or dead, but frozen with distaste at your clumsy fumblings."

"Frozen indeed. I feared you were going to give Master Longstaff a fatal case of frostnip."

"Master Longstaff! Ha! Don't flatter yourself."

Austyn summoned up a feral snarl with little effort, his narrowed gaze promising revenge for that snippet of sauciness.

Eugene stepped between them, plainly fearing they were on the verge of flying at each other's throats and depriving him of his own diabolical pleasures. "If you loathe your wife as much as you claim, Gavenmore, why have you come rushing so gallantly to her aid?"

Austyn did not have to fake his icy sneer as he turned his attention to Montfort. "For the same reason I came rushing so gallantly to wed her. Gold. How long do you think her father will let me keep that dowry if she gets her witless self killed? And I've earned it, by God, for being forced to endure the lash of her barbed tongue all these weeks."

Holly leaned around Eugene and stuck out that luscious, pink tongue at him. Austyn shifted in the puddle of water, wishing he hadn't chosen such an inopportune moment to recall the delicious torments it was capable of inflicting.

To hide his consternation, he gave the manacles a violent tug, as if he'd like nothing more than to wrap them around his wife's elegant neck. The right manacle rewarded him with a tantalizing inch of give.

He ceased his struggles as Eugene drew a small silver dagger from his belt. "Allow me to put your mind at ease, sir. You'll be heartened to know that I've no intention of murdering your beloved bride."

The blood rushed from Austyn's pounding head, leaving him dizzy with relief.

Eugene tested the blade against his thumb, then smiled tenderly. " 'Tis you who disgraced my good name before the crowd at the tournament and 'tis you I'm going to kill."

Holly's horrified gasp nearly betrayed them, but she recovered quickly, clapping her hands with childish glee. "Oh, joy! And I had feared I'd be stuck with the lummox for all eternity."

Even Eugene eyed her askance at that bit of bloodthirstiness. "Remind me to sleep with the candles lit when I take you to my bed, dear."

Austyn began working the right manacle back and forth with excruciating slowness, but increasing desperation. If he could just coax a few more inches of slack into the chain before Eugene came to finish him off . . . "If you're fool enough to bed that witch," he said, "you'll soon be begging someone to gut you in your sleep. I'd almost prefer death to a lifetime of hell spent listening to her nag."

Holly lunged for him, her fingers curved into

claws. "Give me the dagger and let me at the wretch! I'll put him out of his misery."

Eugene grabbed her around the waist. "Not so fast, love. Wouldn't you rather make him suffer?"

"What did you have in mind?" Austyn growled. "Forcing me to swive her again."

"Only in your dreams!" Holly retorted.

She fought back a shiver of revulsion as Eugene's grip mellowed to a mocking embrace. "On the contrary," he said, rubbing his cheek against her temple. "I thought you might like to watch while I did the honors." His eyes never left Austyn's as he slid a hand upward from her waist to cup the underside of one of her ripe breasts.

Holly's gaze was also riveted on her husband's face. She dared not even breathe. She knew a single visible flinch, one whispery thread of the whimper caught in her throat, would be the ruination of them both.

Austyn's face, so quick to mold itself to a scowl of anger or to dimple in delight, did not betray even a flicker of emotion. 'Twas so still its unholy beauty might have been set in mortar.

He raked her with a contemptuous glance, coldly dismissing the sight of Eugene's hand kneading the softness of her breast. Straining against the manacles, he flexed his arms and yawned like a big, sleepy bear. "Suit yourself, Montfort. Just don't forget to wake us both when you're done."

Stiffening with rage, Eugene gave Holly a shove. She stumbled to one knee, but was too awash in triumph to feel a drop of pain.

"The two of you deserve each other," Eugene

snarled. "A shrill harpy and a merry cuckold. You'd be enough to milk the joy out of dipping a virgin in boiling oil."

Holly grinned, savoring his petulant rage. But her smile faded as he marched resolutely toward Austyn, brandishing the dagger. "If you only knew how much I loathe wasting a quick, clean death on the likes of you . . ."

Austyn began to struggle against his chains in earnest, his forearms bulging with the effort. He shot Holly an imploring look. She knew him well enough to recognize 'twas not a plea for assistance, but a desperate decree for her to stay her hand.

Holly had no time to seek a weapon. No time to scream or mumble a frantic prayer. Eugene whipped the dagger back, aiming its blade at her husband's heart. Ducking beneath the baron's elbow, she threw herself across Austyn, wrapping her arms around his waist and burying her face against the consoling warmth of his chest as she awaited the plunge of the knife between her shoulder blades.

Except for the thundering of Austyn's heart beneath her ear, the chamber went as silent as a tomb. Then a breathy chuckle coaxed the hairs at her nape to tingling life. Still clinging to Austyn's waist, she turned her head to find a sneer of gloating triumph fixed on Eugene's lips. She could almost feel his invisible snare tightening around her throat.

"How perplexing. You claim to care nothing for your husband, yet you've proved yourself willing to die for him." He tapped the hilt of the dagger against his chin. "Let no one say the baron of Montfort is not a romantic at heart. I shall reward your noble sacrifice by letting him live."

The tears poised on Holly's lashes spilled down her cheeks in a torrent of relief. Austyn rubbed his chin against her curls, the only show of solace allowed him.

"Live, Gavenmore," Eugene said, mesmerizing them both with the virulent softness of his voice. "Live knowing that every time you look at your wife, you'll remember her on her back with her legs spread wide for another man. Live with the fear that she secretly relished my attentions, that she writhed and moaned not in pain, but in ecstasy. Live with the doubt that the babe she'll bear nine months from now may not be the true Gavenmore heir, but only the sniveling bastard of a man you despise."

Through a mist of dawning horror, Holly felt every muscle in Austyn's body go as rigid as steel. As Eugene pressed the blade of the dagger to her throat and tore her away from him, he bucked against the chains, bellowing with rage and anguish.

Holly thrashed and kicked and flailed, no longer caring if she incited Eugene to murder her. She would rather die than force Austyn to endure what to a Gavenmore man would truly be a fate worse than death. The tip of the blade bit into her throat.

"Holly, look at me!" Her husband's roar of command was so irresistible that even Eugene stopped dragging her along to gape.

Austyn's gaze burned with a sweet, holy fire. "Listen to me, angel," he said fiercely. "Don't make him hurt you. Do whatever he wants." He blinked furiously to clear his eyes of tears. "Your life is of more value to me than your virtue. He'll never touch what I adore in you. You will always be pure and lovely in my sight."

"How revolting!" Eugene spat.

Holly's knees crumpled beneath a staggering siege of love. Her husband's generosity had left her with no choice but to offer him a sacrifice of her own.

She drove her elbow hard into Eugene's codpiece. As he dropped to one knee, grunting an oath, she broke from his grip and stumbled toward the window.

She scrambled up on the ledge. The wind tore at her hair and molded her gown to her legs just as it had on that summer afternoon at Gavenmore when the beauty of the day had reminded her that despite its hardships, life was too precious to forsake without a fight. She refused to look down at the cobblestones below.

Instead, she whirled to face the tower, smiling through a veil of tears at the man whose faith had given her the courage to continue the battle.

"No," Austyn whispered, riveted by his wife's tender smile. "Oh, God, please, no . . ."

"Don't be a fool, you bitch," de Legget snapped, clambering to his feet. But Austyn knew he was never going to reach her in time.

Austyn strained at the manacles with all of his weight, panic numbing him to the rivulets of blood trickling down his wrists.

Eugene lunged for her. Time lurched to a halt as Holly touched her fingertips to her beautiful lips, then backed off the narrow ledge, disappearing into thin air.

CHAPTER 32

Austyn roared Holly's name. Fueled by an inhuman surge of agony, he ripped the manacles from the wall in an explosion of mortar. Eugene had time to do little more than emit a strangled cry of surprise before a free length of chain whipped around his neck with a nasty crack.

Austyn lowered the baron's limp form to the floor, then charged to the window. Bracing his palms on the ledge, he sucked in shuddering gasps of air, keeping his eyes squeezed shut until he could work up the courage to look down at the cobblestones below.

"Austyn?"

At the tentative whisper, his eyes flew open in horror. The cheerful blue sky mocked his grief. Dear God in heaven, he thought savagely, was he to be allowed no interval of mourning before the ghost of his beloved wife began haunting him?

"Austyn!"

The second plea sounded both more corporeal and distinctly more annoyed. Austyn slowly lowered his gaze to discover Holly tangled in a curtain of ivy a mere arm's length below the window. One of the vines snapped off in her hand, eliciting a very mortal squeal.

Trembling with disbelief, Austyn stretched out his hand. She seized it, the desperation of her grip assuring him that she was no ghost. He shouted with jubilation as he hauled her against him in a fervent embrace. They went tumbling to the floor of the tower in a breathless tangle of arms, legs, laughter, and tears.

She nuzzled her lips against his throat, as if starved for a taste of him. "I thought you were going to leave me dangling out there all day. I had no idea if the stuff would hold, you know. If you'd have dawdled any longer, I'd have gone *splat* on the cobblestones like one of Winnie's fig puddings."

"Nag, nag, nag," he murmured, kissing her lovely brow, her precious ears, the tip of her impertinent nose.

"I just knew that if I provided you with a sufficient distraction, you could best the wretch." She splayed her palms against his chest and smiled up at him adoringly. "I had nothing but the utmost of faith in you."

Austyn sobered. "And I in you, my lady." He smoothed back her windblown curls, searching her face—a face that had become dear to him for far more than its striking beauty.

Their lips brushed and lingered in tender accord. As they drew apart, gazing deep into each other's eyes, a golden haze claimed the tower. Austyn might have taken it for nothing more than sunshine striking the motes of mortar drifting through the air were it not for the gentle ripple of laughter that echoed in their ears.

He and Holly clutched each other, their eyes widening with dawning astonishment as the shimmering outline of a woman appeared before them. The wheaten silk of her hair danced around a face so exotically beautiful it made Holly feel no more comely than a troll. She tightened her possessive grip on Austyn's arms without realizing it.

Austyn would have known her voice anywhere— rich, melodious, slightly mocking. " 'Twas all I asked, Austyn of Gavenmore. That you put your faith in the constancy of a woman's heart."

The vision wavered, but before it could fade into obscurity, Austyn found himself gazing into the forgiving eyes of his mother. His heart swelled with gratitude at the generous and unexpected gift.

The ethereal halo of light vanished, restoring the mundane gloom of crumbling stone and mortar dust. A flea-bitten mouse sat up on its hind legs, sniffing the air where Rhiannon had disappeared.

Austyn and Holly exchanged a wondering glance.

"You were truly cursed," she whispered, as if the Welsh faerie might still be eavesdropping.

"Aye." He traced the curve of her cheek with one

reverent finger. "But thanks to you and your unwavering faith in me, my lady, now I am truly blessed."

Holly flung herself into his arms with a sob of joy. Austyn gathered her against him, squeezing his eyes shut against a rush of raw emotion. As their lips met, the air resounded with a flourish of trumpets.

'Twas a dazed eternity of bliss before either of them realized the trumpets' fanfare was no celestial celebration of their love, but a call to war.

The glade below rang with angry shouts and threats of impending chaos. Still hand in hand, Austyn and Holly shot to their knees and peeped over the window ledge.

Two armies poured into the clearing from opposite directions, sending de Legget's henchmen scattering like rats into the shadowy forest.

From the east rode a mammoth company of knights, their banners rippling in splashes of saffron and purple, their shiny plate armor glinting in the sun. At the head of their precise formation sat a squat figure on a magnificent gray stallion, proudly bearing the Tewksbury standard.

Holly bounced up and down with excitement. " 'Tis my papa come to rescue me!"

"He might have spared a decade from my life had he come with a bit more haste and a bit less pomp," Austyn muttered, squeezing her hand.

From the west came a motley group of men mounted on sturdy plow horses, drooping nags, and lathered donkeys. They were armed with naught but rusty hoes, tattered brooms, and smithy hammers, yet their stern Welsh visages looked no less determined than the faces of their English counterparts. Their general was none other than a fair-haired Viking who drooped over the pommel of his saddle like a withered daffodil, his ribs bandaged and his left arm supported by a makeshift sling.

"Damn his obstinate hide!" Austyn exclaimed. "Emrys promised he'd lock him up to keep him from following me."

"Would that be Emrys there just behind him? My goodness, his head is nearly as shiny as my papa's armor." Holly pointed. "And look, there's Winifred beating on a kettle with an iron spoon. What a splendid Amazon she would have made!"

The two armies met in the center of the glade, showing dangerous signs of clashing.

Austyn sighed. "We'd best get down there before they annihilate each other for the common good." Ignoring Holly's squeal of protest, he swept her into his arms. "I'll be afraid to put you down for fear someone else will carry you off."

She twined a tendril of his hair around her finger, secretly delighted. "Now that you've proved your faith in me, sir, you shall never again be plagued by jealousy."

He stepped over de Legget's body without a second glance and gave her a devilish wink. "Rhiannon never promised that."

"She's *my* daughter! I shall lead the charge into the tower!" the earl of Tewksbury was bellowing when Austyn carried Holly from the castle, a beaming Elspeth trotting at his heels.

"Like hell you will," Carey shouted back, his

words still slurred by the various indignities suffered by his lips. "She's *my* lady! I'll lead the charge."

"Charge, ha! You can barely walk."

Austyn tapped the earl on the shoulder.

He turned around and thundered, "Not now, lad. Can't you see I'm busy?"

Austyn waited patiently for him to swing around the second time. His beady little eyes broadened at the sight of his daughter in Austyn's arms.

"Baby!" he cried, an angelic smile wreathing his dwarfish face. "My precious little baby!"

Holly squirmed in mingled delight and embarrassment as he threw his arms around her and smothered her face with kisses. Austyn demonstrated absolutely no desire to relinquish her to her father's arms. Holly feared if either one of them loved her any more staunchly, she would have been tugged in two.

"How did you know, Papa?" she asked, settling back in Austyn's arms to pat his weathered cheek. "How did you know I needed you?"

The company of knights parted to reveal a litter borne by four grumbling foot soldiers. Its occupant struggled to a sitting position, clutching a heavily bandaged chest. "'Twas I who told him."

"Nathanael!" Holly breathed. "Good God, I thought you were dead."

"So did I." He held up a heavy chain. "But it seems my crucifix deflected the worst of the blow." He grinned sheepishly. "I hope I didn't scare you too badly. I must have fainted from the pain." At a snicker from one of the foot soldiers, he snapped, "Well, it was quite intolerable."

Her father glowered at the priest. "We'd have

been here sooner had he not led us on such a merry chase. We were halfway to Scotland before we realized we were heading the wrong way."

"Now, sir, you know I've a deplorable sense of direction." Nathanael's eyes darkened as he lifted them to the tower. "The baron?"

"He'll not trouble anyone again," Austyn said firmly.

Both the earl and Nathanael nodded their approval while Carey limped over to slap Austyn on the back.

The earl's gaze traveled from Holly's face to Austyn's. "Come, child," he said in a voice that brooked no disobedience. " 'Tis time to get you home."

Holly twined her arms around her husband's neck and rested her head on his shoulder, giving her father the reassurance he sought. "I am home, Papa."

Austyn kissed her hair. "Let's not be so hasty to spurn your father's invitation. A sound night's rest in a fluffy feather bed might be just the thing." The flash of his dimple warned her that a sound night's rest was the furthest thought from his mind.

"Sounds good to me," Carey mumbled, rubbing his ribs.

"Me, too," said Nathanael, reclining on the litter.

But as Austyn sought to pass, the priest's hand shot out to capture Holly's arm. Holly felt Austyn tense, but the wistful shadow in Nathanael's eyes was brightened by his sheepish smile. "I hope you'll allow me to bestow my heartfelt blessing . . . upon the both of you."

As Austyn carried Holly toward his destrier with both her father's and the priest's blessing, he nuzzled her ear and whispered, "Perhaps tonight will give you time to get reacquainted with a friend of mine. A certain Master Longstaff who is only too eager to seek redress for a rather unkind slur you've cast upon his honor."

"I can assure you I'm more than willing to soothe the saucy fellow's vanity," she whispered back.

At her chiming laughter, a flushed young knight slid back the faceplate of his helm, hefted his lance in salute and shouted, "To Lady Holly, who possesses the fairest face in all of England!"

The rousing cheer that went up was stifled midnote by the sweeping look Austyn leveled on the crowd. Holly's breath caught as his gaze lowered to caress her face with irresistible tenderness.

"To Lady Holly," he proclaimed, his rich voice tolling like a bell in the crystalline silence, "who possesses the fairest heart in all of England."

That heart overflowed with love as Holly welcomed her husband's kiss.

This time there was no quelling the exultant roar that resounded through the forest as Welsh and English voices united in tribute. As Austyn swept Holly in front of him on the destrier, a joyous fanfare rippled through the air, leaving the heralds staring dumbfounded at the shiny horns hanging limp from their hands.

EPILOGUE

❧

"Holly Felicia Bernadette de Chastel!"

Holly hid her smile behind the tiny coif she was embroidering as her husband came stalking across the meadow. His handsome face was set in a fierce scowl, but he might have looked even more intimidating were it not for the three-year-old who had secured her perch on her papa's massive shoulders by tugging at his ears.

He stopped at the edge of the blanket to avoid trampling his infant daughter, who slept in a basket with her thumb nestled between her cherubic lips, and dangled a sheaf of parchment in front of Holly's eyes. "Do you know what this is?"

Laying her embroidery aside, Holly absently twirled an ebony curl belonging to the six-year-old napping in her lap. "A letter from the Baron of Gloucester," she speculated. "Ruminations on the weather. A snippet of gossip about the king's mistress. Complaints about the size of his goiter . . ."

Austyn snapped open the missive, but had to pry his daughter's hands away from his eyes before he could read it. " 'Don't think me impertinent, Gavenmore,' " he read, " 'but it has come to my attention on more than one occasion that your eldest would make a suitable bride for a lonely widower such as myself.' A lonely widower indeed! A desperate old lech, he means!" Austyn wadded the letter into a ball, growling beneath his breath.

His daughter batted gleefully at his hair. "Papa's a big ole growly bear!"

"Papa's not a growly bear, Gwynnie. Since the king restored his title, he's a growly earl." He gently disengaged her from his shoulders and sent her off to toddle in the grass with a pat on the rump before sinking down beside Holly on the blanket. His expression was bleak. "It's starting already, isn't it? I thought we'd have a few more years of peace."

Holly leaned her head against his shoulder. " 'Twas inevitable, you know. Why Felicia and Bernadette are nearly eight."

Austyn frowned. "Where are the twins today?"

"They're off with their uncle Carey, learning how to shoot a bow."

Austyn shuddered. "I hope he wore his padded hauberk."

"I'm sure he did. I think he learned his lesson

when they dropped the tub of poppies on his head. I've not seen him without his helm since. And then there was that little incident when they burned down the north tower while roasting chestnuts on the hearth."

Austyn shook his head. "I never have figured out how that sheet got stuffed up the chimney . . ."

Holly bit off a piece of thread and murmured something noncommittal. She much preferred the spacious solar Austyn had built in place of the tower. A solar whose door was never locked unless they wished to steal a few precious hours of privacy away from the inquisitive eyes of their offspring.

Austyn ruffled his sleeping daughter's hair, then ran a finger along the baby's downy cheek. "They're all so beautiful."

Where once there would have been despair in his voice, now there was only pride and a perpetual sense of wonder that their love had brought such grace into the world. Even Austyn's father had shared a brief taste of it. After tenderly cradling his first granddaughter in his arms, Rhys of Gavenmore had died quietly in his sleep. He now rested beneath a blanket of anemones at his wife's side, at peace at last.

Holly reached up to caress the tendrils of silver at her husband's temples, thinking as she always did how very striking they were. "I fear that in the next few years you're going to come to learn that there are more vexing trials than possessing a comely wife. Such as fending off the suitors of six lovely daughters. I hope you don't fancy yourself still cursed."

Austyn drew her into the warm circle of his arms. "You and the girls will always be my dearest blessing."

He brushed her lips with his, igniting the passion that still flared so quick and bright between them.

The thunder of hoofbeats disturbed their tender reverie.

"Oh, Austyn, you didn't!" Holly exclaimed as the fully armored rider approached, the celestial turrets and graceful arches of the newly completed castle providing the perfect backdrop for the dainty warrior.

He shrugged, bestowing upon her one of those crooked smiles she never could resist. "Your father donated the armor, but it had occurred to me that one of our daughters should be able to fend off her own suitors."

The lithe rider brought the horse to a prancing halt, then reached up and dragged off her helm, sending a torrent of raven curls cascading down her back.

An impish giggle bubbled from her lips. "I saw you kissing Papa, Mama. How disgusting!" She tilted her pert nose in the air, sniffing with disdain. "I shall never bestow my kisses on any unworthy man."

Austyn grinned. "That's my girl."

Holly pinched him.

The rider wheeled the horse around and urged it into a canter. Wrapped in each other's loving embrace, Austyn and Holly shook their heads in wry wonderment as they watched her gallop fearlessly around the outskirts of the curtain wall encompassing their home.

She had inherited her mother's grace and sense of mischief along with her father's jousting skills and stubborn courage. Several minstrels and a handful of poets had already pronounced the dark-haired, blue-eyed sprite the fairest lady in all of England. Holly was only too eager to relinquish the title to her beloved eldest daughter, who had been conceived twelve years ago in one of the softest, fluffiest feather beds at Tewksbury . . .

Lady Ivy of Gavenmore!

ABOUT THE AUTHOR

A self-professed army brat and only child, TERESA MEDEIROS spent much of her childhood talking to imaginary friends. She's now delighted to have a chance to introduce them to her readers. She wrote her first novel at twenty-one and enjoyed an earlier career as a registered nurse before realizing her dream of writing full-time before the age of thirty. She lives in a log home in Kentucky with her husband Michael, five neurotic cats, and one hyperactive Doberman.

If you loved FAIREST OF THEM ALL,
don't miss

A Breath of Magic

a bewitching new
romance from the
superb Teresa Medeiros.
Look for this Bantam Book
in early 1996.

The girl plopped down on the broomstick. Her skirts bunched around her knees, baring a pair of slender calves shrouded in black stockings. A stray gust of wind ruffled her hair, forcing her to swipe a dark curl from her eyes.

The dying leaves still dripped with the morning's rain. A stiff autumn breeze raised gooseflesh on her arms.

Shaking off the foreboding pall of the sky, she gripped the broomstick with both hands and screwed her eyes shut. As she attempted the freshly memorized words, a cramp shot down her thigh, shattering her concentration. She tried shouting the spell, but the broomstick did not deign to grant even a bored shudder in response.

Her voice faded to aching hoarseness, then to a defeated whisper. Disappointment swelled in her throat, constricting the tender membranes until tears stung her eyes. Uncurling her stiff fingers, she tugged irritably at the laces holding the coarse homespun tight across her breasts.

She reached inside her bodice, toying out of long habit with the emerald amulet suspended from a delicate filigree chain. Although she kept it well hidden from prying eyes, she still felt compelled to wear it over her heart like a badge of shame.

"*Sacrebleu,* I only wanted to fly," she muttered.

The broomstick lurched forward, then jerked to a halt. The amulet lay cool and indifferent over her galloping heart.

Afraid to heed her own fickle senses, she slowly

drew the gold chain over her head and dangled the amulet from her tensed fingers.

Leaning over the weatherbeaten stick, she whispered, "I only wanted to fly."

Nothing.

She straightened, shaking her head at her own folly.

The willow broom sailed into the air and stopped, leaving her dangling by one leg. The stick quivered beneath her, the intensity of its power making the tiny hairs at her nape bristle with excitement.

"Fly!" she commanded with feeling.

The broom hung poised in mid-air for a shuddering eternity, then aimed itself toward the crowns of the trees. It darted to a dizzying height, then swooped down, dragging her backside along the ground for several feet before shooting into another wild ascent.

She whooped in delight, refusing to consider the perils of soaring around a modest clearing on a splintery hearth broom. The wind rushed past, capturing her cries. The harder she laughed, the faster the broom traveled until she feared it would surely bolt the clearing and shoot for the distant moon hanging in the afternoon sky.

With a tremendous effort, she heaved herself astride the broom. She perched in relative comfort for a full half a second before the curious conveyance rocketed upward on a path parallel with the tallest oak, then dove downward with equal haste. The ground reached up to slam into her startled face.

She wheezed like a beached cod, praying the air would show mercy and fill her straining lungs. When she could finally breathe again, she lifted her throbbing head to find the broom lying a few feet away.

She spat out a mouthful of crumbled leaves and glared at the lifeless stick.

But her disgust was forgotten as she became aware of the gentle warmth suffusing her palm. She unfolded her trembling fingers to find the amulet bathed in a lambent glow. Her mouth fell open in wonder as the emerald winked twice as if to confirm their secret, then faded to darkness.

She was too captivated by her discovery to see the gaunt figure who unfolded himself from the shadows of the forest. A grim smile of triumph twisted his lips as he turned toward the village, the half-light of the rising moon caressing the elegant threads of silver at his temples.

If anyone had informed Miss Arian Whitewood that it might prove hazardous to study magic in the colony of Massachusetts in 1689, she would have scoffed in their face with all the saucy immortality of any twenty year old. Anyone, however, did not include her stepfather, for whom she harbored a great deal of respect and a somewhat stilted affection. So she sat in the ladder-backed chair facing the stone hearth, her hands folded demurely in her lap, and listened wide-eyed to his diatribe against Satan's servants and black magic.

His rehearsed speech seemed to embarrass him more than it did her. He clutched a slim prayerbook in one hand while fidgeting with his iron-gray hair with the other. His gaze persisted in straying to a spot just over her head.

Arian's buckled shoes tapped out a merry rhythm on the freshly sanded floor as her stepfather raved on about some irksome cow that refused to give anything but curdled milk for Goody Hubbins. As she glanced at the willow broom leaning innocently against the hearth, her lips twitched with remembered amusement.

"Arian!" Marcus Whitewood bellowed, his faded blue eyes capturing her gaze. "Have you not heard a word I have said? Do you not realize your soul is in grave danger, child?"

She sighed. "Forgive me, Father Marcus. My thoughts wandered. Pray do continue."

Her bored resignation sent Marcus's hand shooting through his hair again. "Only yesterday Goodwife Burke claimed her Charity was reading her catechisms when you did pass by the window and the girl went into fits."

"Fits of boredom most likely," Arian muttered beneath her breath. She didn't dare tell Marcus that the horse-faced Charity had come pounding at their door only two nights ago, begging Arian to cast her future in a cup of moldy tea leaves.

"I accuse you of nothing, daughter. But I thought you safer warned of the talk in the village. 'Tis not only your soul I am troubled for."

Arian groaned. "I shall never be a Puritan and they know it. I only attend their interminable Meeting to make life easier for you. They've hated me from the moment I arrived in Gloucester."

Marcus's frown softened. He remembered that moment vividly although it had occurred over ten years ago. He had stood on the dock, wringing his hat in his hands until it was past all repair. A silent prayer had risen unbidden to his lips when a tiny vision in scarlet had come sauntering down the ship's ramp, clutching a valise with the bored assurance of a practiced traveler.

His rehearsed words of welcome had died in his throat as the jaded pygmy had surveyed him from heels to head and demanded in a voice two octaves too deep for its owner's petite stature, "Where is my mama? Has she run off again?"

His stepdaughter had grown several inches since then, but her husky voice and snapping dark eyes could still make a man swallow his words.

She folded her arms over her chest in a gesture of rebellion Marcus had come to know only too well. "'Twas my fluency in French and my ruffled petticoats they didn't care for. My grandmama believed a traveling child should be well dressed."

"Your grandmama also believed in magic, young lady." He shook a forefinger at her. "She was a fanciful old Frenchwoman who poisoned your innocent mind with her black arts."

"White arts," Arian bit off. "Grandmama was a Christian. It broke her heart to send me away."

Arian blinked back unexpected tears. Her dear, pudgy grandmama had not known she was sending Arian to a stern stepfather she had never met and a mother who would be dead before she arrived.

Marcus tilted her chin up with one finger, forcing her to meet his gaze. "I promised your mother I would

offer you both a home and a name. Even when Lillia
was too weak to speak without coughing up blood, he
thoughts were of you. She had great hopes of buildin
a life here for the three of us."

His wistful smile gave Arian a glimpse of the adora
tion that had drawn her frivolous mama to this plain
stoic man. She looked away, knowing herself an in
truder on his lost passion for a woman Arian ha
hardly known and never liked.

Marcus gruffly cleared his throat. "You are an in
nocent, Arian. An easy mark for the devil. He coul
prey upon your childish potions and playacting. I know
you intend no harm, but the villagers do not. They se
a willful girl who is different from them and it make
them afraid."

"But I haven't concocted a single potion since yo
burned my powdered mice feet and poured out my
bat's blood," She assured him earnestly.

He shuddered and placed a firm hand on he
shoulder. "Allow me to pray for your soul, daughter
Let us kneel and ask the Almighty Lord to purge you o
the seeds of black magic your grandmother planted i
your heart."

Even as she slipped obediently to her knees, Arian
silently cried, *White magic!*

Knowing protest was futile, she arranged her
skirts to cushion her knees for an ordeal that could las
for hours. Marcus eased into a steady drone, repeating
prayer after prayer from the slender book. A trickle o
sweat crawled down Arian's side beneath the scratchy
linsey-woolsey.

She opened one eye to find Marcus's head bowed

nd his eyes closed. Eager to test her newfound discovery, she drew her folded hands inward until she could grasp the emerald amulet through the coarse cloth of her bodice. She narrowed her eyes, focusing all of her concentration on a pewter candlestick that rested on the mantel. Her fingers began to tingle.

A gap slowly widened between the gleaming base of the candlestick and the wooden shelf. A mischievous smile curved Arian's lips. She swung her head from side to side, sending the candlestick into a sprightly jig.

"Arian!"

Marcus's roar splintered her concentration. The massive candlestick crashed to the hearth only inches from his kneeling form.

Arian gasped. "Forgive me, Father Marcus . . . oh, please . . . I never meant to . . ."

Her protest faded as he scrambled to his feet, his face ashen. "You seek to do me harm, daughter?" Throwing a hand over his eyes, he cried, "I cannot bear it!"

He stumbled to the door and fled into the windy night, leaving Arian to wonder if she had just alienated her only ally in this heartless land.

The moon had drifted high in the sky before Arian heard Marcus's disheartened tread on the stairs. She sat before a cheval glass in her shadowy loft, working a hairbrush through her mass of frizzled curls. The brush caught in a painful tangle as Marcus's bedroom door creaked open, then shut with a mournful thud.

Taking up her single candle. Arian paced to the shuddering windowpane, her eyes searching the night for an unknown comfort. Resting the candlestick beside her, she curled up on the narrow sill and dragged a threadbare quilt around her shoulders. Clouds sped across the moon, making her wish she could fly away with them.

She had thirsted for magic most of her life, believing its power might quench the yearning in her soul. A yearning honed by years of being shuffled from household to household at the whim of her mother's wealthy lovers. Her only stability had been a battered book of fairy tales sent to her on her third birthday by a grandmama she had yet to meet.

She had immersed herself in the exotic kingdoms ruled by wizards, witches, and raven-haired princes, far preferring them to the whirl of frenzied gaiety punctuated by her mama's brittle laughter, the clink of wine glasses, and unfamiliar masculine tones.

The rabid snarl of quarreling voices had shattered her sleep more often than not, leaving her trembling in the darkness and trying to remember where she was. It was only after she had fumbled to light a candle and began to leaf through the gilt-edged pages of her beloved book that she would begin to remember not only where she was, but *who* she was as well. Or at least who she longed to be.

Often after such a night, her mother would emerge, her ethereal beauty only enhanced by tragic pallor, and inform Arian that it was time to pack. Before the day was over, Arian would be settled in another house and her mother in another man's bed.

Arian rested her forehead against the cool glass. Her precious book of fairy tales had been lost during the grueling voyage to the Colonies and her mother now slept for all eternity beneath the stony Massachusetts sod. All that remained of her past was an emerald amulet—a trinket she had always regarded with a curious mixture of pride and contempt.

Arian drew the amulet from her nightgown, regarding it with newfound respect. Until that afternoon in the clearing, her clumsy attempts at spellcasting had always failed her. Perhaps she had just needed an object to focus her attentions upon, she thought. She shivered with mingled fear and delight to remember the strange experience. The thrill of the amulet's raw power strumming across her nerves had been a bit like being kissed by a bolt of lightning. She longed to discover what other wonders it might be capable of, but after her disastrous encounter with Marcus, she feared invoking it without a powerful reason.

She closed her fist around the gem, wondering if it could be a source of comfort as well as a source of contention.

Her eyes slowly fluttered shut as she snuggled deeper into the quilt. But instead of dreaming of a raven-haired prince who possessed the power to break Gloucester's dark enchantment with a single kiss, she dreamed of a man with hair the color of sunlight and eyes the color of frost.

She moaned softly in her sleep as the wick of the tallow candle sputtered in its drippings and drowned itself into darkness.

The Meeting House was cool, the oppressive heat of summer vanquished by the autumn winds. Arian smoothed her skirts and stole a glance at the man beside her.

Her stepfather's profile was as impenetrable as it had been at breakfast. Her cheery attempts at conversation had been rebuffed by the stony set of his jaw. He had left the hot corn mush smothered in the sugary molasses he loved untouched on his wooden trencher. Draining the well water from his mug, he had risen and started for the Meeting House without word, giving Arian no choice but to slap a white bonnet askew on her head and trot after him.

The Reverend Linnet's voice swelled, its arresting timbre undiminished as he plunged into the third hour of his sermon. As he accented his threats of fiery retribution by slamming a fist on the pulpit, his words penetrated Arian's fretful musings for the first time, sending a shiver down her spine.

"Aye, my brethren, the Almighty Lord led us to Gloucester. He rescued us from evil and delivered us from the temptation of lives of ease bought with the lifeblood of our faith. He carried us over the sea to this new land. He protected us from tempests and disease."

Arian thought grimly of her mother, who had died choking on her own blood.

"But wherever there are godly men on this earth there are devils to tempt them." He lowered his voice to a hollow whisper that could still be heard throughout the hall. "Never forget the words of the Lord written in Job—'When the sons of God came to present themselves before the Lord, Satan came also among them.'"

Arian glanced at the rapt faces around her, both

gusted and slightly envious that they could find a
rthy message in the man's theatrics.

"It is because we are good that Satan sends his
rvants among us. Satan is clever. He knows what
npts us. I hasten to remind you that Lucifer was the
ost beautiful angel in the heavens. No star shone
ighter than Lucifer's glorious face. Never forget lest
u be drawn into beauty's snare. Would Satan send
dliness among us to lead us astray? Would he send a
inous monster to plague our cattle and cast our inno-
nt children into fits?"

A blanket of ominous silence drifted over the hall.
ople turned to one another, their eyes questioning.

"No!" The Reverend's voice rang out in a shout.
here is beauty among us. And there is evil among
, too. There is evil in this very room."

A collective gasp rose from the pews. Arian drew
a ragged breath, but found herself unable to release
as the Reverend Linnet looked straight over the
ads of those seated in front of her, paralyzing her
th his gaze.

"Satan's angels stalk us. Wild and wanton crea-
es fly in the night, howling at the moon. Simple
ls dance with a life of their own. We can deny it no
re. Satan and his servants are abroad in Glouces-
." Then more gently, "Now bow with me and repeat
e Lord's Prayer."

Arian sat frozen, the breath oozing from her body.
arcus's head bowed with a terrible finality. Only one
ad remained upright. Only one pair of eyes remained
en. The Reverend Linnet stood tall and straight at
e pulpit, his eyes devouring her with an unholy hun-

ger. The Lord's Prayer flowed smoothly from his lip
blatant mockery of his searing gaze.

Arian choked back a cry, terror rising in
throat. She rose and fled down the long aisle betw
the pews, mercifully unaware of the hollow silence
in her wake. A single tear splashed on Marcus Wh
wood's folded hands.

Arian ran toward the only home she had know
this foreign land. Marcus's clapboard house sat p
idly in the middle of the clearing, the sparkling indif
ence of its windowpanes mocking her agitation.

She clutched her aching side as she flew up
stairs to the loft, half expecting to hear the angry r
of a mob behind her.

Autumn sunshine beamed through the wind
thawing the numbness from Arian's mind as she pa
the narrow attic, reviewing every scrap of thought
had ever had concerning the handsome minister w
had come to their village the previous spring.

He had spoken to her often as she left the Meet
House, clasping her hand in his warm, dry palm. Ch
ity Burke had simpered each time he took her ha
while Goodwife Burke had whispered to Arian that
had received several invitations to marry since arriv
in Gloucester. Now Charity was having fits and nam
Arian as her tormentor.

Arian's hands shook with impotent anger. She l
to admire Linnet's craftiness in making his accusat
prior to the Lord's Prayer. Everyone in Glouces
knew that a witch could not recite the Lord's Pra
aloud. The hundreds of times she had repeated

rayer in the past would be forgotten as word of her ight from the church spread on the wings of malice.

But why did Linnet seek to destroy her? she wondered wildly. Did he truly believe her a servant of Satan?

Arian paused at the window as Marcus rounded the bend, his shoulders set in sharp angles of defeat. After several moments, his heavy footsteps sounded on the stairs. As the door creaked open, Arian turned to face him.

He gazed at the floor, his hands hanging limp at his sides. "I sought the good Reverend's help last night. I did not know he would make my confession public."

"It seems the good Reverend surprised us all."

Marcus lifted his head. His pale blue eyes were darkened by torment. "He convinced Constable Ingersoll not to come for you. He agreed I should be the one to fetch you for questioning. The villagers trust me." The burden of their trust lowered his shoulders another inch.

Arian dreaded his answer, but was still compelled to ask. "Do you think me wicked?"

"I think you are playing a child's game your grandmother taught you. But I know you have powers. And such powers cannot come from God." His voice cracked beneath the strain. "The Good Book speaks plainly on the subject of witchcraft."

" 'Thou shalt not suffer a witch to live.' I am familiar with the scripture." Arian rested a hand on his forearm, thinking it odd that she should be the one to comfort him. "Shall we go?"

He pressed his lips briefly to her hair, murmuring, "Do not cry, child. I could not bear it."

"Don't be absurd, Father Marcus. Witches don't weep."

Arian's trembling lips belied her words.

DON'T MISS THESE FABULOUS BANTAM WOMEN'S FICTION TITLES

On sale in July

DEFIANT
by PATRICIA POTTER
Winner of the 1992 *Romantic Times* Career Achievement Award for Storyteller of the Year

ly the desire for vengeance had spurred Wade Foster on, until the last of
men who had destroyed his family lay sprawled in the dirt. Now, badly
unded, the rugged outlaw closed his eyes against the pain . . . and awoke
the tender touch of the one woman who could show him how to live—
d love—again. ____ 56601-6 $5.50/$6.99

STAR-CROSSED
by nationally bestselling author SUSAN KRINARD

"Susan Krinard was born to write romance."
—New York Times *bestselling author Amanda Quick*

captivating futuristic romance in the tradition of Johanna Lindsey,
elle Taylor, and Kathleen Morgan. A beautiful aristocrat risks a for-
dden love . . . with a dangerously seductive man born of an alien race.
____ 56917-1 $4.99/$5.99

BEFORE I WAKE
by TERRY LAWRENCE

"Terry Lawrence is a magnificent writer." —Romantic Times

vard-winning author Terry Lawrence is an extraordinary storyteller
iose novels sizzle with irresistible wit and high-voltage passion. Now, she
aves the beloved fairy tale *Sleeping Beauty* into a story so enthralling it
ll keep you up long into the night. ____ 56914-7 $5.50/$6.99

Ask for these books at your local bookstore or use this page to order.

ase send me the books I have checked above. I am enclosing $____ (add $2.50 to
ver postage and handling). Send check or money order, no cash or C.O.D.'s, please.

ame _____

dress _____

ty/State/Zip _____

nd order to: Bantam Books, Dept. FN159, 2451 S. Wolf Rd., Des Plaines, IL 60018
low four to six weeks for delivery.
ices and availability subject to change without notice. FN 159 7/95

DON'T MISS THESE FABULOUS
BANTAM WOMEN'S FICTION TITLE!

On sale in June

From the blockbuster author of nine consecutive *New York Times* b
sellers comes a tantalizing tale of a quest for a dazzling crystal.

MYSTIQUE by Amanda Quick

"One of the hottest and most prolific writers in romance today."—USA To
Available in hardcover   ___ 09698-2 $21.95/$24.95 in Ca

VIOLET by Jane Feather

"An author to treasure."—Romantic Times

From the extraordinary pen of Jane Feather, nationally bestselling author of *Va
tine*, comes a bewitching tale of a beautiful bandit who's waging a dangerous g
of vengeance—and betting everything on love.   ___ 56471-4 $5.50/$6

MOTHER LOVE by Judith Henry Wall

"Wall keeps you turning the pages."—San Francisco Chronicle

There is no love as strong or enduring as the love of a mother for her child.
what if that child commits an act that goes against a woman's deepest beli
Is there a limit to a mother's love? Judith Henry Wall, whose moving sto
and finely drawn characters have earned her critical praise and a devoted re
ership, has written her most compelling novel yet.   ___ 56789-6 $5.99/$

THE WARLORD by Elizabeth Elliott

*"Elizabeth Elliott is an exciting find for romance readers
everywhere . . . . Spirited, sensual, tempestuous romance at its best."*
—New York Times *bestselling author Amanda Quick*

In the bestselling tradition of Teresa Medeiros and Elizabeth Lowell,
Warlord is a magical and captivating tale of a woman who must dare to l
the man she fears the most.   ___ 56910-4 $5.50/$6.99

- -

Ask for these books at your local bookstore or use this page to order.

Please send me the books I have checked above. I am enclosing $____ (add $2.50
cover postage and handling). Send check or money order, no cash or C.O.D.'s, ple

Name _____

Address _____

City/State/Zip _____

Send order to: Bantam Books, Dept. FN158, 2451 S. Wolf Rd., Des Plaines, IL 60
Allow four to six weeks for delivery.
Prices and availability subject to change without notice.   FN 158 7